Piers Anthony was born in Oxford in 1934, moved with his family to Spain in 1939 and then to the USA in 1940, after his father was expelled from Spain by the Franco regime. He became a citizen of the US in 1958 and, before devoting himself to full-time writing, worked as a technical writer for a communications company and taught English. He started publishing short stories with *Possible to Rue* for *Fantastic* in 1963, and published in SF magazines for the next decade. He has, however, concentrated more and more on writing novels.

Author of the brilliant, widely acclaimed *Cluster* series, and the superb *Tarot* trilogy, he has made a name for himself as a writer of original, inventive stories whose imaginative, mind-twisting style is full of extraordinary, often poetic images and flights of cosmic fancy.

D1323754

By the same author

PIERS ANTHONY

Book Six:
Incarnations of Immortality

For Love of Evil

GRAFTON BOOKS
A Division of the Collins Publishing Group

LONDON GLASGOW
TORONTO SYDNEY AUCKLAND

Grafton Books
A Division of the Collins Publishing Group
8 Grafton Street, London W1X 3LA

A Grafton UK Paperback Original 1989

Copyright © Piers Anthony Jacob 1988

ISBN 0-586-20682-5

Printed and bound in Great Britain by
Collins, Glasgow

Set in Times

Contents

1
Parry

There was a knock at the door, so hesitant as to be almost inaudible. Parry opened it.

A girl stood without, huddled and childlike. Her flowing honey hair was bound back from her face by a fillet: a narrow band of cloth that circled her bare head. Her frightened eyes seemed enormous, the irises grey-green. 'I am Jolie,' she whispered, her hands making a tentative gesture towards her bosom.

She had come! Suddenly Parry's mouth felt dry. He had known she would, yet doubted. He had wanted her to, yet been afraid. Now the test was upon him.

'Please come in,' he said, his voice sounding considerably more assured than he felt.

She gazed at him. Her face crumpled. 'Oh, please, my lord, please let me go! I never did you harm, or even spoke ill of you! I never meant to give offence, and if I have, I apologize most abjectly! Please, please do not enchant me!' She put her face in her hands, sobbing.

Parry was taken aback. 'I am not going to enchant you, Jolie!' he protested. 'I have no grievance against you.'

Those marvellous eyes peeked from between her fingers. 'No?'

'None. I know you have done me no harm. I want only to –' He found no appropriate word. 'If you will come in, I will explain.'

Her tears ceased, but not her fright. 'The Sorcerer said I would not be hurt,' she said somewhat defiantly.

'My father spoke truly,' Parry said. 'I mean only to talk with you. Please come in; it is warm inside.'

She hesitated. A gust of wind tugged at her garment,

and she shivered. It was evidently her best dress, but it was somewhat soiled linen, given shape only by the cord at her waist. It was inadequate protection against the chill of the fall evening. 'You order me, lord?'

Parry grimaced. 'I am no lord, Jolie. I am the Sorcerer's apprentice. I am hardly older than you. I cannot order you, nor would I if I could. I only want your company this night.'

Her face crumpled again. 'Oh, please, spare me this! To you it may be nothing, but to me it's my life!'

Parry had realized that there would be difficulty, but he had not properly appreciated its nature before. The girl believed that she was doomed if she set foot inside his house.

He could let her go. But that would mean the loss of what might be his sole opportunity, and failure in his first significant challenge. The Sorcerer had little sympathy for failure of any type.

'How can I persuade you that I mean you no harm?' he asked. 'I swear to you that I will do nothing to you without your leave, and that I will not force that leave-giving.'

'Will you swear by the Blessed Virgin Mary?' she asked disbelievingly.

'I swear it by the Blessed Virgin Mary.'

She watched him for some sign of disaster, but there was none. He had not been smitten for false swearing; therefore it must be safe. Still, her doubt loomed almost tangibly.

'Come in before you freeze,' he urged. 'I have a fire within.'

That did it; her shivering was not entirely from fright. 'Remember, you swore,' she reminded him nervously.

'By the Virgin,' he agreed.

She stepped in through the doorway, her eyes fixing on the fireplace within. There was indeed fire, radiating

8

flickering heat. He had banked it so that it gave off little smoke and warmed the chamber without depleting the air; it was one of the arts the Sorcerer had taught him.

Jolie knelt before it, extending her hands to the warmth. Now the threadbare nature of her garment became evident; and the light of the fire shone through, showing her thin arms, and there were holes. But she was oblivious; for the moment that warmth was all that she craved.

Parry closed and barred the door against the wind. It was of stout oak, and clinked around the edges, but some draughts still leaked through. He went quietly to his pantry, which was a niche to the side, separated by a dark linen curtain. He brought out a loaf of bread, a cup of butter, and a jar of blackberry jam. He set these on a tray and added a pitcher of goat milk and a knife and two mugs. He brought these to the main chamber and set them on the wooden table.

'I have food,' he said.

Jolie tore her rapt gaze from the fire and turned to him. For a moment her eyes met his; then she turned away without speaking.

'For you,' he clarified, picking up the sharp knife.

She looked again – and screamed. She lurched to her feet and ran for the door. She would have been out and away, but the bar baulked her.

'No, wait!' Parry cried, dropping the knife and hurrying to join her. 'I meant – '

Perceiving herself trapped, Jolie turned on him a stricken countenance, then fainted.

He caught her as she fell. It was no ruse; her body slumped in rag-doll fashion. He had to transfer his hold from her shoulders to her midsection as she sagged. She was so light she seemed indeed like a doll; there was little flesh on her bones.

He tried to walk her to a stool, but couldn't make it

work. Finally he picked her up and carried her. He eased her down by the fireplace, propping her against the warm hearth wall, then fetched pillows for comfort.

In a moment she recovered. Her eyes popped open, and she glanced about like a snared bird.

'You are safe, Jolie,' Parry said quickly. 'You swooned, but you are safe.'

'The knife – '

Then it burst upon him: the knife! He had been about to slice the bread, and she had thought he meant to use it on her. No wonder she had spooked!

'I gave my oath,' he reminded her. 'No harm to you.'

'But – '

'I was cutting bread for you.'

'But the sacrifice – '

'My oath,' he repeated. 'By the Holy Virgin. You can trust that.'

'Yes,' she agreed dubiously.

'I'm going to cut you a slice of bread,' he said carefully. 'Or you may do it yourself, if you prefer.'

'No . . .' she said, evidently afraid that the knife would turn in her hand and seek her innocent blood.

Parry picked up the knife, slowly, and oriented on the hard loaf. He sawed through it, severing a thick slice, and set down the knife.

Jolie's eyes remained locked on the knife throughout. She relaxed only when it left his hand.

'Would you like butter on it?' he inquired. 'Or jam?'

'Oh, my lord . . .' she demurred.

'I am no lord,' he repeated firmly. 'Call me Parry.'

'Oh, I could not!'

Parry smiled, a trifle grimly. 'Call me Parry,' he said, touching the knife.

'Parry!' she cried, shrinking into her dress.

'That's better,' he said. 'You know I am only a year older than you. I see you as an equal.'

'But you are the Sorcerer's son!'

'Butter or jam?' he asked. 'Or both?'

'For me?' She simply could not believe.

'For you. I will have a separate slice. Here, I will cut it now.' He picked up the knife.

Again her eyes locked on it, and her breath became shallow. It was as though he were torturing the loaf.

'I will put the knife away,' he said as he finished. He carried it back to the pantry and set it behind the curtain, safely out of sight. Only then did the girl's breathing revert to normal.

He used a wooden spatula to spread butter generously on both slices of the coarse black bread, then poured jam on each. He picked up the slices and walked to her, proffering one. 'For you,' he repeated. 'I will sit on the other side of the fire and eat my own.'

Hesitantly, her tiny hand came up, as if ready to dart away at the first sign of menace. Her whole arm was shaking. He set the bread firmly in it, then took his place on the other side as promised.

He had been uncertain how to proceed, but now he felt more confident. 'Jolie, I would like you to understand me. May I tell you my story?'

'Yes, lord,' she said. Then, as his glance went to the table where the knife had lain, 'Parry!'

He smiled. 'You learn quickly, Jolie. That is one of two reasons I asked for you.'

'You gave your oath!' she cried.

'I asked only for your company this evening. Your father owed my father, and this is the manner of the payment: your visit here. After this you will be free; we shall never require this of you again.'

'Oh, please – I never harmed you!'

'And I will not harm you!' he snapped. 'Eat your bread and listen; then perhaps you will understand.'

11

She looked at the bread she held as if seeing it for the first time. 'I – really can eat?'

'Slowly,' he cautioned. 'One small bite at a time. Like so.' He took a delicate bite of his own. 'Chew it well before swallowing.' He was aware that a hungry peasant tended to gulp good food, fearing it would vanish. He did not want the girl to make herself sick.

She took a bite, emulating him exactly.

'Fifteen years ago, the Sorcerer was preparing a major spell,' Parry said. 'For this he required a blood sacrifice. So he bought a baby. As you know, such babies are for sale by poor families who have too many to feed already.'

She knew. She chewed deliberately, watching him.

'I was that baby,' he continued. 'It was my destiny to be cut and bled on the altar, my life's blood lending substance to the potency of the spell. I believe it was a weather spell; there had been a drought, and the Lord of the Manor feared for his crops and the wild animals on his preserve. He did not want to suffer poor hunting. So he hired this service of the Sorcerer, in the year of our Saviour 1190. The sacrifice was to be private, because the Holy Church frowns on human sacrifice.'

He paused, glancing at her. She watched him as if mesmerized, slowly chewing.

'But the Abbot somehow learned of it,' Parry continued after a moment. 'He showed up at the site in person. "What's this noise of sacrifice?" he demanded. "You know it is forbidden to cut a living human baby!" And naturally the Lord had to disavow it, because the Abbot could make things very difficult for the progress of his soul to Heaven. "No, no, Abbot, you misunderstand!" he protested. "This is no human sacrifice! We have a fine sheep for that!" And he signalled his minion to fetch a sheep from the herd.

'"Then what is this human baby doing here?" the Abbot demanded, for he was no fool. The Lord had to

12

think fast. "Why, this is the Sorcerer's newborn son," he explained. "But the Sorcerer is not married," the Abbot pointed out. "That is why he is adopting this fine baby," the Lord said.

'The Abbot looked at the Sorcerer, whom he didn't like because magic was, strictly speaking, forbidden outside the auspices of the Church. But on occasion the community did need the professional touch, as now, so the Sorcerer was tolerated. The Abbot saw a way to make the Sorcerer really uncomfortable, and he pounced on it. "I am very glad to hear that," he said, rubbing his hands together. "Children are the Lord's blessing. I shall perform the ceremony of adoption straightaway." And the Sorcerer was trapped in this bed of thistles of the Lord's making; he would have to adopt and raise the sacrificial baby. Thus was my life spared, and I have not had occasion to regret it.'

He looked again at Jolie, and caught her in a tentative smile. He smiled in return, encouraging her. She was now halfway through her feast of bread, still chewing deliberately, as directed.

'The sheep arrived, and the sacrifice was made,' he resumed. 'And do you know, the weather did turn, and rain came within the day. It seemed that the sacrifice had been effective. The Abbot performed the ceremony of adoption, and I became the Sorcerer's son. I understand it was difficult for the Sorcerer to mask his scowl, or the Abbot his smirk. Even the Lord, when he pondered the matter, considered it a fine joke. But he remained neutral, for he required the good offices of both the Abbot and the Sorcerer. He went so far as to guarantee a nominal stipend for the care of the boy, so that he might never be in want. The Abbot matched him by guaranteeing a proper and churchly education for the lad. Thus I received both material and spiritual blessings, to the discomfiture of my adopted father. It was impossible for him to renege, or to dispose of me privately; the Abbot watched like a hawk. Thus the joke became a fact, and I was indeed the heir to the Sorcerer. But do you know, I somehow never did take a liking to the notion of human sacrifice? I am not certain I ever quite figured out why.'

Now Jolie could not prevent her laugh. Her face illuminated with the momentary pleasure of it, becoming pretty. She had finished her bread, while Parry's had only one bite from it.

'Here, take mine,' he said, offering it to her. 'I find I would rather talk than eat; you are a good listener.'

She tried to demur, but she remained hungry, and her protest lacked force. She accepted the bread, and ate it with better confidence.

'Then the oddest thing developed,' Parry said. 'I turned out to have a talent for magic. It was as if God had chosen this way to provide the Sorcerer an heir that he would never have chosen for himself. The Abbot died when I was ten, and the Lord when I was twelve, but the need for any coercion had long since passed. My father now saw to my education and welfare with enthusiasm, and indeed, I have never wanted for either. I have long known the truth of my adoption, and have no resentment on that account; I know that had I not been sold for sacrifice, I would now be a completely ignorant peasant, or perhaps dead of a fever. I believe the Lord in his mercy and discretion did intervene to make of my life what it could be. I was never in danger of death from the knife; God knew that, if the others did not.' He smiled again. 'But you may be sure that when I pick up a knife, it is to cut bread, and not to harm a visitor. Do you believe that now, Jolie?'

'Yes,' she whispered.

'Will you have some milk? I have plenty.'

She nodded mutely, seeming afraid to speak such greed

14

aloud. He got up and went to the table and poured a mugful. He brought it to her.

She took it, and sipped carefully. He knew she was honouring his cautions, which she took to be meaningless; but he knew also that she was far more likely to keep the food down if she went slowly. She was a typical peasant girl in that she had seldom if ever been properly fed.

'And so I learned the disciplines of law and medicine and magic,' Parry said. 'Also combat – and the arts. The art of communication among them. I doubt you have had much difficulty understanding me.'

She nodded, her smile coming more freely now.

'But I suspect you are wondering why I asked for you.'

The fear flared up again, and the remaining milk slopped in the mug. 'I have done you no harm!'

'And I shall do you no harm,' he replied automatically. 'I am fifteen years old now, and in good health. I am becoming a man. That means I am ready for a woman.'

Now the milk slopped over the brim. 'Oh, please, lord – '

'Surely you know that my father would have brought me any woman I wished,' he said.

She nodded, her hands still shaking.

'Obviously I asked for you. Why do you think I should want an illiterate peasant girl one year my junior?'

Her breathing was becoming laboured. 'Oh, please – '

'Stop that!' he snapped. 'Answer the question.'

She took a shuddering breath. 'Be – because I am the only virgin without disease in the village.'

'No.'

'But it is true, lord! No man has touched me.'

'I know it is true, but that is not why I asked for you. Try again.'

'Because my father owed – '

'No! *All* the villagers owe the Sorcerer!'

She shrugged. 'Then I do not know, lord.'

15

'Parry! Call me Parry! That's my name. I am low-born, like you.'

'Parry,' she agreed faintly.

'I asked for you because I want the best woman I can get, and you are that one.'

Now she laughed. 'You do ill to tease me so, lor – Parry.'

'It is true that you are young, but so am I. You are potentially the smartest and the prettiest woman of the village. *That* is why – '

This time her laugh was wholehearted. 'I am the thinnest and dumbest waif in the village!' she protested. 'How can you pretend otherwise?'

Parry leaned forward, reaching for her. She shrank away, but he persisted, catching hold of a hank of her hair at her shoulder. 'Look at this,' he said earnestly. 'Golden tresses, like few known here in the south of France. Look at your face; perfect. Not even any scars from the pox.'

'I have scars,' she said, almost eagerly. 'But they don't show.'

'All you need is some feeding, and you will flesh out into sheer loveliness. You have the frame already; I can see it clearly.'

She drew her dress more closely about her, fearing that her body showed. 'You shouldn't look!'

'Figuratively, I mean. I have learned to see folk for what they are and for what they can be; my father taught me that. He had me look at the villagers whenever we were in the village, and choose the best woman. Had I chosen wrongly, he would have served me as I deserved for my error.'

She was not persuaded, but she was flattered, and curious. 'How would that be?'

'He would have delivered that wrong girl to me.'

Again she laughed. 'And so he did!'

'No. I have no doubt of this. You are the one.'

Her doubt remained, but she was beginning to accept the fact that he believed. 'What will you have of me, then?'

'Your love.'

She looked stricken, having briefly dared hope for escape. 'I dare not deny you, Parry.'

'I said your love, not your body! I want you to love me.'

'I fear you,' she said. 'Is that enough?'

'No. You must come to know me, and to love me.'

She spread her hands slightly. 'You promised never to summon me again, after this night.'

'And I shall not! You must come only if you choose.'

'If the Sorcerer chooses.'

'No! It must be free. It *shall* be free.'

'I do not understand you.'

Parry got up and fetched a sheet of paper, one of the valuable supplies his father provided him with. He took a stick of charcoal and began to mark it, gazing intently at her. 'I have been trained also in the art of persuasion,' he said. 'This is my test: to persuade you. If I prove unable to do so, then I will fail, and my father will be disappointed. I must not fail, for there is no other woman as right for me as you. I must have you with me as I step out into the world as a sorcerer.'

'I have no truck with magic!' she exclaimed with some asperity. 'It is the work of the devil!'

'No. Black magic is the work of the devil. White magic is the work of the Church. It is white magic I am learning. It is beneficial to man and good for the soul.'

She shrugged. 'I wish you would let me go. I fear what sorcery you may work on me.'

'Give me one more hour,' he said earnestly. 'If I cannot persuade you in that time, then I will know it is not to be.'

'You talk so foolishly! I am not to be persuaded! I am here to be – ' She hesitated, then forced herself to finish. 'Taken.'

'Persuaded,' he said firmly. 'Just as I was given a far better life by the intervention of the Lord God, so may you also be. I can offer you good food, better than what you have just eaten. Good clothing, better than what you wear now. The warmth of the fire, every night. The respect, even the awe, of the villagers – '

'Why torment me like this?' she protested. 'I know none of it can be true!'

He set aside his charcoal and turned the paper to her. 'What do you see?'

Her eyes rounded with surprise. 'You drew this?'

'You saw me doing it. Who is it?'

'The Madonna!' she exclaimed. 'You *can* draw! But you had no model!'

'I had a model.'

'But you were looking at me – ' She faltered. 'It cannot be! She is so lovely!'

'It is you, Jolie – as you can be. When properly fed and dressed. When your beauty manifests to others as it does to me now.'

'No!' she said, bemused and flattered.

'It is what you will be, if you come to me. If you love me, and let me love you. It is the potential I see in you, that I know will appear if it is allowed.'

She stared at the sketch, fascinated. 'You believe this?'

'I know this. Yet this is only the lesser half of it. Even as the soul is more than the flesh, your mind is more than your body. You can be brilliant!'

'I cannot even read,' she said. 'Or figure.'

'I can teach you these. I know you can learn. I believe you have the desire. Will you not allow me to try?'

Her gaze became canny. 'So I will return to you every

18

night for your pleasure? You would fool me with impossible promises, so that this night will be not the end, but only the beginning?'

'Only the beginning,' he agreed. 'But not of delusion. All that I have told you is true – or will be true, if you accept it. Please, I beg of you – give me this chance!'

'You beg of *me*? You have no need to beg, only to command. You know that.'

'A command is made to an unwilling person, without love,' he said. 'A plea is made to a person one respects.'

'Peasants are not respected!' she exclaimed.

'Jolie, I will offer you a job, so it is legitimate. To be my servant. I will pay you a fair wage. I will give you a coin tonight, that you can take home and show as evidence. Then will you return?'

'But you said you don't want my body, you want my love. A servant doesn't love.'

'It is only a pretext. I will not treat you as a servant. I will treat you as an apprentice.'

'An apprentice! To be a sorcerer?'

'And to be my wife.'

'Blessed Mary!' she breathed, staring at him almost in shock.

'What more can I promise you?' he asked. 'I want your love. I want you to know me and to love me. I will do anything you ask.'

She sighed. 'I know my place. I am a poor, ignorant peasant girl. I know that none of this is to be believed. I wish you would just do what you mean to do and let me go, so that I need not fear evil any more, because it will be behind me. You have no cause to mix up my mind.'

Parry saw her slipping away despite his best effort. He could not let it happen. He realized he would have to do what he had sought to avoid. He would have to enchant her.

'What do you fear of me?' he asked.

19

'I cannot tell you that! The uttering of it might make it come true.'

'Do you fear that I will ravish you and cast you out despoiled, so that your father will beat you for being of lesser value on the marriage market?'

She nodded, agreeing without uttering.

'Do you wonder why I have not done it long since, instead of talking with you?'

'I have been asking you that!'

'Can you not accept that what I am telling you is true?'

'I can not.'

'Then let me show you the nature of my power.'

She tried to shrink back against the hearthstones. 'I believe it already!'

'Look at me, Jolie. Gaze into my eyes and do not flinch.'

She nerved herself for the inevitable and obeyed.

Parry invoked the magic of mesmerism. He accessed her mind through her eyes and made it responsive to his verbal commands. She would now obey any reasonable directive, and any unreasonable directive if it were suitably couched to seem reasonable. Almost anything could be done with a mesmerized person, if the sorcerer was sufficiently skilled.

'Listen to me,' he said. 'Believe what I say. Do not question it.'

She nodded, her eyes fixed on his.

'I am about to teach you to fly,' he said. 'Follow my instructions, and you will fly. Are you ready to fly?'

She hesitated, obviously wishing to question this, but constrained by his injunction against that. She nodded, ill at ease despite the power of the spell.

'Spread your arms,' he said. She did so. Now the holes in her dress were revealed; she had held her arms close to her body before, hiding the condition of the dress. Stitching had made up much of the damage, but it was not enough; he could see a portion of her right breast through the stitching. The breast was small, because she was young and because she was ill nourished; still, it threatened to distract him from this demonstration, so he forced his gaze away from it.

'You are now poised for flight,' he said. 'When you flap your arms you will rise into the air. Be careful, because the space is limited here; you do not want to bang into the roof. Do it slowly and remain in control.'

Still she looked doubtful.

'Flap your arms,' he said.

She lifted and dropped her arms, imitating the motion of the wings of a bird, awkwardly.

'You are now rising from the floor,' he said. 'Look down. What do you see?'

She remained on the floor, moving her arms. But her face as she looked down changed. Sheer wonder showed. 'I – I am hovering in the air!' she exclaimed.

'I have taught you to fly,' he said. 'But you are as yet clumsy. It takes practice to do it well. When you can do it well, we can fly outside. Now come down, carefully.'

She changed her motions, then her knees bent and she almost lost her balance. She recovered, and stood normally, her bosom heaving. 'I am down!'

'The lesson is over,' he said. 'Do not attempt to fly again tonight. Fix this experience in your memory. When I snap my fingers you will be free of my power.'

He waited a moment, then snapped his fingers.

Her attitude changed. She looked warily at him. 'You enchanted me!' she exclaimed.

'I enchanted you,' he agreed.

'But I flew!'

'You did, and you did not. It is a matter of perspective. I made you seem to fly, but later I can make you fly in reality. This is an aspect of my power.'

She looked about the room. 'It was so real! But I didn't really fly?'

'You had a vision of flying. It would not have been safe for you really to fly at this time. You aren't dressed for it.'

She glanced down at herself, and quickly pulled in her arms, covering the flaws in her dress. 'Why did you do this to me?'

'To show you the kind of power I have, taught me by my father, the Sorcerer. I appeal now to your logic: if I can make you believe you are flying, do you understand I could make you believe that you must undress and do whatever I ask of you?'

She considered. 'Yes,' she whispered, awed.

'Can you now believe that what I am telling you is true? That I value your person, and want your love, not your enchantment?'

'Almost,' she whispered.

'That I will teach you these things I know, that you may join me in the practice of this kind of magic, for the good of the village?'

'Almost.'

He saw that it wasn't enough. If she had this doubt immediately after the experience, that doubt would grow when she went home. His effort of persuasion had not been sufficient.

He had only one more thing to try. It seemed the weakest of his devices, but it was all that remained. If it failed, then he would have to admit defeat.

'I will sing to you,' he said. 'Then you may go, your father's debt acquitted. But here – I promised you a coin, in token of the employment I offer you. In token of all I ask of you. Take it, and return to me if you will.' He fetched the tiny copper coin from his pocket and gave it to her.

'You are letting me go, without – ?'

'After my song.' Then he breathed deeply, twice, and sang. He composed the words extemporaneously, and the melody; it was a thing he had always had a talent for. That was part of what the Sorcerer had discovered in him. There was assonance and meter in the language he used – French – but those hardly mattered; the sentiment would manifest in any language. Yet the words were only the lesser aspect of it, a convenience of the moment, tuned to this passing purpose.

The song filled the house, for it was buttressed by the sorcery he had mastered best: the ethereal accompaniment. It was as if the finest musicians of the realm sat behind him, playing their instruments in perfect accord, buttressing and amplifying his voice, making of it a sound no natural human throat could issue. The power of that orchestra infused the building, making the floor vibrate and the low fire quiver in resonance. There was, literally, magic in it.

> Jolie! I sing of the beauty I see in you,
> Of the glory in you, waiting to be evoked,
> Of the joy I would have of you,
> If only you could love me.
> If only you could love me.
>
> Jolie! I sing of your elegance to come,
> Of the envy of those who once knew you,
> Who will take you for an Abbess,
> If only I may love you.
> If only I may love you.

The girl stood as if transfixed, listening. Her tresses seemed to waver with the sound, and faint washes of colour crossed her eyes. She was indeed beautiful, and intelligent; only the poverty of her situation had masked her qualities. With food and care and confidence she would be a woman to reckon with. Parry had not deceived her in that; she deceived herself. He did want her love, for he knew her to be a treasure. Her name meant 'Pretty', and that she was, in many senses. His comprehension of this infused his song with passion; he loved her already.

He finished. He said nothing; he walked to the door and lifted the bar, and stood aside, waiting for her to leave.

Dazed, she clutched her dress about her and walked out.

She hesitated just outside, afraid of the night, shivering with its chill. Parry took a cloak from a hook and carried it to her, and set it on her shoulders.

Still she stood. He realized that she was now concerned for the creatures of the darkness. The village dogs knew her and would not attack, but they were not out now, which meant that wild animals could encroach. The village was some distance from Parry's house. It could be dangerous for a woman to walk alone.

He took down a cloak for himself, and fetched a stout staff. Then he joined Jolie. Without a word he set out for the village.

She followed, grateful for the protection. He slowed, encouraging her to catch up. Then they walked together, silently. The distance had seemed formidable; now it seemed short. No animals encroached.

When they came to her house, he stopped. She paused, glancing at him, then removed her cloak; it was not hers to keep. Gravely, he accepted it. Then he turned and walked away.

Would she come to him again? She had been moved by his song; he knew that. But how long would the effect last? She was free now; she had paid her father's debt.

Parry slept irregularly. He had put himself across as a urbane young man of considerable power, and he was that, but this was his first attempt to accomplish a major thing by himself. It was his rite of passage as a sorcerer –

and it was something he truly wanted. Jolie was the best possible woman for him in the region; with her he knew he could achieve happiness. There would be a great deal of work to develop her, of course, but there would also be much pleasure in the doing of it. He did not know what he would do if she did not come to him. He had at the moment no other ambition than to bring her to his house and keep her.

He woke before dawn, and dressed and ate and performed necessary tasks, his mind elsewhere.

The day passed with routine chores. One villager had chickens who ranged too far; neighbours had complained and threatened to kill them for their own pots, but the hens were undisciplined and could not be restrained. The man had paid the Sorcerer for a solution to the problem, and the Sorcerer had given the task to Parry for practice. If he bungled it, the Sorcerer would make it right, but Parry intended to handle the matter competently himself.

He pored over his text on law, and in due course found it: a procedure covering exactly this situation. It was not known locally, but had been used in other countries, and it had the force of common law. It was this: the owner of the hens had to stand at the ridge of the roof of his house, and pass his right arm under his left, and reach up and grab his own hair. Then he was to take a sickle by its point, in his left hand, whose motion was at this stage restricted. He would fling the sickle as far as he could, and its landing would define the distance his hens could go with impunity.

It happened that this particular peasant was athletic and coordinated; he would, with a little practice, be able to fling the sickle quite far. That should give his hens enough room to range. The Sorcerer would advise the client of this, privately; then, in a few days, present the procedure. It would be done in public, so that all the villagers would see how the man vindicated his chickens.

Once again, the Sorcerer would earn his fee. The Lord of the Manor, seeing the matter settled amicably, would not interfere; he might even come to watch the sickle-throwing himself.

Parry was well satisfied. But as evening approached he became nervous. Would Jolie come? He thought she would, but also he doubted. He had done the best he could to convince her; if it wasn't enough . . .

The day waned, but the girl did not show. Parry's gloom deepened. He had tried so hard to persuade her! What could he have done differently? He had a whole life to live with her, if only she chose it.

He lit a fire on the hearth. The air was turning chill, but that was not what motivated him. It was that he had had the fire going when she had come before, and she had sat beside it. Almost he could visualize her there! But he stopped that vision; a sorcerer had no business succumbing to the illusions he foisted on others. A sorcerer had to deal in reality, whatever it was, wherever he found it, being always undeceived. Magic, science, law and illusion were merely tools to be understood and applied. Reality was his truest master.

Even the reality of a woman who chose not to come.

But he had pinned so much on this! He *knew* she was right for him; he knew he could offer her a better life than any peasant of the village could. But did *she* know?

The fire blazed up, and smoked, and gradually settled into place as the draught became established. The average peasant cottage had no internal fire; it would have been dangerous for the thatched roof. But Parry had been raised in comparative luxury – a luxury he had hoped to share with –

He stiffened, listening. Was that a knock? He doubted it, for the sound had been so faint as to be coincidence, but he hurried to the door anyway and threw it open.

Jolie stood there. 'Did you mean it?' she asked timorously.

Parry opened his arms to her, realizing even as he did it that he might be making a mistake. He had asked for her love, but promised her only a job.

She stepped into his embrace. Her action, like his, was answer enough.

2

Crusade

There was not much more to it, that night. They embraced, then separated, aware that such intimacy was premature. She had only come to inform him that her father had acceded to her employment by the Sorcerer's son, and wanted to know the rate of pay. She would come in the morning for work.

'Yes, of course,' Parry agreed. He was so relieved that she had come that he had no concern for the details. He guided her to the fire, and brought her bread and milk.

'I should do that,' she said.

'Tomorrow you shall,' he said, smiling.

'My father thinks I am to be your mistress,' she confided. 'He wants an extra coin for that.'

'He shall have it!' Parry agreed before he thought.

She averted her gaze. 'Then it is true?'

'Only if you wish it. I told you before – '

'You desire me?'

'Yes.'

'But will not force me?'

'Yes.'

'And if I do not wish it?'

Parry spread his hands. 'I want only what you wish to give.'

She shook her head. 'I do not understand you, Parry.'

He tried to explain. 'I could pay a village girl, and she would do whatever I asked, because of the money. But she would not love me, only my money. I want your love, and that I can not buy.'

'I wish I could believe.'

'I wish I could make you believe.'

She glanced sidelong at him. 'I thought you would give me a reason.'

He was puzzled. 'What reason?'

'That you wished to catch a unicorn.'

He laughed. 'And for that I would need a virgin! I should have thought of that!'

'Is it true?'

'That you can catch a unicorn only with a virgin? Yes, in a manner. It is possible without, but the animal is killed in the process.'

'I meant, that this is why you want me?'

He spread his hands. 'No. I could have got an ugly or stupid virgin for that. You are neither.'

'But you could make me feel safer with you if you tell me that it is for the unicorn.'

'It is an assurance I cannot give you.'

'Then why do I feel reassured?'

'Because you realize I am telling you the truth, and that is more important than a facile rationale for your presence.'

She considered. 'Am I really neither?'

'Neither what?' he asked, unable to follow her thread.

'Ugly or stupid.'

Oh. 'Yes.'

'You could take me now, and I would not protest.'

'Do you love me?'

'I fear you.'

'I will wait for your love.'

'But I fear you less than I did.'

'That is good.' He liked the fact that she spoke her mind directly. Some in the village evidently took that for social ignorance, but he took it for innocence.

'I must go home now. But I will return in the morning.'

'I will walk you home.'

'No. It is not fully dark yet, and I must conquer my fear.'

29

'Then let me give you a spell to ward away bad animals.'

She considered again. 'Yes, that would help.'

He gave her a pouch that exuded a foul odour. 'Open this at need. Hang it outside your cottage, or it will drive out your family.'

She tittered. 'Bad animals!'

He nodded. 'The smell is versatile.'

She departed, and he clenched his hands together in an expression of sheer joy. He would win her!

Jolie came the next morning, and the morning thereafter. He prevailed on her to wash herself; she was distrustful of this peculiar requirement, but acceded and became clean in the new dresses he provided. Her hair became lustrous, and her skin as smooth as milk. But when she went home each evening, she donned her old garment and smudged her face with dirt, so as not to cause suspicion.

She was, as he had judged, a bright girl, and Parry used mesmeric techniques to teach her more rapidly and fully, just as the Sorcerer had used them on him. There was an enormous amount to learn, for sorcery was mainly a matter of knowledge and experience in the correct lores; true magic could be mastered only by those with special talents and dedication. Few folk had the cleverness or the patience to do it well; most who claimed to be adept were to some degree charlatans, buttressing their minimal magic with illusion. She learned to read, and to fight, and the arts, so that she could study on her own or defend herself from molestation or play prettily on the little harp he gave her. Her flesh quickly filled out, because of the good feeding, and she became the woman of his picture; not the Madonna, but as beautiful.

This progress did not pass unnoticed in the village, despite her effort to conceal it. Rags and dirt could hide only so much. The peasant boys oriented on her, and

Parry had to give her a spell to repel them. But he knew this would not be effective for long, for she was nubile and the other girls her age were getting married.

Jolie's emotional progress was as dramatic as her physical and intellectual progress. One day she accompanied him with her harp as he sang, and drew on the magic she was learning to make of it far more than a single instrument. He had always had a fine voice, but with her it was better than ever. The music was truly beautiful.

Then she set the harp aside. 'Parry, today I am fifteen. Will you marry me?'

He choked. She had caught him entirely off guard.

'You said you wanted my love,' she continued. 'You have not touched me, because you wanted my love, not my body. I love you now, and give you all that I have. Please marry me.'

He gazed at her. She was no longer pretty, or beautiful. She was stunning. All that he had foreseen in her had been realized in greater measure than anticipated. He had loved her virtually from the start, for her potential, but had reined it in in the interest of giving her room to grow. His love had become direct as her potential was fulfilled.

He could have said a great deal. He did not; it wasn't necessary. 'Yes, Jolie. I will marry you.'

She flung herself at him. 'You had me worried!'

He had had *her* worried?

They kissed. Jolie's original fear had become an equal measure of passion. But in a moment he drew back.

'You have second thoughts?' she asked, perhaps having one herself.

'I want to marry a virgin.'

'And you think I am not?'

'I think you will not be, if we embrace much longer.'

'But I would be cheaper if despoiled,' she pointed out teasingly. Her confidence had grown enormously. He

31

realized that it was her attitude that accounted for much of her beauty; now she believed in herself.

'It is a burden I must bear,' he said with mock sadness.

They risked another kiss, but kept it restrained.

Parry had to pay an exorbitant bridal price for her, because of the enhancement of her value he had fostered. But the Sorcerer, pleased with his son's judgement and success, arranged it, and the ceremony was held.

Some anonymous party, perhaps jealous, arranged to have a unicorn driven at the group. The ploy failed; Jolie, radiant in her bridal gown, called to the animal, and it came to her and suffered her to stroke its head. All the nasty gossip about her relationship with Parry was by this stroke abolished, and its perpetrator made ludicrous; now none could doubt she was still a virgin. Parry was especially pleased by the look of astonishment on the face of Jolie's father, who had thought that he was overcharging for her, and that Parry had paid only to maintain the pretence of licit dealings.

Parry and his bride retired for the evening to their house. Seldom had such a precious commodity been thrown away with such abandon!

The following two years were for them such as legends could be fashioned from. Parry became a full sorcerer in his own right, and Jolie joined him in his practice. For appropriate fees they saw to it that the local weather was good for crops, that the King's taxes fell on the village less strenuously than before, and that the Lord of the Manor prospered. So did the local peasants; their dire poverty became only nominal, and some individuals even became fat.

But their main effort was shrouded from village view. The Sorcerer precipitated it. A few days after the wedding, he paid a call on his son. He was now a venerable figure with a white beard. He had been travelling widely as his son took up the burden of local service, and had been absent for weeks at a time.

'As you know, Parry, I did not adopt you by choice – but had I the choice to make again, knowing how it turned out, I would have done it eagerly. You have been a source of great pride to me.'

'Thank you, sire,' Parry replied. The Sorcerer seldom expressed himself so directly and positively.

'Not the least of it has been your way with this woman,' the Sorcerer continued. 'You fixed on her with unerring accuracy, and developed her with consummate skill. As a result, you now have far greater power than you could otherwise have had.'

'And joy, too,' Parry murmured. Jolie arranged to flush prettily, though her naïveté had been among the first of her qualities to change. She now knew, indeed, that she had been the best Parry could have chosen, and that she had lived up to her potential. He had been the diamond cutter; she had been the diamond.

'I do not begrudge you that joy,' the Sorcerer said. 'But it was for another purpose I challenged you to acquire the best possible woman. Even as I adopted you for cynical reason, and gained more joy out of it than I deserved, you acquired her for reason, and your joy of her is incidental.'

Both Parry and Jolie gazed at him, realizing that his visit was not at all social. Something serious was afoot.

'Through my arts I divined that the Horned One has slated great evil for this region,' the Sorcerer continued. He did not name Lucifer directly, because that would invite mischief.

'But this is a poor region, even after our efforts,' Parry protested. 'What interest could such a being have here?'

'It is the entire southern region of France that has evoked the interest,' the Sorcerer explained. 'Our village is not the object, because I have laboured long to mask its improvement from the notice of the Crown, for tax purposes. But elsewhere in the region peasants and their masters are doing well, too, partly because of the Albigensian heresy.'

'Heresy?' Jolie asked. Parry kept silent, because he knew something of the matter. Heresy meant trouble, certainly!

'You of the country and village remain loyal to the tenets of the Church, but in the growing towns men are becoming more liberal. They question the corruption of the priests, and indeed the entire priestly hierarchy. They are dualists, seeing only good and evil without shades between, and to them the choices are clear enough without the intercession of the priests. Indeed, they see little need for any interpretation between themselves and God.'

'But that means there is no need for –' Jolie said.

'For the Church,' the Sorcerer concluded. 'And that is heresy, plain and simple.'

'But if they do honour God –'

'Forgive me if my cynicism offends your sensitivities, daughter.' The Sorcerer had called her that since her marriage to his son. 'I do not subscribe in my heart to any religion; I cannot afford it, professionally. I see no reason why a man should not honour God directly, in his own way. But consider the welfare of the Church, if the people should choose to bypass it. If they no longer tithed. No longer attended services or honoured the sacraments. No longer heeded the word of the Pope.'

'Why, it would destroy the Church!' she exclaimed.

'Therefore the very notion is heretical. The Church cannot tolerate that which would destroy it – and the notions that are prospering among the Albigenses would indeed destroy it. The Church has kept its place by being vigilant in the suppression of rival notions, and it shall

34

surely continue so. Its power is being threatened, and like any creature it will react with ferocity.'

'But are the Albigenses so bad?' she asked.

'No, they are not bad at all; they are good folk, as these things go. They are industrious and increasingly educated, and though they subscribe to asceticism, those who associate with them are more tolerant of wealth. In fact, some of the Lords are using the precepts of the Albigenses to avoid the payment of taxes to the Crown.'

Trouble, compounded! Parry had to speak. 'So the Evil One sees an opportunity for mischief, because of the irritation of the Church and the Crown!'

'It is not smart to annoy both at once,' the Sorcerer agreed. 'The times are changed; any spark will set things off. Now that spark has occurred, and I recognize the handiwork of the Evil One. He cares nothing for Church or State, only for mischief, for in troubled times his harvest increases.'

'Spark?' Parry asked.

'A Cistercian monk has been murdered. That provides the catalyst for action. We cannot abate it now.'

'What will happen?' Jolie asked.

'There will be a crusade against the Albigenses. They did not kill the monk, but they opposed his teachings, and they will not be able to defend their innocence. The Pope will determine that the Albigenses must be abolished. They must recant their heresy, renew fealty to the Church, and pay their taxes, which are in arrears.'

'But they will not do that!' Parry exclaimed. 'They are stout folk, firm in their belief and their independence, and they have powerful support.'

'Hence the crusade. They will be converted by force. Their heresy will be abolished. But there will be much pain in the doing of it. That is why we must prepare.'

'A crusade,' Parry said. 'Troops will come here?'

'Yes. We are on their main route; this I have determined. Our time is limited; within a month they will be here. I regret I was involved in absorbing research and did not survey the political situation earlier; the crisis was well-developed before I was aware.'

'How can we prepare?' Jolie asked.

'We must get away from here with our valuables,' he Sorcerer said. 'Quietly, leaving no trail. In the north the disruption will be minimal; we can survive there nicely.'

'But what of the folk here?' Parry asked. 'They cannot move.'

'They are lost. They cannot be helped.'

'But surely if the warning is given – '

'That will only make our own escape complicated. We cannot afford to alert them.'

Parry knew his father. The Sorcerer was not an evil man, but a practical one; if he said the local folk could not be helped, it was surely so. Yet he had to argue. 'The Lord of the Manor – he could do something! If we tell him privately of the threat – '

'I have done so. He refuses to believe there is genuine danger. He will not change.'

'Change?'

'I explained to him what would be required to save his demesnes and the welfare of the villagers. He and all others must renounce the Albigensian heresy. They must swear renewed fealty to the Christian doctrine as espoused by the Church. They must pay taxes and penalties.'

'But such penalties can be ruinous!'

'True. Therefore he will not budge. But he courts disaster. I gave him good advice.'

Parry nodded. The cost of compliance was too great; the Albigenses and the Lord of the Manor preferred to take the risk of noncompliance. They lacked the perception of the Sorcerer; they did not accept the full validity of his divinations. 'Then we must flee,' he agreed.

'But I cannot desert my family!' Jolie protested.

The Sorcerer stood. 'Talk to her, son. She must be persuaded.' He departed, for he had preparations of his own to make.

Parry talked to her. It was no good; she was too much a creature of her community, and she loved her family. It was one of the good things about her, and he could not fault her for it. But he knew they had to get away.

He compromised. He fashioned a temporary retreat in the forest whose location was secret from all but himself and Jolie and his father. When the soldiers of the crusade came, they would hide there. After the soldiers passed, Jolie's family would either be all right or it wouldn't; she would be free to leave then, having remained near during the crisis.

To this she agreed. They set about their preparations for the disaster.

The soldiers of the crusade evidently had advance information. They struck first at the Sorcerer, knowing that the most effective local resistance would be organized here. They could handle peasants, but magic was more formidable. They sent a mission to burn his house and slay him, before moving on to the Manor.

The Sorcerer had seen them coming, of course. This had required not divination but plain common sense. He had moved his key supplies and texts out long before, but to allay suspicion had left enough of the lesser material at his residence to give the impression that he had been caught by surprise. For similar reason he had to defend it. Parry was there to assist, while Jolie hurried afoot to the village to bring out her family. She had not yet mastered form-changing, so was limited by her human body.

Parry and his father would change to avian form and fly away after making a respectable and unsuccessful defence of the Sorcerer's house. It was a loss that had to be taken; after that they should be free of pursuit, and could relax. They would seem to die here, so that no fear of them remained. Their route north had been planned; they knew at which taverns to stop, and where to stay for the nights. They would be like other refugees, unidentified.

They watched the troops arriving. It was a contingent of about a dozen: common soldiers wearing helmets, hauberks and boots, carrying bills.

Parry studied the soldiers. He had in the course of his education learned the basics of military outfitting, as well as those of combat itself. 'Never can tell when such knowledge will be important,' the Sorcerer had told him. Now he appreciated that importance, for he was able to determine the nature of the force ranged against the house.

These were common soldiers from all over France. Their helmets were standard sugar-loaf types, basically metal caps shaped like the pointed end of an acorn. Knights had better headgear, but commoners could not afford it. Their hauberks were long coats of mail worn over their jacks: quilted garments that protected the body from bruising when the mail was struck. This, again, was standard, though the quality of individual hauberks varied. The main distinction was in their weapons: the bills. These were assorted pole arms, with heavy curved blades mounted on poles, buttressed by points and spikes. The helms and mail might be provided by the one who organized the crusade, but the weapons tended to belong to the individual soldiers, who became proficient by long familiarity and practice. Each local smithy had his own variant, and the locals swore by it, and used it in preference to other variants. The particular curve of the blade, the sharpness of the hook, the length and stoutness of the spike – these served to identify the regions from which the weapons came. The bill had started as an agricultural implement, and some were still used as such, but most had been modified for war. Certainly it was an effective weapon in the hands of one who knew how to use it.

Parry had entertained a notion of fighting off the soldiers and saving his father's house, which still contained much of value. He saw now that this had been unrealistic; only formidable magic would suffice, and the makings of that would be better saved for later use. The Sorcerer was correct: they would have to let this house be destroyed, and make it seem that the two of them died with it; it was the only practical way.

'Now we must show ourselves,' the Sorcerer said. 'They have to know we are within when they torch it, so that no doubt of our deaths lingers. This may not be easy.'

Parry swallowed. He was aware that their supposed deaths could all too readily become genuine if they miscalculated in any way, or simply had bad luck. Escape was easy; escape after seeming death was more complicated.

The leader of the squad hailed the house. He wore a surcoat over his mail, which meant that he did not expect to fight. 'Sorcerer! Come out and renounce your heresy!'

It was a ritual challenge, done in the name of the crusade, which was theoretically to convert the heretics. Once the demand had been made and rejected, the soldiers would be free to do what they had come for, in the name of God. Normally they would take plunder, for this was the most substantial part of their recompense, but the orders for this mission were surely to destroy the house and occupants without ceremony or delay. They would not want to give the Sorcerer opportunity to demonstrate his power.

The Sorcerer opened the door and stepped out. Parry followed. Neither was armed with any physical weapon. 'Will you spare my life and that of my son if I do?' the Sorcerer called.

The leader seemed to consider. 'Funny you should ask that.' Then he gestured to his men. 'Take them.'

The soldiers came towards the two, their bills poised. They looked grim.

'Do I have your word you will not harm us if we submit?' the Sorcerer asked.

The leader did not answer. The soldiers closed in. That was answer enough.

'That's what I thought,' the Sorcerer said. He flung out his right hand, throwing powder. It glinted in the sunlight, forming the shape of a dragon that glowered at the soldiers.

The men backed hastily away, their fear of the Sorcerer becoming justified.

'Don't be fooled by his tricks!' the sergeant cried. 'It's illusion! It has no substance! Just march right through it and cut him down!'

The men hesitated, but then, at the continued urging of their leader, they braved the dragon and found it was true. It was only a spectre fashioned from the powder, having no more substance than that powder. It was theoretically possible to conjure real animals, but this was well beyond the Sorcerer's ability, while illusion was cheap.

But the delay had allowed Parry and the Sorcerer to retreat into the house. Stage One had been negotiated: the soldiers now had no doubt of the Sorcerer's presence and nature.

'Surround the house,' the sergeant commanded. 'Don't let them escape.'

Parry watched from the windows as the men spread out. They remained wary, though they had overcome the illusion of the dragon.

'Now torch it,' the sergeant said. 'And kill them as they come out.'

'But what about spoils?' a soldier demanded. 'There must be good stuff in there!'

'Our orders are to kill the Sorcerer and destroy his house,' the sergeant said firmly. 'No spoils here. Anything you took could be enchanted to kill you in your sleep. That's how they operate.'

The soldier was silent. His fear of the supernatural overrode his greed. That was just as well, for the Sorcerer would have had to kill any men who entered the house, lest they interfere with the escape.

They hauled brush and straw to the walls of the house, half the men working while the others guarded them with their bills. When they had a fair pile of dry material, they brought a torch and started the fire. It blazed up vigorously, sending clouds of smoke aloft.

The Sorcerer turned to Parry and nodded. This was exactly what he had planned for. They had navigated the situation without a hitch.

They waited until the fire was raging all around the house. Then they climbed to the loft, where the Sorcerer opened a panel he had prepared. They had an avenue to the outside, now concealed by the billowing smoke.

The Sorcerer changed form, becoming a hawk. He spread his wings and flew up into the swirl. Parry became a crow, and followed. Changing shape was relatively easy, once the appropriate level had been achieved; it was the change of mass that was difficult, and the mastering of the ability to use the altered body to fly. As far as Parry knew, they were the only two human beings in France who could do this. In time Jolie, too, might accomplish it.

'There they go!' a soldier cried.

'I got the hawk,' the sergeant snapped. 'You take the crow.'

Parry saw to his dismay that they had two crossbows, and seemed competent in their use. The sergeant let fly his shaft, and it transfixed the hawk. Parry swerved – and

41

the shaft intended for him missed, brushing his right wingtip.

The Sorcerer fell. Parry could not help him, for he was defenceless against the deadly shafts of the crossbow. He winged strongly towards the trees, losing himself among their branches before the soldiers could reload.

The soldiers had known what to expect! They had come prepared for the form-changing. This had been a more competent trap than the Sorcerer had realized. Their accuracy of information was unnerving, apart from its effect on the Sorcerer. Most ignorant peasants believed that sorcerers could accomplish anything, no matter how outlandish; most educated folk prided themselves on their ability to doubt, so professed not to believe in magic at all. Between the two extremes, a clever sorcerer could prosper, as Parry's father had, using only that minimum of magic required to accomplish his purposes. But this party had targeted him precisely, and so accomplished the mission: Sorcerer dead and house destroyed.

Parry had escaped largely by luck. He had been the second to fly, so the less-accurate soldier had been assigned to him. He had dodged involuntarily, and thereby saved his life.

He soon lost the soldiers; it was impossible to pursue a black bird flitting through low shadows. When he was sure he was safe, he paused to rest and take stock.

Then the full realization of his father's fate struck him. The Sorcerer was dead! All his plans for escape and success elsewhere were ended, by that single shot from the crossbow.

Parry's surge of grief was overridden almost immediately by rage. He would go back and destroy those foul soldiers! He would make a fire that would engulf them, as their fire had engulfed the house! It required only minimal magic to start a fire; then it fed itself. His father would be avenged!

But then a new concern overtook him. Jolie! She was at the village, and if they had known of the Sorcerer, they might know of her, too. If they sent a contingent to the village –

He spread his wings and flew into the air. The crow could travel more swiftly than the human being, cross-country. Part of what made his form so difficult was adapting his consciousness to fit within it; that alone had taken Parry months of practice, but now he blessed that effort.

Even so, it took him many minutes to cover the distance. By the time he reached the village, he knew from the clamour that his worst fear had been realized. The soldiers of the crusade were there, and they were before the house of Jolie's family. Something was happening there, and Parry dreaded to imagine what.

He landed and returned to his human form. He was naked. He had not yet developed to that sophistication of transportation that enabled him to change his clothing, too. But he had prepared for such an event; he had a cache of clothing in a hollow tree just beyond the village.

He hurried to this now. Just as he was reaching into it, a harsh voice sounded: 'We have you, Sorcerer!'

Parry jumped up, whirling on the man, but found himself facing a cocked crossbow aimed at his chest. He froze in place.

'Before you try magic, know this,' the crossbowman said. 'We have your girl, and she will die the moment you oppose us. Then we shall hunt you down, too; we know how to do it.'

Evidently they did! Twice now, in two places, the soldiers of the crusade had sprung successful traps. They had known exactly where to find his father and himself, and who else to look for. It was too neat. There had to be magic involved – and until he knew its source and nature, he would have to cooperate. Unless his hand was forced.

43

They marched him, naked, into the village. None of the villagers was in evidence; the soldiers had evidently cowed them and sent them to hide in their cottages while waiting for Parry. Now they had him. He could change form and escape, or conjure a weapon and attack; he was not at all helpless. But he was sure they were not bluffing about Jolie, and he could not risk precipitating harm to her.

They did have her. Another sergeant held her by the arm. Her dress was torn, and the other soldiers were ogling what showed. She had evidently fought, but had been overcome; the white cross on the sergeant's tunic was smeared with dirt. Because she lacked the ability to change form, she had been unable to escape that way. How he wished now he had taught her that, and let some of the other arts wait.

Still, she did have effective abilities. She could mesmerize, if she could gain and hold the direct gaze of a single person. If they could manoeuvre things so that she could stun her captor with a glance, then Parry could change to a horse and carry her swiftly away.

'Bind him!' the sergeant commanded. 'Blindfold him, too; that will stop his magic!'

They were wrong in that; Parry had limited second sight, so that he could see almost as well without eyes as he could with them. They were underestimating him, and that was an asset. He needed every advantage he could muster!

They bound him tightly with rope, and put a hood over his head, tying it closely about his neck. They thrust him against the wall of the cottage.

'I don't know,' a soldier said. 'I've heard those sorcerers cannot be bound if they don't want to be. How do we know he isn't pretending helplessness until he's ready to wipe us out?'

The sergeant considered. 'You're right. We were warned to take no chances. If anything goes wrong at the old sorcerer's place, we want to be sure we've got this one

44

secure. So we'll test it. Keep the crossbow on him, and kill him if he moves.'

'But he could wait till night, then make a vision to distract the guard and break away,' the soldier pointed out.

That soldier was too smart!

'I had a good test in mind,' the sergeant said. 'I'm going to take the wench inside and have some fun with her. If he can get free, that's when he'll do it. If he doesn't budge, we'll know he's secure.'

The sergeant was too cocksure. He knew less about sorcerers than he thought. Parry could break free any time, but he would not – because it was not his safety but Jolie's he was concerned with. But the sergeant was giving her the opportunity she needed. The moment he tried to rape her, she would mesmerize him. Because they would be out of sight of the soldiers, she would be able to stun him and tie him up. Then Parry would burst free and change and carry her away.

Ah, but there was the crossbow. With his second sight, he could see the soldier clearly. Parry was facing away from him, but it didn't matter; second sight did not depend on direction.

He generated an image that caused his own body to seem to blur. The soldier blinked, but this blurring was not of his eyes but of the subject. Parry's form wavered rhythmically, in a manner that induced mesmerism. The soldier's mind became clouded, and then the soldier drifted gently to sleep, his eyes still open and his weapon still pointed. But now he would not fire when Parry moved.

Parry diverted his sight to Jolie. Her parents' cottage was empty, or perhaps the people were bound in the stall half of it, leaving the living chamber clear. Jolie was tied, her hands bound up behind her head, her ankles crossed and tied in that position. That made it possible for her legs to spread, but not to kick. She was lying on the straw bed.

The sergeant was in the process of removing his hauberk. The mail garment covered him from head to knee, and was heavy; a sexual act would be problematical in it. So the sergeant drew it off over his head, and pulled his arms from the mitten-sleeves. Now he stood in his jack, the padded undergarment.

He approached Jolie. He took hold of her shoulders and made her look him in the face. 'Scream, wench!' he said. 'I want your man to hear!'

She did not scream. She stared at him, using the mesmerizing gaze.

The sergeant laughed. 'Your tricks won't work on me, wench! I have an amulet to protect me from them!' He touched a silver medallion that hung from his neck. 'We were warned about your kind!'

Parry had not thought of that! Most of the power of mesmerization lay in the recipient's belief; a counter charm destroyed that belief, and therefore the effect.

The amulet dangled near her face. Jolie lifted her head and took it with her teeth. She wrenched it away.

The sergeant cursed. He grabbed for the amulet, but Jolie's gaze caught his own, and now her power was unfettered.

The sergeant threw himself back, and brought up his hands, covering his eyes, breaking the contact.

She scrambled up as well as she could with wrists and ankles bound, pursuing him. She had to catch his eyes again, to complete the mesmerization. Then she could make him untie her, and she would be ready for Parry to act.

But the sergeant, aware of this threat, scrambled to fetch his sword. His hand caught it as Jolie made it to her knees and lurched to her feet despite the bindings. She hopped at him.

Parry realized he couldn't wait. He drew on his reserve of strength and snapped the rope that bound his hands. Then he snapped his feet free. This was more physical discipline than magic; the cords that were effective against the average man did not have too much extra capacity.

'He's escaping!' a soldier cried. 'Shoot him!'

The crossbowman, jolted from his trance, pulled the trigger. The arrow fired out. But Parry was already out of its line, and it struck the ground. He ripped the hood from his head.

His second sight remained. While he moved, avoiding the soldiers, he saw the sergeant lift the sword and jam it at Jolie's approaching body.

Parry leapt for the door, changing to wolf form as he did. But fast as he was, he was too slow. As he burst inside, the sergeant's sword plunged through Jolie's chest, and was withdrawn: a swift but deadly strike. The man oriented for a second, more precise attack.

Parry reached the sergeant. His teeth closed on the sergeant's throat and sliced through the flesh, tearing out the jugular vein and puncturing the carotid arteries. The sergeant was dead on his feet.

But so was Jolie. She and the sergeant fell together, their blood mingling.

Parry sniffed Jolie. The sword had driven through her right lung. She was grievously wounded, but alive.

He shifted to human form. 'Jolie, look at me,' he said, taking her head in his hands.

Her pain-glazed eyes gazed into his. Instantly he mesmerized her. 'You feel no pain,' he said. 'Your body will bleed no more. You will sleep in stasis until I wake you. I love you.'

Her eyes closed. Her bleeding slowed. She would endure for the time required. This had been part of her training: to respond instantly to healing mesmerization.

Quickly he took the soiled sword and used its edge to

47

slice the mattess. He cut stout strips and fashioned them into a harness.

A soldier's face showed in the doorway. Parry glanced at him, and exerted his power of mesmerization. 'I am your sergeant,' he said. 'I have dealt with the sorcerer. I have not finished with the wench. Remain clear until I emerge.'

The soldier nodded and retreated. Parry returned to his work. It was easy to deal with a single enemy, but difficult to deal with many in this manner, because he could focus his mesmeric gaze on only one at a time. The single soldier's intrusion had been a stroke of luck in an otherwise disastrous situation; it gave Parry time to do what he needed.

He rigged the harness to support Jolie's body. Then he formed the long straps of it into two great loops, such as might encircle the body of a horse. He fitted Jolie into her part, then stood in the loops, draping one around his neck and the other around his midsection. Then he heaved Jolie up to his back, bent forward, and changed to horse form.

His abruptly larger body took up the slack, filling out the loops. Now Jolie was bound to his back. He shook himself, nudging her into proper place so she could not slide around and down. Then he leapt out the door.

The soldiers gaped. Parry took advantage of their momentary inaction to locate the crossbow and stomp it with a forehoof. Then he galloped out of the village, unscathed.

He was in animal form, but his human intellect remained, as it had in the other forms. That was a key part of the magic. A person who transformed without making allowance for the mind could be in bad trouble! But it was not easy to master, and this was one reason that Jolie had not yet reached this stage. If only Parry had realized earlier that she would need it!

There was no pursuit. The death of the sergeant and the speed of Parry's escape must have thrown the soldiers into confusion. That enabled Parry to go almost directly to their prepared retreat in the forest.

Once there, he reverted to his human form and took Jolie down from his back. He carried her into the shelter and eased her to the mattress.

Now he drew on his expertise in medicine. He had herbs and elixirs to reduce pain, cleanse infection and promote healing. Few folk realized the importance of cleanliness in such matters; the worst threats to life were not huge monsters, but invisibly small ones that multiplied in dirt. The wound was bad, but his magic should fix it.

But he realized now that the trip to the retreat had been hard on her. Had he attended to her immediately, in the village, he could have done her a great deal of good. But he had had to use a stopgap measure, and then carry her, and she had bounced on his back. Her wound had been aggravated, and the blood had flowed despite the control lent by her mesmerized state. Now she was in serious trouble. Her breathing was laboured, for only one lung was functioning adequately.

He worked desperately, but there was much he could not do. His father had greater expertise – but his father was dead. Parry didn't know how to make up for the extensive internal bleeding he realized had occurred. He had no substitute for blood! He would have given her his own, but knew that wouldn't work; the humours of one person inevitably fought those of another, and made the transfusion worse than none at all. She had to survive on her own blood – and she no longer had enough.

Perhaps if he gave her plenty of nourishing liquid to drink it would restore the blood. But to do that, he would have to wake her. He didn't like that, because she would then become aware of her pain; yet there seemed to be no choice.

He prepared broth, thick with the needs of life. He set a warm bowl of it beside her. Then he roused her with a word. 'Wake,' he said. 'Wake, Jolie.'

Her eyelids flickered. 'Parry,' she breathed – and winced.

'You were wounded,' he said quickly. 'A sword thrust. You have lost blood. But I have you safe, and if you will drink this good broth – '

Slowly, she shook her head. 'Parry, I hurt,' she gasped. 'Please let me die.'

He was horrified. 'Jolie, I'll never let you die!'

'It is no use,' she whispered with half a breath. 'I love you, but I cannot – cannot survive. The pain is ter – terrible. Kiss me and let me die.'

It was worse than he had supposed. She would never have yielded to mere pain; she was a stout girl at heart. She knew her body, and knew it could not be saved.

He had to honour her last request.

He leaned forward and kissed her with infinite tenderness. He felt her response. Then she sighed and sank into unconsciousness.

A hooded figure stepped through the wall.

Parry started up, astonished and dismayed. He had not heard the soldiers coming!

But this was no soldier. It was a man in a voluminous black cloak, with a deep cowl that hid his face in shadow. He leaned over Jolie, one hand reaching for her.

'Stop!' Parry cried, outraged in his grief. 'She is my love and my wife! I will suffer no stranger to touch her in her last moment!'

The figure turned to him as if in surprise.

The surprise was mutual. Now Parry discerned the face – and it was a fleshless skull.

'I am no stranger,' the bare teeth said. 'I am Thanatos. I have come for this woman's soul.'

It had to be true. The figure had stepped through the

wall without disturbing it, at the very moment Jolie was sinking into oblivion.

He remembered something his father had told him. There were Incarnations, and Death was one of them. But he came personally only for those whose souls were in doubt.

'Jolie is a good woman!' Parry protested. 'She has been everything to me! How can her soul be in doubt?'

The hood tilted. 'I shall ascertain that for you.' The hand moved again, this time reaching into Jolie's body and catching something there. In a moment it emerged, holding something like a netting of glowing spider web. It was her soul.

Thanatos studied it. 'She *is* a good woman,' he agreed. 'There is virtually no blight on her soul. Yet I was drawn to her. Let me investigate.'

Then, suddenly, the world stopped. Parry was frozen in place, unable to move, even to breathe, yet was in no discomfort. It was as though time had stilled. This was magic of a far superior order!

Then, after what could have been an instant or a day, motion resumed. 'I have inquired,' Thanatos said. 'She is not evil, but the circumstances of her death precipitates monstrous evil. We do not know its nature, for we find no current evidence of it, but it is nonetheless present. When it coalesces, it will be known that this was the site of its initiation. Therefore the goodness of her soul is balanced by the evil of its situation and I was summoned.'

'She can not go to Heaven?'

'I think she can not escape the mortal realm,' Thanatos replied. 'She must remain as a ghost, until the evil abates.'

'Then let her stay with me!' Parry cried. 'I will care for her ghost!'

Thanatos shrugged. 'Take a drop of her blood on your wrist,' he said. 'She can inhabit only her own essence.'

Parry touched his left wrist to Jolie's wounded breast, picking up a smear of blood.

Thanatos set the soul against that smear. It shrank into the blood and disappeared.

Parry was silent, gazing at the blood. By the time he thought to ask another question, Thanatos was gone. Parry was left with Jolie's body, and his grief.

Then he heard the soldiers coming. He had to flee, for they would kill him on sight. He could not even remain to give his beloved a decent Christian burial. That was grief upon grief.

He became the wolf and leaped from the shelter. An arrow sought him, but missed. In moments he was away and hidden among the trees. He escaped unscathed – in body.

3

Franciscan

He ran till he was leagues from his home region; there was no longer anything to hold him there. His father, his wife –

He paused in his motion, to revert to his natural form. Now his grief struck with full force. What was he to do, without Jolie? All his other losses he could handle, but hers he could not. He had based his future on the assumption that she would be with him.

He sank down to the forest floor and wept.

Then he heard the baying of the hounds.

He did not need to guess their quarry. The Soldiers of the Cross had picked up his trail and were closing in. He would not be permitted even his hour of grief in peace!

He was tired, for the physical exertion was wearing, and so was the energy required to change form. But he changed into his crow form, spread his wings, and ascended to the open sky. He flew at right angles to his prior trail, so that the dogs would have no hint of his location.

He reached the edge of a village north of the one he had left, and landed. He reverted to man again.

He was naked; he would have to get some clothing. His cache of valuables was back in the retreat, now forfeit. He would have to scrounge.

There was a cottage outside the main village area. It was a standard peasant dwelling, with stout posts buttressing thin logs, the walls chinked with twigs and mud, the roof thatched with straw. The occupant might be friendly or unfriendly; Parry would just have to risk it.

He went up and knocked on the twisted board that

served as the door. In a moment an old woman appeared in the dark interior. She stared at him apprehensively.

'I have lost my clothes,' Parry said quickly. 'I – I'm a refugee from the soldiers. They killed my wife. If you have anything I can wear, I will work for it.'

The woman considered. He knew she was trying to judge whether he spoke the truth, and whether it was safe to help him.

'Are you Christian or heretic?' she asked at last.

'Christian, with heretical leanings.' That was the literal truth. 'Whatever kind of Christianity the crusade represents, I'm not it.'

'Get in here, then,' she said, and lifted the board clear.

Parry ducked his head and entered the cottage. This was the stall chamber, and several sheep were in it. Their manure flavoured the air.

They passed into the second chamber, which was the residential one. The woman evidently lived alone; there was a single bed of straw at one side. She dug out a ragged old tunic. 'My husband's, rest his soul.'

Parry accepted it and quickly donned it. 'My thanks, good woman. I will earn it.' The thing was patched and restitched and dirty, but did not seem to have fleas; it had been too long unused. That was a blessing.

She found some battered shoes. 'You're about his size.'

He tried them on. They were a bit tight, but would do. 'This is more than I – '

'You hungry?'

Parry realized that he was; he had been too busy to eat recently.

She fetched a soiled wooden bowl and poured some cold pease porridge into it. Parry tilted it to his lips and took a swallow. It was bland, formless stuff, but it was food, and he was duly grateful.

But before he finished, there was the sound of baying

dogs. 'Oh, no!' Parry exclaimed. 'They are after me again, and I have brought mischief on your house!'

'Run out and lead them off,' the woman said. 'Then loop back; you owe me some work.'

'Agreed!'

He hurried out. He realized that the boots would mask his smell, so he took them off and carried them. Then he walked quickly through the village, attracting no attention; ragged peasants were common, especially now that war had come to this region.

The sound of the dogs was coming closer. He walked on beyond the village, until out of sight of it. Then he walked into the forest on the left, looped about, intersected his own trail and put on the boots. He tromped back across the road to the right, finding a passable path. He followed this back around the village.

He heard the dogs arrive at the village. Then, as he moved back the way he had come, they progressed forward the way he had gone. He smiled briefly; they would encounter the loop, mill about uncertainly, and the handlers would conclude that he had changed to avian form and flown. End of that trail! They would not suspect a pedestrian ruse from a sorcerer. At least, that seemed worth gambling on. He was too tired to fly again, when the old woman had offered him further hospitality.

He returned to the cottage. He knocked on the door.

'Get in here!' the woman snapped. 'They'll be back.'

He got in. 'Hide under the straw,' she said. 'Till it's clear.'

He wedged under the matted straw, and arranged it to cover him. Now he could not see out, but he could hear. If they came back, and the woman betrayed him, he would be helpless. But what motive could she have for that? He owed her some work for his clothing.

Shortly they did return. He heard them at the door.

'Keep those dogs clear!' she screeched, outraged. 'They'll spook my sheep!'

There was a muttering outside he could not hear.

Then the woman spoke again: 'Of course he's not here! What do you think I am? May the wrath of our merciful Lord Jesus fall on me this instant if I speak falsely!'

She was baldly lying, compounding it by invoking Jesus! This was not an ordinary peasant woman! Yet she had asked if he were a Christian, and he had assumed that it was the positive aspect of his answer that had persuaded her to take him in.

Her vehemence evidently convinced the pursuers, for the sounds of the hounds departed. The woman remained for some time at the door, perhaps watching to make sure they were not lingering. Then she returned to the living chamber.

'Very well, boy, they're gone,' she said. 'Now get up and tell me why they want you so bad.'

Parry climbed out and shook off the straw. 'You lied for me,' he said.

'A villein hag can't afford integrity,' she said. 'But you're no serf. Honour means something to you.'

'How can you be sure of that?'

'I worked for years as bondswoman to the Lady of the Manor, minding her children till they came of age. I can spot the manner at a glance, and I got a good glance at you.'

Parry grimaced. He had stood before her naked.

'You had no calluses and not much dirt, and your posture was that of no peasant. When you spoke, you had the inflection of education. And you were being chased. They don't chase dispossessed serfs; who cares about them? They chase those who are dangerous to them: the lords and their leading servants. A lord would have honour, a servant maybe not. When you kept your word and came back, I knew you were no servant.'

'Maybe I just wanted shelter for the night.'

'At a hovel like this? With company like me?' She laughed, a hideous cackle. 'You'd go to an inn and talk the serving wench into your bed for the night.'

Parry had to smile. 'If I had the money.' But as he spoke, the word *wench* brought about a chain of thoughts that brought him quickly low. The crusade sergeant had called Jolie a wench, and then –

'Say, lad, I didn't mean to insult you,' the woman said. 'I just meant – '

Parry realized that his horror of the memory had shown on his face. 'My – my wife – '

'Oh, I shouldn't have joked about a wench! I'm sorry, lad.'

'They took her to – to rape, and when I tried to save her, the sword – she was the most beautiful woman of the region, with hair like honey and eyes like tourmaline, and – '

'The Lady Jolie!' she exclaimed. 'She who married the Sorcerer's son!'

'The same,' he said, startled.

'And you are that son!' she concluded triumphantly. 'The one who picked out a villein girl and made her the loveliest creature of all France! Now I know you!'

'Now you know me,' he agreed heavily. 'Are you sorry you helped me?'

'I'm glad I helped you! I have no truck with magic, but your father's a good man.'

'He's dead, too.'

'Yes, he would be the first they would kill, and you the second. He brought good weather to the region, so our crops prospered, our village as well as yours. I never heard a tale of either of you wronging a villein.'

'Villeins are people, too.'

'Not that any lord knows of! I gave the best years of my life to mine, and raised his children right, and I thought

57

he would take care of me when they were grown. But he married me to a field bondsman and forgot me, and the grown children never looked at me again. I was just lucky my husband was a decent man, so I got by.'

Parry realized that the Lord of her Manor might have rewarded her in this fashion, by giving her a decent man for a husband in her retirement. But it did not seem expedient to argue that case at the moment.

'Then my husband got the fever,' she continued. 'I prayed for him, day and night. I used our last coins to buy holy candles to burn to our Saviour, that my husband might live. But the Lord Jesus let him die, and now I am alone, and winter coming.'

So she remained a Christian, but a disaffected one. That was why she was willing to swear falsely by Jesus' name. 'The Lord Jesus does not seem to have his eye on southern France at the moment,' he said wryly.

'And this crusade is a pot of sheep manure,' she continued. 'They're out to get the Albigenses, who are good folk, and they're laying waste the countryside while they go about it. I wish they'd stayed at home!'

'So do I!' he agreed.

'I did figure when I saw you that anybody the crusade didn't like might be someone I'd like. Well, I know what it's like to lose a mate. I'll help you all I can, Sorcerer.'

'You helped me before you knew who I was,' he said.

'I did not know your name, but I knew you were someone.'

'I can return the favour, perhaps in greater measure than you hoped for.'

'All I wanted was for some good wood for the winter. I've got this ague in my bones, and when I go out in the cold I get the chills so bad – '

'I'll fetch you wood,' he agreed. 'But you know I can do magic. If there is something more I can do – '

She nodded. 'Let me think about it. It's late, and you

are tired. Sleep the night, and in the morning we shall see.'

Parry was glad to do that. She fetched some fresh straw for him, and he lay on the other side of the chamber from her bed. At first sleep would not come, because of the horrors of the day. Jolie . . .

Then he mesmerized himself, making the memories distant, and fell out of consciousness immediately.

In the morning she fed him more gruel and some sheep's milk. Then he went out to gather wood from the forest, bringing back many armfuls of sticks. 'But you know,' he said, 'you could make do with less fire, and less smoke, if you had a warmer house and warmer clothing.'

'I was thinking the same,' she said. 'Does your magic conjure good clothing?'

'No. If it did, I would not have come to you naked! I can mesmerize, and change my form, and transmute certain substances to certain others – '

'Lead into gold?' she asked eagerly.

'No, unfortunately. My father was working on alchemy, but had not progressed to that level, and I am far below it. Water to wine is my level.'

'I'll take it!' she exclaimed. 'Wine should warm me up!'

'I'm not sure that it really would,' he said cautiously. 'My observation is that it may make a person feel warmer, but that the effect is illusory.'

'I'll take it,' she repeated. 'I have water skins!'

'Very well. I'll transmute them. Then we can see about insulating your cottage.'

She brought a skin full of water. He invoked the magic ritual, and the skin warmed and quivered as if something had come alive within it.

'That's it?' she asked.

'That's it. Magic doesn't have to be spectacular when it's not for public show. I merely draw on the ambient

59

power that exists, and channel it to my purpose. You could do the same, if you studied the technique and had an aptitude.'

'Glory be!' she breathed.

'Try some. See whether the flavour is right.'

She squeezed some into her mouth. She smacked her lips. 'Best wine I ever tasted! Ah, my winter seems warmer already!'

She had two other water skins. He converted them, then went out to fetch more wood. Had he learned to conjure, he thought ruefully, he could have brought good wood into the cottage with far less effort. But he was as yet only an apprentice sorcerer. It took decades to become truly adept, and then only with the proper application and training. He had planned to get into more advanced techniques at the same time Jolie did . . .

He had to invoke his mesmerization again to restore his equilibrium. His future was in ruins, his love destroyed. Why didn't he simply lie down and die?

He pondered that as he gathered the dry sticks. It was because, he realized, his skein had not yet run its course. At the moment he was destitute and grief-stricken, but his life had been spared. Thanatos himself had come for Jolie, and revealed that there was some great evil associated with her death. Certainly Parry regarded her death as evil! He had to live to discover the nature of that evil, and to set it right. To settle his account with whoever and whatever was responsible for that evil. Until he accomplished that, he could not lay down his life. He had to be strong, and survive his losses, until he could accomplish his settlement. And what a settlement that would be, once he came to it!

He glanced down at his left wrist, where the stain of her blood remained. Was her spirit really there in it? Or had Thanatos merely tried to make him feel better by the suggestion of her presence? Certainly no such presence had manifested.

Regardless, he would avenge her murder. Even if her ghost should come to him, what good was that? It was her living self he craved, his lovely and accommodating wife!

First he would have to get himself suitably situated. Then he would have to extend his second sight, to spy out the source of the evil. Then –

He paused in his reflections. Was that the sound of baying?

Yes, it was. The hounds were moving again – and coming this way!

He dropped his bundle of sticks and ran for the cottage. But he was some distance from it, having wandered far in his quest for fallen wood, and the dogs were moving rapidly. By the time he got in sight, they were there.

He ducked behind a large tree, knowing it would be folly to show himself. He could do nothing at the moment.

'We know you have him!' a soldier was shouting at the door. 'You lied to us, old crone! Bring him out now!'

Parry couldn't hear her reply, but he saw its effect. 'Then we'll roust him out the easy way,' the soldier said grimly. He gestured to a companion. 'The torch!'

Suddenly a torch was flaming. They touched it to the thatch of the cottage, which blazed up. In a moment all of it was burning, sending coils of smoke into the sky.

Parry could do nothing. He lacked magic potent enough to douse a fire of that magnitude, and had he had it, he could not have got close enough to use it without being spotted and captured or killed by the soldiers. His best choice was to wait until the soldiers departed, then help the woman craft another shelter. He was sorry he had brought this mischief upon her.

How had they known of his presence? They had been turned away before, but this time had been certain. No one had seen him except the woman, and he knew she had not betrayed him. They had erred only in their conviction that he remained in the cottage. That had saved him – but cost the proprietor.

Yet where was she? He saw the soldiers, but not the old woman. She would not have remained within the burning house! But she did not seem to be outside it, either.

He watched with growing alarm, then with horror. The woman had *not* emerged! Had she refused to leave her only refuge, or had the soldiers cruelly kept her in there to die in the flames?

At last the flames had died down. The house was gone; its straw and wood had been consumed, leving only the shoring of mud. Satisfied, the soldiers departed.

Parry was going to check the ashes, but now the villagers were coming out. They had to have seen the fire, but wisely stayed clear until the soldiers were gone. What would they make of Parry?

He doubted they would be kind. He knew he was responsible for the old woman's death. She had refused to tell the soldiers where he was, so they had burned her out. Perhaps they had stabbed her, so that she fell back into the flames and died. He had not thought to use his second sight – and what good would it have done, anyway? It would only have fixed his blame more precisely. It was his fault, regardless of the details. The woman had helped him, and he had tried to help her, and for that she had died. To his grief for his father and his wife was added this score for the old woman, whose name he had never learned.

There was nothing remaining here for him. He would have to get far away from here, where the soldiers did not know of him and did not seek to kill him.

He could change form and move rapidly. He had been restored, physically, by the food and the night's rest. But that would cost him the clothing the woman had given him, and he was reluctant to lose it. It was tattered material, and the shoes chafed, but it *was* clothing, and it was all he had left of the generosity of this brief acquaintance.

But to trudge afoot, with the shoes wreaking blisters on his feet – that was not ideal either. He considered, then retreated to the deep forest and got out of the clothing. He formed it into a bundle, the shoes inside the tunic, and gripped it with his teeth. Then he changed form to a small horse, still holding the bundle, and set off north at a trot. He could travel a long distance rapidly this way.

He did so. By nightfall he was many leagues north. But he could not keep running forever; though he was very like a horse in this form, he had not perfected a horse's digestion, so could not graze. He was tired and hungry, and had to revert to his natural form for the night.

He did so, when his ears told him he was near a town. He pried the bundle from his locked teeth and untied it. He donned his tunic and shoes. Now he had to find a decent inn, and find a way to pay for his keep. He did not relish the notion of cheating the innkeeper, but he had no money.

He scouted about and found a naturally faceted stone. He concentrated on it, transmuting its silica to glass. It was harder to change a solid than a liquid, but silica was close to glass in composition, which facilitated the process. Soon he had a pretty faceted glass stone, translucent with a blue tinge.

He walked towards the town. He was in luck; there was an inn at the edge. He entered.

The innkeeper eyed him warily. 'Refugee, eh? Let's see the colour of your coin.'

'I am a refugee, and I have no coin,' Parry said. 'All I have is this pretty stone I found. I doubt it is worth much, but if you would be kind enough to accept it in lieu of payment for the night's lodging – '

The man peered at the stone. He brought it to the fireplace and held it before the dancing flames. The light refracted, and the blue showed through.

'One night?' the innkeeper asked. 'Then on in the morning?'

'I'm travelling north,' Parry agreed. 'As I said, that stone may not be worth much, but it is pretty, and – '

'Done.' The man pocketed the stone. 'Go ask the wench for soup, and she'll show you your room after.'

The wench . . .

Parry quelled his surge of grief. All day he had kept it at bay, focusing narrowly on his effort of running, of finding his way along little-used back trails so that he would not encounter many people. A runaway horse was fair game for anyone! But now, abruptly, that grief threatened to overwhelm him.

He went to the girl, who was a blotchy-faced creature with just one fetching feature: a deep cleavage that she flaunted knowingly. She leaned forward to serve him a bowl of soup, and he gazed down the proffered valley, not because of any interest but because it would have marked him as odd had he not done so. Satisfied that she had his proper attention, she straightened up so that the view suffered. She was a natural tease. What a contrast to –

Again he clamped down on it, and marched to a solitary table with his brimming bowl. As he slurped the soup, he saw the innkeeper showing something to another man. The stone, surely. Well, Parry had never told him it was valuable; he had protested that he thought it wasn't. If the man had convinced himself it was a diamond, worth an abbot's ransom, could Parry be blamed for that? The innkeeper thought he was cheating an ignorant refugee peasant. It served him right.

Still, Parry felt some guilt. Then he realized that the man would probably sell it to some equally ignorant trader, and make a tidy profit on the deal. The stone might in time become as valuable as others thought it was, and no one would suffer.

He had a good meal, and a good night, except for the looming anguish of his memories. Again he looked at the smear of blood on his wrist. Perhaps he was just being foolish, but it seemed that his wrist was warm in the vicinity, as if heated by a kindred spirit. Jolie . . .

But just before dawn he came abruptly awake with another concern: had he heard the baying of hounds? No, of course not – and even if it were true, they would not be after him. Not this far from his origin.

Still, he scrambled into his shoes and hurried downstairs. The innkeeper was up already, stacking loaves of bread in his pantry. 'If I may have one of those, kind sir, I'll be on my way,' Parry said.

He needed no second sight to fathom the man's thought process. One loaf was a cheap price to be so readily rid of his patron, so that no one would know the origin of the precious stone, or be able to reclaim it. He handed Parry a loaf.

'I thank you most humbly for your generosity,' Parry said, tucking it under his arm. Then he hurried out.

The dogs were definitely closer. Parry walked on through the town, ducking around corners. Then, unable to control his suspicion, he looped back until he could see the inn from cover at the rear.

The dogs appeared, with soldiers holding them on leashes. They looked like the same soldiers who had pursued him before. How could they have followed him this far?

Then he heard loud voices. 'Sorcerer . . . killed a sergeant . . . price on his head . . .'

Now there was no doubt. He was the one they were after!

Parry moved away; this was no safe place for him. But as he fled, he wondered: how had they traced him down so fast, so accurately? And, that being the case, why did they not realize when he was right within sight or hearing? Twice they had run him down, only to overlook him when he was virtually under their noses. How had they even known he was alive, after burning down the villein woman's cottage? For all they should have known, his charred bones were there with hers.

Yet obviously they *did* know – and as obviously, they had no really precise fix on him. That was why they used the dogs, who nevertheless could not penetrate the mask of his changed shoes. It was as though the were hunting a fox, who had been spotted in the vicinity but now was hiding well. They knew he was here, but not accurately enough to nab him. What could account for this odd combination of precision and imprecision? He thought he had escaped cleanly when he fled as a wolf, and then as a crow, and then as a horse . . .

Then, abruptly it burst upon him: the transformations! *They were tuning in on the magic!* The exercise of magic had its own aura, that a sorcerer could detect, even from afar. His father had known that there was no other of his calibre in the region, because he would have detected the magic. But obviously the crusaders had a competent sorcerer, who was spotting the magic of others, so that those others could be tracked down and killed. What a way to abolish effective resistance! No wonder they had fixed so swiftly on his father, and then on Parry himself! Every time he performed magic, he made a beacon for them to orient on.

He had transformed to his own form after running as a wolf, and they had come; he had thought it was a straight tracking, but now saw that it was not. He had flown from them, and they could not follow, but they had noted the location of his transformation back to a man, and sent a party there in the morning. Or perhaps they had overlooked the form-changing, and picked up his transmutation of the water to wine; the timing made more sense that way. Even the best of sorcerers could not remain on watch all the time; he had to sleep. So he watched mostly by day, and gave the soldiers a fix when he picked it up. He would have noted Parry's changing to horse form, but of course the soldiers could not keep that pace. So they had followed more slowly. Then Parry's transformation back to his natural form had registered, too late for them to reach the town that day, but they had made sure to close on it first thing in the morning, hoping to catch their quarry asleep. And they had almost done so!

So now he knew his liability. A powerful sorcerer was watching, with his own version of second sight. The soldiers were not apt; they merely went where directed, with the dogs confirming what scent there was, and inquired. Thus Parry had escaped, narrowly, twice.

What could he do, against determination like this? They really wanted him dead!

He knew what he had to do. He had to hide, long and well. To do that, his first step was to do no more magic. The magic he had used to help the villein woman had cost her her life. Future magic would surely cost him his own life.

How, then, would he survive? He had no money, no assets. He would soon enough starve, unless he found some gainful employment – and if there were a price on his head, how could he risk that?

Then he heard faint music. Someone was singing. The sound was strangely evocative. Parry paused to listen, though he feared that any delay was foolish. Then he walked towards the sound.

It was a friar, a singing friar, with an alms bowl. He was begging musically for his breakfast. But his voice was strangely good; it was a pleasure to listen.

Then it burst upon him: he, Parry, had an excellent voice! He could sing for his sustenance! Who would suspect a poor singing friar of being a sorcerer?

He approached the friar. 'Oh, holy man, I have heard your singing and admire it. What denomination are you?'

'No denomination, my son,' the man replied. 'I am not a holy man, merely a member of the Brotherhood.'

Such a brotherhood might be easy to join. 'Do your accept converts?'

'We welcome them! Can you sing?'

'Very well, Brother.'

'Let me hear you, then.'

Parry sang the refrain the friar had just rendered. He was apt at music, and could repeat anything he heard. He sang it well; indeed, surely better than the friar had heard it done before.

'Come with me!' the friar exclaimed, excited.

As they moved, they exchanged introductions. The friar was Brother Humble; he explained how they adopted appropriate names at the time they joined the group, to exemplify their intentions.

'Then I think I would be Grief,' Parry said without feeling any cleverness or delight.

'As you wish. We do not inquire into our backgrounds; the name signifies the devotion.'

They went to the local Brotherhood headquarters, which was merely a stone and wood house of the type becoming common in towns: more permanent than the country cottages but just as dirty. Another friar was there, introduced as Brother Lowly.

'I would like to be called Grief,' Parry said.

Brother Lowly looked at him, nodding. 'The mark of it is on you, Brother Grief.'

'Here we each contribute what little we have to the group, and take what little we need,' Brother Humble explained.

Parry took the hint. 'I have this loaf of bread. I give it to the group.'

'Bless you, Brother,' the man at the house said gratefully. 'We knew the Lord would provide.'

Other friars appeared as if by magic. They shared the loaf, and soon it was gone.

'Brother Grief has the finest voice I have heard.' Brother Humble said. 'I believe we should work as a group today, to show him our way, and to benefit from his ability.'

The others were agreeable, and so was Parry; this would be the perfect concealment.

Then they found a bowl for Parry, and a hooded cloak, marking him as a lay friar. They went out into the town for the day's work.

The routine was simple. Wherever there was a reasonable group of people, such as a shopping mart, the monks would start singing, forming an impromptu chorus. Parry picked up their melodies quickly, and developed appropriate counterpoints that amplified the effect.

The result was dramatic. Parry had always had the ability to project his music, making it seem to the listener as if there were an accompaniment. Now, for the first time, he was using his talent for other than selfish purpose. Whether it was because of this, or because of the added feeling his grief lent to it, or because he was singing in company with others, or because the Lord approved and augmented their effort, the music became more than it had in the past. The voices of the other friars assumed greater stature, becoming closer on key, and blended more harmoniously with each other. The music they made together was truly beautiful.

The audience responded immediately. The shoppers formed a circle around the friars, and when the song was done, dropped small coins into the extended bowls. The friars glanced down, evidently trying to mask their surprise; they had not been this generously rewarded before.

Brother Humble squeezed Parry's arm. That said it all: recognition that Parry's voice had made the difference. The other friars, somewhat reserved before, now welcomed Parry completely. They might have dedicated their lives to God and poverty, but they saw no point in taking the latter to extremes.

The day was a success. As they retired for the evening meal, they had more than they ever had before, for the coins had bought decent food instead of the usual scraps. More than one friar approached Parry with a message like this: 'I deeply regret the sorrow that brought you here, Brother, but there can be some good even in the worst of cases. Welcome to our Brotherhood!'

Parry's grief was real, and his faith was suspect, but he was as quick as the others to recognize a good situation. He had a new home.

If only he could have shared it with Jolie!

A year passed. Parry practised no magic, protecting himself from discovery by the searching sorcerer. He sang with the friars, and their group flourished. They travelled from town to town, singing and preaching the glory of God, because he was certain that no just God would have allowed a crusade in His name to wreak the kind of havoc it had in southern France, or to kill as perfect a creature as Jolie. But he preached the word too, for to do otherwise would have made him suspect. The sentiments were easy enough to cover: that God in His greatness deplored the conditions of the world, and required a return to the fundamental values of generosity and forgiveness.

But a strange thing happened as time passed. Parry discovered that his belief began to follow his words. Generosity *was* good, forgiveness *was* good, and the ways of the Lord might be strange at times, but perhaps did have merit. He could not accept the loss of Jolie, but he was coming to accept the notion that his present life might be doing more good in the world than his past one. Before, he had helped the folk of a single village, for suitable fees; now he helped the folk of the entire nation to see the error of their ways, so like his own of prior times.

Yet the evil of the deaths of his father the Sorcerer, and Jolie, and the villein woman who had helped him could not be justified by this. Had God simply come to him and asked him to become an impoverished friar, he would have done so; it had not been necessary to have good folk murdered. This was not the way of the kind of God he could accept.

Where, then, hd the evil originated? Parry thought about that increasingly, as the cutting edge of his grief abated and left his mind free for thought. He considered and reconsidered every aspect of it, and slowly came to the conclusion that only one entity could be responsible. That was Lucifer, the figure of evil. Lucifer must have seen the advantage in turmoil and warfare, so had generated a situation that brought war to southern France. The crusade, waged in the name of God, had actually to be the work of the Lord of Evil.

This was a phenomenal revelation, and one he dared not publicize. He had trouble, initially, believing it himself. How could God tolerate such an inversion?

The answer had to be that God was not paying proper attention. God was starting worthy projects, but Lucifer was perverting them almost as fast as they developed, so that in the end the gain was Lucifer's. Thus the worthy crusade becamed unworthy almost as it formed, and Parry's grief was only a tiny part of the result.

Another strange thing happened in this period. The drop of blood on Parry's wrist continued to heat, seeming to possess a kind of life of its own. Finally Parry realized that it might be Jolie's spirit trying to communicate with him. 'Jolie,' he said. 'Come to me!'

That was all it took. Her ghost rose from the blood and hovered before him, vague and wavering, but definitely present. Thanatos had spoken truly; she was with him, in the blood!

The ghost could not speak or act. But as time passed he encouraged it, speaking to it, loving it as the remnant of his wife. Gradually it learned to manage, until it was able to assume her living form. Bit by bit, she learned to talk, not verbally but by sending her thoughts to his mind as if in speech. Progress was slow, so that later he could not remember when the stages of her renewed presence occurred. But he had his wife again!

But his grief for her remained. This was the mere shade of Jolie, and could never match the living presence of yore. Still, it was a great improvement, and it enabled him to deal with his grief more efffectively, and to focus instead on what he intended to do about his vengeance. He still did not dare to practise magic himself, but he continued to rehearse the spells in his mind, perfecting them for the time when he could safely practise sorcery again.

That year a former Italian soldier, who had renounced his ways and become devout, set out to preach. He was Giovanni di Bernardone, and when he took his small band of followers to Rome, he was permitted to form a band of friars. Now his mission was spreading to other countries, and a group came to France. The originator called his mother the Lady Poverty, and his father the Lord Sun, and his values seemed much like those of the Brotherhood Parry associated with. They called themselves the Franciscans, because of Giovanni's father's travels in France.

The local friars considered, and decided to join the Franciscans. In this manner they achieved the approval of the Church. They continued their singing and preaching much as before, but now their influence was greater because of that approval.

In 1213 Simon de Montfort, the leader of the crusade, won a victory at Muret that made the fate of the Albigenses certain. Parry felt private anguish, but said nothing. As long as the crusade continued, he had to remain in hiding.

In 1214 King Philip of France won the battle of Bouvines, and established the French monarchy as dominant in Europe. Parry continued singing, preaching and thinking.

In 1216 Dominic Guzman, of Castile, who had been preaching to the Albigensians, was given a house for his growing band. Parry attended, providing moral support as a representative of the Franciscans. The Dominicans, officially the Order of Preachers, became known as the Black Friars, because of their black mantle over the white habit. They were more interested in the philosophical aspects of evil than were the Franciscans, who simply preached the virtues of poverty and humility.

In 1221 Dominic died. The Franciscans held an assembly, becoming more formally organized. Parry, as a member in excellent standing, could have stepped into higher office. But his thinking about Lucifer caused him to do something others might have deemed foolish: he decided to leave the Franciscans and join the Dominicans, because they seemed to be orienting more specifically on the problem of evil.

Parry had never forgotten the injury Lucifer had done him. Now he was ready to begin moving more directly against the Lord of Evil. Lucifer had to be made to pay. But first it was necessary to study the ways of evil, to ascertain exactly how Lucifer operated. Once the enemy was truly known, he would be vulnerable. Parry intended to be there for the counterstrike against the Kingdom of Evil.

Parry had survived more than a score of years after the loss of his father and Jolie. But he had a secret: the soul of Jolie. She had learned to travel increasing distances from him, and to bring him news of far folk and far places. She could do what he could not: search out the source of the enemy sorcery. The time was coming when he could accomplish his purpose.

4

Inquisition

In 1230 Parry and another friar, Father Service, were dispatched by the Dominicans on what was expected to be a routine case. As it turned out, it was not. For one thing, Jolie had indicated that there was something special about this one. She had been searching for the mysterious sorcerer who had brought them so much mischief in the past, and his aura seemed to be associated. That was enough for Parry; had he not been assigned, he would have petitioned to accompany the friar who was. If he could locate that sorcerer . . .

The local magistrate had arraigned a wealthy lord on the charge of heresy, and sought to confiscate his possessions for distribution to interested parties. This sort of thing was becoming more common, but the action could not be completed without the approval of the Church. Therefore it was necessary for a priest or other appropriate figure to examine the case and make the final decision.

Jolie did not like the routine dispossession of accused persons of their assets, and therefore neither did Parry. He lived ascetically himself, owning nothing, his very clothing technically the property of the Church. But she reminded him that property was a necessary thing for those who existed in the material realm, and fairness in its disposition was essential. Too often, folk were deprived on trumped-up charges so that their accusors could benefit. Something like that had happened to Jolie's own family.

Father Service, in contrast, tended to bear down hard on any accused, and to exact the maximum penalty. He had no villein-girl conscience to ameliorate his dedication to what he knew was right. Parry found that problematical; he did not wish to affront his companion, but he suspected that there was such a thing as being too certain in one's sanctity.

The fact that this particular pair had been selected for this mission was significant, for their attitudes were known. That meant that the Dominicans suspected that this was an invalid case, and depended on the two of them to deal with it appropriately. That Parry intended to do, despite the predilection of his associate.

'You know that people are often condemned on very slender evidence,' Parry remarked as they rode their donkeys, starting what he knew would be an argument. But the long, slow ride was dull, and this would enliven it slightly.

'Better that than to risk the proliferation of heresy,' Father Service said piously.

'Pompous ass!' Jolie exclaimed.

The friar turned his head. 'What?'

'My mount is becoming wilful,' Parry said. Had Father Service actually heard Jolie's remark? He hesitated to inquire. As far as he knew, he was the only one who could perceive her, but he was not sure whether that was because he was specially attuned, or merely because she manifested only to those she chose. There were intriguing mysteries about her, in death as there had been in life.

They arrived at the local monastery, and began the tedious process of reviewing the evidence. It was the usual assemblage of rumour, hearsay and speculation. He wondered whether there was any connection between the terms *hearsay* and *heresy*. His mind drifted, speculating on that. What an indictment of the system that could be! Suppose that all heresy turned out to be illusory?

'Where there's smoke, there's fire,' Father Service said, satisfied.

'The idiot!' Jolie snorted. 'You have to do better than this, Parry!'

Parry sighed. He knew that the worst smoke sometimes occurred after the fire had been doused. 'I shall have to interview the witnesses directly,' he said.

'Why?' Father Service asked. 'We have their depositions. This many witnesses cannot be wrong.'

'I don't care if there are a thousand ignorant depositions!' Jolie fumed. 'These aren't grounds to condemn anyone!'

'We wouldn't want to leave any possible grounds for later criticism,' Parry said smoothly. 'It is better to nail it down absolutely. I believe I can develop firmer testimony.'

Father Service blew out his cheeks. 'Very well, Father Grief, if you insist.'

'This one,' Jolie said, pointing to one of the depositions. 'I have a feeling about her.'

Parry picked up the document. 'Fabiola,' he read. 'Her testimony seems to be crucial.'

'So it seems,' Father Service agreed. 'That alone is sufficient to seal the case.'

'Then we are agreed; she must be interviewed.'

Father Service opened then closed his mouth. He had had no such intention, but was now in an awkward position to deny it.

They reviewed other documents. 'It appears that Lord Bofort stands to gain somewhat from this transaction,' Parry remarked. 'His lands are adjacent to those of the accused. I begin to suspect a motive.' Indeed, Jolie was growing excited; she suspected Lord Bofort.

'Such suspicion is inappropriate to men of God,' Father Service protested. 'Lord Bofort is not on trial!'

'Perhaps not,' Parry agreed. But if he turned out to be the one . . .

In due course the woman stood before them. Fabiola

77

was young, no more than seventeen, but looked older. Her hair was bound back by a fillet and hanging loose behind, in the fashion of unmarried girls. Her tunic was in fair condition. She stared at the two men behind the desk with great frightened brown eyes, reminding Parry momentarily of the way Jolie had been when he first summoned her to his house. Even after twenty years, such memories were poignant.

'She's been tortured,' Jolie said.

Tortured! Parry wanted to ask for more information on that, but could not speak in the presence of the others. His ability to talk with his dead wife would not have been understood by the men of his order!

'According to this deposition,' Father Service said to her, 'you have testified that the accused has had communion with devils, and that you have seen this yourself. Is this true?'

'Yes, Father,' she said, almost whispering.

'And that when the accused discovered you observing him, he sent one of his devils after you, and the devil caught you and raped you?'

Her pallor faded as she tried to show some colour. 'Yes, Father.' It was a difficult thing for a woman to confess rape, because it reflected on her more than on the rapist.

Father Service turned to Parry. 'We have documentation of the rape. She was examined by Lord Bofort's personal physician, who verified it.'

'She was raped,' Jolie agreed. 'But the deposition says nothing about torture.'

Parry nodded. 'Fabiola, we are not here to add to your burdens,' he said gently. 'We wish only to ascertain the truth. I am not certain that your deposition covers all of it.'

Her eyes widened with something like terror. 'Please

Father, I have told all! All! I swear it!' She was eager not to be tortured again, of course.

'I doubt this,' Parry said firmly.

'Oh, Father, what is it you wish me to say?' she begged. The significance of this phrasing was not lost on Parry; she was ready to say anything she was directed to say, because her will had been broken.

'Only the whole truth, Fabiola.'

'But I –'

'I see nothing in this document about your torture.'

Father Service started, but remained silent. This line of questioning had caught him by surprise, but it interested him.

The girl tried to shrink into herself. 'I have not been –' She could not continue, for obviously she had been threatened with more torture if she told of the first.

'She's marked on the belly,' Jolie said.

'Remove your tunic,' Parry said.

Now, Father Service had to protest. 'We are men of God, Brother! We cannot expose this woman to –'.

'True,' Parry agreed. 'We must clear this chamber of all but the essential parties.' He glanced around to where guards and servitors stood. 'Depart, we shall call when we require your presence.'

'But Father!' the sergeant said.

Parry simply turned his gaze on the man, making a slight frown. The sergeant quailed, knowing the trouble he would be in if one of the friars reported him for insubordination. The power of the Church was supposedly neither physical nor political, but in truth it was both, and all knew it. Peasants were not the only folk subject to torture.

In short order the chamber was emptied of all but the two friars and the girl. 'Remove your tunic,' Parry repeated softly.

'Oh, Father, why do you seek to shame me?' she cried.

'We are men of God,' Father Service said sharply. 'There is no lechery in our gaze. We seek only to ascertain the truth.' He had had enough experience with Parry to know that Parry never made foolish demands, and of course he had to support the authority of the Church. This had become an issue; therefore he defended it.

Trembling, the girl drew off her tunic. She wore only a bandage beneath it, stained cloth wrapped around her abdomen. Her body was so thin and dirty that it was no incitement to lechery. 'A knife, I think,' Jolie said. 'But she wasn't cut deeply; there must be something else.'

'You said you have not been tortured,' Parry said. 'Why then, do you wear a bandage?'

'Oh, Father, the demon did it to me!' she exclaimed.

'Did what?' Father Service asked, getting into it now.

'He – it – it clawed me when it – '

'Woman!' Parry snapped, causing her to jump guiltily. 'Do not attempt to deceive men of God!'

She broke into tears.

'Fabiola, look at me,' Parry said.

The girl wrenched her gaze up until it met his own. She seemed like a bird before a serpent.

'There are two kinds of damnation,' Parry said. 'One is the damnation of the body, and I see you have suffered that. The other is the damnation of the soul and you are in danger of that.'

'Oh, please, Father, mercy!' she screamed, terrified anew.

'The Lord Jesus is merciful,' Parry said sternly. 'But He requires truth. Tell the truth now, and your soul shall be removed from peril.'

The girl sobbed, but did not speak.

'There is something else,' Jolie said. 'I think she's been threatened. Or maybe her family.'

Parry nodded. 'Do you fear to bring destruction on

80

your family if you tell the truth?' he asked quietly. 'Remember, God is your judge.'

Her mouth worked. 'I –'

'I give you my word that no harm – no further harm shall come to you or your family if you confess the whole truth before us now,' Parry said.

A tiny flicker of hope showed. 'Your word, Father?'

'And mine,' Father Service said. 'You have nothing to fear from us.'

Still she hesitated. 'You swear?'

Father Service stiffened, but Parry cautioned him with a touch on the arm. 'Lucifer can be cruel to the ignorant, Brother,' he murmured. 'She is not conscious of questioning our word.' Then, to the girl: 'We swear, before God and the Holy Virgin, child. You and your family will be protected. All it requires is the whole truth.'

Even that did not seem to be enough. The girl stood there, obviously wanting to cooperate, but unable to take the necessary step.

'You know we are not alone in this,' Parry said. 'Look at me, child.' He brought out a small silver cross.

She looked, and he fixed her with his mesmeric gaze. 'In a moment you will see this cross begin to glow. It will be a sign from God to you personally, that all will be well. Look at the cross now, child.'

She transferred her gaze to the cross. In a moment her face seemed to illuminate. She was highly suggestible, as the ignorant tended to be. 'Oh it glows, it glows!' she exclaimed.

Parry extended the cross towards her. 'Take it child. Feel the warmth of it. This is God's protection, as long as your faith is strong.'

Hesitantly she took it. 'Oh, it is warm!'

'As warm as our Saviour's great and blessed love for you,' Parry said. 'He will protect you always, if your sins be confessed and your heart pure.'

'But I am full of sin!' she cried. 'Terrible sin!'

'Confess that sin, that it may be freely forgiven. Our Lord Jesus died, that this be possible. He welcomes the penitent sinner,'

Then the floodgate was opened. 'They made me do it!' she said rapidly. 'They stripped me and put the knife to my belly, and they cut me, and it hurt but I could not scream because they bound my mouth, and they said they would cut a hole in me and draw out my gut and tie a horse to it and strike him with a whip so that he would gallop away and draw out my life and they brought up the horse and oh, I had to do it!'

Father Service's mouth fell open. But Parry, prepared for this, took it in stride. 'We understand, child. Put your clothing on again, and we shall discuss the details. You have done well to tell us this.'

Fabiola scrambled into her tunic, and the interrogation resumed. They learned that Lord Bofort, the accuser, had done this, threatening to do the same to each member of her family if she failed to testify as he wished, and if she spoke one word of this to any other party. Lord Bofort was the nemesis of this region; she knew he could and would do all of it. There were stories.

'But I have not been raped,' she had protested as she learned the story she had to tell.

Whereupon one of Bofort's men had raped her. She, seeing the knife and the horse nearby, had not dared protest. Therefore she knew that by contemporary custom she had not truly been raped, for she had technically acceded to it. But she would be sure to tell the story they demanded of her.

Parry turned to his associate. 'Are you satisfied, Brother?'

'No,' Father Service said. 'Justice has not yet been done.'

Parry nodded. 'And it had better be initiated before

this girl leaves this chamber.' He raised his voice. 'Magistrate!'

The magistrate entered. 'The girl has satisfied you?'

'In a manner of speaking,' Parry said drily. 'We are satisfied that we now know the truth of this situation. You will arrest Lord Bofort, for he had incited false testimony. You will also extend protection to this witness and her family, lest there be misfortune.'

'But I do not take orders from you!' the magistrate protested.

Parry turned that disconcerting gaze on the man. 'Of course you do not, magistrate. You merely do what you know to be proper. We merely advise. The Church does not interfere in the concerns of men.'

The man became as uncertain as the girl had been. 'You really think – ?'

'We believe that the truth will manifest in due course, and would not want it to be said that any party interfered.' Parry continued to gaze at the man.

'Uh, yes, perhaps it would be best to – I will see to it.' He hurried out.

Father Service shook his head, bemused. 'Brother, you certainly have a way with you! First you caused the girl to reverse her sworn testimony, then you – I could not have done it!'

Parry smiled. 'Surely you could, Brother, if you saw the need.' He was fortunate that his associate could so readily be managed. That was a common trait of those whose views of right and wrong were narrow.

But it turned out that Lord Bofort was not so readily arrested. He resided in a castle that was defended by a host of a score or more of knights. It would take an army with siege equipment to fetch him out – and by the time that could be arranged, his potent political connections would have got him off.

Parry realized that his promise to Fabiola would be worthless unless he got Lord Bofort out of the way. The moment the friars departed, those knights would swoop down and wreak vengeance on the girl and her family. The magistrate would bend to the most proximate power, and not interfere. Parry had kept the girl in the vicinity, knowing that it would not be safe to release her until the matter was resolved. She was looking better, having been fed and cleaned, and her confidence in the cross he had given her almost made her glow. That glow would quickly fade if Bofort got hold of her!

However, he had come prepared for this kind of encounter, thanks to Jolie's suspicion about this assignment. 'I shall simply have to go and fetch him out,' he told the magistrate, 'and deliver him to you for trial.'

Father Service coughed. He was firm in his faith, but not a fool.

The magistrate shook his head. 'Begging your pardon, Father, but you can't do that. He has little respect for friars. He would have you beaten, or worse.'

Parry affected surprise. 'But I am a man of God.'

'Father, we are far from the centre of things. The power of God sometimes has trouble making itself felt here,' the magistrate said.

'The power of God is without limit,' Parry said righteously.

'All the same, Father – '

'Perhaps we should merely report this to – ' Father Service began.

'No, this is a thing that must be done,' Parry said firmly. 'But I agree, Brother, it should be reported. Suppose you return to make the report to our Order, while I go to bring the man to justice?'

'You must not go alone!' Father Service said, agitated.

'I will not go alone,' Parry said. 'I will go in the company of God, than which there is none better.'

'Yes, of course! But even so – '

'Then it is settled. I will see Lord Bofort to justice here, while you relay word to our Order, who will advise the Pope, who I am sure will be pleased. It is not every day the Church is able to act specifically in the cause of justice.'

'Not every day,' Father Service agreed hollowly.

'Really, Father – ' the magistrate started.

'No more of this,' Parry said briskly. 'My course is clear. Merely show me the way to Lord Bofort's demesnes, and I shall pursue the matter as God directs me.'

'I can show you, Father!' Fabiola said. 'I live near there.' Which might have been the main reason she was selected as a key witness. Why travel far to induct a peasant girl when one was close by?

'Excellent, child; you shall be my guide.'

Father Service exchanged a look with the magistrate. Both evidently thought Parry had lost his wits, but neither was in a position to make an issue of it. They thought he was going naked into the lion's den.

However, he reminded himself, there had been one who had gone into the lion's den before, and had tamed the lions.

In due course they set off, the girl leading the way, the man riding the donkey. There had been one who rode a donkey into town, too, he remembered.

And, gazing at Fabiola's thin back, he was reminded again of Jolie, as she had been during their first interview.

That thought evoked Jolie. 'Now don't go getting notions!' she chided him.

'None, my love,' he murmured.

Fabiola turned. 'What, Father?'

'It is all right, child. I was merely talking to myself.'

But the girl continued to gaze in his direction. 'Who is that great lady, Father?'

'You see her?' Parry asked, startled

'Of course she sees me!' Jolie said. 'You gave her the cross.'

'So I did,' he agreed, doubting that that could be the reason. Father Service had a similar cross and had not seen Jolie. Then, to Fabiola: 'The lady is my wife, when she was your age. She has been dead more than twenty years, but she guards me yet.'

'Oh.' Fabiola faced forward again and resumed walking.

'What do you have in mind, love?' Jolie inquired. 'You know that evil man is not going to come out just because you ask him to.'

'I know. But if he is, as we strongly suspect, the sorcerer who spotted us, and led to your death and my father's, he cannot withstand exposure. That may be my major weapon against him.'

Fabiola turned again. 'Lord Bofort is a sorcerer, Father?'

He had forgotten, carelessly, that the girl could overhear him when he spoke to Jolie. Yet was there harm in it? Fabiola was dependent on him for her security and that of her family; she would support him absolutely.

'Yes, child, I believe so. So am I – my magic is white, in support of God, while his is black, supported by the forces of evil.' Parry had made a considerable study of evil; on occasion other friars had even teased him for his supposed love of evil because of his finesse in ferreting it out, as in this present case. He had learned well that evil was not always where one expected it, or of the nature one anticipated.

'I would like to see the man who was responsible for denying me my life with you brought to justice,' Jolie said. 'But still, I don't see why mere exposure should hurt him.'

'Because he once worked in support of the crusade,' Parry explained. 'That was actually a work of evil, but

86

was believed to be good. He would therefore have seemed to be aligning himself with good, and surely he would not thereafter declare himself to be the opposite. His present situation is evidence that he professes to be a good man. If his servants or knights knew that he was not, and that the whole countryside was about to know that truth, they would not support him. So exposure could cost him greatly at the outset; his own men would turn against him.'

'I would love to see that!' Fabiola exclaimed.

Surely she would, for she had been tortured and raped by Bofort's men.

'Do you know, Parry, we might be able to use her,' Jolie said.

'Use her?' he repeated, startled.

'Use me?' Fabiola asked. She evidently understood that he was answering questions she could not hear.

'I believe I might be able to speak to her, if I floated through her head,' Jolie said. 'Then I could tell her what to say. It might make a difference.'

'I don't know . . .'

But Jolie was already floating towards the girl. Her form fuzzed as it overlapped the head, then shrank into it.

Fabiola abruptly straightened up. Then she turned to look back at him. 'Hello, my love,' she said with Jolie's voice.

Parry almost fell off the donkey. 'Get out of there!' he sputtered. 'That's too much like possession!'

'No, it's fun,' Fabiola said in her own voice. 'I can hear her now, and feel how she wants me to speak. I think I would know a demon. Jolie is good!'

'But the implications – '

The girl stood, evidently listening. Then she said: 'I suppose that's true.' She was talking to the ghost within her. 'But it seems like trying to vamp a holy man.'

'Get out of there!' Parry repeated.

The girl glanced at him, forming a marginal smile. 'Can you make me, Parry?' she asked in Jolie's voice. Now her features seemed to resemble Jolie's too.

He jumped off the donkey and strode to her. He took her by the shoulders. 'By the greatness of God, depart this vessel!'

Jolie reappeared in the air above the girl's head. 'You exorcized me!' she exclaimed indignantly. 'I'm no demon!'

Fabiola began to cry. 'I didn't mean any harm! It was only a game, she said!'

Parry turned her loose. 'Some games we do not play,' he said shortly, and returned to the donkey.

'Don't be so stuffy!' Jolie said. 'I was only showing you what could be done. I can help you directly, if I work through her. I'm not going to corrupt her, and it might make a difference if Bofort proves harder to deal with than you think. Anyway, what do you suppose you are going to do with her, after she brings you to the castle? Turn her loose so the knights can run her down?'

Parry had to concede there was a merit in her position. 'You're sure she isn't being imposed on? I gave her my work to protect her from that.'

'No, it's fun,' Fabiola said. 'I feel like a woman when she's with me.'

That was part of the problem. Parry had lived for twenty years without any women in his personal life, wanting none after Jolie. The sudden manifestation of Jolie's personality in a girl close to her age when she lived had jolted him, arousing reactions he had thought long forgotten. Fabiola resembled Jolie in no other respect; she was neither pretty nor bright. If such a manifestation could provoke such a reaction in him, what would a closer match have done? *He was a man of God now!*

Jolie floated over to him. 'You started to see her as woman?' she asked softly.

Parry nodded grimly.

'I'm sorry. I hadn't thought it through. It was almost like being alive again. I won't tease you any more.'

'Thank you.' He did not look at her.

'But I really do think she could help us – and it *isn't* safe to let her go, yet. That Bofort is a bad enemy.'

'Agreed.'

'Then it is all right to – ?'

'Do what you believe is best, Jolie,' he said, yielding reluctantly.

She drifted off. In a moment Fabiola straightened again. 'Oh, I wish I were like you!'

Surely so, Parry reflected. He was not at all sure how he felt about this development.

'Now I can remain with Fabiola, or I can explore the castle, when we get there,' Jolie said through the girl's mouth. 'What do you wish?'

'I'm not sure,' Parry said. 'I won't be able to speak to you there, lest I give away your nature, so you'll have to use your judgement. Probably you should circulate, to see what is around us, that I may not be able to see, and report to me, but at other times remain with her.'

'I will do that.'

'Fabiola,' he said. 'Are you sure you wish to enter the castle? They will not like you there.'

'I have the cross you gave me, Father,' she said promptly. 'I cannot be harmed.'

'That is true – so long as your faith is firm. But if you begin to doubt, that protection will falter. Jesus cannot help those whose faith is not pure. They will try to make you doubt.'

She gripped the cross, holding it high. 'They cannot make me doubt.'

Parry hoped that was the case. He knew they could not

make *him* doubt, but her faith was of recent vintage. Still, with Jolie to guide her, she had a chance.

They arrived at the castle. It was not any giant of its type, but it was imposing enough, a motte and bailey with forbidding stone walls. Like any castle, it was highly defensible; twenty men could hold off an army here.

They were evidently expected, for the drawbridge was down and the gate guards snapped to attention as they approached. 'Our master bids you welcome, Father Grief,' a guard said. 'We shall take care of the donkey and the wench.'

Parry stiffened momentarily; even after the score of years, that term *wench* bothered him. But he forced himself to relax. 'Thank you; the donkey you may care for, but the young woman will remain with me.'

The guard paused, assessing the situation. It was not unknown for friars to abridge their vows of chastity when opportunity offered. Parry had investigated more than one such case, and taken the appropriate disciplinary action; it was galling to have such suspicion adhere to him now. But perhaps that was better than the alternatives; at least it give a pretext to keep the girl close.

They were ushered into the main castle. As they walked down the long entry passage, Jolie floated away, then returned. 'They are drawing up the bridge,' she announced.

Parry nodded, as if to himself. He had expected as much. The lion did not wish his prey to escape without a reckoning.

They came to the main court, which was elegantly furnished. Illustrated tapestries hung on the walls, and the floor was polished wood. Lord Bofort had excellent taste – and the ill-gotten wealth to indulge it.

'There are bowmen watching from concealed recesses,' Jolie said. 'Crossbows.'

Parry reached into an inner pocket and took his large

silver cross. He doubted that anyone would fire at him yet, but there was no sense in taking unnecessary chances. Fabiola felt the same way; she clutched her small cross tightly.

Lord Bofort awaited them at a great oaken table. He was a stout man of perhaps fifty, very well dressed with embroidered robes. 'Welcome, Father Grief,' he said expansively. 'To what do we owe the honour of this visit by a man of the cloth?'

'Bofort,' Parry said without preamble, 'there is a warrant for your arrest for abuse of your power. I have come to take you to the magistrate.'

'Friar, you are overstepping your bounds,' Bofort said curtly. 'You have no business meddling in my affairs.'

'I shall be satisfied to let the magistrate decide that,' Parry said. 'I ask you to leave this castle and come with me now to the town, so that this matter may be settled.'

'Because of the reckless charge of a foolish young girl? Surely you know better than that, friar.'

'You were satisfied with her testimony when you meant to use it against your neighbour,' Parry reminded him. 'Now we have ascertained that that testimony was perjured, the result of the torture and threats you made against her. She is a more credible witness against you than she was against your neighbour.'

'I think she will not be a witness at all,' Bofort said grimly. He made a gesture, and two guards stepped forward.

Fabiola straightened, and Parry recognized Jolie's aspect. She lifted the small silver cross. 'Creatures of hell, touch me not, lest you be chastened,' she said.

The guards hesitated.

'Do not be daunted by a superstition!' Bofort snapped. 'Take her!'

The guards resumed their motion. Fabiola fixed her

gaze on the face of the nearest and swung the cross, shoving it against his forearm.

The man screamed and fell back, holding his arm.

Parry knew that Jolie had drawn on an item of magic they had learned since her death: the mesmeric burn. The guard had not really been hurt, but he had felt the pain where the cross touched – because of the guilt on his conscience. He had known it was wrong to interfere with a witness protected by a friar. Superstition had indeed daunted him.

'So it is of this manner,' Bofort muttered. He made another gesture.

'Deflect!' Parry cried, warning Jolie.

Two crossbow shafts came down from the bowmen in the alcoves. The arrows swerved slightly and thudded into the wall on either side of the girl. Jolie had invoked the spell of deflection, causing the barbs to miss. Conjuration or levitation was difficult magic, but deflection was its simplest aspect, and they had had more than a decade to study it.

'If your guilt were in doubt,' Parry said, 'that doubt has been resolved by your action. Come with me.' He strode around the table towards Bofort.

'Clear the court!' Bofort cried. 'I will talk with this man alone.'

The guards and attendants hurried out, as did the bowmen. In a moment Parry and Fabiola were alone with Bofort.

'Who are you?' Bofort demanded. 'I know sorcery when I see it!'

'I am sure you do,' Parry agreed. 'You have practised it for decades.'

'On behalf of the Church!'

'On behalf of Lucifer.'

'How dare you charge me with that? I gave invaluable magical aid to the crusade!'

'You systematically eliminated your competition – in the guise of that support. That was the work of Lucifer.'

'Who are you?' Bofort repeated. 'I know of all competetent sorcerers, and there are none among the monks!'

'I am the one that got away. You killed my father and my wife. Now I bring the power of that God you wronged, to see that justice is done.'

Bofort reflected. 'There *was* one that escaped! A novice, a stripling, who murdered a crusader and slipped the noose. I had all but forgotten.'

'I had not forgotten,' Parry said grimly. 'Now you will come with me voluntarily to the magistrate, or I shall reveal your nature to the personnel of this establishment. That will demolish your reputation as well as your estate.'

'You seek to make a deal, friar?' Bofort sneered.

'My calling requires mercy for the sinner, no matter how grievous his sins may be. Confess your sins, and accept your punishment, and I shall not add to it. Come with me now, and some part of your estate may survive.'

'I cannot come with you,' Bofort said. 'You know whom I serve.'

'I serve a greater one.'

'No, you merely serve a different one.'

'Must we try our strength? My Lord supports me; does yours support you?'

Bofort thought about that a moment. It was known that Lucifer quickly lost patience with those who were clumsy in the pursuit or practice of evil. 'Perhaps we can after all deal. I will give you information that is worth far more than I am, if you will depart in peace.'

'I seek no deal, merely justice. Come with me; perhaps you can make a deal with the magistrate.'

'The magistrate? He goes with the politics of the moment! You have incited the town against me; there will be no justice there.'

'It's true, Parry,' Jolie said through Fabiola's mouth.

'The townsmen are massing now to march on this castle. It seems that quite a number of them have suffered at the hands of this man, and now they see their chance to bring him down.'

'So you are finished, sorcerer,' Parry said. 'Come with me.'

'I tell you, you would be better off to make the deal,' Bofort said. 'I can tell you of the greatest scourge ever to strike this fair land, now in the making. You may be intimately involved; what irony! You can save yourself and all you hold dear, if you know its nature.'

'I make no deals with your kind,' Parry said. 'Now come; I will protect you from the malice of the throng.'

'Well, if I must,' Bofort said, and turned as if to walk.

Then a bolt of energy lanced at Parry.

It bathed him in fire, then died. He was untouched.

'So you are braced against physical assault,' Bofort said. 'But perhaps not against this.' He made a sign.

Parry held up the cross. Something struck it, invisibly, and bounced back.

'Why you cunning – Hell and damnation! Damn, damn, damn – rascal!' Bofort exclaimed. 'You used a mirror spell to send the curse back at me! There is no cure!'

'Come with me,' Parry repeated.

'I shall not – God be cursed! Lucifer be worshipped! Damn, damn, damn! – come with you, friar! The peons would – animal fornication! Black Mass! Damn, damn, damn! – tear me apart!'

'Then I shall go without you,' Parry said. 'Come, Fabiola; our business here is done.'

'For the love of – damn, damn, damn! – what do you expect me to do?' Bofort cried in desperation.

'I expect you to suffer to the precise degree of those you have afflicted with this curse in the past,' Parry said.

They walked from the chamber, Lord Bofort ranting behind.

'Father, what's wrong with him?' Fabiola asked, awed.

'The curse he sought to inflict on me,' Parry said. 'My research in the documents relating to this case suggested that he had used it on others, so I prepared myself against it. It causes the victim to swear uncontrollably when he tries to speak. Such a person cannot hide, for his mouth soon gives him away. Lord Bofort is finished; his own retainers will not serve him now. I doubt he can do much magic, for the interjections will ruin both the spells and his concentration.'

'Serves him right,' Jolie said. 'You really fixed him.'

'I did nothing to him,' Parry demurred. 'He did it to himself.'

'You are a man of God,' she said smugly. 'You have left worldly passions behind. But I am only a vengeful spirit; I glory in our enemy's downfall. It was long in coming, but nonetheless satisfying.'

Parry let it go at that. He did not want to explore his private emotions more closely.

They departed the castle without opposition; the guards had seen enough to realize that it would be extremely bad form to oppose the powerful friar. Outside, they soon encountered the advancing throng. 'Do not seek vengeance,' Parry urged them. 'The man had brought mischief on himself.'

They milled uncertainly, not wishing to oppose him but also unwilling to give up their satisfaction.

But the matter soon became academic. News came from the castle: Lord Bofort had lambasted his guards and servants in the foulest possible terms, then stabbed himself. His body, they claimed, had turned to charred ashes before their eyes, as if burned in the fires of hell itself.

Parry saw Fabiola back to her family. 'Keep the cross, my child; it will protect you always, as it has today.'

95

'Oh thank you, Father!' she exclaimed. 'And the Lady Jolie!'

'God bless and keep you, child.' Parry remounted his donkey and rode away.

'You put on a humble front for the populace,' Jolie said. 'But you know that the legend of Father Grief has been started, and will last long in this region.'

'Perhaps it is time that the power of God manifested in the hinterlands.' he said.

'This won't do you any harm in the hierarchy of the Dominican Order, either,' she continued.

'It is true that there are projects I have wished to pursue. Perhaps God has chosen this way to forward them.'

So they chatted as they travelled home to the monastery. Parry tried to maintain a humble pose, but deep down he was extremely gratified. The action of the day did not restore Jolie or his father to life, but it went far to alleviate an abiding frustration. He had finally settled with the one who had brought such mischief on him.

Yet there was a dark current, too. Thanatos had said that there was great evil attaching to Jolie's death, so that her soul was in near balance instead of being free to float blithely to Heaven. So far he had not fathomed that evil; what he had done following that tragedy had been manifestly good. Could Thanatos have been mistaken? So it seemed – yet somehow he doubted it.

His success did indeed have impact. The following year, in 1231, he was invited to meet with Pope Gregory IX. He explained to the Pope the necessity for a more ardent pursuit of evil, because Satan had many tools among disaffected folk. Lord Bofort had become such a tool (Parry was not free to say that he believed Bofort had always been such a tool, because the Pope had endorsed the crusade of his predecessors), and was constantly

96

seeding evil in others. Only the most constant vigilance and understanding of the problem could keep the works of Lucifer at bay. He expressed his conviction that the Dominicans, as the order that had studied this issue most scrupulously, should be formally assigned this duty. As it was at present, the Dominicans lacked the authority to pursue the evil of heresy to its limit. Stronger measures were required.

The Pope listened, and seemed impressed. But he would not act without further deliberation. He thanked Parry and dismissed him. But Parry had the impression that the Pope intended to act, and was gratified.

Two years later, in 1233, that action came: the *inquisitores hereticae pravitatis* were henceforth to be Dominicans, appointed by the Pope and subject only to him. Parry was not the friar placed in charge, but he was the mover behind the scene, which was exactly as he wanted it.

Now at last he could go after the ultimate source of evil, of which Lord Bofort had been only a symptom: Lucifer himself. Parry intended to discover the nature of the scourge Bofort had spoken of, and to foil it. The Inquisition had gained teeth.

5
Scourge

In 1239 Parry rode his donkey to the Germanic realm. It was fall, and the countryside was turning beautiful. He was alone this time; the monastry had not been able to spare another monk for such a long journey, and it was known that Father Grief could take care of himself despite his advancing age. 'He brings grief to any who oppose him,' it was said, without complete humour.

'Whose chestnuts are you pulling from the fire this time?' Jolie inquired, manifesting as a ghost floating before him. The donkey, used to this, merely twitched an ear and plodded on, ignoring her.

'The Emperor's,' he replied, knowing what was coming.

'Frederick?' she asked. 'But he's been excommunicated!'

'Twice,' Parry agreed equably.

'So how can you, a devout man of God, go into his realm?'

She was badgering him, but he liked it. 'Because the realm of the excommunicated is where the light of God is most needed,' he replied. 'My journey here is not to be construed as support for Frederick II, though in truth he is not an evil man, but as an effort to abolish heresy wherever it is found. The Holy Roman Empire does not question the authority of God, or even of the Church; it merely seeks to increase its temporal power at the expense of that of the Church.'

'Big distinction! How can the Emperor fight the Pope and not be an evil man?'

'Because good and evil do not lie in the material realm. If Frederick stopped pushing his influence farther into

Italy's rich northern lands, the Pope would soon enough find him to be a worthy man.'

'You sound as if you are criticizing the Church!'

He turned a bland countenance to her. 'Surely you misunderstand, my dear! How could I, a Dominican friar, dedicated as I am to the eradication of evil, possibly do that?'

She laughed. 'I wish I were flesh again, Parry! I'd corrupt you so rapidly!'

He nodded. Jolie was great company in spirit, but would have been much better alive. He had done well as a monk in large part because of her advice, and because he had no interest in mortal women while Jolie was with him. If she ever should leave him, appearing no more in her ghost semblance, he would be in trouble, for even at age forty-nine he did notice the young women.

'But I don't think you ever really answered my question,' she continued. 'What is your present mission?'

'As you know, I have laboured diligently to extirpate heresy from the fair face of France. Most heretics are simple, uneducated folks who accede readily to correction when it is made; they merely have known no better. Thus my labours are mainly of enlightenment and persuasion.'

'You're stalling, Parry! Don't use your Guest Lecturer pose on me. What's so special about this case?'

'Well, some few are hardened in their error, resistive to the amelioration of normal efforts. Such cases are referred to the higher structure of the Inquisition. I have shown a certain talent in this regard, so have been assigned increasingly to the most difficult cases.'

'Parry, you know I know all this!' she exclaimed in exasperation. Then her eyes narrowed. 'Is it a female heretic? A luscious young woman who –'

Now he laughed. 'I love it when you're jealous, Jolie! But I must confess I have an additional motive: not only do I wish to abolish heresy wherever it sprouts in its weedlike profusion, I seek to discover Lucifer's larger purpose. Do you remember Lord Bofort?'

'That girl!' she exclaimed. 'What's her name – Fabiola! The one that demon framed! I knew you had a woman on your mind!'

'That was years ago, and I only remember her because you animated her. Oh, Jolie, if you ever *could* return to life –'

'I could only do it halfway, with the consent of the living body. And that would ruin your celibacy. You're better off with me dead.' She lifted her head with a flirt of her hair. 'Now stop changing the subject and tell me about this particular mission.'

'From Lord Bofort, before I left him, I learned that Lucifer is up to some terrible scourge. I refused to deal with him, yet always since have regretted it. What did he know, and why did he think I should have any connection with it? That haunts me. This upcoming heretic may be a genuine agent of Lucifer; there are certain signals. If so, I may at last learn from him the nature of this thing. *That* is what makes this potentially significant, for me, and perhaps for the world. All I know now, from those scattered hints I have gleaned from recanting heretics, is that this scourge will devastate all Europe, perhaps destroying the Church itself, and that it will occur about a decade from the time I first learned of it. That was nine years ago.'

'So you still have one more year to ferret it out.'

'No, not necessarily. It could happen before the time expires, or after. I can't afford to let it go any longer than absolutely necessary. Suppose it happens this year?'

'Is there any sign of such monstrous evil?'

'No, there isn't. That's the most disturbing aspect of all. I see nothing capable of devastating the entire continent and delivering the majority of its souls into the power of the archenemy. To the north I see King Henry

III of England squandering the purse of that nation in foolish wars and pointless extravagance; he lacks the wit to bring such disaster on any except his own head. To the south I see the Christian states of Castile, Aragon and Portugal wresting the Iberian peninsula from the Moorish infidel; that is hardly any tragedy. Here in France Louis IX is close to an ideal King; when he has had more time to establish himself, France will benefit greatly. To the east is the Emperor, who has too much to gain from controlling central Europe to risk destroying it. In short, I see no sign of any evil so monstrous as to devastate the entire continent and deliver the majority of its souls into the power of the archenemy. Europe is its usual chaotic self, neither better nor worse than it was the century before. The matter baffles me! Yet I am sure it is not bluff; somewhere, somehow, a terrible scourge is in the making.'

'I hope you find it out, Parry,' she said, and faded.

He hoped so, too!

Near the border Jolie brought another matter to his attention. 'There is a group of orphan children that need to be taken to a nunnery to the east,' she announced. 'But the nun who is supposed to take them is afraid to travel through the Black Forest without an armed escort, and there is none available.'

Parry sighed. 'What do you want of me, Jolie?'

'Why, I think you could readily convey those poor children. No robber would dare to bother *you*.'

'I appreciate your confidence,' he said drily. 'Where are they?'

'Right this way, noble knight!' She floated before him, guiding him. Parry was just thankful that he had taken the trouble to learn the language of German, for this was surely a German nun guiding the children to her home nunnery.

The nun was only too glad to accept his offer. She knew that a Dominican friar was the best available company for a dangerous trip. Once again Jolie had served as his conscience, alerting him to a deed he would not have thought of on his own. He was a better man and a better friar because of her, he knew. That was ironic, because he would never have become a friar if she had lived, and would not have remained one had she somehow been restored to life.

There turned out to be eight children, all girls, ranging in age from five to twelve. They were barefoot and in rags, but reasonably healthy and clean. The nun had taken good care of them, to the best of her resources.

They started along the path. Parry offered his donkey to the nun. She accepted, but did not ride herself; instead she put the smallest two girls on it.

The forest closed in densely soon after they left the village. The road degenerated to a trail, so that they had to go single file. Parry led the way, and the donkey brought up the rear, with the nun keeping a wary eye from the middle. They had hoped to reach an established camping spot by nightfall, but a sudden storm drenched them and made the trail a wash of mud. The children began to whimper. It became obvious that they would have to camp for the night in the wilderness.

'There are edible berries,' Jolie said. 'And some ferns. We can feed them and bed them down.'

Parry relayed her suggestions, and soon the girls were foraging for their supper and sleep. Under his guidance they managed to form crude shelters from boughs and sticks, and to gather sufficient fern for comfort.

Then the shapes and sounds of the dusk manifested. There was an eerie howl that sent the girls clustering together, terrified, and rustlings amidst the foliage of the trees.

'These are merely wild creatures,' Parry said. 'They will not harm us.'

'The holy man says not to worry,' the nun told the children. 'Now settle and sleep.'

They settled, clustering together in their shelters. Parry considered, then hoisted himself into a tree. Safely out of sight of the party, he could change into the form of an owl and roost with relative comfort and safety. One of the pleasures of recent years was his renewed facility with magic, now that he no longer feared being tracked down by the mysterious sorcerer. He used magic only for proper purpose, of course, and always discreetly; it was too easy for ignorant folk to assume that *any* magic was evil. The truth was, the Church was based on magic, from the simplest rituals in the Mass to the full-scale miracles; without it, the Church would soon falter and fail. That was one of the most compelling reasons to extirpate heresy: if folk were permitted to practise magic independently, the monopoly would be broken. And, of course, without the guidance of the Church, folk would inevitably drift into evil magic and Lucifer would profit. Good magic was a marvellous tool, but evil magic was treacherous.

There was a commotion at the shelters. The nun muttered, evidently investigating. Then there was a piercing scream.

Parry flung himself out of the tree. That had been the nun screaming!

She had cause. In the slanting moonlight was the shape of a wolf.

Stories about wolves abounded, but Parry had taken the trouble to research the matter and knew that wolves almost never attacked man, only man's domesticated animals. That was why a lone shepherd boy could protect a flock of fat sheep from predation; it was not his presumed skill with a weapon, but the fact that wolves feared man and avoided him whenever possible.

With certain key exceptions. When an animal was inhabited by a demon, it was no longer in full control of itself and acted irrationally. The demon did not care for its welfare, and indeed soon ground the animal to a miserable death. In the final stages the animal foamed at the mouth, and fled water. But before it died, it tried its best to bite some other creature, such as a man, by that action transferring the demon to the man. Thus the course continued indefinitely, with relatively few demons causing misery and death for an endless chain of victims.

This was of course a job for the friar. No wonder the nun had screamed; she, better than any, had known the creature for what it was: a sending of Lucifer.

'Do not move,' Parry said clearly. 'Motion attracts it. Remain where you are, and I shall deal with it.'

The nun crossed herself. The wolf's head snapped about to orient on her. 'No motion!' Parry cried. 'The cross only baits it! Demons are infuriated by the cross!'

The nun froze, realizing the truth of his cautioning.

Now Parry advanced slowly on the monster. 'Orient on me, demon,' he said. He brought out his own silver cross. 'Gaze on this, O accursed one! These good children shall not be yours!'

The wolf did orient on him. Its eyes seemed to glow, but it maintained its uncanny silence. No growl, no sound of breathing, just that silent assessment. What was it waiting for?

'Parry!' Jolie cried, manifesting. 'There are others behind you – and not just wolves!'

Parry turned. There were two other wolves – and above them, hovering low, several dark bats. All centred on him unwaveringly.

Parry realized that he was up against no ordinary thing. This was a deliberate, concerted effort. In fact, it was a trap. Lucifer was moving against him directly.

'Behind!' Jolie cried. He whirled. The first wolf was

almost upon him, jaws open, faint bubbles showing. He brought the cross down, and the creature bristled and withdrew, grudgingly.

'Behind!' Jolie cried. 'A bat!'

Parry whirled again, lifting the cross as the bat swooped at his head. The thing shied clear, but not before the malice showed in its tiny eyes. A drop of saliva splatted against Parry's cloak.

Then he returned to the wolf, who was crouching, about to spring. He thrust the cross at its snout, and it snarled silently and ducked away.

'Another wolf! Behind!'

He parried that one with a quick motion, then whipped the cross back to counter the first again. He would already have been bitten, had not Jolie been present to watch his rear.

So Lucifer had at last realized the effectiveness of Parry's quiet campaign against evil, and was acting to eliminate him. This was a compliment, of a sort! But how was he to escape this dreadful trap? He knew that a single bite of any one of these possessed creatures would doom him; the process might take days or weeks, but there was no cure for this type of malady.

'Behind!' Jolie screamed.

Parry jumped aside, so that whatever was coming at him would miss, and held the cross towards the wolf in front that was already tensing for a leap. The tactic worked; the bat spun by his ear, only its wingtip touching. But the wolf was unable to halt its coordinated action; it sprang, and its body struck Parry's hip.

Parry chopped downward with the cross. It rammed against the wolf's back. There was a kind of flash.

Now the creature made a sound of pure anguish, as the demon within felt the power of that enchanted talisman. It twisted to the ground, shuddering and stiffening. Ordinary folk were affected primarily by their own belief, but

105

truly possessed creatures were literally smitten, being animated by the humours of Hell.

But the others were closing in from every point of the compass. Parry saw there was no way to thwart them all physically. He had to have some more effective measure against them. But what was there?

'Sing, Parry!' Jolie cried.

Then he knew what to do. He drew upon his lifelong ability to sing and improvise, and he set aside his inhibitions and unbound his voice. He sang to the wolves and the bats:

> Creatures of the wild, hark unto me!
> I am not your enemy!
> Your enemy is the demon inside each one of you,
> Who leads your soul to damnation!

His voice reached out into the gloom of the forest, gaining authority and conviction. He saw the children staring raptly, and the nun with eyes and mouth open in astonishment. The Dominican friars did not sing, only the Franciscans!

The wolves stood at bay, and the bats hovered uncertainly. They were listening, but not in a position to respond. They were waiting for their chance to charge again.

> Creatures of the wild, hark unto me!
> I am not your enemy!
> Rise, throw out the evil spirit within your body!
> Cast it out, and be free!
>
> God forgives the worst human sinner who is penitent;
> Even so will God forgive you.
> Cast out the unnatural thing that possesses you
> Cast it out, and be natural!

He was pleading to the hosts that the demons were using. He doubted that the animals could understand his words, but they understood his message, for the song was imbued with it. Possession of this nature was thought to have no cure, but now he was going to try to change that.

> If your demon is too strong,
> If it strangles you rather than be evicted,
> Come to me, and I will banish it
> With the touch of the Holy Cross.

The song was having its impact! The possessed creatures were struggling to banish their demons, and could not; but neither could the demons make them attack the singer.

> If you cannot come to me,
> Wait where you are.
> I will come to you;
> I will touch you and heal you.

But when he approached the nearest wolf, it shied away. Still the demon was too strong, or the faith of the wild creatures too weak. More was required.

'Be like them!' Jolie cried. 'Show them, Parry!'

Parry nodded. As always, Jolie's advice was good.

> Creatures of the wild!
> I am your friend!
> I know your natures!
> I am one of you!

Then he stopped singing and transformed himself into the form of a wolf. The cross remained in his right paw; he lowered his head and took it between his teeth.

He approached the nearest wolf, and this time the creature stood its ground. The silver cross touched its nose. There was another exclamation of anguish – but this time the demon spirit fled. The wolf collapsed, but it was free.

107

Parry approached the second wolf, and touched it similarly. Then the third. Now all three lay panting, exhausted by the terrible animation they had suffered, but restored to their natural states.

Parry changed to bat form. He was a huge bat, because the cross was too heavy for a small one. He flew slowly up, approaching one of the hovering bats, and touched it with the cross. It screamed silently and fell to the ground, but the other two did not flee. They hovered where they were, able to balk the demons to this extent. He approached and touched each, and each fell to the ground.

Now Parry returned to his human form. 'Rise!' he cried to the wild creatures. 'Go your ways, and suffer no demon spirits again! Live your lives as they are meant to be, far from the human kind!'

The creatures stirred. The wolves climbed to their feet and walked unsteadily into the darkness. The bats paused, then launched themselves one by one into the air and flew away.

All that remained was the group of staring children, and the staring nun.

'I think you have some explaining to do, love,' Jolie said, fading out with an impish grin.

Surely so! Parry turned to face the small audience. 'What did you see?' he inquired, as if this were routine.

For a long moment there was silence. Then the smallest child piped, 'Wolves!'

The next smallest added 'Bats!'

'Demons!' several chorused.

'An angel!' another breathed.

'That was the Madonna!' the oldest corrected her. 'And she warned you when things were behind you!'

'And she told you what to do!'

The others nodded. They had seen it too. They turned to the nun inquiringly.

The nun spoke with difficulty. 'I saw – a vision,' she said. 'Perhaps Father Grief will clarify for us its nature.'

So she hadn't seen Jolie, but realized that the children had seen something. She surely had seen Parry change form, but hesitated to proffer an explanation for that, in case the others had not seen the same.

He would put them all at ease. 'It was a vision,' he agreed. 'Evil stalked us in the form of possessed wild creatures, but it was put to rout by the power of Jesus.' He held aloft his cross. 'That is all that happened, but the manner the struggle between good and evil manifests is subject to individual perceptions.'

The younger girls looked blank.

'Each person sees it her own way,' Parry said quickly, and the blank looks cleared. 'No way is wrong; each is suited exactly to the person. So some of you may have seen wolves and bats, while others saw infernal creatures animating them. Some may have seen and heard an angel helping me, while others saw the Madonna. It does not matter; the important thing is that God saw the need, and extended His help by advising me and enabling me to drive off the creatures.' He smiled. 'Some may even have seen me change form, to carry the cross to the creatures in their own semblance. This too is fair.'

Now the nun nodded. It seemed that that was the form of the vision she had seen. The girls, being more innocent, had seen the angel. Jolie was seldom apparent to adults, who were inevitably corrupted by life and cynicism, but children retained the openness to see spiritual things.

'And you sang, Father!' a girl exclaimed. 'When the demons were closing, you sang the evil from them!'

'Song is a wonderful force for good,' Parry agreed. 'Remember that, when it is time to sing in a service at the nunnery.'

Again the nun nodded; she approved of that. These children should be model students, because of their experience here. But there seemed to be a certain reservation about her, and Parry understood that too. He had demonstrated too much magic for comfort.

They completed the trek through the Black Forest without further event, and delivered the girls to the nunnery. Parry wished there was more he could do for them; he knew that they faced a life of only slightly diminished privation, for the nuns had little to offer in the way of material things. But the face of each child shone with an inner joy and wonder that had not been there at the start of the journey. The vision evidently remained with them, and perhaps that was enough.

Jolie manifested as he resumed his donkey ride alone. 'Parry, I'm worried,' she said.

'I had not realized that spirits were capable of worry,' he remarked.

'I'm serious! Lucifer never went after you directly before.'

'True. Obviously he knows my mission. That must be a good sign.'

'A good sign? Parry, you have done well all these years because you have never taken proper credit for your accomplishments. Lucifer never realized that you were the one responsible for all that good. But now, if he knows, he'll be out to get you. The demons in the forest may be only the beginning!'

'It is good, because it means I am at last getting close to the truth,' Parry explained. 'Lucifer does not want me to interview this particular heretic.'

'But it's dangerous! Who knows what horror will menace you next?'

'Accomplishment is seldom without risk. I trust you will keep watch over me, as you have these thirty years.'

'I have no choice,' she grumbled. 'You hold my blood hostage.'

He glanced at the stain on his wrist. Her soul was still housed there. 'Certainly it has been good to have you always with me, always as pretty as you were in life.'

'I think you like me better as a spirit than as a living woman!'

That stung him. 'I would give anything to have you alive, Jolie! But since even the semblance of that poses horrendous complications, I must be satisfied with that aspect of you that is available. Yet if I could release your spirit to go to heaven where it belongs, I would do so.'

'Oh, it's not so bad being a ghost,' she said, mollified. 'Though I do wonder what the great evil can be that keeps me fixed in perfect balance. I have seen no evil in your life since my death, and it is true that I would be old and fat by now if I had lived.'

'And I would not be in the Church,' he added. 'I agree: it was terrible to have you die, but I perceive no evil apart from that. I can only presume that it has not yet manifested.'

'But now Lucifer knows you. Oh, Parry – I fear that evil is close upon us!'

'We shall oppose it together,' he said with conviction.

'Together,' she agreed, and floated close for an ethereal kiss. Then she faded out.

There were no further episodes with evil as he completed his journey. Parry concluded that Lucifer was not truly aware of him, just of the fact that a friar had been dispatched to handle this case. So a contingent of demons had been sent to eliminate that friar. The fact that no others had come meant either that the Lord of Evil had not been paying close attention, this being a minor matter, or that he lacked other forces at the moment in this vicinity. Probably the former. Still, if this heretic did have critical information, and Parry were able to get it, then

111

Lucifer would certainly pay attention. Then things could become difficult.

The heretic was an old man, grey of beard and frail. He was not comfortable when Parry saw him; he was in a dank dungeon, naked on the floor on his back. His wrists and ankles were roped to stakes so that he could not move them. There was a flat board on his front, and on this were set metal weights. The man was breathing only in shallow gasps, unable to inhale properly because of the pressure on his chest.

'What is this?' Parry demanded, outraged.

'It is the *peine forte et dure*, Father,' the gaoler said. 'The strong and hard pain.'

'I know what it is!' Parry snapped. 'What I mean is, why is this punishment being practised on this person? I was told he has not made a plea.'

'This is not punishment, Father. It is merely an inducement to cause him to make his plea.'

'An inducement? It looks like torture to me!'

'By no means, Father. He is not being cut, his bones are not being dislocated, he is not being burned or starved. He is merely being encouraged to plead.'

'Because if he does not plead guilty or innocent, you cannot try him,' Parry said, disgusted.

'True, Father. Criminals are becoming obstinate; they dally forever, clogging the processes of justice. They must be made to plead.'

'But under such duress, any man would plead, even if he had no guilt!'

'No, Father. Some die rather than plead.'

'So most plead guilty? What happens to them?'

'They forfeit all their goods, and are let go.'

'And what of those who plead innocent?'

'They are found guilty, and punished for their intransigence, and their property is forfeit.'

'I can see why they try to avoid making pleas,' Parry

said drily. 'Their alternatives are starvation or torture and starvation. Did it ever occur to you that a man might be innocent, undeserving of any punishment?'

'No, Father,' the gaoler said, surprised by his naïveté. 'We have only guilty here.'

Jolie appeared. 'Stop talking and get him out of this!' she exclaimed. 'The poor man!'

Parry agreed. 'Release the prisoner,' he said.

'But he has not yet made his plea!'

'I wish to talk to him. That would be hard to do if he can't breathe.'

'Oh. In that case I will lessen the weights just enough to enable him to answer.'

'No. Remove them all, and unbind him. I want him free of fetters.'

'But Father, this is most irregular!'

Parry delivered a steely stare. 'Gaoler, do you value your soul?'

The man gave way, grudgingly. In due course the prisoner was free. But he was unable to rise; he lay where he was, his gasps diminishing.

Parry tried to help him, but the man groaned. He had been bound so long that the circulation had suffered in his hands and feet, and his joints hardly functioned. Parry had to let him be; it was the kindest thing he could do.

'I have come to talk to you,' Parry said gently. 'I regret that you were put under such duress; I did not know of it until I saw you. I will do what I can to help you escape this situation, if you will return to the bosom of our Lord and tell me what I wish to know.'

'I cannot!' the man gasped.

'Surely you can,' Parry said gently. 'God is forgiving, for the truly penitent.'

'No, I cannot, for I dare not make a plea!'

Parry nodded. If the man confided that he had had dealings with Lucifer, that would be confirmation of his guilt, and the savage retribution of the law would wipe him out. If he denied it, and in so doing swore falsely, there would be no salvation for him. It was certainly a difficult situation.

But the order thought there was evidence that this was a true heretic, and Lucifer had tried to prevent Parry's arrival to interview him. This could be the source of the information Parry had to ferret out. He could not let it go without making his utmost effort.

'Let me speak candidly,' he said. 'It is my desire to save your soul from the eternal fires of damnation if at all possible. It is also my desire to learn certain information. I am not without influence. Cooperate with me, and perhaps your situation will ameliorate.'

The man's eyes flicked to the gaoler. He looked like a hunted animal. He did not speak.

That was enough for Parry. The suspect *did* know something!

Parry addressed the gaoler. 'Allow me to interview this man alone, if you please.'

The gaoler's look was crafty. 'I do not please, Father. This criminal is dangerous! I must remain here to protect you from possible harm.'

'This man can hardly breathe, let alone stand,' Parry pointed out. 'He is alarmed by your presence; I believe he will talk more freely in private with me.'

The canny look intensified. The gaoler thought there might be revelation of hidden money. 'I cannot – '

Parry fixed him with an imperial glare. 'Leave us!'

Reluctantly, the man retreated. He exited the cell, but stood just beyond it, well within hearing range.

'Go elsewhere,' Parry said, his patience fraying.

'But I cannot leave the cell unlocked!'

'Lock it, then!'

The man hauled the heavy door shut, and barred it from outside. Parry knew he was standing just beyond it,

114

his ear straining, but was assured that low voices would not carry sufficiently to satisfy the man.

'Now the gaoler is gone,' he told the suspect. 'You may speak freely to me, and I will keep your confidence.'

'I – wish I could,' the man said.

Parry realized that the man needed help. 'I understand the situation you are in. You can not plead, because no matter what you plead, they will deprive you of your property and perhaps your life.' He saw the agreement in the haunted eyes. 'You have perhaps a family, who would suffer privation, and you do not wish that.' Again the muted agreement. 'But if there were only some way you could get out of this without hurting those you love, you would take that course.'

'Yes!' the man breathed. Now he was recovered enough to struggle to sit up, and Parry assisted him.

'Therefore your problem may be material rather than spiritual. Suppose you were to be found innocent of the charge against you?'

For a moment the man brightened; then he slumped.

Parry continued to read the signals. This man *had* dealt with Lucifer! But now regretted it.

'You were in need – your family was in need – so you did what you thought you had to do, to deliver them from grief. What did you offer Lucifer? Surely not your soul!'

'Not my soul!' the man agreed.

'But what else would the Lord of Evil desire of you?'

The man struggled. 'My – my silence.'

Parry concealed his mounting excitement, and spoke calmly. 'Your silence about what?'

'I – ' But the man balked, hesitant to convict himself.

'And for your silence on this score, Lucifer paid in gold,' Parry said, as if there had been no balk. 'It came as if by accident; you found buried coins – ' The man was nodding as he spoke; he was hitting close enough to the mark.

115

'And when you spent them, the neighbours became suspicious, or rapacious, and turned you in, hoping to gain those coins for themselves'

'Yes!'

'And now if you confess to dealing with Lucifer, you are lost, and if you do not confess, you will be tortured until you do confess. In either case you will lose the money, and your family will be worse off than before you started.'

'Yes, Father.'

Parry fixed him with a gentle variant of his stare. 'Did it not occur to you that Lucifer broke his bargain with you? He gave you the money – then alerted the neighbours so that you would lose it and be worse off than before.'

The man's mouth fell open.

'Lucifer reneged,' Parry continued relentlessly. 'You owe the Lord of Evil nothing!'

'Nothing!' the man echoed.

'But you may redeem your soul and perhaps your family if you cooperate with God. God does not renege. God will welcome you back to His fold. All that He requires is genuine repentance and dedication to His will.'

'My family . . .' the man said, daring to hope.

'First we must ascertain what we have,' Parry said. 'Tell me the thing about which Lucifer bought your silence, and I will see what I can do.'

Suddenly it poured out. 'Father, I am a historian! All my life I have studied the scrolls of the ancients, and tried to fathom the courses of mankind. I have questioned travellers, learning about their homelands, piecing together the tapestry of the mortal realm. Oh, the tragedies that abound, the wasted lives! But recently I learned of a terrible scourge that is building – '

The man paused to recover his breath. That was just as

116

well, because Parry needed a moment to steady himself. The scourge! Here it was at last!

'And I saw that it was coming this way,' the man continued. 'Others have not noticed, because it is as yet far away. But it is coming here, to the ruin of us all! I sought to publish my discovery, but lacked the money, and then – '

'Then Lucifer proffered much greater wealth – for your silence,' Parry said.

'Yes. He came to me in the form of an ordinary man, but I knew him for what he was. He told me where to find the coins, and said I could do whatever I liked with them, as long as I kept silent about my discovery. And I – my wife was ailing, she needed better food – '

'And you realized that if you did not agree to do as Lucifer wished for gold, he might coerce you by some less amicable means,' Parry said.

'Yes. He – he frightened me! I did not want to deal with him, but – '

'My son, you did wrong,' Parry said. 'But your deed was understandable. What was the nature of this scourge?' He hoped that the man did not balk now!

'It is the heathen Tartars,' the man said. 'They come from afar, as they did eight hundred years ago, but they come in terrible strength. Then they destroyed the empire of the Romans; this time they will destroy all that remains. Already they are overrunning the lands of the Moors, making pyramids of their severed heads! The Moors are our enemies, so our kings are not concerned about their problems, but the Tartars are a worse threat than the Moors! In one, perhaps two years they will come here, and there will be carnage such as we have never seen before!'

And there it was: the scourge of which Lord Bofort had hinted! The alien Tartars – coming at last to Europe! Suddenly it all made sense. Parry had studied some history himself; he knew how ferocious had been the invasion of the Tartars before, then called the Huns.

But more information was needed, and there was not much time. One or two years? It would take that long just to prepare a respectable defence, assuming the proper ears could be reached.

'You can document this?' he inquired. 'You can prove your case to those in a position to understand it?'

'Oh, yes, certainly! But – '

'But you fear the reprisals of Lucifer or the law,' Parry concluded. 'Do not be concerned; I will protect you from these. You must come with me, to give evidence about this matter. We must prevent the ravaging of Europe.'

'But my – '

'We shall provide for your family before we go.' Parry walked swiftly to the door and rapped on the wood with his knuckle. 'Gaoler! Bring the prisoner's clothing! I am taking him out of here!'

'You have no authority, Father!' the gaoler cried. 'The criminal is ours!'

Parry paused to take stock. It was true that the Church did not like to intervene in secular matters directly. He realized that the gaoler and his superiors were greedy for the spoils of the prisoner's property; they would not let him go without a horrendous struggle. He didn't have time for that; he had to get the man to his Order as soon as possible.

'Jolie,' he murmured.

'He has summoned guards,' Jolie said, manifesting. 'They will not let you take him out.'

Parry nodded. 'Then I am constrained to use magic.'

He returned to the prisoner. 'I must put you in my pocket for a time,' he said. 'Do not be afraid; it is temporary.'

'Anything is better than the torture!'

Parry touched the man's shoulder, and transformed him

118

to a mouse. The creature squatted on the dank floor, astonished. Parry reached down to pick up the mouse and put it in a voluminous pocket. 'There is a piece of bread there,' he murmured. 'Eat of it, and be welcome. But make no sound.'

Then he gestured at the floor, and the likeness of the prisoner appeared there, lying bound as before.

He turned and strode again to the door. 'Then keep what you find here!' he called. 'I'll have no further part of this.'

Now the gaoler hauled up the bar and hauled open the door. His gaze darted past Parry as he spied the illusion. 'I'll see you out, Father!' he said, eager to be rid of this interference so that he could resume the pressure on the prisoner.

Parry marched sedately out. Soon he was back with his donkey, riding through the town.

He went to see the local magistrate. 'The disposition of the one you charge with heresy has been taken from your hands,' he said. 'His property is not to be attached until the Church has come to a decision in this matter. His family is blameless, and must be left alone.' He knew that when the magistrate learned of the disappearance of the prisoner he would suffer all manner of frustration, but would not dare to go against the expressed wish of the representative of the Inquisition. The Church had ways of enforcing its measures.

Meanwhile, he would carry the prisoner directly to the monastery in France. The man would realize that both he and his family were better off with this separation; it would not be safe for him to show his face locally for some time.

The Tartar campaign, as Parry came to understand it, was a juggernaut; a new tribe of heathens, the Mongols, had taken over and was fashioning the most massive and savage empire the world had yet seen. This was indeed the scourge, and Lucifer was shaping its thrust to overrun Europe in the course of 1241 and 1242. At the moment the eastern portion of the Saracen domains were captive, and the Russian principalities were being subjugated. The Mongols were leaving no nation untouched; they were incorporating the entire continent into their cruel empire. Their manner of dealing with resistance was simple: they cut off the heads of the resisters and potential resisters. There were no rebellions in their lands; all who might or could oppose them were dead.

Yet despite the formidable array of information Parry generated, he was unable to convince his superiors of its importance. 'The kings have many troops, well seasoned in battle,' he was reminded. 'The Asiatics have never encountered real Christian fighting men before, and will quickly retreat before them. Meanwhile, if the Saracens are discomfited, so much the better. That may save us the effort of mounting a crusade against them.'

This was sheer folly, Parry knew. But he also knew that if he could not convince those of his order, who were most concerned with heresy, he would have no better luck with the secular authorities. By the time the magnitude of the menace was properly appreciated, it would be too late. That was what had happened to the Saracens.

But he could not stand idly by while this disaster loomed. Lucifer obviously intended to reap a lavish harvest of souls as the Mongols decimated Europe. Surely evil would flourish under that cruel yoke, without the authority of the Church to suppress it. The Mongols were said to be tolerant of religion; that meant that they would permit any form of it to prosper as long as it did not conflict with their rule. Thus they were like the Holy Roman Empire, only more so. What heresy would manifest under that alien umbrella, unchecked! Truly, Lucifer had crafted a scourge.

There was no help for it: he would have to do the job of saving Europe himself. All he needed now was to figure out how.

6
Dvina

By late 1241 Parry knew that the campaign was almost lost. He had not been able to find any way to stop the approaching Mongol horde. It had annihilated resistance in Poland and Hungary during the summer, and now was orienting on the Holy Roman Empire. The Mongol leader Batu was intent on conquest, and his general Subutai was a military genius. The Europeans remained generally complacent, hardly looking beyond their own borders, but Parry understood now that there was no general and no army who could stand against the Mongol thrust.

'Well, at least you tried to alert them in time,' Jolie said, trying to console him.

'Even if they had marshalled the finest joint army possible in these two years, it still might not have been enough,' Parry said, remaining dispirited. 'The Mongols have routed every type of force, in every type of situation. They conquered the Russian states in a winter campaign; no one has done that before, and it may never be done again. I have learned that they are even now pressing for Cathay. They are simply the most effective military force ever seen, because of their training, dedication and leadership. It may have been already too late to stop them, by the time I learned of the menace.'

'But surely Lucifer cannot have the victory so simply!' she protested. 'If it was inevitable, why would he have worked so diligently to conceal it?'

That made him pause. It was true that Lucifer had kept the threat of the scourge hidden for years, and had tried to prevent Parry from learning of it from the accused heretic. If the decision were sure, Lucifer should have gloried in it, encouraging mortal folk to switch loyalty to him from God. Lucifer had not done that, and was not doing it now.

'There must be a weakness,' he said, his pulse accelerating. 'Lucifer must have reason – good reason, if that is not a contradiction in terms – to keep the secret longer. But what could it be?'

'Something that could even now turn the Golden Horde aside,' she said.

'There is nothing that can turn it aside,' he said. 'Had any such thing existed, someone would have used it by now. Subutai awaits only the thawing of spring to move against the Empire and thereafter France and the Papal State. Indeed, he may not wait till then; he is the master of strategic surprise.'

'You keep thinking in terms of force,' she chided him. 'Isn't there any other way to settle a war?'

'You mean to try to buy the Mongols off? They seem to be virtually incorruptible; all they want is conquest, until nothing remains to conquer.'

'Suppose something happened to their leader?'

'You mean, assassinate Batu? That is not a course I would approve, but I'm sure it has been tried. The Mongols are fanatically loyal to their leaders. The fact is, leaders do die, but the campaign continues; they really don't seem vulnerable that way.'

She sighed. 'Still, there must be something. Some way to stop them, that we might use, that Lucifer is hiding.'

'I wish I knew how to find out what it is!'

'Could you do a divination?'

'The Church really doesn't approve of such magic. In any event, the scale of operations is so vast that I would hardly know how to approach it. It is necessary to have a most specific question in mind, or divination is virtually useless. Many people are worse off with divination than without it, because they misunderstand what it reveals.'

'Perhaps I could look,' she suggested. 'I can travel far now, and swiftly.'

Parry knew that was true. She had laboured over the decades to extend her range, and now could fly to any region of the mortal world. But he remained negative. 'Where would you look? You face the same problem as the divination.'

'I might watch Lucifer's mortal minions. If they abruptly stir, that might be a clue.'

Parry nodded. 'That may be our only chance.'

'But of course I'll have to spend most of my time away from you. Can you endure that?'

She was teasing him, but there was substance in it. 'Your presence and company have sustained me all these years. I will miss you – but for the preservation of our society from evil, I am prepared to endure it.'

She smiled, and brushed his lips with the image of hers, and faded out.

In December Jolie brought news: the minions were stirring. They were active in a pattern of locations forming a rough shield towards the east.

'Surely *they* aren't trying to stop the Mongols!' he exclaimed.

'No, they are operating well within the Mongol sphere, behind the armies. They seem to be alert for something from the east, though. They are at the stations of the major trade and travel routes.'

'They must expect something from the east,' he said. 'But it is winter; the trade routes are mostly shut down. Only a few hardy travellers are abroad now, and the Mongol messenger cadre – '

He broke off, staring at her. 'A message!' he exclaimed. 'They want to intercept a messenger!'

'That must be it,' she agreed. 'But why? What message?'

'We must find out! That is surely the news Lucifer fears!'

'I will go look,' she said excitedly, and faded out again.

She was gone for several days, and Parry was lonely. He had not realized how much he depended on her company! He had been devastated when she died, but her return in spirit had alleviated much of his grief and enabled him to follow his present course. He wondered how the other friars managed, without spiritual women. Some, he knew, cheated, seducing innocent girls on the sly, but others seemed genuinely uninterested in such relations. Did other friars wonder about him? He had been true to Jolie throughout – because she was always with him. But sometimes he dreamed of living women. He knew he was not a natural celibate; had it been feasible for Jolie to resume mortal form, he would have had to leave the Order to rejoin her. Sometimes he almost wished she would animate the body of a mortal girl for a few hours, so as to –

But such notions were forbidden! He steeled himself and went about his business, which at this stage was mainly paperwork. Had he not known better, he would have been tempted to think that the parchment and quill were works of Lucifer, devised to destroy men with sheer tedium.

At last she manifested. 'Parry, I found it!' she said, excitedly. 'The Great Khan is dead! The messengers are riding out to all parts of the Mongol empire with the news!'

'The Khan Ogedei?' he asked, amazed. 'The leader of all the Mongols?'

'The same! Batu is chief only of the Golden Horde; he owes allegiance to the Great Khan! He will have to return to help elect a new Great Khan!'

'Then what of the thrust against Europe?' Parry asked, and answered it even as he spoke. 'It will have to halt,

125

because their leader is dead, and the new one might have different notions! This is what Lucifer has been waiting for. But – '

'But why should Lucifer be so interested in the stopping of the thrust against Europe?' she put in. 'He wants it to continue!'

'Which means Lucifer intends to stop the message from getting through!' Parry concluded. 'Then the thrust will continue, and by the time the news of the Great Khan's death gets through, it will be too late for Europe!'

'Yes, even if the Mongols withdraw, the damage will be so great that there will be chaos, and Lucifer will reap a monstrous harvest!'

He nodded. 'Now we know. Now we must act. How much time do we have?'

'Those riders are professionals,' she said. 'They are using horses in relays, and galloping from station to station. But the stations are farther apart in the wilderness, so they have to rest their horses more. I think it will take about a month to get all the way to Poland; it's over a thousand leagues.'

'But for a message of this importance, they might move faster,' Parry said. 'Also, they could have magicians to transmit it instantly across some sections.'

'Yes. Lucifer's minions are acting as if they expect the messengers in just a few days.'

'So we may not have much time at all. We have to stop Lucifer's minions from ambushing those messengers.'

'But wouldn't Lucifer be on guard against that?' she asked. 'Lucifer has been setting up for this for many years, ready to take advantage of the situation; surely he will not readily be balked.'

'You're right, Jolie! He will be watching! In fact, he will probably be subtle; he won't waylay the messengers, he will simply distract them momentarily and substitute false documents for the originals. Ones that say that the

126

Great Khan is preparing a celebration and wants Europe conquered as swiftly as possible for the occasion. The messengers of course will not know the contents of their packets; those would be only for the eyes of those in charge. We shall have to be as clever as he is – and switch back the original messages.'

So they agreed. Jolie went out again, and used her ability to penetrate the message packet of one of the riders, and memorized the content of the key document. It was written in Uigur script, which complicated matters; she had to describe parts of it, and return for more, in a number of stages. Parry drew on the services of a scholar monk who understood the language to re-create the document.

By the time they had a reasonable imitation, their deadline was close. Lucifer had made the exchanges, and the messengers were riding towards Europe. It would be impossible to intercept each messenger; they were widely separated, taking different routes, using the major trade lanes. Lucifer, with his many minions and many years of preparation, had been able to cover every one, but Parry could only do one.

He decided on the one who was now passing through the chief city of the Russian Principality of Novgorod. That was the northernmost trade route, the one that connected to the Baltic Sea. Sections of that route would be virtually impassable in midwinter; if Lucifer's minions were to be careless about any messenger, it would be that one. He might not even get through in time to have any effect; one of the more southerly messengers would be there first.

'But if false messages arrive first, Prince Batu won't believe the true one!' Jolie protested.

'He's no fool, and certainly General Subutai isn't! They will know something is amiss, and will investigate before acting. That's all we need!'

127

'I hope so,' she said doubtfully.

'It is all we can do on this short notice. We are going to have to work closely together, and your part is vital.'

'Oh?' she asked archly.

He explained the plan he had worked out. 'Oh,' she repeated, no longer archly.

He changed to duck form and set off. The duck was not the most impressive of birds, but was equipped to fly steadily over a long distance, and so represented his fastest and least conspicious mode of travel.

He flew all day, and came to roost exhausted; he had tried to remain in condition, but he had few opportunities as a monk to fly, and he was now fifty years old. The night was freezing. His down insulated him, but foraging and roosting was no fun.

In the morning, tired and stiff, he resumed his flight, northwest towards Novgorod. He made less progress than the prior day, because of his fatigue and the rising winds, but he fought on. He knew that the fate of Europe was at stake; this was his only chance to blunt Lucifer's malicious device.

So he continued, struggling, Jolie floating along with him. Every so often she vanished, going to verify the progress of the Mongol rider. That man, too, was cold and tired, but he was toughened to it, and closed inevitably on the city of Novgorod.

As Parry flew, he reflected on what he knew of Novgorod. About four hundred years before, the Vikings from Sweden had thrust up the river routes of northern Russia, establishing colonies and a trading empire throughout the region. The town of Novgorod became their headquarters, and then the town of Smolensk farther south, and finally Kiev to the south of that, on the approach to the Black Sea. Kiev became the capital of a flourishing empire with strong links to the Byzantine empire of the Mediterranean region. When Kiev broke up, the other cities formed principalities, and Novgorod developed a vast northern fur-trading empire. In recent years, under Prince Alexander Nevski, Novgorod had aggressively extended its domains – until the Mongol onslaught. In 1238, during their winter campaign against the northern principalities, the Mongols had come within twenty leagues of the city of Novgorod. But Alexander had been saved by the luck of the season: the Mongols were steppe fighters who flourished in dry country and in the frozen steppe regions, but were wary of being bogged down and trapped in the marshes by the spring thaw. So they had retreated, sparing Novgorod. Prince Alexander, however, no fool, had yielded sovereignty to the Mongols and paid tribute. Thus they had spared him their next season for campaigning, and moved instead to the west.

Parry nodded internally. Prince Alexander had been wise indeed, for Novgorod retained its strength while the other states were being sliced to bits. Similarly the Principality of Polotsk, now taken over by the Principality of Lithuania, had been spared – but no one doubted the power of the Mongols here, and the Mongol agents were unquestioned. So this was Mongol territory, though it had not felt the Mongol sword directly. Just as much of Europe would be, if Parry's present mission did not succeed. Lucifer had planned well!

By the time Parry reached the border of the Principality of Lithuania, he knew he was not going to make it. The document packet, light enough for a duck to carry, now was weighing him down intolerably. But Jolie hovered with him, spurring him on with words and gibes, so that he dragged himself onward. But soon even her encouragement was not enough, and he had to come to ground at the frozen-over waters of the Western Dvina River. He had not quite made it to the Republic of Novgorod. He was exhausted, and dared not change from his duck form because as a man he would be naked to the snows.

129

Meanwhile, the Mongol rider had reached the town of Novgorod and delivered his message packet to the next rider, who was now riding southwest. Parry's chance to make the exchange in the night was gone.

'But the messenger must pass this river!' Jolie said. 'We can intercept him here!'

'In the form of a duck?' he asked dispiritedly. He did not actually speak; he merely thought it, and she was able to hear, being hardly more than thought herself. This was another refinement of their interaction they had developed over the years.

'You said that I would have to make the actual exchange,' she reminded him. 'That I would have to find a local woman and arrange to animate her body long enough to do it. Why can't I do it here?'

'Because there is no woman,' he replied. 'And if there were, it still wouldn't do, because the messenger will be riding right across the river without pausing. He will be a professional, not stopping for anything until he meets his relay in Vilna. No hope to make the substitution here!'

'Surely there is!' she persisted. 'If I can find a woman, and intercept him here – '

'He would not stop. Not even if you stood naked in the snow. These men simply do not dally; their heads would be forfeit if they did. It is discipline, perhaps more than anything else, that makes the Mongols so formidable.'

'There has to be a way,' she said. 'Maybe you could use magic to stop him.'

'I lack the strength to do more than mild illusion or divination.'

'Illusion,' she said, musingly. 'Much can be done with that, properly applied.'

Now at last her attitude struck a spark. 'The semblance of a barrier!' he thought. 'If the way seems impassable – '

'The river!' she responded. 'If there seemed to be a thaw, so that he could not cross – '

'Except by boat, which his horse could not manage – '

'Unless a local girl knew the only safe route across the loosening ice – '

Parry would have kissed her if he could. She had found the key!

In a moment they had their plan. Parry marshalled his strength for a suitable effort of illusion, while Jolie ranged out to find a suitable local peasant woman for her purpose.

Soon a figure approached, swathed in furs. Parry, foraging at the snowy bank as well as he could, tried to hide, but it hailed him in French. 'Parry! It is Jolie!'

Already! Amazed, he came out to meet her. This was a young woman, a maiden, with girlishly fair features. Even the bundled fur clothing was unable to mask completely the healthy lines of her.

'She has agreed to let me use her body for this occasion,' Jolie said. 'She doesn't speak our language, but I was able to make our need plain. But we must give her something.'

Parry nodded his duck head. No one did something for nothing. 'What did you promise her?' he thought warily.

'I'm afraid it was a pretty important gift. The ability to form a ball of ice, and gaze into it, and see the best location for good firewood under the snow. That way her family will not be cold this winter.'

Parry nodded again. How cleverly Jolie had managed it! This was in fact a minor thing to do; he could readily craft it, even in his present state. But of course it would loom important to the peasant girl, whose horizons were limited. 'It shall be done,' he agreed. 'I shall instruct her now, before the rider comes.'

So he did. If the girl thought it strange to be educated by a duck, she did not show it; evidently Jolie's presence in her mind reassured her. Parry thought his instructions to Jolie, who relayed them to the girl. Because they were concepts rather than words, the girl could understand.

She formed a ball of ice. Actually, it was a ball of solid snow, but that was sufficient. She stared into it, and Parry showed her how, via the channel of Jolie's understanding, to see the visions in it. When she pictured the kind of wood she wanted, the spell enabled her mind to range out ethereally, much as Jolie's did, and orient on that substance. It was borderline magic, actually more of an extension of the natural power latent in every person; they were merely showing her how to exploit it. It was much easier to train her in this, because of Jolie's presence and experience; they accomplished in an hour what might have been difficult in a lifetime for a person instructed only by words.

'But now we must prepare for the interception,' Jolie said. 'The rider is approaching.'

Parry crafted his prepared illusion: the air seemed to warm, the fog coalesced, and the ice of the River Dvina developed seeming cracks through which clear water welled. It looked dangerous for a horse to attempt to cross. He gave Jolie the document packet.

The Mongol messenger arrived; Jolie had tracked him all along. He drew up at the shore and peered ahead, dismayed. He had understood that this river was completely frozen over, and here it was half liquid. He did not want to ride around it, for that would take him many leagues out of his way and cost him time, ruining his schedule. He could go upstream to the city of Polotsk, where a ford would certainly be available, but then he would have to ride extra time to return to his route.

Jolie, in the guise of the peasant girl, walked by, carrying an armful of wood.

The horseman's thought processes were almost visible. A local girl who lived along the river; she would have

132

intimate news of this inexplicable thaw. 'Girl!' he called gruffly, in his own language.

Jolie paused, as if startled; she had not, it seemed, realized that a man was near. She backed away, frightened.

The rider guided his horse to intercept her. Terrified, she dropped her bundle of sticks and stared at him.

'The river – you know it?' he demanded. His gesture made his meaning clear: he wanted to get across.

She nodded affirmatively, making a gesture to signify that she lived on the other side, and was only an innocent maiden gathering wood for her family's hovel.

'You know where to cross? Where the ice is tight?'

Again she nodded.

'Show me!'

Now she hesitated, glancing here and there, signifying that the route was tortuous, hard to describe to a stranger.

Abruptly suspicious that she meant to mislead him, perhaps getting him on to thin ice where the weight of his horse would break through and cause them both to drown, he acted with dispatch. He gestured her on to his steed, behind him. That way she would face the same danger he did, and would not betray him.

Afraid to deny him, she approached and suffered herself to be hauled roughly up. She clung to him, afraid of this height. But she indicated the correct route.

Sure enough, she did not betray him. She guided him through the fog without mishap; nowhere did the ice thin and break. He watched carefully throughout, perhaps not unmindful of her arms clasping his body and her pneumatic front pressed so firmly against his back. Indeed, it was almost like affection, the way she pressed so closely in to him. It would be nice to pause, to get her to embrace him face to face, to open their clothing enough to –

But no, he was disciplined, and refused to yield to such a distraction. He only thought about it, enjoying the way

133

her arms moved against his torso, the way her front rocked against his back as the horse moved. He was alert, but he fell into a kind of secondary reverie, thinking about what he might have done had his mission not been so pressing.

And by the time he was safely across, the packet had been exchanged for the one in his travel pouch, he none the wiser. He set her down on the ground, gave her a small coin, and urged his horse onward. He had not after all lost his schedule. Perhaps the girl would meet him again on the return ride, when he would have more leisure.

Parry had followed, staying hidden in the fog, and rejoined her. 'That was beautiful!' he thought.

She smiled. 'My host agrees. I have explained to her how important this matter is. She doesn't like the Mongols; already their tax agents are driving the farmers to ruin. She asks whether you would like to come to her house, where it will be warm, to rest in your natural form.'

The girl must have had considerable prompting for all that! But he was so tired and cold, and aware of the forbidding distance to France; he needed restoration before he attempted that trip. Perhaps he could reward the girl's family in some additional manner for their hospitality; rested, he could perform more formidable magic. 'Yes, if she offers it freely,' he thought.

'I have told her what a good man you are,' Jolie said, still speaking through the body of the girl. 'But not the nature of your profession.'

Because it might be awkward having a Dominican friar visit, he realized. He appreciated her discretion. By being anonymous, he could accept the family's hospitality and repay them with some additional favour, and not only would he not make it unduly awkward for them, he would be away from the notice of Lucifer. For Lucifer should be furious when the 'wrong' message made it through, and Lucifer would be scouring the route for some hint as to what had happened. Better to have everyone involved anonymous!

Jolie picked him up and carried him under her arm, walking back across the frozen river towards the peasant girl's home. Who would have believed that the duck was actually a man, and the girl actually a ghost who resided in a drop of blood on the duck's wing? Fortunately no outsider needed to believe it!

Actually, no outsider was present. They were alone on the river as the evening closed and the chill of winter intensified. The illusion of melt had dissipated, leaving only the troubled landscape of ice. He was glad they would be getting inside; the very prospect restored his strength somewhat.

In due course they came to the residence. It was a typical hut, fashioned of wood and thatch, largely buried under the snow. 'Oh, we forgot the wood!' Jolie exclaimed.

'Perhaps I can make a heat spell for this night,' Parry said. 'But first you had better get me something to wear, so that I don't shock the good peasants when I revert to my natural form.'

'Why not use illusion for clothing?'

'Illusion isn't very warm.'

She smiled and set him down. 'We'll fetch a blanket.'

She entered the hut. Parry heard muffled talk as the girl explained things to her family. Then she emerged with a tattered quilt, and held it out for him.

Parry shifted to human form. The chill clasped his naked body immediately, but Jolie wrapped the quilt about him and opened the door.

The peasant girl's parents stood there: an old man and an old woman huddled in bedraggled furs like her own.

The girl spoke to them in their own language. They

nodded. They accepted Parry as a stranger their daughter had befriended, who could pay for his keep for this night. How his nakedness was accounted for he did not know.

'Do the heat magic,' Jolie murmured.

Oh. Yes. Parry drew on his talent and cast a spell that caused the walls and floor to radiate heat.

Jolie or the girl – he suspected that they switched control in and out as necessary – held her hand near a wall, showing how it was warming. The old folk did the same, and exclaimed with surprise and pleasure; this was magic they liked!

They had a supper of gruel and water; indeed, the Mongols had not left much in the region for sustenance. But Parry enhanced it with a spell of seasoning, and they all enjoyed it. There was not much conversation, because he did not speak their language; he had to sign to Jolie, who translated for him. He gathered that she had told them that the visitor was under a vow of silence. Again he appreciated her finesse.

He discovered that he was experiencing a deep satisfaction. He realized why: this was like mortal life, with normal folk. He was for the moment no longer a monk, and Jolie was no longer dead. Indeed, the very features of the peasant girl, who now doffed her heavy outer furs to reveal more of those attributes that belonged only to youth, seemed to resemble those of Jolie.

After the meal there was nothing to do but retire, as the gloom was thickening and candles were obviously too precious to waste for mere light. Parry stepped outside to attend to a call of nature, then returned to lie down in a vacant corner. The old folk had a rack of their own, and the girl settled on a bed of straw near them.

But when the darkness was total, the girl came silently to him, tugging at the wrapped quilt. Was something wrong?

'No, Parry,' Jolie said, manifesting momentarily in her

spirit form. 'I have come to be with you, as in the old days.'

He opened his mouth to protest, but the girl put a finger on his lips. She did not want him disturbing her parents.

But you can't use her body this way! he protested mentally. *And I – I am a friar!*

She got his quilt open and crawled next to him. Her body was hot and emphatically female.

Jolie! What are you doing!

But it was clear what she was doing. She had not loved him physically for thirty years; she intended to do it now. She had evidently made some arrangement with the peasant girl, who perhaps was not averse. Chastity was a virtue few peasants could afford; Jolie herself had been unusual in that respect, perhaps because he had caught her young enough, before the full bloom of her womanhood.

Parry wrestled with his conscience and his long training, but the battle was so uneven as to be token. He had known all along that he could never withstand Jolie in life, and now for a night she was alive. He clasped her and kissed her with the ardour of three stifled decades, and plunged into the rapture of the body. She responded with total eagerness. So potent was their penned desire for each other that it refused to abate after a single bout, or a second, and a fair portion of the night was expended before they were able to sleep.

But by morning she was back in her own corner, and he remained in his. If the parents had any knowledge of the night's activity, they kept their own counsel. They probably understood as much as they cared to.

He shared another meal with them, improving it magically, then performed some magic in return for their hospitality. In addition to the ability of the girl to locate good firewood under snow, he gave her the power to

137

identify the best bargains of several proffered at the market. That, too, was mainly an extension of her natural abilities, with very little actual magic; but it would enable her to profit significantly by avoiding bad deals or outright cheats. It would help her family through the winter, and more than recoup the value of the food shared with him.

But the use of her body during the night – how could he repay that? What deal had Jolie made for that? Suppose she should conceive by him? In the night he had not seen fit to question the matter, but now by day he was having serious second thoughts.

The girl spoke to her parents, then took his arm. Parry was now garbed in shaggy furs borrowed from the man; they were uncomfortable and riddled with lice, but served adequately. He needed to return them, but could not until he changed form.

They left the house. Jolie wasted no time coming to the point. 'She has an illness I told her you could cure,' she said. 'It is apt to make her barren, but you can abolish it and restore her fertility.'

'But to do that, I would require sustained contact with her for a full day and night,' Parry protested. 'You know that, Jolie! Healing magic of that type cannot be hastily accomplished.'

'Yes. We must remain for another day,' she said. 'I have started the process, and you have given her of your substance. Remain long enough to keep it active, and she is well repaid.'

'But I must return to the monastery!'

'You are too fatigued still to fly.'

She was right. He was as yet only partially restored. He could not yet undertake that journey, lest he fall and die on the way.

Jolie released the girl, who tried out her talent for finding wood. She fashioned an ice ball and stared into it, then moved purposefully through the trees while Parry followed. In moments she had found an excellent cache of sticks, exclaiming with pleasure. It worked!

Parry helped her carry the wood back to the hut. This would keep them warm another day, and there was more where that came from.

Then they went to the nearest market, a league's trudge down the rivershore. The girl had only the coin the Mongol rider had given her, but she was determined to spend it wisely. She turned down the first proffered deal, and the second, finally accepting one for bread, and carried her prize away. The proprietor shook his head, evidently feeling bested. This gift, too, was working.

That night she came to him again in the darkness, sharing the quilt. He did not argue; it was obvious that the girl was satisfied with the deal she had made, and did not mind this part of it. She had evidently had some experience before. Perhaps she was accustomed to rougher handling, and appreciated his gentleness and obvious delight, despite the knowledge that it was really Jolie he was embracing. But he did concentrate on the curing of her malady, which was not difficult to treat at this stage, and by morning he knew she was free of it. He had, indeed, rendered a suitable return service.

Next day his strength had recovered, and he knew he could fly back to France. He bid silent farewell to the family and stepped outside. He changed to the duck form, and the girl collected the clothes. She smiled as he spread his wings, evidently in response to Jolie's leave-taking; then Parry was up and away, and Jolie hovering with him.

Now the realization he had suppressed for two days burst upon him: *he had violated his oath of celibacy!* Technically, celibacy meant the state of being unmarried, but in practice it meant abstinence from carnal relations. For two days he had become married again, and made love to his wife. He had forfeited his right to be a friar.

139

'I shall have to leave the Order,' he thought to Jolie. 'I am undone!'

Jolie was unpenitent. 'I have always loved you, Parry. Now that I know how easy it is to love you physically, I want to do it again. Leave the Order and be with me! I will find a young girl to – '

'But I must remain to fight evil!'

'You have foiled Lucifer's dire plan. Now at last you can relax.'

'But the Order has become my life!'

'It never was *my* life, Parry! I supported you because I love you, but now that your work is done – '

'My work is not done! Lucifer must be constantly fought!'

'But there are other ways to fight him, are there not?'

'Not as effective as this! Oh, why did I give in to the wiles of the flesh!'

She gazed at him, then turned away as she faded.

'Jolie!' he cried, stricken. 'Come back! I didn't mean – '

But she was gone. He had hurt her feelings, and she would not return until she chose.

It took him longer to return than it had to make the outbound flight. He tired faster, and had to land often to rest and forage. But it gave him time to ponder, and when he finally reached the monastery he knew what he had to do.

He had to confess his sin before the head friar and beg absolution.

But at first, when he was back, he just had to recuperate from his arduous excursion. He rested and ate and slept for several days.

Jolie returned. 'I am sorry,' she said. 'I see now that I was wrong. I should not have tempted you into sin.'

That made him argue the other side of it. 'You are my

wife!' he protested. 'Nothing you could lead me to could be wrong!'

'No, you are correct. The situation changed when I died, and I had no right to return to the flesh after all these years, knowing that – '

'You borrowed a living body so that you could enable me to complete my mission! Without you I could not have done it! There can be no fault in you for that!'

'But after it was done, and the messenger went on, I had no right to – '

'You knew I was exhausted to the point of collapse, and would die in the snow if not given warmth and food and rest. You acted to save me, not hurt me!'

'But during the night, possessed of a living young body, I should not have come to you.'

With that he had to agree. 'You should not have, Jolie. But there was no way you could have tempted me, had I not been willing, even eager. The sin was mine!'

'It was ours,' she said.

'Ours,' he agreed.

'Yet such is my depravity, I cannot hate what we did. I love you so much, Parry, and want to be with you – '

'You are with me always, Jolie.'

'In the flesh,' she finished.

'And I want you – in the flesh.' Now it was out. Not only had he sinned, he knew he would do it again if given the opportunity.

'What will happen now?'

'I must leave the Order,' he said. 'I thought I could make confession and beg absolution, but now I know I cannot do that, for the sin remains with me. I can no longer be a Dominican friar.'

'But the good work you are doing – the foiling of Lucifer's mischief – who will do that if you do not?'

Parry put his head in his hands. 'No one, I fear! No

other friar has made the same study of evil that I have! How ironic that I should fall prey to evil myself!'

'The evil of loving me.'

'No!' But there was truth in it. He was a friar; he had no business loving a woman. 'Jolie, you are my conscience. What would you have me do?'

'I am not your conscience!' she flared. 'I am your wife who has led you into sin!'

'What would you have me do?' he repeated grimly.

She paced the air, distraught. 'There is sin in what I did with you, and would do again. But there is evil in letting Lucifer plot without hindrance. I think the sin must be tolerated for the sake of the good you can do in your present office.'

They hashed it over, but could come to no better conclusion than that. The great good ends justified the means of keeping silent about one small sin.

So Parry made no report, knowing that he had compromised his honour as a Dominican friar. He knew the doctrine of ends and means was fallacious, but hoped that in this case it was justified.

Indeed, as the weeks and months passed, it seemed so, for the Mongol juggernaut halted, and finally reversed. The message of the Great Khan's death had got through, and Europe was saved from Lucifer's scourge.

But neither his doubt nor his renewed passion for Jolie's living flesh faded. Parry knew he could not remain in this hypocritical existence. He had to find some means to resolve his savage internal conflict.

But *what* means?

7

Lilah

In the spring of 1242 Parry was taking a walk out around the monastery grounds. He sought, as always, to reconcile the evil he found in himself with the good work he was doing. He had continued to deal with heretics, garnering their conversions when others had failed. Why was he unable to resolve the sin on his own conscience?

'Because you do not wish to, Parry.'

He jumped. There beside him was the figure of an attractive young woman. He had not seen her at all; indeed, there should be none here, not even a nun. He stared at her.

She smiled back. She wore the long flowing hair, bound back by no more than a fillet, and the single long dress of the ordinary unmarried girl. But she was hardly ordinary! Her hair had the lustre of gold, and her eyes seemed golden too, glowing like tiny discs of the sun, and the contours of her body thrust against the silken cloth of her garment, making of it a statuesque configuration. She reminded him somewhat of Jolie, as she had been in the day of her mortal beauty. But this woman was more than that, physically; she was like Venus clothed.

He fought past his amazement. 'There can be no woman here!' he exclaimed.

'Really?' she asked, her lips quirking with amusement. 'What of your ghostly lover?'

'Who are you?' he demanded.

'I am Lilah, sent to corrupt you.'

He had expected some sort of evasion; this brought him up short again. 'You are a – a sending of Lucifer?'

'That is true, Parry.'

143

Could it be? Certainly that would explain her sudden appearance, and the way she knew his private name, never voiced in the monastery. Still –

'Lucifer works by deception,' he said. 'If you are from him, you should not tell me so!'

'Lucifer is the Father of Lies,' she agreed. 'But the truest lies have the semblance of truth. We underlings are not permitted to lie freely; that is the province of the Master. Thus I will always speak the truth to you, though you may not always wish to hear it.'

'I don't believe you!'

'You will, in time.'

'A problem, Brother?'

Parry turned guiltily. Another friar was approaching. How would he explain the woman?

But the other gave no sign of seeing the woman. 'I saw you pause and gesture as if disturbed. Indigestion?'

'I thought I saw something,' Parry said lamely.

'You are equivocating,' Lilah remarked. 'You do not *think* you see something; you *do* see a demoness, here where we are not supposed to be able to intrude.'

She had him dead to rights.

The other friar looked around. 'I see nothing out of order. What was its nature?'

'Evil.'

The other man's brow furrowed. 'Evil? Here? Surely you are mistaken, Brother.'

'I must be,' Parry agreed.

'Now you are lying,' Lilah said.

She had scored again. 'That is, I saw a figure of a woman, an evil figure,' Parry said. 'A – a demoness.'

The other friar looked at him with concern. 'I fear you have a problem, Brother.'

'I fear I do,' Parry agreed.

'But the cross will banish the vision.' The friar brought out his silver cross.

'Yes,' Parry agreed, relieved. He brought out his own and swept it through the region where Lilah stood. She vanished without a sound.

'Gone now?' the other inquired.

'Gone,' Parry agreed. 'I thank you, Brother.'

'We are all troubled on occasion by doubts and bad memories,' the other said. 'But our Lord Jesus is proof against them all.'

'Yes!' Parry agreed fervently. He walked with the other back to the buildings. But he remained in doubt, knowing that his own doubts and bad notions had not been abolished by his faith in Jesus. The fault, he knew, was not in Jesus but in himself; his faith was flawed.

When he was alone in his chamber, Jolie appeared. 'Oh, that was horrible!' she exclaimed. 'I couldn't come out while she was with you!'

'You saw the – the apparition?' he asked, startled.

'Lilah the demoness. Of course. The aura of Hell surrounded her. Oh, Parry, what does she want with you?'

'She said she was sent to corrupt me.'

'She can't corrupt you! You are a good man, and a Dominican friar. You are proof against evil.'

'Not necessarily,' Lilah said, appearing. In that instant, Jolie faded.

Parry fetched out his cross. 'Begone, demoness!' he cried, thrusting it at her. Lilah vanished.

Jolie reappeared. 'What an infernal creature!' she exclaimed. 'I cannot co-exist with her!'

'The cross banishes her,' Parry said. 'I will use it until she gives up this harassment.'

'But why should she come for you now?' Then she reconsidered. 'The scourge! Lucifer has ascertained your part in foiling that!'

'You've got it, ghost,' Lilah agreed, her appearance causing Jolie's disappearance.

'Begone!' Parry cried, jabbing the cross at her. She clicked out of sight.

Jolie reappeared. 'You foiled Lucifer, and now he is angry. He has sent his minion to wreak vengeance on you.'

'He can't touch me, or you,' Parry said. 'We are secure in the bosom of Jesus.'

'That's what you think, hypocrite!' Lilah exclaimed.

Parry lifted the cross. The demoness retreated to the farthest corner of the chamber.

'No, don't drive her out yet,' Jolie said, reappearing translucently. 'Find out how she thinks she can do it.'

Parry looked from one to the other. 'You can co-exist after all?'

'She is fundamentally good; I am fundamentally evil,' Lilah said. 'We co-exist; we are merely unable to be close to each other.'

'Then what of me?' he asked.

'You are mortal.'

'That makes a difference?'

'That makes *the* difference. Good and evil co-exist in all mortals. It is the struggle between the two that makes mortality what it is. Mortality is the battleground. You know that, Parry; you have studied evil more than any other living man.'

Parry nodded. He did know it; he just had not been thinking coherently. 'How is it that you are able to come here, to the order dedicated to the eradication of evil?'

'Dedicated to the eradication of *heresy*,' Lilah said. 'The distinction is significant.'

She was entirely too sharp! 'To corrupt me,' he continued. 'How can you hope to do that?'

'Because you have planted the seed of evil in yourself. I am here to make it grow. Without that seed, I would be powerless against you. The corruption had to start within yourself.'

'What corruption?' Jolie demanded.

The demoness eyed her knowingly. 'You should know, pretty spirit! You started it.'

'The loving!' Jolie cried, stricken.

'The sex,' Lilah said. 'To love is holy, if it is of a good person or good cause. But to tempt a man into sinful sex – '

'Oh!' Jolie's exclamation was pure anguish as she faded out.

'She could not have done it had I not cooperated!' Parry said. 'She is good; she meant no harm!'

'True, Parry,' Lilah said, advancing. 'She is good; she meant no harm. In addition, she is beyond adjustment of her balance; it was set at the time of her death. But you are mortal; you knew it was sinful, yet you did it, and did it with sinful joy. Two nights, each a multiple effort.' She glanced sidelong at him. 'A surprising performance, considering your mortal age. And then – '

'Enough!' he cried, lifting the cross.

'Do you use the cross to banish the truth?' Lilah asked as she retreated.

Parry turned, found his bed, and sat down on it, hard. It *was* the truth. He had done wrong, knowingly.

The demoness advanced again, unchallenged. 'But it was not the sin that made the opening, for the mortal flesh is ever weak. Had you succumbed, and repented, and confessed, and done proper penance, you would have been absolved, and this too you well know. The opening was made by your decision to conceal your weakness. When, knowingly, you failed to seek absolution, you practised deliberate deception. And that, my dear mortal, provided my Lord Lucifer His wedge against your soul.'

Her truths were hammering at his mind. He *had* done it; he *had* practised deceit, which was a lie. That lie had put him into the power of the Lord of Lies.

'I must seek absolution now,' he said.

'And give up all you have gained, discrediting yourself, your monastery, and indeed the Dominican order?' the demoness asked derisively. 'I think not.'

'Better that than the lie!' he cried.

'And that is another lie,' Lilah said.

Again, she was devastatingly accurate! He knew he could not do that to his work or his order. He could not throw away thirty years of his campaign against evil, at a single stroke discrediting everything. He was locked into his lie, because of the enormous cost of its expiation.

'Lucifer is having his way with me,' Parry said brokenly.

'You flatter yourself, mortal,' Lilah said. 'Lucifer has not yet begun to have His way with you. This is only the opening. Have you any notion how angry He is with you?'

Parry recovered a portion of his humour. 'I daresay you will inform me, demoness.'

'After the scourge failed, my Lord made a thorough investigation. He discovered that not only had an obscure Dominican friar almost singlehandedly foiled His greatest ploy, that same friar had wreaked mischief throughout his career. Right here, virtually under Lucifer's nose, this friar had plotted with angelic cunning, and sown a harvest of good that very nearly cancelled my Lord's activities of the past half century. Lord Bofort, the heretics, the conversion of His wolves and bats – thirty years of mischief. One lone friar! My Lord has not before been this angry in this same half century. All the fires of Hell were enhanced for several infernal nights. That is why He deliberated long, pondering suitable retribution against this insolent mortal. That is why He finally decided on the worst of all the routes available. The one that was appropriate for this case.'

She leaned forward, so as to speak almost in his ear. 'That is why He sent me to corrupt you.'

Parry glanced up at her – and found his nose almost in a cleavage such as he had not imagined in thirty years.

Lilah's outfit had changed; she now wore a tight bodice open at the top.

'Get away from me, harlot!' he exclaimed, almost spitting into that awesome channel.

'Make me, mortal!' she taunted him.

He jerked the cross up, aiming for the centre of her body. But she was gone.

Jolie reappeared. 'Oh, Parry, what have I done!' she wailed.

'You did nothing blameworthy,' he snapped. '*I* committed the sin!'

'But I enabled it! Oh, Parry, I wanted you so much! I knew it was wrong, but – '

'It was not wrong of itself. We are married. But my decision to cover it up, to go on as if it hadn't happened – Oh, Jolie, I made a sin of what had been natural! What a price I must now pay!'

'But what can she do, actually?' Jolie asked, taking faint heart. 'No one else can see her or hear her, and your cross banishes her. If you don't listen to her – '

'That's right, ghost-girl,' Lilah said, reappearing across the room. 'Just don't listen to me – or look at me – and you cannot be corrupted. Your lie only opened the way; it did not complete the course.'

Parry glanced directly at her, about to make a sharp retort. But it was stifled unspoken.

This time the demoness was naked. Lusciously so. Her full breasts did not sag in the manner of most mortal breasts; they were erect and proud. Her belly did not protrude; it was almost flat, just slightly rounded. Her hips flared in a manner that –

'Damn,' Parry muttered, wrenching his gaze away.

'You are learning the language,' Lilah said.

He ripped the cross from its chain and threw it at her. The demoness faded. The cross struck the wall and fell to the floor.

Parry felt a pang of guilt and remorse. That was no way to treat the cross!

Lilah reappeared, immediately before him, still naked. 'You treat your silly icon the way you treat your silly order: with contempt,' she said.

'Get out, spawn of Lucifer!' he cried.

'I told you before, Parry: you have to make me.' She put her hands on her hips, her legs well spread, and inhaled.

He swept his hand up. But he no longer held the cross. His fingers struck her in the crotch, which was furry and warm. He had expected her to vanish before his hand swept through that region. For a moment, he was too appalled to move.

She snapped her legs together, pinning his hand. 'Well, now, that is more like it, lover! I thought you would be more reticent at first.'

He yanked his hand back, but she remained clamped; he only succeeded in drawing her more closely in to him. She fell towards him, smiling, her breasts swinging close to his face.

'Damn you!' he repeated.

'Yes, lover, I am damned,' she breathed. 'And you will be too, when you accept me.' She caught a hand behind his head and pushed his face forward, into her bosom.

Parry was not so far addled as to compound his error. 'Bless you!' he exclaimed.

Abruptly she was gone. He was left hunched forward, one hand extended.

There was a knock at the door. 'Brother Grief!' a friar called. 'Are you all right? I heard you cry out.'

'A bad dream,' Parry called back, hastening to get up, cross the chamber, and pick up his fallen cross.

'Every lie you tell brings you closer to Hell.'

Parry froze, then realized that it was not the friar but the demoness who had reappeared across the room. Yet

150

again, she had him dead to rights. But how could he tell the truth?

'Very well,' the friar said, and departed.

Now Parry advanced on the demoness, cross extended. 'You are the spawn of hell indeed!' he said, keeping his voice low. 'But you shall not remain in my presence.'

'Parry, you don't seem to understand. I have been sent to corrupt you, and that I shall do. I think we have an excellent beginning.'

'You can't corrupt a man who doesn't want to be corrupted!'

'True, Parry. I am certainly in luck.'

'Your tricks and wiles will not work! I shall drive you away until you stay away.' He reached her and stabbed with the cross.

She vanished. 'Parry, why don't you put down that thing and give me a chance?' Lilah asked from the far side of the chamber. 'I can be very nice, and the soul of discretion.'

He stalked her again, cross extended. She vanished again.

'For example, in bed,' she said. He turned to see her lying on his bed, her legs spread invitingly. 'Set it down over there, and come to me here, and I will show you how obliging I can be.' She ran her hands down her torso suggestively.

Parry found himself reacting. He was a friar, but he was also a man, and not yet so old as to be beyond awareness of the flesh, as recent events had shown. He realized now that much of the reason he had endured celibacy was that he had never been truly tempted. The moment Jolie had assumed mortal semblance, he had succumbed, and now this demoness was arousing him despite his efforts to banish her.

'What do I have to do to be rid of you?' he asked.

'You think I won't answer, but I will,' she said smugly.

'On condition you put down that weapon and behave yourself.'

'What?'

'Parry, you know a girl doesn't like to act under duress. You would not like it if I demanded information of you at the point of a sword. Why do you think I like it any better?'

'I am not using a sword!'

She sat up, her breasts shifting and quivering with her motion. She extended her right arm, and a great long sword appeared in her hand. She swung her legs to the floor and stood. The sword glinted. 'Talk, miscreant, or I'll run you through!' she exclaimed.

Parry held the cross before him.

'Ah, so it is that way!' she snarled, and hurled the sword directly at him.

Parry jumped aside – but the sword faded out before reaching his vicinity. It had been illusion, banished by the nearness of the cross.

'The difference is,' she said calmly, 'that my sword cannot harm you, but your icon is intolerable to me. So if you want to talk to me, you must have the courtesy to set aside your weapon.'

Grudgingly, Parry realized that there was merit in her argument. It galled him to accede to even the simplest request of the demoness, but he did want to be rid of her and she had spoken the truth to him so far. 'Put on some clothing,' he said.

'Anything you wish, Parry.' As she spoke, she was garbed in a matronly robe that masked her physical attributes.

He set down the cross and walked to the bed. He sat down on it.

Lilah joined him. 'Isn't this so much more civilized?' she said. 'Now, what was it you wanted to know?'

'How do I get rid of you?'

'That is very simple, Parry. You must abolish evil from your heart. Then there will be no point in my presence, for I will have no further hope of corrupting you.'

'I have been trying to do that!'

'No. You have been making a show of trying, but you have not truly wished to be rid of that evil – or of me.'

He stared at her. 'How can you say that?'

'I can say it because it is true. I am a creature of evil; I am attuned to the evil in you. It is small, but persistent; the seed is sprouting, and in due course it will bear its fruit.'

He found himself unable to deny it. 'Be more specific.'

'Your ghost-girl borrowed mortal flesh and reminded you of what you had been missing. Now the desire for that has fixed in your mind. But you know there are hideous complications in the borrowing of the flesh of a mortal woman, for you are no longer in distant foreign territory. A local woman might tell. So you cannot indulge in the flesh while being true to your dead wife – but the urge of the flesh remains. You must have a woman.'

Parry started to protest, but she only gave him a knowing glance, and he stifled it. She could indeed read the evil in his heart.

'But you wish to continue the work you have been doing,' she continued. 'You are no longer young, and you have a comfortable existence here, and you value your reputation and that of your order. So you cannot resign. That puts you on the path of deceit, and I am the realization of that path. I can give you the gratification of the flesh you crave, and I will not betray your secret in any way. Therefore –'

'You are evil!' he exclaimed. 'You seek to undo me and my work, to achieve Lucifer's vengeance on me! Of course you will betray me in any way you can!'

She shook her head, and her robe fell open. She had conjured no underclothing, of course. He tried to avert

153

his gaze, but could not. 'I do not seek to undo you, Parry. I want you to remain in your present position, and even to improve upon it.'

'That's impossible!'

'You are not thinking clearly, Parry.' She leaned towards him, further clouding his thinking. 'Lucifer has need of agents in the enemy hierarchy. The more trusted and powerful they are, the better. You will be ideal. I will facilitate your career in every possible way.'

'This is outrageous!'

'This is reasonable.' She put her hand on his arm, encouraging further closeness. 'What your ghost-girl has done for you, I can do better, for I am not limited in substance. I can become solid, and perform any function, and fade away without leaving any guilty trace. I can advise you on your most effective course, without suffering the restriction of conscience. And this is only the beginning.'

'I must be rid of you!'

'Now be fair, Parry. I am not forcing anything on you, ever. My semblance of flesh is yours to enjoy whenever you may desire, but you need not avail yourself of it. The sensible thing for you to do is try me, and if I do not please you, dismiss me.'

'I am trying to find out how to dismiss you now!' he flared.

'And I am answering you. Merely ask me to depart for a time, and I will do that.'

'But I did – '

'No, Parry. You did not ask, you ordered. Only my Lord Lucifer can order me. Others must enlist my cooperation.'

Parry tried it. 'I ask you, demoness, to leave me alone.'

Lilah stood, drew her robe together and smiled. 'I leave you, Parry, for one day. I hope you will consider what I offer in the interim.'

She faded out, leaving him amazed.

Jolie reappeared. 'That was awful!' she exclaimed. 'I couldn't come out when she was close, and I couldn't even be near when she was touching you.'

'You shouldn't react like that. You should remain to oppose her.'

'It's not that. It's – her evil just overwhelms me, like a fire too hot to tolerate. She really is from Hell, Parry.'

'I have no doubt of that. How much of what she said did you hear?'

'After she got you to set aside the cross, I heard nothing. What happened, Parry? How did you get rid of her?'

'I asked her. She said she would depart for one day. She – ' He paused, uncertain how much he should tell her.

'I can guess,' Jolie said. 'She vamped you.'

'Yes. She said she wants me to remain in my present position, so that Lucifer will have an agent here, and that – ' he shrugged. 'It is no secret what such creatures offer.'

'Did she tell you how to be free of her?'

'Yes. I must abolish all evil from my heart. Then she will have no power over me. But she is certain I cannot do that.'

Jolie nodded. 'Because of what I led you into.'

He was unable to deny it. 'The seed of sin is within me, and I fear I lack the power to banish it.'

'Unless you absolve yourself and resign your position, and let all your prior good works be disgraced.'

'That is the case. I can absolve my personal evil only by inflicting a greater evil on my career and the Order.'

'But what is the alternative, Parry? If this is a mission of Lucifer's to wreak vengeance on you, you surely must get free of it any way you can.'

He clapped his hands in sudden decision. 'Yes! Now

155

that I know that Lucifer wants me here, I must depart! I will wrap up my affairs and go to the Abbot.'

'Then we can go somewhere and I can find a woman and we can be together again,' Jolie said, brightening.

Parry doubted that it could be that simple, but he set about concluding his current business and putting it in order for other friars to take over. His heart was heavy.

There was more of it than he had thought; he was unable to conclude it by the day's end. He slept, and resumed in the morning. Still it stretched out; every matter had to be organized just so, or it would be bungled by the inheritor. He had forgotten how many heretics he had dealt with, and how many still bore watching, in case of relapse. Jolie was unable to help in this; only he knew the necessary details.

'Hello, sinner.' It was the demoness.

'You said you would remain away for – ' Parry broke off, realizing that it was now the same hour that she had left the day before. She had been true to her word.

'Let me help you with that,' Lilah said.

Parry smiled grimly. 'You can't, and if you could, you wouldn't. I am preparing to make my absolution and depart the Order, so that the evil may be gone from me.'

'You can't do it,' she said confidently. 'The knowledge of what I offer you is percolating through the layers of your desire, and you must accept it.'

'What do you offer?' he flared. 'Tawdry sex – at the expense of my soul! And even that I can have with my beloved wife, after I leave the Order, without compromising my honour or my soul.'

'Tawdry sex has its appeal,' she said. 'Gaze at me and tell me that you have no interest.'

He glanced at her. Sure enough, she was naked again. Her body glistened as if she had just come from a swim in a lake of oil, and every part of her was full and vibrant.

156

Parry was silent. He knew she would give the lie to any denial he tried to make.

'And this is hardly all I offer,' she continued. 'I told you it was just the beginning.'

Parry knew that he should fetch out his cross and banish her, but he did not. 'You offer damnation,' he said shortly.

'That, too, of course. But damnation is not really that bad. I am damned, but quite satisfied with my limited existence. Lucifer can be an excellent Master for those who serve Him well.'

'You have always been damned, beyond any hope of redemption; therefore you cannot know the joy of salvation. You are no judge of it.'

'By that term you mean residence in the upper region after death?'

He looked at her again – and regretted it. She was now quite close to him, opening her arms in invitation. Her effort to tempt him was obvious – but that hardly diminished its effect.

'You cannot say the words *salvation* or *Heaven*?' he asked.

'That is correct. Or the term for your icon, or any number of words relating to the other power. Sometimes I can use variants if I mean them ironically, such as *angelic*. But I am no more limited than you in this respect.'

'I can say any word I choose!'

'Oh? Then try this one.' She paused, then spoke a word of such horror and evil that Parry was appalled.

She smiled. 'That is too strong? Then let's make it easier. Say "Curse ****."'

'Curse what?'

'The four-letter name of a variant of your god, which I cannot say.'

157

'I can't do that!' he exclaimed, then realized that he had conceded her point.

'But I was about to explain what else I offer you.' She stepped towards him.

He grabbed for the cross.

'Wait, Parry! Of course I can't show you if you do that, any more than you could show me anything if I held you at bay with an infernal talisman! You must be fair.'

'Why should I be fair to a demoness?'

'Because if you are not, that is a signal of evil. A closed mind is open for evil; you know that.'

He did know that. 'What, then?'

She stepped towards him again, and put her arms around him briefly. He tried to suppress his consciousness of her beautiful body, knowing that it was only a construct of ether.

'There,' she said, satisfied. 'Have you a mirror?'

Mirrors were rare, but he did have one, used occasionally in researches. He brought it out.

'Look at yourself.'

He looked at his face. A young stranger gazed back at him. 'You have enchanted me!'

'No, only your aspect. I have restored to you the semblance of your youth. Now you look half your present age.'

Parry looked down at his body. It felt lighter and stronger, but he could not tell whether it had changed.

'Take off your robe,' she said.

'What, in front of a – '

She laughed. 'A woman? Parry, you know I am not a woman! I am nothing more than a foul spirit whose presence you may ignore.'

She was right again. Overcome by curiosity, Parry doffed his robe and looked down at his naked body.

It was lean and firm – a contrast to his present corpulent and wrinkled one.

'It can perform as youth does, too,' Lilah said, stepping into him and embracing him.

'Hey!' Parry reached for his cross, but could not find it.

'You set the icon aside with your robe,' Lilah reminded him. 'But do not be concerned; I will tell no other person what you do with me.' She rubbed against him. 'See – you have excellent reaction time now.'

Parry wrenched himself away and dived for the cross. As he touched it, Lilah vanished and his body reverted to its normal state. He scrambled back into his robe.

'I regret I cannot give you extra life,' Lilah said from across the chamber. 'Only my Lord Lucifer can do that, and He really does not have that in mind for you at this time. But you can have much greater joy of your present life.'

'Get away from me, temptress!' he gritted.

'Now, Parry, you know I do not respond well to that type of demand.'

Parry nerved himself and forced a smile. 'Please, if it pleases you, depart for a time.'

'That's better.' She disappeared.

Jolie returned. 'I am almost afraid to ask what happened this time.'

'I'm almost afraid to tell you! She – she made me seem young again.'

'She is getting to you,' Jolie said sadly.

'No!' But they both knew that wasn't true.

Parry wrapped up his documents by nightfall. 'Tomorrow morning I go to the Abbot,' he said.

Jolie didn't answer. She just gazed at him with love and resignation, and faded out.

He woke in darkness. A warm body was with him.

'Jolie!' he exclaimed.

'Guess again, lover,' the demoness replied. 'Though I will, if you ask me to, emulate her form and manner for your pleasure. I have absolutely no pride about that sort of thing; I want only to please you.'

'But a day and night have not passed!'

'I did not promise you a day this time, Parry. I promised you only a time. That time is done. Now I have returned to bring you all the joy your ghost-girl cannot bring you.'

'Get out!'

'This game becomes tiresome. Make me.' She rolled over, plastering a hot breast against him.

Parry opened his mouth – and she kissed it. He moved his legs – and she covered them with her own. He struggled, but she held him like the succubus she resembled.

He finally got his hand on the cross and brought it in.

'Oh, don't do that, lover,' she protested. 'Not when we are so close to making it.'

He hesitated, then with sudden decision brought the cross down against her back. And she was gone, leaving him with an erection and sweaty covers.

Jolie did not appear, and for that he was thankful. The demoness was aggressive and blatant – but she had an impact. He *had* desired her infernal body! Had he been deliberately clumsy in finding his cross? Had he purposefully delayed in applying it? He was afraid he knew the answer.

There was indeed evil on his soul, and the demoness was exploiting it mercilessly.

In the morning Jolie returned. 'She came to you at night,' she said flatly.

Parry nodded. 'I thought for a moment it was you. I finally drove her away with the cross.'

'Finally?'

'Jolie, I am a man! I thought I was a friar, but now I know I am not. I will take my disgrace and go away with you; then she will leave me alone.'

'Will she, Parry?'

'She will have wreaked Lucifer's vengeance on me and the Order! I will be of no further use to her! And I will be with you when you are reanimated. Proof against further evil.'

She relaxed. 'I hope so, Parry!'

He squared his shoulders and walked out of his chamber and down the hall to the Abbot's office. He had not requested an audience, but knew the Abbot would see him. Indeed, Parry himself could have had the office, had he desired it. Now he was glad he had not; that diminished the potential disaster somewhat.

The demoness appeared before him, discreetly clothed. 'You can't do it, Parry. You have too much to lose.'

'The world has too much to lose if I do not,' he said gruffly.

'But the world need lose nothing! I will help you in any way you desire.'

'To fight your evil master? I doubt it.'

'Try me, Parry.'

'Don't try her, Parry!' Jolie protested. 'She only means evil!'

'I know that,' Parry said. He pushed on, leading with his cross, and the demoness vanished in her normal manner.

And reappeared elsewhere, also in her normal manner. 'Parry, you have not given me that chance,' she said urgently. 'Parry, with my help you could become Pope!'

'You'd like that, wouldn't you!' he muttered. 'A corrupt Pope, in liege with Lucifer!'

'It would not be the first time.'

Parry halted. 'You lie!'

Her lips twitched. 'May **** strike me down if I have not spoken the truth.'

'It's irrelevant,' Jolie said. 'We must get this done. Obviously it will be effective against her, or she wouldn't be opposing it so.'

'You are right, ghost-girl,' Lilah said, grimacing. 'He will be of little use to my Master if he loses his position. There would then be nothing for it but to proceed to the lesser aspect of His vengeance, and send in the vampires.'

'Vampires?' Jolie asked faintly.

'I have fought off possessed creatures before,' Parry said.

'These are not possessed,' Lilah said. 'They are the real thing. They would come first for your animate ghost-girl, depriving her of her new body. You might find her less appetizing then.'

Parry felt a chill of apprehension. The possessed could be cured, but true vampires were beyond that. There were ways to resist them, but it would be difficult for one of flawed virtue. The threat to Jolie –

'No,' he said firmly. 'This is a scare tactic. It shall not move me.'

But Jolie, beside him, was fainter.

He reached the Abbot's door. He lifted his knuckle to knock.

'I will show you how to make your Inquisition truly effective against heretics,' Lilah said.

'Why should you do that?' Yet Parry knew that the fact that he even questioned her meant that he was in doubt about his course.

'Because heretics are nothing to me or my Master, but your corruption is everything.'

'A likely claim,' Parry said, beginning to move his knuckle.

'Don't you understand, Parry – most heretics are incompetent ruffians. Seldom is a truly educated and dedicated man brought into Lucifer's service. You are worth more than all the rest.'

'Before you said that it was Lucifer's vengeance that brought you here.'

'That, too, is true. But His mode of it is devious. He

162

never wastes an opportunity. He much prefers to corrupt you, so that not only do you serve His purpose, you know it is the worst possible perversion of your nature and of the faith of those who believe in you. You will suffer that realization for the rest of your life, even as you do ever-greater evil. That is the most exquisite nature of His vengeance. Perhaps you will even do such harm to the cause you once served that it makes up for all the mischief you have caused my Master.'

'How can you tell me this, knowing I must reject this course?' Parry asked, appalled.

'That is part of the torture,' she said. 'You must know that you could have avoided all of it – and chose to enter into it instead, for the basest of reasons.'

'*What* basest of reasons?' Parry demanded.

'Lust for a creature of Hell, despite the availability of the woman you loved in life.'

'That's preposterous!'

'Is it, Parry? Then knock on that door.' Lilah smiled cruelly, and her dress disintegrated, leaving her voluptuously naked.

Parry's arm muscles tensed – but his knuckles did not touch the door. He tried again, and again his hand did not move. He could not knock!

He looked around, seeking Jolie, but she was gone.

'No good, lover,' Lilah murmured. 'She knows what you know: you have accepted what I offer in your soul, and she is doomed.'

'Jolie!' he cried with horror.

'Do not wail for her, mortal man. She has completed her onus, that bore down her soul despite an exemplary life. She has at last brought you to the evil you were destined for. Now she is free to go – and perhaps, if she is fortunate, my Lord will not treat her harshly.'

'Jolie can't go to Hell!' he cried.

'She surely can't go to the other place.'

'She must stay with me, to be my conscience, as always.'

'Your conscience is doomed, Parry. You are one of us now.'

'No!'

'No? Then knock on that door.'

Again Parry tried, and again failed. Even to save the soul of his wife, he could not do it.

He collapsed against the door, wracked by sobs. What an awful failure this was, this failure of his will!

The demoness embraced him, stroking him here and there, stirring his lust despite his grief. 'Lover, this is only the beginning,' she assured him. 'You will rue this hour the rest of your life.'

Parry was all too certain this was true.

8
Lucifer

Lilah led him back to his chamber. Parry went without resistance, stunned by his inability to do what he knew was right. The demoness really *had* corrupted him!

In the chamber, Lilah turned, her clothing fuzzing to fog and wafting away. 'You have joined us, Parry, and now I shall reward you.'

Parry gripped his cross. 'No!'

She walked towards him, her torso moving with rhythms of its own. 'Yes.'

He jabbed the cross at her midriff. It passed through her without effect. She neither vanished nor screamed; she merely waited. 'But – the cross!' he exclaimed, stunned.

'Parry, your icon is only as potent as the faith behind it. You have lost your faith. You can no longer invoke your prior god in your defence.' She moved on in to him, and her hands went to his robe, opening it.

'Jolie!' he cried.

'She is gone, lover,' Lilah said. 'I am your woman now. But I want you to think of your ghost-girl as you indulge your carnal lust with me, so that you can really appreciate the irony. She started your corruption, and I am completing it.'

'Get away from me!' he cried, pushing at her. But it did no good. His right hand, holding the cross, was unable to touch her body at all, passing freely through it, while his left came up against her plush right breast. There, the touch was all too tangible.

Meanwhile her hands were busy, efficiently baring his body. She moved the rest of the way in to him, pressing against him from thigh to breast, while his right hand continued to flail helplessly within her substance as if it did not exist. Then she quivered, and her belly seemed to stroke his while her hips rotated slowly.

'I beg of you – ' he gasped, finally letting go of her breast.

She drew back. 'I will always do what you ask, when you phrase it that way, Parry. But I believe you would really rather move on to the culmination.'

'I am a friar!'

'You are a man.' She glanced at his body significantly. 'You can see that your body wants me.'

Parry grabbed for his robe, to cover his aroused body. 'You are a damned succubus!'

'Faint praise, Parry! I am much more than that. But if you really wish to wait for the raw sex, I will wait. I have no carnal desire of my own, of course; I am only acting as my Lord Lucifer directs, to corrupt you suitably, and this is merely a single aspect of it. What other aspect would you prefer to start with?'

'No aspect! I don't want to be corrupted at all!'

'You are lying, Parry. That is good; you do need practice in that.' Her left hand caught his right wrist, and lifted his hand back towards her left breast.

'I'm not lying!'

She smiled. 'I have no need to prove my point, but it entertains me to do so. Doff your robe again, stand before me, and tell me that you do not wish to partake of my body.'

Parry did not answer, aware that he could not pass such a test.

'But you know that my body is infernally crafted to evoke the basest lust in a mortal man,' she continued. 'You know the route you are headed when what rises is not your soul but your member.'

'Damn you!'

'Thank you.'

'Go away!' he said, closing his eyes.

'Why, when you really do not want me to?' Her lips brushed against his.

'Please, demoness, leave me!'

'That's better, Parry. I will return when you retire for the night. I think you need time to yourself to adjust to your new reality.'

He remained with his eyes screwed closed. She did not speak again. Finally he opened his eyes, and verified that she was gone.

'Jolie?'

But Jolie did not appear. He knew why: she had been banished by his accession to evil. She knew what he refused to acknowledge: the demoness had aroused his lust, and he could not free himself of it.

Was it too late to leave the Order? He walked to the door – and stopped, unable even to start towards the Abbot's office.

He dropped to his knees and prayed. 'Oh, Lord, grant me release from this bondage!'

'Now that would be foolish, wouldn't it.'

Parry glanced up, startled.

There hovered a small black cloud within the chamber. As he gazed at it, it sprouted horns.

'No!' Parry hurled himself away.

The cloud laughed and dissipated.

The wrong Lord had answered his prayer. His orientation had changed; he now answered to Lucifer instead of to God.

How could such a calamity have happened? He had laboured so hard for the cause of God! How could a single episode of love with his wife bring such ruin on him?

But he knew the answer. He was a friar, and celibate. What Jolie had offered had been sinful, and had his faith

167

been true, he would have rejected it. His faith had not been true, and this was the proof of it. His inability to give up his position as an important Dominican was another proof: he had succumbed to worldliness in the guise of holiness.

Still, he did not regard himself as an evil man, merely as a fallible one. Granted that he fell short of perfection, he could still do much good, just as a tree that was rotting at the core could still cast good shade and bear good fruit. Perhaps, if he continued his good works, he would in time recover his prior orientation and rejoin God.

He felt better. He went about his business of the day, labouring for a cause that he knew was good even if he himself was not.

But when he sought to retire at night, the demoness was in his bed, as warm and luscious as ever. 'Are you ready to enjoy me now, lover?' she inquired.

'No!'

'Your body says otherwise.'

'My body lies!'

'Your mind lies, not your body. That's lovely.'

'May God banish you, temptress!'

'Your terminology has no power when not backed by faith.'

Obviously that was true, for she remained warm against him. 'How can I make you go?'

'You really do not need to ask again, Parry. You know the answer.'

'But you always return!'

'That is the nature of evil.'

'I beg of – '

She silenced him with a hand on his lips. 'Parry, we must end this charade. Do the forthright thing: accept your situation, and get on with it. I return so insistently only because you desire me to.'

'That's – '

'The truth.' She embraced him and kissed him, ardently.

'No!' he exclaimed when able to wrench his face free.

'Would it help if I took the initiative?'

'I – ' He was unable to answer.

'That is a useful device for reticent maidens, who are constrained not to confess the base desires they feel. They would have it that they are powerless to prevent being ravished, but that is a legal fiction. We are experienced in all manner of fictions, in the Kingdom of Lies.' She stroked her body against his.

Parry knew he should protest, but he did not.

She proceeded to make love to him, while he lay almost unmoving. Technically, she was doing it, not he – but he could no longer deny that she was doing what he desired.

She brought him to a phenomenal climax, enhanced by its great guilt. 'I had hoped you would be more of a challenge,' she remarked sardonically as he was in the throes of it. Then, as he spasmed, she faded away, leaving him to foul himself.

That, of course, was the finishing touch. He felt completely dirty and ashamed. 'Never again!' he swore – but knew even then that he swore falsely.

In the course of the night, he succeeded in coming to terms with himself: the demoness had evoked his lust, and there was no staying it. It was better simply to indulge, leaving his mind clear for better things.

She reappeared at dawn. 'Well, Parry, ready for the day's mischief?' she inquired brightly.

The sight of her evoked his lust as if it had never been sated. That, too, it seemed, was an attribute of the gifts of Lucifer: temporary satisfaction, lasting guilt. 'Yes,' he said tightly, and stepped towards her.

But she became smoke in his arms. 'No, no, Parry,' the smoke spoke, as to an errant child. 'I gave you a mere sample. To obtain more, you must please me, and if you please me sufficiently, I may even remain throughout the night. Would you like that?'

He was done with lying. 'Yes. How may I please you?'

'By doing a significant deed of evil in the name of good. As it happens, there is a case just now coming up: a heretic who refuses to recant. You must make him recant.'

'But that will be a good deed!' he protested.

'For him, perhaps; not for you.'

Parry found that confusing. He shrugged, and set about making the journey. He rode the donkey, as before, but now it was Lilah, not Jolie, who accompanied him. She chatted freely about all things evil, and it was amazing the breadth of things that included. She seemed to know all the gossip about prominent figures, and she clarified with quite believable precision exactly which aspects of it were true. Parry was disgusted with himself for listening, but nonetheless fascinated. Thus he was immersed in news of evil throughout, and knew this was further corrupting him, but he could not resist it. Each time he thought to reject it, Lilah's body became naked and suggestive, and his lust rose up, and he knew he had to have her no matter what the cost. He also knew that that cost would be ever-greater evil on his soul, leading inevitably to eternal damnation. That appalled him – but he had tasted her wares, so to speak, and now was addicted.

That was the ugliest part of it: he knew exactly what was happening, yet could not wrench himself out of the process. Lucifer's minion was doing her job perfectly.

The heretic had pled innocent, and no amount of suasion had been effective. That was why Parry had been assigned. To this extent this was a normal case.

'But fair reasoning will not sway this one,' Lilah said with satisfaction. 'Neither will brutal torture; he will die first, and be lost to your former master. You must of course prevent that.'

'Why do you care?' Parry demanded, knowing the nature of her answer but compelled to ask anyway. If there could be some way out, some way to please her without further damning himself . . . but he knew there was not, for her purpose was to damn him.

Parry went into the dungeon and interviewed the captive. The man showed the ravages of his interrogation; he could no longer stand or feed himself, for the bones of his limbs had been dislocated by the procedure known as squassation: he had been hauled up on a pulley, with weights attached to his legs, and then dropped suddenly so that his feet did not quite reach the floor. This had been done three times, destroying his limbs, and it was obvious that he would not survive another. Despite the excruciating pain of this, he had refused to implicate any other heretics. This was a problem, because the local authorities were running out of heretics, and needed the revenues generated by continued confiscations of properties.

Parry shook his head. He had helped start the Inquisition in order to purify the faith, not to extort wealth from victims. The secular authorities might have base motives, but the Inquisition had only lofty motives: the salvation of the individual's immortal soul, and the purity of the faith.

'But you will help change that,' Lilah said. 'The desire for wealth is one of my Lord's principal tools in the corruption of men. So you must get this man to implicate others, that the chain of extortion may continue and grow, in the end corrupting the Church as well as the individuals.'

The corruption of the Inquisition itself! Parry considered that, and balked. 'Demoness, you demand too much! I'll not turn against – '

171

He broke off, for she was floating in the air, on her back, and spreading her legs towards him. His lust surged up like a living entity, paced by his guilt. Damn her!

He would have to make the prisoner talk. That would maintain his reputation as the interrogator of last resort, and would bring him the favour of the demoness. He hated both aspects of it, but knew he would do it.

But how could he persuade a man who was ready to die under torture rather than implicate another person? That was the problem that had brought him here.

'Remember,' Lilah reminded him. 'You are no longer constrained by ethical considerations. My Lord believes in effectiveness, and therefore can accomplish things your prior lord cannot.'

Parry sighed. He knew what would do it. The heretic had a small daughter. He did not want her to suffer; that was the source of his stamina.

But corrupt as he was becoming, Parry would not torture an innocent child! That might make the heretic give evidence, but would be no credit on the Church or himself.

'Remember, my Lord is the master of deceit,' Lilah said.

She was giving him strong hints, but leaving him to figure it out for himself, because corruption had to come from within. Now Parry realized what she was driving at. Truly, it was infernal – but it would surely work. And it seemed he had no choice, if he was not to give up what he could not give up. For the love of evil, he was damning himself.

'Can you assume the form of the heretic's child?' he asked her.

'I thought you would never ask!' she said brightly. She became the child: a string-haired waif of about five years, with big grey eyes and a tattered dress and a straw doll.

172

Parry took the waif's hand and led her into the chamber where the heretic lay. '*Père!*' she cried.

The man's sunken eyes opened. He gave a start of recognition.

The waif took a step towards him, but Parry held her back. 'Silence, brat!' he snapped. 'You will have your chance to talk soon enough.'

She began to cry. The prisoner gazed at her with alarm. 'You would not – ?'

Parry reached down with his free hand and grasped the waif by the hair. He hauled her up off the floor while she screamed piercingly. He glanced meaningfully at the ropes and pulleys at the far end of the chamber.

The prisoner capitulated. 'I will give the names!'

Parry smiled with cruel benificence. 'May God have mercy on your soul.' And on his own, he thought. But there was little chance of that.

The rest was routine. Parry escorted the mocked-up child out, leaving the local personnel to take down the information. The heretic would be required to sign a statement (they had been careful not to break the fingers of his right hand) that he had given testimony freely and without duress, and to testify against those he implicated as companion heretics. Then he would be allowed to retire to prison for the remainder of his life. His family would not be bothered, once their property had been taken. His soul had after all been saved for eternity.

Parry received his reward in full measure; the demoness was pleased with him, and she had ways of expressing that pleasure that transcended the powers of mortal women. She gave him the semblance of youth, and the vigour and potency of youth, and she became a succession of luscious young women who availed themselves freely of that potency with ever-increasing imagination. He found himself doing things with her whose very description would have evoked the Index, and that no decent person would have cared to imagine.

But the knowledge of the cruel trick he had played on the heretic haunted him; truly, this was a device he would never have thought of, let alone practised, in his day of serving God. Worse, he knew that he would use similar devices in the future, for the demoness had as cruel a hold on him as he had had on the first heretic: illusion that cut through to the core.

Five years passed in this slow descent. Parry never sought personal aggrandizement, preferring as he had before to be the power behind the power, but in private he wielded critical control over the Inquisition in France, the Holy Roman Empire and Italy. Under his direction, money became the engine that drove the Inquisition; the spoils were the estates of the accused heretics, and the requirement that each confessed heretic implicate others guaranteed that the proceeds would be ongoing. The Inquisition was now on a sound financial footing – and well on the way to ultimate corruption.

With each successful case, Lilah became more ardent. Parry was becoming older, but he felt younger, because of the magic of the demoness and his infatuation with her. A billy goat seemed to have taken up residence within him, so that in those moments when he could not be fornicating with her, his mind remained on the subject. He suspected that this was an enchantment placed on him, to greatly enhance his lust, but he did not care. He lived to indulge it.

The first part of Lucifer's vengeance was complete: the man who had done most to organize the Inquisition as a force for good had now reorganized it as a force for evil. That evil was self-sustaining; it would feed on itself and continue long after Parry himself was gone.

'My Master is pleased with you,' Lilah said. 'It is time for an audience with Him.'

Parry was not eager for that, knowing that there could

be little benefit in it for him. But this was not a thing he was in a position to refuse.

Lilah made a circle in the air of his chamber with her finger. As that circle closed, the circle filled in, becoming a disc. She hooked her thumb into the side of that disc, and it swung open like a door.

Beyond it was a tunnel. 'After you, lover,' she said, gesturing into it.

Parry climbed in. At first the tunnel was large enough only for his body on hands and knees, but soon it widened, so that he could stand. Lilah joined him, showing him the way.

They followed a descending spiral down through an increasingly intricate network of chambers and passages. They were, he realized, on their way to Hell.

At length they reached a grand nether audience chamber. There, on a golden throne, sat the Prince of Evil, Lord Lucifer. He was a darkly handsome figure with well-defined horns and tail, exactly as represented in contemporary paintings. Obviously the artists had had infernal inspiration.

'Bow down,' Lilah whispered. 'Prostrate yourself before the Son of the Morning.'

Parry hesitated. 'The what?'

'My Lord Lucifer, the Morning Star, as he was known before the Fall. *Get down!*'

'So the friar shows doubt,' Lucifer boomed. 'For that will I do him one disfavour. Friar, I tell thee what thou dost not wish to know: the date of thy death. It is precisely three years hence, at the hour of – '

Parry dropped to the floor, prostrating himself before Lucifer, and the malignant voice cut off. The Lord of Lies was satisfied.

The Lord of Lies. Did that mean that this cruel information was a lie? That Lucifer was merely taunting him with a fallacious date of demise?

'The frair still doubts!' Lucifer boomed again. 'To Hell with him!'

Suddenly flames rose up around Parry. They closed in on him, their heat excruciating. His robe caught fire. He scrambled to his feet and leapt out of the circle. He struck the ground rolling, but the material of his robe blazed up again the moment it was upward. He tore the robe off, getting free of the agony only when naked.

And found himself the cynosure of a multitude of eyes. They belonged to young women, naked themselves, who gazed at him in shocked confusion. Each held a three-tined pitchfork. Parry tried to cover himself, but had nothing other than his hands. He realized the effort was pointless, and desisted; after all, they were as embarrassed as he.

He was in a more literal version of Hell. There was choking smoke and smouldering fire all around, extending endlessly. The fire was contained in circular pits, each tended by one of the maidens.

The nearest pits blazed up vigorously. The girls squealed in dismay, and returned to their labours, using pitchforks to scoop ashes from the edges into the centre of each fire. This had the effect of damping the flames, though there was a compensating increase in the vile smoke, causing the girls to cough uncontrollably. Most of the ashes sifted down between the widely spaced tines, which hardly helped, but they had no other tools.

So his appearance here had distracted these damned souls, causing them to neglect their fires, and they had been punished by increased heat and smoke. Obviously they had to keep constantly at it, or they would very soon be even more uncomfortable than they were.

Lilah appeared. 'I have prevailed on my Lord to give you another chance,' she said. 'Considering that this is your first visit here. Apologize to Him, and He will grant you the intended audience.'

Parry realized that this was the best course. Obviously Lucifer could read his mind, and he had indeed doubted what Lucifer had told him.

Then he noticed something about Lilah. Her normally perfect tresses were in disarray, and there were marks on her body. She was a demoness; no mortal could muss her or mark her, as he had long since discovered.

'You were left with him,' he said. 'Did he hurt you?'

'Of course not,' she said quickly. 'I cannot be hurt.'

'But he did something to you! You're changed!'

'I am His creature,' she reminded him. 'I never suggested otherwise. He can do what He likes with me.'

The nearer fire girls were becoming distracted again, overhearing this dialogue.

'What did he do to you?' Parry demanded.

'Nothing I was not made for,' she said defensively. 'Look, Parry, this is dangerous. Just apologize to Him, and – '

'How did you get him to reconsider?'

'Parry, you know I have only one way to – '

'You had sex with him!' he cried, in a sudden fit of jealous rage. 'You prostituted yourself to him!'

'That term has no meaning for my kind. Please, Parry, be reasonable, lest – '

'You whore!' he screamed.

The visage of Lucifer appeared amidst the hovering smoke. 'Methinks our friar hath not quite yet relinquished his monkly ways,' the Lord of Lies said. 'Let him remain here for eternity, then!'

'My Lord, no!' Lilah cried. 'It is not yet his time!'

'And thou with him, strumpet, for thy failure,' Lucifer intoned, and faded out.

Lilah tore at her hair in a remarkably human gesture of remorse. 'Now look what you've done, Parry! We'll never get out of here!'

Parry's rage evaporated. Of course she was a creature

177

of this nether region, and sexual fidelity had no meaning for her. He had reacted possessively, when he had no right to be. She had never told him that she cared for him at all; she had only rewarded him in a calculated manner when he did what she wished. Whore? She had never claimed to be anything else! She had acted in her fashion to try to obtain a reprieve for him, and had succeeded – and he had thrown it away by his narrowness.

'I apologize to you, Lilah,' he said. 'But not to him.'

There was a smattering of applause from the surrounding women. Then they hastened back to their work.

'It's too late to apologize to anyone!' she snapped. Yet she seemed mollified; she had always reacted positively when he addressed her in a polite manner. It was evident that demons did not get much respect, and craved it. 'We're both stuck here with the adulterous wives. In a moment the warders will assign us to our separate places.'

Parry had been almost ready to accept this chamber of Hell, if it was to be in Lilah's company. Now he realized that of course it would not be; Lucifer would hardly allow him to have that satisfaction.

'Maybe we can escape,' he said.

'Fool – there is no escape. The attempt would only aggravate the warders.' She looked him for a moment in the eye. 'But I will say that your jealousy was very flattering. You know I am not worthy of it.'

It was almost as if she were human! Their common plight had for this moment put them on an equal basis. 'I think you are,' he replied.

'A demoness? I am no more than a tool in my Master's hands. I have no soul, no conscience, no imperative except to do His will. His will is that I corrupt you, and that I am doing. Certainly you owe me nothing; I extract payment from you in full measure for every reward I return.'

Absolute truth. 'Yet you are very good at what you do,' he said.

'I certainly am. Too bad I will not be allowed to do it any more.'

'So you do have pride in your work.'

'Pride is one of the basic sins.'

'And one of the basic virtues.' But of course she would not regard that interpretation with favour. 'Why did you try to get me another chance with Lucifer?'

'Because your failure is my failure. I had to give you a chance to show that I have done a proper job corrupting you. Then I could continue.'

'Why not just let me go, and start with another assignment?'

'Well, I – '

'You're lying,' he said.

'I never lie!'

'Then tell me that you care nothing for me. That I'm only an assignment.'

She opened her mouth, and paused. Then she laughed.

'You're doing it back to me! You're corrupting me with words!'

'I have had excellent teaching,' he replied drily.

She considered. 'As a demoness, I have no mortal emotions, only emulations I use to deceive mortal folk like you. But I do have an abiding desire to accomplish my purpose, which is to please my Master. I see in you the potential for enormous evil; therefore your corruption will accrue equivalent power to my Master, and He will be equivalently pleased. I believe my Master errs in throwing you away. Therefore I tried to persuade Him to allow the process of your corruption to be completed. I care for you in the manner you might for an exceedingly precious gem, or a unique tool to accomplish your purpose. It would be foolish to mistake this for caring for you personally. I am incapable of that.'

179

Parry nodded. That had the ring of authenticity. 'I know you for what you are, Lilah. But I *am* mortal, and human. I hate you for what you have done to me and my spirit wife, but I care for you too, and hate myself for that. So just let me delude myself that there is some spark of human sentiment in you, masked by your demonic nature.'

'Delusion is the hallmark of this realm,' she reminded him. 'Here comes the warder.'

The warder was a huge masculine demon bearing a three-tailed whip, which he lashed about routinely, striking the flanks of the labouring women. The women screamed piercingly; but the manner in which they cringed from the warders suggested that the whip was not the worst they feared from these. One woman even stumbled into her pit; there was a horrible hiss as her feet burned, and her scream redoubled as she scrambled out.

These were damned souls, Parry knew; they had no mortal flesh. But they looked physical, and evidently felt so. They were truly being punished for their failure to remain loyal to their home hearths. As was Parry himself, now that he had taken the demoness as his lover. Lucifer was a cruel and somewhat arbitrary master!

'This way, sludge!' the demon rasped, tagging Parry on a buttock with a casual flick of the whip. Pain lanced through Parry's flesh; he bit his tongue in his effort not to scream. 'What's a male soul doing here?'

'Lucifer has a warped sense of humour,' Parry replied as his agony abated.

The demon raised the whip for a more telling strike – and recognized Lilah. 'What are *you* doing here, Lil?' he demanded. 'Slumming?'

'I failed to corrupt this mortal sufficiently,' she explained. 'So I am incarcerated here with him.'

'Ho, ho! That means you are finally subject to *my* lust,

you snooty creature. I have lusted for a piece of your posterior for centuries. Come here!' He grabbed for her.

'Down dog!' Lilah snapped. 'I'm not for the likes of you!'

But the demon caught her and hauled her in for a tusky kiss. Parry realized that she could not dematerialize here in the nether spirit realm; not now that she had been classified as an inmate rather than a favoured creature. She could not avoid the demon as she could a mortal man on the surface.

Before he knew it, Parry grabbed a fork from the nearest woman and launched himself at the demon. He stabbed it at the creature's rear.

But the fork passed through without resistance. The demon, intent on Lilah, hadn't even noticed; his flesh was untouchable by local artifacts. But it was evident that Lilah's substance was touchable. She was struggling valiantly, but the demon was overpowering her, and in a moment would have his will of her.

Parry had to do something – but what? On one level he knew this was utterly foolish, because Lilah was an infernal creature who could hardly be hurt by the act of the demon. Human standards did not apply here. Yet she was in her singular fashion *his* female, and he could not stand to see her ravished. It had been bad enough knowing that Lucifer had used her. This time the horror was occurring right in his sight.

He had no weapon that could prevail against the warder. He could not even touch the warder! How, then, could he bring the creature up short?

His mouth opened, and he began to sing.

> Creature of Hell, hark unto me!
> Turn not against your own kind!
> Consider how all of you are minions of Lucifer,
> How all labour for a common cause.

The warder paused. Parry was improvising in the same manner he had when protecting the children from the possessed animals, using the mode of address that had been effective then. He was trying the pacify the evil spirit, to make it respond to his own will. He was putting magic into his song, reaching out to the demon not in enmity but in understanding.

> Creature of Hell, remember that favour is fickle;
> As you treat your associate, so may you
>   sometime be treated.
> When Lucifer's favour orients again on her,
> What you do now may be remembered.

The warder froze, evidently shaken. As Parry continued singing, the warder let Lilah slide from his grasp. She stepped back, staring at Parry.

Parry took Lilah's hand and led her away from the stunned warder, still singing. She walked with him without resistance, her eyes fixed on him. They wound through the chamber, and all the women stared likewise at them, their fires untended. But, while he sang, the fires did not blaze up.

They came to the chamber wall. There was an opening in it, guarded by another warder. Parry continued singing and improvising, and the demon watched without moving. They entered the opening, and walked down a passage. When the entrance to the tunnel was small in the distance behind, Parry stopped singing.

Now Lilah took the initiative. She moved ahead, still holding Parry's hand, tugging him along in the route she selected. They turned a corner at an intersection, then another, and another, wending through the labyrinth. Now the general trend was upward.

At last they emerged from the final tunnel, and stepped down into Parry's chamber in the monastery. Lilah turned, closed the door and erased it with a sweep of her hand.

They had won their freedom from Hell after all.

Lilah spoke no word. Instead she embraced him and kissed him with unusual intensity, and made love to him with a passion bordering on ferocity. It was of course her way of expressing pleasure with him; she knew no other.

Later, as he drifted to sleep with Lilah snuggling close, Parry considered what had occurred. He had succeeded in singing the demons of Hell itself into quiescence! How could that have happened? The surface of the world was the mortal realm, where mortals and demons could interact in limited ways; human magic could prevail against demon spirits if appropriately exercised. But Hell? That was hardly to be believed! If the damned souls could escape, they would be doing so in droves.

Of course he was not yet a damned soul; he was a mortal. Perhaps, then, Lucifer had been bluffing; he could not hold the souls of the living in Hell. That meant that Parry's singing could have been incidental; all he had had to do was walk out.

But Lilah – she was of Lucifer's domain. Surely Lucifer could hold her if he chose. Had Parry got her free despite Lucifer's sentence on her – or had that, too, been a bluff? For once Parry got free, who would corrupt him if not Lilah? Perhaps Lucifer had had to let her go, once Parry made his move for freedom. Therefore all of this could be less than it seemed.

Still, suppose he had not tried to make the break? Suppose he had simply stood and let Lilah be raped by the demon? Would he ever have escaped then? He wasn't sure. Lucifer, the master of deception, had tried to deceive him into believing that he was a prisoner in Hell, and it had come closer to success than Parry liked to imagine.

He had done what he had done because of the threat to Lilah. That had perhaps been an act of folly. But it had demonstrated the extent of her hold on him, and she was duly pleased. She was after all a demoness; her power lay in her influence over him. Thus neither his action nor her reaction reflected favourably on either of them.

He tried to be angry with her. But his hand stroked her warm, plush bottom, and his lust, so recently sated, rose again. She responded, encouraging it. His anger turned back on himself, but did not cause him to desist. His need for her was beyond outrage.

Parry realized that his corruption was proceeding apace.

Parry was slated to die in 1250; he no longer doubted Lucifer's word on that, for such knowledge was a most insidious torture. That meant that his time with Lilah was limited, for he knew that once he died, her assignment with him would be over. He was desperate to please her, so as to gain as much of her semblance of love as he possibly could while he could. He knew it was not real, for a demoness was incapable of such emotion, but he cherished the illusion. It was all he had to pursue.

Indeed, she acted like a woman in love now, and she was letter perfect at it. She no longer teased him by fading out just before the culmination of their sexual unions; she remained with him throughout, making each fulfilment as compelling as the arousal. She did whatever he asked, whenever he asked, being completely malleable to his will. If he asked her a question, she answered; if he asked her to leave him for a time, she did so.

'But what do *you* want?' he asked, perplexed by the consistency of her attitude.

'Just to hear your voice, Parry,' she replied. 'Sing to me, as you did in Hell. I thrill to the suggestion of the Llano.'

'The what?'

'The Llano, the ultimate song. Sing to me again.'

Technically, he had been singing to the warder demon,

but it had been on Lilah's behalf. He was curious about this special song she spoke of, but did not care to advertise his ignorance lest it in some way benefit Lucifer. He sang to her extemporaneously, and she simply watched him with a look of adoration on her face.

Parry did not fully trust this, so he was careful to keep trying to please her exactly as if she still rewarded him only on performance. He searched for new evil to do, so that she would know he was on the job.

He found a beauty. King Louis IX of France was the most chivalrous monarch of Europe, lofty of character and an excellent King. He was working hard to establish proper justice in the kingdom. This tended to inhibit the developing procedures of the Inquisition, and certainly it was not good for Lucifer's operations. If Louis could be removed from the scene, it would be a coup!

He worked out the way. A crusade! There had been talk of such an effort for years, but it hadn't materialized. Now Parry used his influence as a leading friar and got the crusade moving. In 1248 Louis set sail for the Holy Land by way of Egypt.

In 1249 the Nile Delta city of Damietta was taken by the crusaders without a struggle; all seemed to be going well. But Parry knew that this was a trap. The crusaders marched south towards Cairo – and were routed. The army was massacred and Louis was captured by the Saracens in 1250. The job had been done.

But Parry was out of time. His ageing body was breaking down; his breathing was hard, even when Lilah gave him the semblance of youth, and he knew his lungs were deteriorating. His heart was going, too; he could feel its too rapid flutter.

'Now you are dying, thoroughly corrupted,' Lilah said. 'You know you are destined for Hell.'

'I know. But these nine years with you have been worth

it. Mock me as you will, demoness; I would do it again. Will you visit me in Hell?'

'I think not.'

He sighed. This was of course part of his punishment: to long for the demoness and be forever denied her.

'Will you kiss me once more before I go?'

He expected another refusal, as she savoured the last dreg of her victory over him, but she got down close to him. Her eyes seemed luminous. 'Parry,' she whispered, 'it doesn't have to be!'

He tried to laugh, but only gagged. He was in the last hour of his mortal life, perhaps the last minutes. He had to die, and he surely was not going to Heaven!

'Parry,' she repeated urgently. 'You are a sorcerer! A potent one! You could be the best, if you tried! The way you sing – that suggests your potential. Use what you know to – '

'What is this?' a new voice interrupted.

Lilah shrank away. It was Lucifer himself.

Parry coughed and managed to clear his throat enough to speak. 'You come for me personally, Lord of Lies?'

'I always come for My vengeance personally,' Lucifer replied. 'What would existence be like without the pleasure of the torment of Mine enemies? You have served Me well, mortal, and now you shall pay for that with eternal torment in the most excruciating fires of Hell.'

'I am ready,' Parry wheezed.

'But you have a few minutes remaining to suffer in this life. I want you to understand your situation exactly.' Lucifer's baleful gaze moved to Lilah. 'Wench, revile him.'

Wench. Old anger stirred in Parry's breast. His blood began to circulate more strongly, and his mind clarified. He knew it was his last effort of life, but he wanted to strike back at his former nemesis and present master. He served Lucifer; that did not mean he liked him.

Lilah stood by Parry's bed, gazing down at him, unspeaking.

What was it she had told him? To use his magic to –

'Speak, slut!' Lucifer said. But still she did not. She merely looked at Parry with that same emulation of adoration she had affected these past three years.

To do what? She had said that it didn't have to be. What could she have meant? That there was some alternative to Hell?

'Do you defy Me, you piece of ether?' Lucifer snapped at Lilah. 'What is the matter with you? Spit on him!'

Still Lilah gazed, and now a tear showed on her cheek.

'You disreputable bitch!' Lucifer exclaimed, amazed. 'You have fallen for him!'

Fallen for him?

Lilah dropped to her knees and embraced Parry's supine form as well as she could. Her tears wet his face. 'Oh, Parry, I cannot say it!'

She was a demoness. She could not say she loved him. But now he realized that she did. Her gazes of adoration had been genuine.

'When?' Parry rasped, as amazed as Lucifer.

'Yes, tell us when,' Lucifer said in such fury that steam was rising from him. 'It is an error I shall never again permit.'

'When you sang me out of Hell,' Lilah said to Parry. 'When you sang to me with the power of the Llano. You charmed the demons – and I am a demoness.'

'When he *sang*,' Lucifer demanded incredulously. 'You deserted Me for a song?'

'I deserted You for a man,' she said.

Lucifer considered. 'A mortal can love, and be in other respects unchanged. A demon can love only totally. When the object of that love is gone, that demon is destroyed.

You have given up your existence for three foolish years with a dying mortal.'

'It was worth it,' Lilah whispered, kissing Parry's lips.

Now Parry knew why she would not visit him in Hell. When he died, she would cease to exist. She had known this throughout, as surely as he had known that his involvement with her would damn his soul. A truer love could not exist.

'But I intend you to suffer!' Lucifer said angrily to Lilah. 'No one betrays Me without punishment!'

'I am suffering now,' Lilah said, clinging to Parry.

'It is not enough,' Lucifer said grimly. He lifted his hand, and a flicker of fire played about it. He pointed at the demoness. 'Burn, bitch, while he watches!'

Parry summoned his last resolve as she hugged him. 'No!'

Lucifer's lip curled into a sneer. 'I will banish her to that very fire awaiting you, mortal fool! But she will suffer only while you remain alive. Then your soul will replace her there, and she will not exist. Take your time about dying!'

Lucifer made a gesture. Lilah clung to Parry. And Parry did the only thing he could think of: he invoked his mirror spell. His shield against hostile magic. All of his remaining strength went into it; he knew that the strain was destroying his heart, and that he would be dead in a moment. But Lilah would spend no time in the agony of the flame.

Lucifer's magic bounced. Suddenly Lucifer himself was bathed in flames. He disappeared, screaming.

Lilah lifted her head. 'You did it!' she cried. 'Take the Office! Take the Office!'

Parry's heart was fibrillating, going into its final throes. 'What?'

'Assume the Office!' she screamed at him.

His brain was clouding. As his consciousness faded, he

made his final effort to please her. 'I – assume – the Office,' he gasped.

Flame coalesced about him, but it did not burn.

'Choose Your title!' she cried.

What was she talking about? 'Look, Lilah,' he gasped 'I –'

'Your title! Your title! It must be now! But different from that of your predecessor. You can be Scrotch, or Satan –'

The second was less objectionable. 'Satan,' he repeated.

'Choose Your form!' she urged him.

'What?'

'It must be now, at the outset! Your true form for the Office. Choose Your form.'

'I – choose the form I was at age twenty-five,' he said.

Abruptly the constriction of his heart eased, and it beat slowly and strongly. Strength returned.

'Choose Your consort!' she cried.

He hardly understood this process. 'I want to be with you.'

She hugged him and kissed him. 'For as long as You want me, my Lord of Evil!'

The bottom dropped out of his equilibrium. 'Who?'

'You have assumed the Office, my Lord! You vanquished the former holder, and now it is Yours. You will be forever as You are now, physically, until some other claimant deceives You as You deceived Your predecessor and disposesses You. But that need never happen.'

'I – am Lucifer?' Parry asked, dumbfounded.

'No, Your title is Satan. You chose it.'

'But I am the – the new master of Hell?'

'The Lord of Evil,' she agreed. 'In Your mortal body as it was at age twenty-five, and I am Your consort. All else is malleable.'

189

'But all I was trying to do was protect you from torture! I never thought my spell would destroy Lucifer himself!'

'You protected me from extinction itself,' she said. 'I have no existence apart from my love of You. Now I will serve You utterly, in any manner You require, just as I served the prior Lord of Evil when I loved him.'

Parry felt dizzy. 'There is something about the way you pronounce –'

She laughed. 'You are now a deity, my Lord! Co-equal with the other one. I refer to You always as such.'

'And – and I am now to run Hell?'

'And forward the cause of evil, exactly as Your predecessor did. As You have done these past nine years, serving him.' The subtle accent that denoted her respect was no longer on her reference to the prior Lord of Evil.

'I don't think I know how to handle this.'

'I will help You in any way I can,' she assured him. 'You will quickly grow accustomed to the exercise of this power. You will come to understand that Evil is the opposite aspect of, of – may I say the word?'

'Say it,' he said, uncertain of his authority in this respect.

'Of Good,' she finished. 'That both are required for either to have meaning. G – G –'

'God,' he said. 'You may say it'

'God. God is the Incarnation of Good, and Satan is the Incarnation of Evil, and the struggle between the two of you is the essence of mortal existence. Your position is as important as his.'

'And I can authorize you to say those words I can say, that no demon otherwise can say?'

'Yes, my Lord Satan. Your power over Your minions is absolute. Your predecessor forbade those words, but Your law governs now.'

Parry shook his head disbelievingly. Then she embraced

him again, and kissed him again, and his young, strong body responded ardently, and he began to believe.

He had completed his progress from Good to Evil. He had become the Lord of Evil.

9
Hell

'What now?' he asked Lilah, after a suitable orgy of celebration over his sudden fortune.

'Now You must establish Your mastery over Hell.'

'Isn't that automatic, now that I have the Office of the Incarnation of Evil?'

She shook her head in negation. 'You have dispatched Lucifer; You have not proved You can fill his boots.'

'Oh? What happens if I don't prove it?'

'You have a thirty-day grace period. If in that time You do not demonstrate Your fitness for the Office, You will be dispatched to that fate Lucifer intended for You, and he will be restored as Incarnation of Evil, unless some truly evil mortal preempts the Office first.'

Parry was abruptly serious. 'You knew this – yet you supported me?'

'A demoness can be a fool; that is one of her few similarities to mortal souls. When I came to love You, I could do no other. Thus I did not warn Lord Lucifer of his danger.'

'His danger?'

'He could not banish You to Hell without first separating You from the soul with which You are bound. I would ordinarily have reminded him of that, just as I will remind You of those things You need to know but may on occasion forget.'

'The soul with which – ' Parry repeated blankly. Then it came to him. 'Jolie!'

'In the drop of blood on your wrist,' she agreed.

'But she went to Heaven long ago, didn't she? Once you made it impossible for her to be with me?'

'No, my Lord. She merely retreated into her drop and slept. She cannot leave You until her onus is abated – and because she is in balance, she cannot be relegated to either Hell or – '

'Say it. Say any word you need, while you serve me.'

'Heaven. She must remain with You, until her balance is changed. She is with You now, though she cannot manifest.'

'She is not suffering?' he asked anxiously.

'No, my lord. She knows nothing now, and will not until she wakes again, which may be only when You retire.'

Parry was relieved. 'And her invisible presence caused Lucifer's spell to bounce?'

'Your spell did that, my Lord. But Lucifer knew of Your spell, and was contemptuous of its feeble power against the magnitude of his magic. But no amount of magic could send Your wife to Hell with You, so your spell assumed far more force than Lucifer reckoned.'

'Like an iron bar hidden in a loaf of bread,' he agreed.

'Yes, my Lord. Had I warned him, he would have severed Your hand first, thrown it away, then banished You with his magic.'

'But she was with me in Hell when we visited. How – ?'

'That was not the same. You may go to Hell of Your own volition, and she may travel with You, because that is not damnation. But she cannot be damned eternally. Lucifer inadvertently tried to do that.'

And Lilah had known. 'So I owe my salvation – ' He paused, reconsidering. 'My present situation to Jolie – and to you. What an unlikely collaboration!'

'True, my Lord. But also to Your own effort, which enraged Lucifer and caused him to be careless in his arrogance. He was past his time, I think.'

'Because he treated you with contempt,' Parry said.

'You might put it that way.'

'Lilah, suddenly I want to know more about you.'

'Ask, my Lord, and I will answer, as I always have.' She smiled and embraced him.

'Exactly who are you? I mean, I know you're a demoness, but what is your history? What is the nature of your association with the Incarnation of Evil?'

She grimaced. 'That would be long in the telling, my Lord.'

'Are you refusing to answer?'

'By no means, my Lord! But if I told You my complete history, I would be talking for the full month, and You would get none of Your necessary work done.'

'Let me put it this way: your defection from Lucifer led to his undoing. I want to understand you well enough to know what would cause your defection from me.'

'That much is simple. I will serve You loyally as long as I exist. You have the power to destroy any demon, me included, and to create any demon from ether. If You destroy me, I will not be able to serve You. If You do not destroy me, but treat me with contempt, in time my love may go elsewhere, and then I will serve You less loyally. But I will never truly betray You.'

As she had not truly betrayed Lucifer, he realized. She had merely failed to serve him completely. The distinction was worth noting. 'Lucifer treated you with contempt?'

'Yes, lately. He took concubines from among the damned souls, and even from among living witches, neglecting me. He assigned me to corrupt a mortal, and did not reward me for my success. He even threatened to confine me to eternal punishment in Hell, and finally with destruction.'

Parry nodded. 'I was that mortal?'

'Yes.'

'So you came to love me when I rescued you from the punishment he inflicted on you.'

'Yes. But it was more than that. I do not desert my

Lord lightly. He cast me off – and You showed me You were worthy. Now You are my Lord, and I will not desert You unless You treat me as Lucifer did.'

'That I can understand and accept. Even in your alienation, you did not oppose Lucifer; you merely failed to volunteer more than he asked.'

'He was my Lord.'

'If I ever treat you as he did, I will expect the same from you.'

'It would be easier for us both, my Lord, if You simply destroyed me and created a new demoness more to Your liking.'

'Lilah, I have no intention of destroying you! But if it became necessary for some other demon – just how would I go about it?'

'That I cannot tell You, my Lord. It is a spell that only a very few know, because of the danger of its use. There would be chaos if any demon or soul could destroy any other.'

'So Lucifer maintained his power because he could destroy any other, but they could not destroy him?'

'Yes, my Lord.'

'An excellent precaution against revolution or coup! I approve of it. But how can I use it if I don't know the spell?'

'You must learn the spell, my Lord. Lucifer did, and all his predecessors.'

'But it is not something that a person could guess, or come upon by chance?'

'Never, my Lord. It must be taught by one who knows.'

'Can you tell me who knows it?'

'God knows it, and Gaea, and Lucifer. Perhaps others have known it, but I have no notion who they might be.'

Parry considered. 'God surely would not tell his arch-enemy! Lucifer – he is now confined to the deepest flames of Hell?'

'Yes, my Lord.'

'I rather doubt that he would tell me! Especially since he stands to recover the Office if I wash out during my trial period. That leaves Gaea.'

'I believe Lucifer learned it from her,' Lilah agreed.

'Then I will have to ask Gaea.'

'I fear she will not give it to You, my Lord.'

'Why not? If I'm an Incarnation, and she's an Incarnation, shouldn't there be professional courtesy?'

'The other Incarnations oppose You, my Lord. They labour only to frustrate Your ambition.'

'But if Lucifer – '

'I don't know how he got it from her. He did not allow me to accompany him. I suspect he charmed it from her, when she was relatively new in office. But now she is old in office, and will not be deceived again.'

Parry sighed. 'Well, I'll just have to see if I can get along without, then. But first, tell me your history; I do want to know, to set the context for our association. Just make a simple summary that covers what you know will interest me.'

'Gladly, my Lord. I am the original demoness, first called Lilith, and sent to be the wife of the first mortal man, Adam.'

'You are that one?' Parry asked, amazed. 'How old are you?'

'As old as man, my Lord. God created Adam, but forgot to create a woman, so Samael fashioned me from ether to be Adam's companion in Eden.'

'Who?'

'Samael. The first Prince of Demons, also known as the Angel of Death.'

'But what of Lucifer?'

'The Incarnations of this office have assumed different names, each choosing the one he prefers, as You have also, my Lord. All are the same in significance.'

'I – that was why you made me choose? Because each has to have a different title?'

'Once he proves himself in office. Any name will do. But it is best to take a familiar one, the way Your Popes do, so that others understand Your nature.'

'I shall keep the one you prompted me to take,' Parry said, realizing that it was her desire to see him succeed in his trial period and become permanent that had prompted her to make him choose all his primary attributes – form, title, consort – at the outset. 'So you were Adam's first wife?'

'I was, and a good one, too. There was no human blood in me, but I was as soft and sweet as any mortal could be, and considerably more durable. I taught him everything he knew about the joys of copulation.'

'I'm sure you did. But didn't God object?'

She laughed. 'God was not as prudish then as he is now! It varies with the Officeholder. He let it be; after all, it did keep Adam occupied and out of mischief. But then I spoiled it.'

'*You* spoiled it?'

She frowned reminiscently. 'Adam – well, he had some crude edges. He got this idea that he was superior, just because he was male. Naturally I couldn't go along with that! He might have claimed superiority because he was mortal, but not because he was male. So I told him to cut out that chauvinism or I'd cut out the pleasure. Stubborn fool, he wouldn't give over, so I gave him a taste of no sex. That drove him wild! But would You believe it, he complained to God that I was uncooperative, and God banned me from Eden?'

'How could God ban a creature Samael had made?'

'It was God's garden. He couldn't legitimately destroy me, but he could exclude me from his property. I didn't like it, and my Master was not at all pleased, but there was nothing we could do. So I left, and God ripped a rib

197

out of Adam's side and fashioned that bone into a golem-girl he called Eve, and you bet *she* had no feminist notions! But I got back at them.'

'Oh, no – not the serpent!'

She smiled. 'Hell hath no fury like that of a demoness scorned; You know that, Parry – I mean, my Lord. I was new then, and had some rough edges of my own. Samael sent me to corrupt Eve – that was my first negative assignment – so I assumed the form of a serpent and tempted that foolish girl to eat of the fruit of the Tree of Knowledge of Good and Evil. You see, they had not realized that all this nakedness and fornication was sinful. Suddenly they knew, and it changed their lives, and God then threw *them* out of the Garden. Thus we had our revenge.'

'You had your revenge,' Parry agreed, amazed. 'You are really that same creature?'

'I am, and I have served every Master of Evil since. Some I married, some I only accommodated. Each tired of me after a few centuries, and lost my guidance, and subsequently blundered and lost his position, as You will too, my Lord, inevitably, for it is the masculine nature to be fickle. But meanwhile we shall have an interesting time.'

'How is is that you have never assumed the Office of the Incarnation of Evil yourself? Surely you have been in a position to!'

'You forget, my Lord: I am a demoness. I have no soul. Only a living mortal can assume the Office.'

'But I am dead!'

'No, my Lord. You are alive. You assumed the Office in Your last moment of life, and became immortal and ageless. Only when You retire can You die – and Your successor may not allow You to die, any more than You have allowed Lucifer to die.'

'I haven't?'

'No. You let him be confined in the manner of a damned soul, but he cannot die until You allow him to. That choice will be Yours after You take permanent possession of the Office.'

'What of the prior Incarnations of Evil? Did they die?'

'Oh, yes, in time. It is safer to let them die, so that none can resume the Office. They now serve in various important capacities, for their expertise in the ways of Hell is matchless.'

'But don't they foment trouble for the current Office-holder? It must be quite a comedown to be a damned soul, after being the Incarnation.'

'That may be, but they are tough creatures. You can trust them, for their ambition is forever stultified.'

Parry had an inspiration. 'Those prior Officeholders! They must know the demon-destruction spell!'

She smiled. 'They know it, certainly, my Lord. But they will not tell You.'

'What, not one of them?'

'None I can think of. They are immune to blandishments. They will serve You from pride, but will not help You gain power. That You must do for Yourself.'

Parry sighed. 'I don't suppose you could charm it from one of them?'

'You forget, my Lord: I have been used for centuries by each of them. I have no mysteries remaining, no allure for them.'

Parry gazed at her, not entirely pleased at this reminder. He was the latest in a virtually eternal line of lovers. No wonder Lilah was skilled in this respect!

'Well, let's get on to Hell,' he said somewhat gruffly.

She took his arm, conscious of his jealousy. 'Do not forget, my Lord: I am made of ether. I have no existence other than this. I was crafted to serve man, beginning with the first, and that I do as well as I am able. I now give to You that same loyalty I gave to each holder of the

Office. You cannot fault me for that, only for inadequate performance in my role.'

Parry relaxed. It was true; he had no business getting jealous of her prior lovers. She was no woman, but a demoness.

Lilah opened the porthole in the air, and they passed through it to the entrance to Hell. But this time they took the scenic route, coming down at the outer boundary of Hell.

The tunnel debouched into an ugly forest whose twisted trees seemed about to clutch at any travellers, and these flinched as the path skirted the trees.

'The newly damned souls?' Parry asked.

'Yes, my Lord. At death they descend, their velocity determined by the weight of evil on their souls, and land in this forest. See, some have problems already.' She gestured.

He looked, and spied several figures struggling in high branches. They had snagged in their descent, and were trying to work free.

Parry and Lilah joined the procession following the path. None of the others took notice. The damned souls looked exactly like living folk, complete with clothing, but were singularly sombre.

The path broadened into a road, accommodating the unhappy travellers. Ahead was a mighty gate, with a giant arch over it. As Parry approached it, he read the words ABANDON HOPE, ALL YE WHO ENTER HERE!

He nodded. The arrivals were evidently of many nationalities, and most were surely illiterate, but it was evident that each understood that dread warning. All those who entered here were damned.

He passed on under the arch. The road brought them to the dismal bank of a broad, brooding river. 'This is the Acheron,' Lilah said. 'The River of Woe that surrounds Hell. We shall have to wait for Charon.'

In due course the ferry came: a raft that nudged barely above the surface of the water. The ferryman poled it along with fair dispatch, then stepped on to the bank and held out his withered hand for payment. His eyes glowed like coals. Each soul had to give a small coin. Those who lacked coins were barred from boarding.

'The coins are from the eyes placed on the deceased mortals,' Lilah explained. 'Unfortunately, not all who die are properly buried.'

'But what happens to them if they can't enter Hell?' Parry asked.

'They must wait until the need to cross becomes too great to resist, as their bodies rot in the ground. Then they must cross as they can, by wading or swimming.'

Parry looked at the river. Now he smelled it: the miasma of the nethermost of sewers. There were suggestive ripples, as of great beasts that swam in the murk, waiting for prey. Indeed, he heard a scream, and saw a woman flail and splash, as if being drawn under.

'But they can't drown,' he said. 'They are already dead!'

'They can't drown, but they can suffer all the agony of drowning, without limit,' she explained.

Parry considered that as he watched the woman struggle and slide under the surface. 'Point taken. But I want that woman rescued.'

'You may direct Charon,' she said dubiously.

'Charon!' he snapped. 'Draw that woman from the water!'

The sinister ferryman looked at him, then looked away, ignoring him.

Parry controlled his anger. 'Am I or am I not the master of this realm?' he asked Lilah.

'You are and You are not,' she said. 'That is, the title is Yours, but You have to prove yourself before Your minions will obey You.'

'And to do that I need the spell to destroy demons,' he said.

'Yes, my Lord. That same spell cannot destroy souls, but can banish them to restricted regions, which has much the same effect.'

'Let's just see what I can do without it,' he said grimly. He strode past the waiting souls and boarded the raft. Charon lifted his ugly head to stare at him. 'Charon, I am the new Incarnation of Evil. If you value your position, you will obey me with alacrity. Pick up that woman!'

Charon turned away, again ignoring him.

'Answer me, spook!' Parry snapped, grabbing at the man's shoulder. But his hand passed right through the ferryman's body.

So it was like that. Parry pondered briefly, then opened his mouth and sang:

> Ferryman, hark unto me!
> I am the Incarnation of Evil.
> Answer to me: you have no choice.
> Fetch out that woman;
> Ferryman, fetch out that woman!

The power of the song reached out and took hold of Charon as Parry's hand could not. Just as his song had stunned the demons of the fire chamber, it stunned Charon. There had always been magic in Parry's music, and it had power here, too.

Slowly Charon turned. He took his pole and used it to shove the filling raft away from shore. They floated across to where the woman was marked by a thin stream of bubbles. Then Charon reached a bony hand down and caught at something under the murky surface. The woman came up, choking; Charon had hold of her wrist. He hauled her to the raft, where she lay gasping. Then he poled it back to the shore to pick up the rest of his cargo.

There was a smattering of applause. Parry had made his point. He had compelled the ferryman to obey.

'In the future, Charon, if any souls become so desperate as to try to swim across, you will pick them up without fare,' Parry said gruffly. 'If you do not, I will remove you from this position. Do you understand?'

Slowly the grim ferryman nodded. Now Parry turned away, and saw a subdued smile of approval on Lilah's face. He knew it was not because he had done a decent thing, but because he had made his power felt.

They remained on the raft while Charon got it loaded. Parry squatted beside the woman he had rescued. 'What is your name, woman?'

'Oh, sir, I am Gretchen. I thank you for paying my fare.'

'I did not pay your fare. I merely directed that you be given passage without fare.'

She lifted her head to stare at him. 'Sir, if I may ask – who are you?'

'I am the Master of Hell.'

Her eyes widened in shock. She collapsed in a faint. The others aboard the raft retreated from him, and some fell into the water.

Parry sighed. He would have to watch that! Naturally he would now be a figure of terror for the damned souls.

'I am not here to punish you, only to inspect operations,' he said to them all. 'You are damned, but I shall not make your fate worse.'

They seemed only slightly reassured. He realized this was because he was also now the Father of Lies. Probably they feared that he was setting them up for worse punishment after tempting them with false hope. But those who had fallen did scramble back on to the raft.

He squatted again by Gretchen, and shook her shoulder. 'Wake, woman; I spoke figuratively. I am not here to do you harm. What brought you here?'

She recovered enough to sit up. 'My Lord, I lied, I cheated, I stole. I knew it would damn my soul, but my family was going hungry, and I had to get food somehow.'

Parry remembered the poor villagers of his original village. They had not been able to afford the luxury of integrity; the feudal system had kept them too low.

'You others,' he asked, looking around. 'Is it similar with you? You were poor, and had to cheat to survive?'

There was a murmur of assent.

Parry nodded. These were creatures of circumstance, damned for lives over which they had had little control. It did not seem right that they be relegated to Hell for eternity. But would he be able to change that? He wasn't sure, and was not ready to inquire.

They came to the inner shore. This was bleak and barren, and crowded with people who merely stood without talking. Nothing seemed to be happening.

'What is this?' Parry asked Lilah.

'This is Limbo, the first and outermost Circle of Hell,' she replied. 'This is where the unbaptized souls remain, neither punished nor rewarded.'

'Unbaptized? Do you mean they are not Christians?'

'Many are not,' she agreed. 'Some have led illustrious and blameless lives, but are damned in death because of their lack of faith.'

'But other faiths are valid!' he protested. 'They have their own facilities for the Afterlife!'

'So one would think,' she agreed. 'I suppose the records have not been clarified.'

'We shall have to see about this. Who is in charge of the records?'

'That would be Beelzebub, the Lord of the Flies, one of Lucifer's predecessors.'

That meant that she had been intimate with him. Parry stifled that thought. 'I shall have to talk with him, in due course.'

'I think You should establish Your position first.'

Surely good advice! But already he knew there would be some changes made.

'Where is the three-headed dog? Isn't he supposed to guard the Gates of Hell?'

'Cerberus? He is in the Third Circle, with the gluttonous.'

'What's he doing there? That's not the Gates of Hell! And since when is gluttony punished by eternal damnation? They would have to fill that circle with Lords and Bishops and even Popes!'

'They are there,' she agreed.

Parry decided not to press the point. 'Cerberus will have to be moved. Who is in charge of the organization of Hell?'

'Asmodeus, the King of devils.'

'Another former Incarnation of Evil?'

'Yes.'

'Let's move on.'

They passed through the Second Circle, where the carnal sinners were. 'Because they lusted, they are damned?' Parry asked. 'What man does not lust, on occasion?'

'Few men go to Heaven,' Lilah said smugly.

'But if so many are damned for normal aspects of the human condition, what of the truly evil ones? The murderers, the rapists, the traitors?'

'In the lower circles,' she said. 'The traitors are in the Ninth Circle, the innermost one, and that is subdivided into four, for the traitors to kindred, or to their country, or to friends, or to their benefactors.'

'These strike me as needless distinctions. Next thing we know, there will be a region set aside for sorcerers!'

'In the Eighth Circle, along with the hypocrites, thieves, barrators, and seducers.'

'Sorcerers are damned?' he demanded, outraged. 'But it is a legitimate profession!'

She shrugged. 'I could not have corrupted You, had You not been already on the path to corruption, and Your sorcery was much of it.'

'We need some revision of definitions! Great numbers of these folk do not belong here!'

She did not answer, perhaps being wiser than he in this respect. They passed on through the Third and Fourth and Fifth Circles, seeing the gluttons, misers, and wrathful souls confined there. In the Sixth they encountered the three winged furies: hideous women with snaky hair. In the Seventh they crossed the River of Blood, for this was where the violent were confined, harried by the Hounds of Hell and harpies and centaurs.

'But this is all confused,' he protested. 'The hounds should be guardians, and the centaurs record keepers, because of their intellectual capacities.'

Now the sand on which they walked became burning hot. A volcano rumbled, and spouted fire, and burning flakes rained down on them. The incarcerated souls cried out in anguish – and so did Parry as a fire flake singed him.

'They aren't supposed to affect You,' Lilah said angrily. 'What mischief is this?'

'The mischief of some entity who doesn't want change,' Parry muttered. 'Naturally the governing demons want me to fail – and until I find that spell, I can't do much about it.'

'This is true,' she said, furious. 'Asmodeus is behind this, I'm sure. He remains loyal to Lucifer.'

'We'd better get out of here.' Parry resumed his singing, and now when the fire flakes came down, they passed through his body without effect. He could do a lot with his voice, but knew that it would not work against one of the ranking spirits. He had seen enough, and learned enough, to know that further exploration was pointless. Hell required an entire overhaul, and he could not accomplish that until he learned the spell he needed to control the demons and damned souls.

Lilah opened a tunnel, and they soon climbed up out of Hell. It was now dark on the surface of the world, and Parry was tired. It was not physical fatigue, but rather the rush of experience. 'Let's go to some comfortable retreat and relax for the night,' he told her. He knew better than to return to his old chamber in the monastery; they would be cleaning that out, considering him to be dead.

Lilah drew a circle on the trunk of a large oak tree, and opened a door there. Inside was a pleasant nook, with pillows. She drew him in and closed the door. He embraced her and fell asleep. Theoretically he no longer needed sleep, but he realized that there were psychological needs as well as physical ones, and his change of circumstance did not change that.

In the morning, emotionally restored, he decided to tackle the problem at the top. 'I have vanquished Lucifer; I should be able to back off the souls *he* vanquished,' he said.

'My Lord, You are as yet innocent in the ways of evil,' she cautioned him. 'It takes time to get fully into it. They have had many centuries. Do not brace them without possession of that spell.'

'But I can sing to them if I have to,' he reminded her. 'That conquered you and Charon.'

'I am a demoness. He is – ' She paused.

'Not a demon?' he prompted.

'Not exactly. But it occurred to me that his mother, Nox, who is an old acquaintance of mine, might know something.'

'Nox?'

'Night. She is the oldest of the deities of our pantheon,

the daughter of Chaos. She goes back before I do, which is pretty far. She married her brother Erebus, who is the Incarnation of the Darkness Between Earth and Hades, that region now parcelled out between Limbo and Purgatory. In addition to Charon they generated the Incarnations of Air, Day, Fate, Death, Retributions, Dreams and others I misremember at the moment. She –'

'The mother of the Incarnations?' he asked, amazed. 'But how, then, can they be offices?'

'Anything becomes boring after a time, unless constantly refreshed. I would be in a bad way if the Incarnation of Evil did not change periodically, bringing me new interest and challenge. The early Incarnations lost interest, so one by one they vacated, allowing mortals to step in and assume their positions as offices. I believe Nox is the only original Incarnation to retain her position, perhaps because of the everlasting fascination of the things she hides. If any immortal knows the secret of that spell, she might.'

Parry kept his hope restrained. 'Nox is an original immortal Incarnation, not a damned soul, but she might have learned it?'

'That's what I think. If the secret were ever uttered under cover of night, she would know it.'

'Well, let's go see her, then!'

'Not so fast, my Lord! I am not certain she would tell You if she did know, or what payment she would demand for it.'

'Payment?'

'The Kingdom of Evil does not flourish on altruism.'

Parry nodded. 'What payment do you think she might ask?'

'I must answer, my Lord, but I do not wish to. She is the one female who knows more of the ways of passion than I do. She is ageless, renewed at every turn of the world. If she found You appealing –'

208

Oh. 'Let's leave her as a last resort. If I stand to wash out, and you prefer to risk Nox rather than let me go, then we can go to her.'

'You are more generous to me than Lucifer was,' she said.

'Lucifer had a turn with Nox?'

'*Anyone* has a turn with Nox, if she desires it.'

'I will stay away from her. But I must tackle the problem of Hell regardless.' Parry got up, pushed open the porthole door, and climbed out of the tree.

It was day outside, and this turned out to be a park. A little boy gaped, then ran back to tell his mommy.

Lilah smiled, emerging and closing the panel. 'She will never believe him.' They moved on.

They bypassed the several Circles of Hell and went directly to the executive office. This was in a pavilion made of ice, set on a frozen lake in the deepest cavern of Hell. There was a huge throne on the ice which was empty: Lucifer's vacated headquarters. Parry had visited him in a different, warmer hall, evidently one reserved for minor audiences. Asmodeus' office was to the right of this.

Obviously Parry's entry had been anticipated, because the office was clear except for Asmodeus. He had wings and horns and a barbed tail: his semblance for this duty.

'You know who I am,' Parry said. 'You knew it was me when you directed the rain of fire.'

'I know thou art a pretender to the throne of one whose spittle thou art not worthy to wipe off thy face,' Asmodeus said evenly. 'Come here at last to the Circle of Traitors, fittingly enough.'

'I vanquished Lucifer!' Parry retorted. 'Now his office is mine, and you are bound to serve me.'

'Thou hast taken advantage of freak luck during Lucifer's carelessness. Now we have to put up with thy

209

posturing for a month until thou receivest thy just desserts. Begone, impostor, before I chastise thee!'

'This is mutiny!' Parry exclaimed. 'You know the penalty for that!'

'Get thee out of my sight, impostor – and that whore who aids thee!' Asmodeus gestured – and a cloud of energy surrounded Parry and Lilah. They were swept up and carried away.

In a moment the cloud dissipated. Parry found himself in a gloomy forest. 'I was afraid of this,' Lilah muttered. 'This is the Seventh Circle.'

'But that was where the River of Blood was, and the rain of fire.'

'First and third rings of it. This is the second ring, which we bypassed before. This is the Wood of the Suicides.'

Parry paused. 'What's so bad about this?'

'Those,' she said, pointing.

From a distance charged a pack of vicious-looking dogs, slaver dripping from their maws as they bayed. 'The Hounds of Hell,' he said, understanding. 'But we can escape them readily enough by climbing one of these trees.'

'And those,' she said, pointing up.

He looked, and saw a bevy of foul creatures perched on high limbs. They had the bodies and wings of gross birds, but the heads and breasts of old women. 'Harpies,' he said, understanding. 'We are caught between the two horrors.'

'As are the suicides, perpetually torn apart no matter where they try to hide,' she said.

'So Asmodeus sent us here, implying that we committed suicide by broaching him.'

'Or as an experiment. If you cannot escape this, then you pose no threat to him.'

Parry realized that it was a fair test. Asmodeus' magic should not be able to overcome the Master of Hell. Only

Parry's unfamiliarity with the ways of his office made him vulnerable. 'But both groups are demons. I can sing them into quiescence.'

'I'm not sure – ' she started.

But Parry was already opening his mouth. He began to sing – and immediately the harpies burst into raucous song of their own, drowning him out.

The Hellhounds coursed on in, their baying no longer audible. They could not hear his song, so were not pacified, and the same was true for the harpies. What a neat trap!

They leapt for the trees. Lilah ordinarily could float or fly when she chose, but evidently here in Hell she was confined to mundane motion. Perhaps Asmodeus had restricted her, so that she could no longer open a tunnel out.

The trees were easy to climb, having huge, gnarly low limbs. But immediately the dirty birds fluttered down, screeching continuously, extending their talons.

Parry found a small dead branch. He broke it off and wielded it as a club, striking at the first harpy to come at him. But the club passed through her body without resistance; she was a phantom.

Then her claws clamped on his arm, and they were like steel. He was no phantom to *her*!

It was the one-sided situation he had encountered before: the creatures of Hell could strike at him, but he could not retaliate against them. That must be standard in Hell, so that the damned souls could be continuously harried by all manner of horrors without having any chance to resist or to strike back. It hardly seemed fair – but Hell was hardly the place for fairness!

He lifted his arm to shake her off, but she clung, coloured spittle spraying from her foul mouth as she screeched, her dugs bouncing as she flapped her wings. Every drop of spittle that touched him burned. He could

211

not get free, and the next was closing on him. Lilah seemed no better off.

Something clicked in Parry's mind. If he could not shake her off, then she was anchored to him – by her claws. He could not touch her directly, but he could affect her.

He lifted his arm, and her with it. Then, as the second swooped in, he swung his arm violently at her.

The first harpy smashed into the second. Both squawked and fell out of the air. Parry was free, for the moment.

But more were hovering close, and they had seen what had happened. Now they swooped down, slashing rather than grabbing. Parry tried to dodge, but he almost fell out of the tree. He had to hang on lest he drop into the mass of hounds that leapt at the trunk immediately below him.

A talon slashed his hand. It was sword-sharp, and evidently some of the poison spittle was on it because his hand flared with pain. He was out of options.

Except – what about magic? He was after all a sorcerer. His song had worked in Hell because of its magic; perhaps his other magic would also be effective.

He crafted a hasty illusion about himself: a huge, glowering bear. The bear swiped at the nearest harpy, growling villainously. She spooked, flying clumsily back.

But in a moment they realized that it was unreal, and charged in again. However, Parry had not wasted his brief reprieve; he was busy crafting other illusions. He made three imitation harpies, who flapped down to buzz the hounds. He also made a hound, who leapt up and caught one of the illusory harpies in his teeth, biting through her wing, then chomping her neck as she flopped realistically on the ground. In a moment her gore was splattered all over; it was a most realistic illusion, and he was rather proud of it.

The hovering harpies, seeing this, reacted with understandable fury. They forgot Parry and swooped down on the hounds, clawing at them. Naturally they thought that the hounds had turned on them, and so they struck back. That aroused the hounds, and soon the battle between them was fairly raging.

Parry was forgotten. He joined Lilah in the tree, then crafted a spell of undetectability for them both. His magic was working perfectly, even if hers wasn't.

That made sense, in retrospect. She was a demoness, subject to the power of the rulers of Hell; he was not even a damned soul, but a living Incarnation. None of his powers had been stripped from him. Asmodeus had done to him what he had done to the harpies: deceived him with illusion. Now he had penetrated it, and escaped the trap.

'Make an exit,' he told Lilah as they walked away from the carnage.

'But my power has been stripped, my Lord,' she protested.

'Mine has not,' he said gruffly. 'I am the true Master of Hell; you may do what I tell you. Your powers are restored. Make an exit.'

She circled with her hand, and the porthole manifested. She drew it open, and they went through.

They were silent as they made their way to the surface, but Parry was conscious of her glances. He had just taken a giant step towards the realization of his powers as the Incarnation, and she respected this.

But all he had done was escape the mischief of Asmodeus. That was a far cry from assuming the true overlordship of Hell! He had to have that spell – and how was he to get it?

'My Lord,' Lilah said as they stood in daylight again. 'I have been foolish to let you suffer such mischief, when the answer may be at hand. I will take you to Nox.'

He nodded. That did seem best.

10

Incarnations

Lilah, wary of the impending interview with Nox, insisted on making love by day. Parry wasn't sure whether this was her effort to deplete his interest in the Incarnation of Night, or from concern that this might be the last time. He had no intention of straying, but his curiosity was increasing.

Of course, he had had no intention of straying from Jolie, either. He still loved the memory of Jolie, but she was gone, and he was now too far corrupted by evil to be worthy of her, so that was done. But if he ever found a way to free her from the drop of blood and allow her to proceed to Heaven, he would do it gladly. Certainly he would not let her be confined to Hell!

Nox lived in Purgatory, where it seemed most of the Incarnations resided. In fact, Parry himself had a residence there, a palatial structure served by unassigned servants: those who were in such balance at death that they had gone neither to Heaven nor to Hell. The surprise with which his arrival was greeted showed that the Incarnation of Evil had seldom stopped by. Indeed, he did not stay long; he moved on to the realm of Nox.

This turned out to be a region of everlasting night. Not a dark cloud, for there was no smoke or fog; a section in which the light faded and the stars shone down, no matter what the time of day. The residence was like a ghostly nebula, a segment of the great Milky Way, glowing yet indeterminate.

Lilah guided him on in with confidence. Inside, they seemed to be floating through the heavens, becoming ghosts themselves.

«A greeting» It was neither voice nor thought, but rather like a memory from a dream.

'Nox, I embrace you,' Lilah said, spreading her arms. Indeed, she seemed to be in contact with something, but Parry could not tell what.

«What is thy business, mine ancient sister?»

Parry started. Sister?

'This is Parry, who just assumed the Office of Evil,' Lilah explained. 'He does not yet understand.'

The darkness intensified, becoming opaque. Now the form of a lovely woman in a cloak stood before him. Her eyes were stars, twinkling as they gazed on him. «You feel for him, Lil?»

'I do. He comes to ask a favour.'

The woman-shape opened her cloak and moved into him. Parry found himself embraced by something at once too diffuse and subtle to comprehend, and unutterably feminine. Something like a kiss caressed his mouth, and something like breasts touched his chest, and things very like seductive legs came up against his as though he wore no clothing. The femaleness of her overwhelmed him, making him react, inciting his desire; suddenly there was no other thing he wanted to do, now or ever, except embrace her as intimately as was inhumanly possible. His mission here had no meaning; there was only Nox, the Goddess of Night. He had never known a woman like her, neither mortal nor immortal; she was all he could ever dream of, the ultimate fulfilment.

Then she withdrew, leaving him longing, desperate with desire for her. He wanted to cry out to her, and could not; he wanted to reach out for her, and could not. She was ineffable, a thing that came only at her own behest, never his, and infinitely desirable because of it.

«I leave him to you, my sister» Nox sent. «He is special»

'I thank you, my sister,' Lilah said, visibly relieved.

Slowly Parry relaxed, as the sensation of the presence left him. He became conscious of his mission.

'We speak figuratively,' Lilah said to him. 'She is the oldest Incarnation; I am the oldest female creature. But she is a goddess, and I only a demoness. We are sisters in age and sex, not substance.'

Parry only nodded, not yet ready to speak. A goddess! No wonder he had been overwhelmed!

'He needs the spell to banish demons,' Lilah said.

«Surely he does . . . I do not have it.»

Disappointment. Parry could not be certain whether his anguish was because she could not help him, or because he would now have to leave her presence.

«Perhaps Chronos.»

'We thank you, Nox,' Lilah said. 'We shall ask him first.'

«Last.»

Lilah smiled. 'Of course. That's what I meant.'

They moved out of the darkness, departing the intoxicating presence. 'She let you go!' Lilah breathed, as if amazed.

Parry didn't want to say that he would have preferred to have been kept by the goddess. But Lilah knew it. 'She has that effect on men,' she said. 'It will wear off, in time. You can now appreciate why I was worried.'

'The allure of the night,' Parry said, speaking at last.

'All the things your kind longs for in the secrecy of darkness,' she agreed. 'No mortal or demon woman can match that.'

He could only sigh acquiescence. It would be a long time before he forgot that sensation!

'Now we have to ask the Incarnations, who will laugh.'

'Why ask them at all, then? If Chronos is the one – '

'Because we must tell him he is our last resort. If you succeed in holding the Office, your friendship with him

216

should count for something. Chronos is not like the others.'

'I don't understand.'

'Chronos lives backwards.'

'I don't see how –'

'Come on,' she said impatiently. 'We might as well tackle Thanatos first.'

'Thanatos – Death!' he exclaimed. 'I met him, long ago!'

'Not since I have known you.'

'It was when Jolie died, over forty years ago. She was in balance, because of the evil associated with her manner of dying, though she had lived a righteous life. I must ask him about that.'

'Ask,' she agreed.

He saw that they were at Death's Mansion. He knocked at the imposing door, and a sepulchral gong sounded within. In a moment a servant opened it.

'I am the Incarnation of Evil, come to seek information of the Incarnation of Death,' Parry said.

The servant closed the door in his face.

Parry stood there, outraged. 'Since when does one Incarnation refuse even to talk to another?' he demanded rhetorically.

'Since the other Incarnation is Evil,' Lilah answered with a wry smile.

'He wasn't this way forty years ago!'

'You were not Evil forty years ago.'

Parry grimaced. 'Still, the least he could do is talk to me. I am simply trying to find a way to do my job.'

'All the others side with God.'

Disgruntled, Parry departed. 'I will not forget this snub,' he muttered.

They followed a twisted path that led shortly to the abode of Fate. It resembled a giant spider web. 'Fate

217

assumes the form of a spider, and slides her threads to her destination,' Lilah explained.

But Fate, too, refused even to meet him. Parry's mood darkened further.

They approached the Castle of War. This time the Incarnation himself came out to meet him. He was a crusader. 'Begone, foul fiend!' War cried, brandishing his great red sword. 'Ere I cut off thy hideous head!'

'I only want to ask – '

Parry had to duck, for already the sword was swishing at his neck. So much for talk!

'These idiots are really asking for it!' he said as they departed. 'I have come in peace, but – '

'What do you expect, from the Incarnation of War?' Lilah asked.

At that he had to smile. 'Still, it ill behooves such powerful entities to operate with their minds closed,' he said. 'Even countries at war negotiate on occasion with their enemies. Otherwise there is chaos.'

'Crusaders have never been known for their common sense.'

At that he had to laugh. 'True words, demoness!'

Now they approached the treelike residence of Nature, perhaps the strongest of the regular Incarnations.

There was no door, just a thicket of brambles. He tried to make his way through it, but the prickles and thorns and nettles seemed to orient eagerly on his flesh. He might be immortal now: indeed, he had forgotten to eat since his ascension, without suffering any hunger or loss of vigour. But he felt exactly as he had in life, and the pain was just as uncomfortable. He surely could plough through this barrier, and the only harm done would be the immediate pain – but to what point? There had to be a legitimate entrance.

'It is her way,' Lilah murmured. 'The secrets of Nature

are not readily discovered, but they are generally worthwhile.'

'I shall play it her way, this time,' Parry said. But privately he expected little; this was merely a gesture of amity, his straightforward effort to make contact with the other Incarnations. So far they had not even done him the courtesy of listening to his plea. In short, they were keeping him at arm's length, evidently hoping he would wash out.

They walked around the brambly region, seeking a path through. They came to a filthy sty where a huge sow wallowed. Beyond it the brambles grew up even worse, becoming truly impenetrable. This was a dead end.

The pig raised her snout. 'Looking for something?' she inquired.

Gaea's sense of humour, evidently. But he replied with a straight face. 'I am looking for an entrance to Gaea's estate, so that I may talk with her.'

'Kiss my snout,' the pig said.

Only his determination to maintain control of his temper kept Parry from showing his anger at being addressed in such manner by a pig. He turned away.

'And I will show you the way in,' the pig concluded.

He glanced at Lilah, and caught a fleeting smirk on her face. Of course he was not going to kiss a pig!

But if that was what Gaea believed . . . why not call her bluff.

Parry set himself, then leaned over the rail. The sow raised her head. Her nose was smeared with mud and garbage from her last meal. He stifled his rising gorge and kissed her snout.

'That way,' the pig said, indicating a huge hole she had dug under the fence at the far side of the sty. It was so deep that its recesses were lost in darkness.

Parry climbed over the fence, slogged through the muck and got down on his hands and knees. He crawled into

219

the hole. Lilah shrugged and followed. She had surely experienced worse than a little muck in the course of her centuries of service to the Incarnations of Evil.

The hole descended, but was not totally dark. He could see the circular cross section of it, and the route ahead. Tree roots braced the top and sides; fish heads and wilted carrot tops lay at the bottom. He had no clearance, so ploughed through it all. The smell was intense.

The garbage at the bottom thickened. Now it was a virtual pool, containing oyster shells, mouldy bread crusts, cheese rinds, spoiled wine, chicken legs and rotten tubers. 'You mortals are messy folk,' Lilah muttered behind him.

On it went, getting worse. The liquid appeared to have become urine, and faeces floated in it. Lumps of brownish substance bobbled, perhaps blood clots. Sections seemed mostly like vomit. His hand, questing for a firm bottom, found something solid but loose. He brought it up – and it was a severed human foot.

But he ploughed on, determined not to be defeated by Gaea's evident discouragements. Just about the time the sewer threatened to fill the passage, it debouched into a nether river, and he was able to stand in a gloomy cavern. They had made it through.

Both of them were sopping and stinking; their clothing dripped. Parry knew he could clean himself magically, but was too ornery to do it yet; he wanted to be sure he had completed the wretched course first.

A path showed the way on. They followed it – until it halted in a cul-de-sac. A blind cave.

No, this cave was artificial. There were ridges in the stone showing where the rock had been hewn away. It should not have been carved, unless there was a continuation.

'Very well,' Parry said loudly. 'What next?'

'I have seen this sort of thing before,' Lilah said. 'It probably requires a spell to open the rest.'

Parry tried a spell, but knew immediately that it wasn't working; his magic was being damped out. It was evident that each Incarnation was supreme in his or her own bailiwick; others could not use magic without the proprietor's consent.

'Maybe if you just asked,' Lilah said.

'I am the Incarnation of Evil,' he said. 'I ask to proceed on through this passage, so that I may talk to the Incarnation of Nature.'

There was no response.

'Gaea is evidently trying to humiliate you,' Lilah said. 'Maybe she requires an obsequious request.'

Parry gritted his teeth. 'This is the Incarnation of Evil. I ask to be admitted to Gaea's presence.'

Still no response.

'I beg to be admitted,' Parry said.

Silence.

His jaw clenched. 'I am the Lord of Faeces, the lowest of the low, humbly begging the indulgence of my betters,' he said.

The stone slid aside. Gaea was satisfied.

But not quite. 'No person may be admitted to the presence without a search for weapons or hostile substances,' a voice said from a curtained alcove.

'A body search?' Parry asked, outraged. Then he realized that Gaea was getting to him. He had come this far; he might as well do the rest.

He entered the curtained alcove. It was completely dark within. Hands touched him, catching at his clothing, removing it. Parry submitted to this, knowing that weapons could most readily be concealed in clothing.

Then the hands slid down his body, checking every part of it. Then –

He jumped. 'What – ?'

'A weapon may be concealed in a body cavity,' the voice said. 'Bend over.'

Quivering with rage at this demand, Parry bent over. A rough finger poked into him, questing for the weapon Gaea had to know wasn't there.

Abruptly there was light. For a moment it blinded him. Then he heard laughter.

He gazed around, blinking. He was in a glass compartment. Outside it were standing the other Incarnations: Death, Fate, War and Nature. All were staring at him with broad smiles.

He was naked, bent over, with that crudely exploring hand still violating his body. He looked back – and saw that it was an ape. He had been demeaned by an animal, in full view of the Incarnations. What a joke they had had, at his expense!

Still he controlled his rage. Now was not the occasion to make a scene that would only make the joke richer.

He straightened and stepped away from the ape with what dignity he could muster. 'Now will you talk to me, Gaea?'

'No,' she replied. The light ceased, and he was left as he was.

Lilah came to him. 'I was afraid of something like this,' she murmured. 'All the Incarnations of Evil learned early not to try to cooperate with the others.'

'Let's just make our way out of here,' he said with surprising calmness. He led the way back through the gruesome tunnel. The Incarnations had had their fun with him, instead of meeting him honourably. This was their day. But they would pay for it. Oh, yes, they would pay!

It was another two days before he went to tackle Chronos. Lilah took him to her nest in the tree, because he wanted nothing to do with Purgatory now. He had come to understand all too well why Lucifer had ignored the

Mansion of Evil there. He was better off in Hell, where he belonged.

Except that he had not yet proven his ability to control it. The Incarnations, actually, had not treated him worse than Asmodeus had. They were all against him.

'Except me,' Lilah said, divining his thoughts. 'I am absolutely loyal to You, my Lord, and will always be, until You cast me off.'

'I will never cast you off,' he said, embracing her. Demoness she might be, but she seemed better than the mortal Incarnations now.

'Oh, You will, my Lord, eventually. It always happens. But it can be close while it lasts.'

'It will last for centuries!' he said passionately.

'It can – if it lasts out the month,' she agreed.

Sound point. He made love to her, seeking that intimacy no mortal woman could give him any more, and tried to allay his own doubt about his chances of success.

Chronos' mansion was less pretentious than some, but it had its weird aspect, Lilah warned him. 'It goes backwards, as does his life,' she explained. 'You will emerge from it before you enter it. Never forget that, lest there be paradox.'

'Before I enter it? That's impossible!'

'Believe it, my Lord! Make allowance, lest you interfere with yourself.'

'Lilah, I know this is not the normal realm. But nothing will make me believe that – '

He broke off, for there, emerging from the door of the mansion, was himself, trailed by a duplicate demoness of stunning proportions.

The other Parry waved, and so did the other Lilah. Stunned, Parry waved back. Then the other two turned aside, and disappeared down an alternative path.

'As you were saying . . .' Lilah said, a trifle smugly.

'Illusion,' he decided. But he did not take a step towards the door.

'It is really not complicated,' she assured him. 'When you share his backward travel, you come out earlier. When he is outside his mansion, he has to reverse himself in order to interact with others. He remembers what is in our future, and has not yet experienced what is in our past. It must be hard for him. On occasion, centuries ago, I – '

'You have been with him, too?' Parry asked, dismayed.

'My Lord, I have been with every man worth being with, and quite a number otherwise. When my masters tired of me, I would stray, for I have needs unlike those of real women. I have never deceived You in this, or in anything. I am Yours now, and for as long as You desire me.'

'Sorry, Lilah. My mortal instincts keep getting the better of me. But if you have – with this man – '

'Once with this one, not long ago. He was especially lonely, and it seemed to be important to him, and my Lord Lucifer was having his fling with – well, never mind. Once I came to love You, I have been true to You, my Lord. In the past I have been with a prior officeholder, this one's successor. With several successors, actually. Chronos is a lonely Incarnation; it is almost impossible for him to have a meaningful relationship with a normal woman.'

'But if you have always served Evil – '

'Good and Evil are not invariable antagonists. They are merely opposite poles of a spread of states. The one cannot exist without the other. All Incarnations are the enemy of Chaos, Nox's sire, and when cooperation is required to prevent Chaos's return, Incarnations cooperate. It is not to Your interest to quarrel with Chronos; remember, he could change your past life with barely an effort.'

'I have not sought to quarrel with any of the Incarnations!' he exclaimed. 'But they have quarrelled with me! Except for Nox . . . and if she is the daughter of the true enemy, why didn't she do something to me?'

'No one quite understands Nox,' she said. 'She is her own creature. Perhaps she finds the current panoply more interesting.'

Parry squared his shoulders. 'We had better get on with it. I hope Chronos helps me.'

'He was the only major earthly Incarnation not present at Gaea's outrage,' she said. 'That could be because he failed to get the news, being on the other side of events, but I prefer to think it is because he respects You.'

'He doesn't even know me!'

'You forget, he could have known you for decades hence.'

Parry sighed. 'I did forget. This may be tricky.'

'Nox did say Chronos would help,' she reminded him.

Nox. Parry found himself being swept back into his memory of that experience. The stuff of dreams!

Lilah jogged him back to the present. 'I know that look on a man's face. Keep her out of Your mind, my Lord, or You are lost before You begin.'

Good advice! They went up to the door and knocked.

The Incarnation of Time himself opened it. He was a man of about Parry's age, with portly figure and grey hair. His suit appeared somewhat out of style, but not archaic; Parry realized that it probably would come into style in a later decade. The man lived backward; he had to keep that in mind!

Chronos took his hand. 'You told me you would be calling, Satan,' he said warmly. 'I am sorry only that our acquaintance must end now.'

'We – have had a long acquaintance?' Parry asked cautiously, hardly daring to rely on the significance of such a statement.

225

'Certainly!' Chronos agreed heartily. 'You have always been kind to me, Satan, and I am not unmindful of past favours. You told me that you would have something important to ask me at this point, and certainly I shall answer to the best of my ability.'

This was almost too easy! Parry hesitated to broach his question, as yet uncertain of the implications. If Chronos had known him long, then he must have survived the trial period and become the regular Incarnation of Evil. Must have maintained the name Satan. Could he trust that?

'And Lilah, you darling creature!' Chronos said, stepping up to embrace her warmly. She, too, seemed uncertain.

'Chronos, remember that this is new to us at the moment,' Parry said. 'We do not know what kind of relationship we shall be having with you. I should advise you that the other Incarnations – '

'Yes, that is awkward,' Chronos said quickly. 'I must not say too much, of course. But I can tell you that you and Lilah have always been true friends to me, for the entire thirty years I have held this office, though of course never intimate in the other sense.' He glanced again at Lilah. 'Not that I could not have wished otherwise, no affront intended.'

Lilah smiled. 'Perhaps, in three or four years, if you are in need, I will come to you one time.' She glanced significantly at Parry, and her prior remarks to him fell into place. She had rewarded Chronos in the past for the favour Chronos was about to do now for Parry. She had not known it at the time, but the retrospective rationale seemed apt. Parry found he could not quite manage to be jealous of it; it was after all a special situation.

Even so, he could not stop himself from wondering which particular time that she had been absent from him she had done it. She had seemed wholly devoted to his corruption; why had she gone visiting with Chronos?

'You will be welcome, Lilah,' Chronos said. It was evident that he understood her nature perfectly, and accepted it. 'I will let you know, if such need occurs.' And there was the answer; Chronos had asked for her, and she, knowing his nature, had elected to cooperate rather than question it. Now Parry was glad she had.

Chronos returned his attention to Parry. 'But I would help you regardless, my friend. What is it you require?'

'The secret of the spell to banish demons,' Parry said.

Chronos pursed his lips. 'That, I regret, I do not know. Neither you nor any other creature has vouchsafed that information to me.'

The disappointment was keen. 'Nox said you might – ' Parry shrugged. 'I just assumed you knew.'

'Nox.' Chronos smiled reminiscently. 'Now there is a creature to conjure with, if I may be excused the notion. She thought I knew it?'

'She said to ask you, and that you might help.'

'Indeed I would help if I could.' Chronos paced the floor. 'Almost, I think, once long ago, you made reference – I thought it of no significance – to – to, let me think now. No, it was something I read in a book left by my predecessor. Let me see.' He hurried from the room.

'A book from the future?' Parry asked, bemused.

Chronos returned, carrying an ornate volume. '*The Collected Edition of the Poetical Works of Percy Bysshe Shelley,*' he announced. 'Eighteen-thirty-nine.'

'What?' Parry thought he had misheard.

'An English poet, as I understand it. Before my time, of course, and after yours. One of my predecessors may have brought the volume to this house and forgotten it. So it remains, becoming further anachronistic each year. There are some fascinating references I don't pretend to comprehend! But my point is, there is a note in the margin of one of the – ah, here it is! The poem "Death" – '

'Thanatos?' Parry asked, not liking this. His respect for the Incarnation of Death had been rudely downgraded recently.

'No, I am in error. It is the sonnet "Ozymandias". See, here is the note: "He knows the secret." I do not know what that can mean, but perhaps it relates.' He brought the open book and showed it to Parry.

Parry stared at the page. 'The calligraphy!' he exclaimed. 'How could the human hand be so precise? Every letter is the same, and tiny!'

'And the pages!' Lilah added, as intrigued. 'Tens, hundreds of them, bound together by one side! What scribe managed that?'

Chronos shook his head. 'Evidently they had ways, in the nineteenth century. That is after all six hundred years from here. Their magicians must have rare competence. It never occurred to me to wonder about it, before.'

The three of them gazed in wonder at the volume for a moment more. Than Parry read the scrawled note, and the poem to which it attached, piecing out the strange lettering in English, not his best language. '"My name is Ozymandias, king of kings:/Look on my works, ye Mighty, and despair!"' He looked up. 'But nothing beside remains, it says; only bare sand.'

Lilah laughed. 'All his works had been forgotten! So much for his arrogance! I remember him, but did not realize that anyone else did.'

Both Chronos and Parry looked at her, surprised. 'You knew Ozymandias?' Parry asked.

'Of course. He was quite a figure in his heyday! I – I explained about that, my Lord.'

She had been with even this long-forgotten historical king! Parry was too amazed to be jealous, this time.

'Do you think he might know the secret you require?' Chronos asked. 'Surely there was reason to make that note.'

'He just might,' Lilah said. 'He was no scholar himself, but he had pride. He wanted to have the best in everything, so he had a battery of scholars of every discipline, and the finest sorcerers. If there was an important secret to divine, he had the means to divine it.'

'But if he died so long ago that all his works have perished and been forgotten, we can hardly ask him,' Parry said.

'Oh, there is no problem about that,' she said brightly. 'He's in Hell now, of course.'

Parry exchanged glances with Chronos. Ozymandias was available!

Suddenly Parry was eager to be on his way. 'I thank you, Chronos!' he said. 'You may have provided me with what I need!'

'I certainly hope so, old friend.' Chronos extended his hand, and Parry took it warmly. He knew he would visit this man again; already he liked the Incarnation of Time. Perhaps the two of them were alike in their isolation, so found camaraderie together while the other Incarnations ignored them.

They stepped outside. There were the prior Parry and Lilah approaching. Parry waved, startling his other self. 'He'll figure it out,' he said, and turned down an alternate path.

Lilah knew where to look for Ozymandias: in the dread Ninth Circle, reserved for traitors. 'He gained his power by murdering his kindred,' she said. 'He usurped the throne, then went on to betray his benefactors, his friends and finally his country, exploiting all its resources for his own aggrandizement. He was an apt ruler, actually, because of his ruthlessness; his empire was the most powerful of those that have been forgotten. I think he angered Fate by his presumption, so she arranged to have his legacy lost after he died. So now he suffers the humiliation of being a nonentity, in addition to the tortures of Hell. It will be nice to see him again.'

Not too nice, Parry hoped. Her complete honesty was somewhat wearing at times.

They returned to the lowest level of Hell, which was frozen over, an indication of its timelessness. Now Lilah peered at the faces of the figures frozen under the ice. 'Hello, Brutus,' she said brightly.

'You knew Brutus – the Roman?' Parry asked, hardly pleased.

'Of course. And Caesar, whom he betrayed. Caesar was really something – every woman's man and every man's woman. I had to change forms back and forth to keep him entertained. I remember the time when I – '

'Never mind,' Parry said harshly. Now he was getting a notion where she had learned some of her more exotic sexual techniques. 'We're not looking for Caesar.'

'And here's Judas,' she said. 'He was the disciple of Jesus Christ, who – '

'Him, too?' Parry asked, appalled anew.

'Of course. Who do you think corrupted him? Beelzebub was very pleased. He – '

'Enough! Just find Ozymandias!'

'Here he is,' she said, stopping over the face of a perpetually sneering man.

Parry peered down. 'But he's frozen! How can I talk to him?'

'I can thaw him,' she said confidently. 'But you may not like the manner of it.'

'I don't care about the manner! Just so long as he'll talk to me.'

'Remember, he is history's most arrogant man. You will have to approach him appropriately.'

'I'll sing him a song,' Parry said shortly.

'That would do it,' she agreed.

She walked across the ice, her outfit modifying as she

moved. It became an ornate dress, with supportive petticoats and a tightly laced bodice. Sparkling earrings appeared, and a shining tiara for her hair. She looked like a princess.

She came to stand directly above Ozymandias, her legs moderately spread. Now Parry realized that the frozen man was gazing up. He appreciated why she had said he would not like this: she was standing so that the ancient King could see up under her dress.

Then she began to dance. She remained in place, moving her body suggestively but travelling no distance. Her hips swivelled, her bosom bounced, her ankles flashed and her long hair swirled about her body. Parry wished he could take her this instant to the nest in the tree trunk.

Ozymandias had a better view. Now Parry saw the eyeballs move, following the play of those legs. The ice had melted in that region!

As the suggestive dance continued, the melting became more evident. The King was heating up, forming a pool around him. No wonder; the same thing was happening, to a lesser degree, elsewhere in the frozen lake. Any man who could get a refractive view of Lilah's dance was responding. It was a dance that could not be denied.

As the ice melted, Lilah had to move to the side, lest she sink in the slush. She did so, but continued to circle the submerged King, lifting her petticoats so that he could still see her legs.

Parry found himself standing in a puddle. His own heat was doing it. What a dance!

Finally the King floated to the surface of the pool formed around him. His head cleared the water.

Now Lilah desisted, her laced bosom heaving prettily. 'O King of the Ages,' she said. 'I have brought one to talk with you.'

The King replied in a foreign language, but Parry

understood him. Here in Hell, all language was common, no matter what its origin. 'After I enjoy thee, luscious handmaiden of my youth!' Ozymandias replied, scrambling out of the pool.

'Yours, my Lord,' Lilah called to Parry, stepping back. 'Unless you prefer to wait?'

Parry had to laugh. If he waited, he would shortly have the sight of the King having his will of the demoness. He could hardly blame the King for trying, but he did not intend to watch.

He took just a moment to organize his thoughts, then sang, adapting his approach to appeal to the vanity of the King. He was gambling that the arrogance of Ozymandias was greater than his sexual drive, despite the superlative provocation Lilah had provided. He formed impromptu verses, their meter and rhyme falling into place in the language of the King, though not in his own.

> O King Ozymandias, hark unto me!
> I come as a supplicant to ask a favour of you.
> You have a secret I need, that no other will provide.
> Listen to me, O greatest of Kings!

Ozymandias paused in his pursuit of the demoness. The flattery of old was registering. 'Make it quick, supplicant, for I have pressing business with the temptress of old.'

Parry did not attempt to talk normally, knowing that that would not hold the King's attention. Song was his strength and his weapon; it was the only effective tool he had for this occasion.

> Great King Ozymandias, hark unto me!
> I have heard that your power was the greatest known.
> That the mighty looked on your works, and
>   despaired.
> Surely you alone of mortals can help me.

> Great King, I know your power extended to
> knowledge too;
> That there was no thing you could not know
> If it was your desire to know.
> You were the Lord of all lands and all information!

Ozymandias turned his head to look directly at him, impressed by his accuracy. 'Out with it, supplicant!' he snapped. 'I have heard not the like of your voice since the Llano! Ask your boon. Perhaps I will grant it.'

> Great King, I need to know the secret,
> The secret of the spell to banish demons.
> You alone of mortals –

He was interrupted by the King's laughter. 'You ask too much, supplicant! No one can help you there.'

Parry realized that he would have to increase the offering. Ozymandias evidently could help him, if he chose. But what was there to give, except the praise he had already expended? He wracked his mind for what would move the King, knowing that his time was very short. Already the ice was reforming, and if Lilah had to dance again to melt it –

Then Lilah was at his elbow. 'The sonnet,' she said.

The sonnet? That had identified Ozymandias, but it would not even be written for several hundred years. What good was that?

'It is the only record of his greatness,' she said.

Then he understood. That was, indeed, the final appeal.

> Hark unto me, O King of the Ages!
> Fate conspired against you in your decease
> Wiping out the record of your greatness.
> I can guarantee that your name will be immortalized
> in poetry –

That recovered the King's attention. 'My reputation restored? Written in literature never to be extinguished?'

233

Now it was safe to talk naturally. 'In a poem that will exist at least through the nineteenth century, perhaps far longer, telling of your memorial and your final words.'

Ozymandias considered. 'This may be illusion, but better than naught. What power have ye to honour it?'

'I will be the Incarnation of Evil.'

The King nodded. 'That will do. Very well, I will share with you the secret. But you will not find it easy.'

The King himself was not finding it easy. Deprived of Lilah's stimulation, he was sinking back into the thickening pool. 'I will do what I must to maintain my power. You understand that sort of thing, Greatest of Kings.'

'I do indeed!' Ozymandias was now waist deep. He glanced around, to be sure that no one else close enough to hear. 'The secret, O innocent supplicant, is that there is no secret. No such spell exists; demons cannot be banished by mortals.'

'But –'

'That is the truth!' Ozymandias said as his body slid down. 'Make of it what you will!' Now only his head was in the air. 'Look on my words, ye mighty, and despair!' He disappeared beneath the surface. The last thing to go was his grim grin. He was enjoying the humour of the situation.

Parry stared after him, stunned. He had no doubt that the man had told the truth, and gained sinister pleasure from it. But what a disaster that truth was!

Lilah approached. 'He gave you the secret?' she asked.

'He did,' Parry agreed ruefully.

'Now you can govern Hell!'

'Now I can govern Hell,' he agreed ironically. Now he understood why the prior masters of Hell never revealed the secret: it would have destroyed their power. Their power had been based on illusion.

Yet it had worked. They *had* governed!

If they had done it, so could he! All it required was

bluff and deceit. If he could pull that off, in the manner they had, he would survive.

He marched across the ice, towards the office of Asmodeus. Lilah, excited, accompanied him. 'Are you going to destroy him, my Lord?'

'That depends,' Parry said grimly.

Asmodeus was there. 'So thou didst get free, impostor!' he said. 'And thou hast the temerity to return here! Well, this time I shall banish thee to a less comfortable region!'

'You do that, fishface,' Parry said. 'You have no power over Me.' He used the self-capitalization consciously, knowing that it was expected of the true Master of Hell.

Asmodeus snapped his fingers. Magic crackled – but Parry was unmoved. 'I am the Incarnation of Evil,' he said. 'You are a subordinate. You cannot banish Me, because I now have the secret. Accept My authority, or I shall demonstrate it on you. I am to be titled Satan, Lord of all these demesnes.'

Asmodeus considered. He knew that Parry had interviewed Ozymandias, and that this was a legitimate source. The denizens of Hell would accept its validity. It was evident that Lilah already did. On the other hand, if Parry were denied the power he claimed, he could reveal the secret to all, and no Incarnation of Evil would thereafter be able to exercise proper power. Furthermore, it would be known that all the prior Incarnations, Asmodeus himself included, had been bluffing throughout. Demons only puffed into nonexistence because they were convinced that the Lord of Hell had the power to destroy them. They were the ultimate victims of Hell's greatest illusion.

Parry lifted his hand, his fingers poised to snap. At that snap, Asmodeus would have either to vanish or to demonstrate that the power was invalid. This was the key trial.

'I have a soul, as all Incarnations have,' Asmodeus said. 'Thou canst not destroy me.'

'Granted,' Parry said. 'But I can destroy all who serve you, and replace them with My own minions. You may know the spell, but you are no longer the Incarnation. *I* am, and the ultimate power is Mine. Deny it if you will.'

And Asmodeus, his bluff called, capitulated. 'The ultimate power is Thine, Satan. Leave me mine office, as Thy predecessor did, and I will serve Thee as I did him.'

Victory! 'Remain,' Parry said curtly. 'I will reassign officers under your authority, as long as you serve Me well and loyally. Hell shall be revamped along more efficient lines.'

'Hell shall be revamped,' Asmodeus agreed.

Parry turned his back. 'Come wench,' he said imperiously to Lilah. He conjured them both to the tree retreat, leaving behind a dissipating ball of fire. The magic was incidental, but the proper flair was not. As Satan, he intended to do things in style.

11
Plague

But as it happened, the revamping of Hell was not readily accomplished. It seemed that Lucifer had let things slide, and the various major figures had developed minor fiefdoms. Hell was vast in extent, and, despite the superficial arrangement in circles, not well organized. Parry discovered that he was in effect striking at a feather pillow; each piecemeal change he made only resulted in a superficial alteration in an unchanging base. He thought he was making progress, but after some time discovered that he really had not accomplished much. The bureaucracy of Hell balked him in its accommodating way.

'Damn it!' he swore one day in frustration.

'Already done,' Lilah murmured. She was at the moment in the guise of Helen of Troy, for his diversion. She was very good at diverting him, and he could not protest because after a day of getting nowhere with Hell he needed it. But he was spending increasing time in such diversion instead of accomplishing his job. The truth was that even that diversion was becoming jaded. Lilah assumed any of a thousand forms for his pleasure, including those of all the most ravishing women of history, and she did whatever he asked with dispatch. But he knew that it was the same old demoness beneath, and the challenge was absent. He was beginning to get tired of her, though naturally he would not say this. He was wary of the peril of losing her support.

'Did my predecessors have the same problem?'

'Of course, my Lord Satan,' she agreed. 'Each of them spent a century or so trying to remake Hell, and another century or so trying to come to terms with God. Then they settled gradually into funks, apart from occasional major projects. That was why Lucifer was so upset with You: You ruined his one significant ploy of the century.'

'The scourge,' Parry agreed. 'I understand his position better now.'

'The fact is, the situation seems largely unchanging, and not merely in Hell. Good is eternal, Evil is eternal, and Mortality is eternally fudging between the two. It is inevitably dull.'

She was in a position to know. No wonder the Incarnations of Evil eventually became careless; ennui set in, and it might have been almost a relief for them to lose their offices to their successors.

Yet he had not fared much better in the mortal world. The other Incarnations, except for Chronos and Nox, opposed him at every turn, seeming to take endless delight in this. As far as he could ascertain, they were not accomplishing more than he was; they were simply stirring their fingers in the pie and leaving it as messed up as before. Probably that was the way they staved off their own ennui. He had no respect for them, but they were canny, and he was unable to embarrass them the way they had him.

Of course he had opportunity when they changed officeholders. He had overlooked it on the first ones, and had not wished to do anything to the new Chronos, who had been his friend throughout his tenure. Then Chronos had been replaced by his predecessor, a thoroughly experienced Incarnation who was also friendly.

'How long have I been in office?' Parry asked suddenly, realizing that time had passed.

'Ninety-five years, my Lord Satan,' Lilah answered immediately.

'Ninety-five years!' he repeated, shocked. 'It seemed like only a few years!'

'It *is* only a few years. Not even a century.'

'I shall have to do something!'

238

'My Lord, you have been trying to!'

'No, I mean something substantial. It is time that Satan made his presence felt.'

'As you say, Master,' she said noncommittally.

She didn't believe he could do it. Angry, Parry cast about for some new approach.

He had two areas of potential impact: Hell and the mortal realm. His prior approaches had been effective in neither. What he needed was superior management. He had been trying to do it himself, and obviously he wasn't good at this. He had depended on Asmodeus, who obeyed his every command but somehow without much effect.

Maybe it was time to replace Asmodeus. But with whom? Mephistopheles would be no better, and he did not trust Lucifer.

Then he had a notion. 'Lilah, go thaw Ozymandias.'

'My Lord?' For once he had caught her by surprise.

'I'm going to put him in charge of Hell for a decade or so, and see how he does. He's a competent organizer, isn't he?'

'Indubitably, my Lord. But – '

'And he will serve me loyally, won't he?'

'In the circumstance, yes. But – '

'Then what's the problem?'

'He's a damned soul. Locked in the ice. You know how I have to thaw him. If he remains thawed, he will expect – '

'Um, yes. We'll have to assign a demoness to keep him warm. Whom would you recommend?'

'My Lord, he will know the difference. He will insist on me, personally. I know him; he always demands the best.'

Parry considered. 'The man has excellent taste. Well, then you keep him warm. I'll borrow another demoness. Or a damned soul. Nefertiti, perhaps. She could be fun.' He had encountered the damned Egyptian soul in the course of his efforts to reform Hell, and she had indicated a willingness to cooperate, in return for better treatment. She had certainly been in Hell long enough to know the nature of the cooperation that would be required.

Lilah stared at him, shifting back to her natural state. 'Are you dismissing me, my Lord?'

'By no means, Lilah! But we must be realistic. If I must do without your services for a time, I must have a replacement. It wouldn't do for the Lord of Evil to be without a consort, or to be known to be sharing one. Or to accept a substitute from the bottom of the heap. Protocol requires only the best, which is of course you, or one of the second best, such as Nefertiti. When Ozymandias tires of you, you may return to me, no questions asked.'

'You are generous, my Lord Satan,' she said with irony. She seemed to be not completely impressed with his elegant rationale.

Parry scowled. 'Lilah, I want to get moving. I'm tired of this stasis! If you have a better way, tell me!'

'I would not presume, my Lord,' she said. 'But you know that Ozymandias is a powerful soul, and I have been known to fall in love with that kind.'

'Not this time, I think,' he said. 'Ozymandias is history; I am not. Go entertain him, demoness; the break should refresh us both.'

She walked out. She could have vanished, but chose to make a more dignified exit. She had reformed nude, so as to give him an excellent view of her posterior as she walked. It was the most shapely and supple posterior known to man or demon, and she knew how to make it smile and frown and dance on its own.

Parry was indeed tempted to call her back, but as a matter of principle did not. He did not want her to think she owned him.

* * *

Ozymandias took hold immediately, glad for the chance to show what he could do. Hell stirred restlessly under his lash, as overseers were replaced and damned souls shifted to new locations. Lilah kept him satisfied, but Parry suspected that he would have continued working regardless, because of his overweening love of the exercise of power. Certainly it was better for him than the ice!

Meanwhile, Nefertiti was an intriguing change-off, partly because she was a good deal more naïve than Lilah and had a certain remaining modicum of queenly pride. Lilah had, he realized, been *too* obliging; there had been none of the excitement of challenge with her. Nefertiti, in contrast, reacted with shock when he essayed certain configurations; it was a challenge and a pleasure educating her. In due course all her barriers would be down; then she would be less intriguing. But with proper management, she could last for a decent interval.

Still, Parry wasn't satisfied. It would be years, decades or even centuries before Hell was fully reorganized, and it was an internal affair. He wanted to make his mark on the mortal realm, and to repay the Incarnations for their early humiliation of him. If only he had an opening!

Then, abruptly, it came. The Incarnation of Nature retired, and a new woman took her office.

Of all the scores Parry had to settle, this one was the most nagging. He owed Gaea a serious humiliation! He had been unable to make headway against the old one, but the new one would be inexperienced, liable to make errors before she consolidated her power. Now was his time to strike! It was true that the new Gaea had done him no injury, but she had been admitted by the old one, and the old one was now a mortal, able to see what happened to her erstwhile office. She would rue the day she retired!

He scouted for prospects. What was in Gaea's domain that the Incarnation of Evil could influence? It was almost impossible to change the operations of another Incarnation unless that Incarnation were careless or inexperienced, which was why the opportunity had to be grasped immediately.

He found a good one. In 1331 there had been a plague in China of a particularly nasty variety. The Mongols maintained trade routes between China and the West, and episodes of that plague had been known along that route. How fitting that this time, instead of arranging for a message to be delivered from the East, he arrange for an illness! The plague should drive Gaea to distraction, and she might prove unable to stop it at all. That would be an excellent humiliation! In addition, it could send a number of souls to the Afterlife before their normal time, confounding Fate's threads and overworking Thanatos. Because those souls would come early, their proprietors would not have enough time to make up for their bad deeds. They would be caught with negative balances, and Hell would profit.

Yes, this was indeed beautiful! All he needed to do was implement it, immediately, before the other Incarnations caught on and acted to nullify it.

Parry took care of it personally. He went to Samarkand in Transoxiana, a nexus of the eastern trade route. The plague had not spread beyond here, because it depended on dense populations for its propagation, and this was a sparsely populated mountainous region. He found a man who had suffered the first fever but had good resistance; his fever was coming down. He was with a merchant party and able to travel, but they would not take a sick man along that rugged trail. This was not because of any spirit of kindness, but because it was too awkward to dispose of bodies appropriately, and the pace of travel would be seriously slowed before the death.

Parry changed to an appropriate mortal form and

approached the caravan master. 'I need a package delivered,' he said in the local language, using his prerogative as the Father of Lies to accomplish his purpose. 'But I do not trust just anyone to carry it. I have found a sick man, whom robbers would not dare approach for fear of contamination. I have given my package to his care. Here is ample gold; will you see that he is conveyed in isolation?'

The caravan master made ready to protest. Then he saw the nature of the coinage proffered. It was three times as much as was warranted, even for a treacherous mission like this. He was a reasonably honest man, and not a murderer; he decided to accept the money and accept the traveller.

The sick man, eager to get home rather than being stuck for three more months here, did not quibble. He took the package Parry gave him. The package was genuine: a precious Oriental gem, for delivery to a jeweller. But it was a pretext, not the real cargo.

Parry departed, not lingering a moment after his transactions had been completed, in order to avoid calling attention to his presence. Though his simulation of a mortal had been impeccable – he had worked hard on such things during off moments in the past century – even casual questioning would reveal that no one of this region knew him. He wanted to evoke no such dialogue. He let his messenger carry his burden.

Months later, the plague struck Asia Minor. It spread through the eastern part of Anatolia and reached the developing Ottoman Turk Empire. The following year it crossed the Dardanelles and infected Constantinople. Now it was in Europe, and on its way. The new Gaea and the other Incarnations were scurrying about like dispossessed rat fleas, trying to stem the black tide of it.

Chronos called on him. 'I do not wish to interfere in

your business, my friend,' he said gravely. 'But if I might ask a favour – '

For Chronos, Parry would grant it.

'It is that you arrange to spare the city and environment of Milan, Italy. This region is destined to become a leading force in the Renaissance, and – '

Parry had no notion what that might mean, but he did not argue. 'Milan will be spared,' he agreed. Then he summoned Beelzebub, and directed him to see to the preservation of Milan from this scourge of the Black Death.

In 1348 it spread throughout the Mediterranean region, wiping out one third of the population. Gaea was distraught; by the time she realized the significance of this invasion, it was beyond her means to cope with it. This was success beyond Parry's expectation!

But there was a strange gap in its progress, or rather an omission. Milan was untouched. Beelzebub had gone there and fashioned a spell that eradicated all the rat fleas in the vicinity; as the Lord of Flies, he had this power. Because the plague was transmitted to man via the bites of fleas, that region was spared the ravage of the Black Death.

Parry also had Beelzebub do his thing in southern France, in the vicinity of Parry's original home. He realized he was being foolishly sentimental, but he did not want his ascendancy to the Office of Evil to penalize the folk of that region. No one he had known remained alive, of course, but still . . .

In 1349 the Black Plague spread throughout Spain and down the west coast of Africa, north across France and into southern England. The other Incarnations remained helpless to stem its progress. Thanatos fell months behind on his rounds, and made increasing errors of classification. A number of souls that should have been relegated to Heaven arrived instead in Hell. Ozymandias had to set up a separate section for them, an emulation of Heaven, with demons masquerading as angels and doing nice things. It was a joke, but it had its appeal; those souls who were favoured were allowed vacations there, provided they kept silent about its true nature. Parry knew that in due course those undamned souls would have to be reassigned to Heaven, and he did not want them to suffer culture shock.

In 1349 the plague spread throughout England and Ireland and the Holy Roman Empire, skipping only Flanders, because Father Grief had had a Franciscan friar friend there.

At this time Parry received a visitor. It was a young mortal woman from the city of Warsaw, in Poland. She had committed her soul not for riches or happiness but for the privilege of this single interview with the Incarnation of Evil.

By an eerie coincidence, the woman bore a resemblance to Jolie, Parry's first love. Perhaps it was no more than the fact that she was of peasant stock, garbed in the rags that were her nearest approach to finery, and was young and thin and terrified. It had after all been more than a hundred and forty years since the frightened Jolie presented herself at his door.

He looked at the spot on his wrist. It was so faded as to be almost invisible against his darkened skin, but it was still there. Was she still present, sleeping in that dehydrated drop of blood? Or had she at last been released to Heaven? Suddenly he missed her with an overwhelming nostalgia. His first love? His *only* love! He had been corrupted by the demoness, and had had much joy of her malleable body, but he had never truly loved her.

'My Lord Satan,' the girl said timorously. 'Before You relegate my soul to eternal torture, I have one – one boon to ask of You, and I – I pray that You grant it.' She was shaking with her fear, but something drove her on.

245

What could such a creature desire so badly that she would throw away the one asset she had, her immortal soul, to gain it? 'Ask,' Parry said, not unkindly. That resemblance to Jolie still shook him.

'Your Lordship, the plague – they say it is Your doing, to get back at those who humbled You.'

'True.'

'But it is hurting everyone, the good and the evil alike, and most of these never tried to humble You. I was visiting in Prague, and – oh, my Lord, if You could only see!'

It was ridiculous, he knew, but Parry wanted a pretext to remain a while longer with this girl. He knew she wasn't Jolie, but the atmosphere of the encounter was so evocative that he could not help himself. Perhaps it was also her innocence that fascinated him, for that was a quality he seldom saw these days.

'Show me,' he said. He stood from his throne and extended his hand.

The girl nerved herself and took his hand.

He worked his magic, and suddenly they stood in Prague, in the Kingdom of Bohemia. As a mortal he had been virtually unable to conjure, but his office enhanced his powers of magic, and he had been at pains to master useful disciplines. Now he could conjure himself and others anywhere with ease, not merely within Hell but in the mortal realm.

It was a horror. There were bodies piled in the street, and these were purplish, almost black in hue, the features of their faces locked in the rictus of their closing agony. Men with wagons were going about, picking up the bodies, piling them up and hauling them to a mass burial pit beyond the city.

They walked through Prague, hand in hand. Parry did not need to maintain the contact to keep her with him, but the girl did not know that, and he did not undeceive her. The feeling of being with Jolie was heart-wrenchingly strong.

They saw the victims in every stage. The early sufferers had headache, aching joints, and a general feeling of malaise. Some had nausea, and some were vomiting. Swollen nodes developed in the groin, some the size of hens' eggs; it was possible to spot a sufferer of the plague by the way he walked. They developed high fever and congestion of the eyes and face. Many suffered from severe thirst, gulping down water that often was simply vomited out again. Their tongues were gross, thickly coated.

Those who were more advanced were exhausted and depressed. Some ran around crazily, as if they thought they could escape their pain. Others seemed dizzy, and some evidently suffered delirium. Then they sank into stupor, and their colour started to turn. That was the signal that death was imminent. Many, Parry knew, required the personal service of Thanatos, for their souls were nearly in balance between good and evil, but Thanatos was not in evidence. That meant added suffering, for they could not quite die until the Incarnation of Death arrived.

Indeed, it was much worse than Parry had thought. He had started the plague, impinging on Gaea's domain, thinking it would embarrass her and cause her mischief, but the ploy had succeeded beyond his expectation. It was wiping out one third of the population it attacked, and doing it in a grotesque manner.

'O my Lord,' the girl said. 'When I think of this coming to my own city, to Warsaw, to Poland – '

Parry released her hand and snapped his fingers. 'Beelzebub,' he said.

Beelzebub appeared. He glanced around. 'Hell on Earth!' he said approvingly.

'Turn off the plague,' Parry said.

Beelzebub had held the office of the Incarnation of Evil in olden times. He had become an increasingly open supporter of the present regime as the plague progressed; Parry was doing the Office proud, scoring a coup against Gaea and Thanatos and perhaps against God himself. This order could hardly have been to his liking! But he had discipline.

'My Lord Satan, the magnitude of it is too great. Only Gaea can suppress it, when she masters her powers. I can halt it only in a limited region, by piping away the rat fleas that carry it.'

Parry nodded, knowing that Beelzebub was giving an accurate report. 'Then save Poland,' he said. 'Make sure Prague is included in the plague-free area.'

'That I can do, though it is the limit of my power,' the damned soul said. He vanished.

The girl turned a wondering gaze to him. 'That demon will stop the plague?'

'In Poland,' Parry said. 'He can do no more. It will proceed elsewhere until it runs its course.'

'Then I am ready for my fate,' she said simply. 'Throw me into Hell.'

Parry took her hand again, and used his magic to take them to Warsaw. Here life was normal; the plague had not struck, and would not. 'Return to your family,' he said. 'You are not dead, and need not die soon. You will never come to My realm, good woman.' He turned her loose.

She stared at him. 'But I gave up my soul –'

'For one interview with Me. I granted the interview, but will not take your soul. You are good, not evil, and do not belong in My realm.' He turned away.

He was about to conjure himself back to Hell, but he paused, lingering one more moment in the presence of this girl who so reminded him of his lost love. He knew he had done the favour not because it was right but because he could not resist the foolish impulse to please her, and thereby in some devious manner perhaps make up for what he had done to Jolie by his defection to evil.

She spoke once more, her voice almost a whisper. 'Thank you, Parry.'

He stiffened, hardly believing what he had heard. Then, slowly, he turned, but the girl was gone.

Had he heard her call him by the name that only Jolie would have known, or had he imagined it? He realized that he might never know for sure, but he preferred to believe that Jolie had awakened for this moment, when he was out of Hell and away from the demoness and doing a bit of good that was out of character for his office, and that she had in that moment animated the girl and spoken to him.

He had had his reward.

The plague did run its course, proceeding through the rest of Europe in 1350 and 1351 but bypassing the huge area of Poland from just north of Prague to north of Warsaw. In 1352 and 1353 it moved on past Novgorod and through Russia, doing decreasing damage. By that time Gaea had gained facility with her office, and though she still had a problem with other illnesses, such as smallpox, she never again allowed as massive a sweep of the Black Plague as had occurred in these eight years. Parry had, in his fashion, his revenge, and now it was done.

He continued to dabble in mortal affairs, exploiting any weaknesses he discovered. His most notable success was in 1378, when he managed to fan the fires of divisiveness within the Church to the point where the Papacy itself split asunder. One Pope was established in Avignon in southern France (Parry simply could not resist putting the land of his birth into the picture again), and the other in Rome in Italy, with the entire continent divided in its loyalties. Heresies flourished, and it was evident that it was no longer possible to suppress them in the manner of the past.

He also made a score in the political arena. His visit to Samarkand had alerted him to the potential of that region, and he fostered the development of a powerful and ruthless lame king, called Tamerlane, who wreaked havoc in that region of the world and generated pyramids of skulls. But this was in the Moslem society, so had limited impact on the Christian framework, and his harvest of damned souls was not what he had hoped for.

In fact, all this fencing with God in the indirect medium of the mortal realm seemed increasingly pointless. It was true, as the Polish girl had said, that innocent folk were the main sufferers. The errors of classification, the inefficient confusions between good and evil – whom did these benefit? The real struggle was between Good and Evil; why not tackle God directly?

The more Parry thought about this, the better he liked the notion. It was time to have the two Primaries settle things in person!

But how should he go about broaching God? Never in his mortal life or in his time as an Incarnation had he ever had direct communication with the Incarnation of Good. He knew that mortal folk often prayed to God, and certainly the Church interposed itself as the mediator between man and God, but all this was based on faith. What tangible response had there been?

Rather than argue the case rhetorically with himself, he went to his friend Chronos in Purgatory. The Incarnation of Time greeted him positively, as always. 'To what do I owe the honour of this visit, Satan?'

'I wish to have a facedown with God,' Parry said, 'so that mortals do not have to suffer the effects of our differences. But I don't know how to approach Him. I hoped you might have an insight.'

Chronos pursed his lips. 'I do not believe I have ever encountered God directly.'

'Exactly my problem. I am prepared to go to meet Him, if I can find the way.'

Chronos frowned. 'I will help if I can, my friend. But perhaps you should explain to me in more detail why a personal confrontation is necessary.'

Parry summarized the questions that had developed in his mind. 'I have been thinking about my purpose as the Incarnation of Evil. Is it to generate evil in the mortal world, or merely to locate existing evil? Am I here to encourage greater evil, or to discourage it by the threat of infernal punishment? Am I supposed to defeat God and become the major figure of the universe, or to be defeated? There is so much I do not know!'

Chronos nodded. 'I have wondered about that on occasion myself, and about my own true mission. It is my job to establish the timing of every event in the mortal realm, and my staff handles most of this; I step in only when the situation is special. But what is the point? Why should events need to be timed at all? I have concluded tentatively that my job is necessary to facilitate the diminution of entropy. Perhaps yours is similar.'

'Entropy?' Parry asked blankly.

Chronos smiled. 'Sometimes I forget that some of my terms are from your future. The complete concept of entropy, I think, would be too complex to define readily. Let me summarize an aspect of it this way: entropy may be considered as a measure of uncertainty. In the beginning, all was without form and void, what we call chaos. Nothing was known or, perhaps, knowable. We are labouring to bring order and understanding to it, and in so doing we are decreasing entropy. We are fighting the natural current, for the universe, left to itself, would in due course relapse back to its disorganized state, with maximum entropy. Eventually, if we succeed, we will accomplish the maximum organization of the universe, and all will be known. Thus all Incarnations, Good and Evil included, may be working towards a common goal.'

Parry nodded. 'You *have* thought about it, Chronos! It never occurred to me that Good and Evil might be on the same side, but perhaps that is so. But why, then, should we oppose each other?'

'I suspect we should not. But perhaps my theorizing is mistaken.'

'I doubt it! Maybe it is just that because we have been assigned to different aspects of reality, and have assumed different identities, we believe that we are differing forces. We become competitive, each trying for a greater share of power. This may be folly!'

'This may be folly,' Chronos agreed.

'Here I am, fighting God for a greater share of mortal souls – and why? What do I want with yet more soiled souls? What does He want with yet more pristine souls? Why should either of us care how many souls the other has? As you say, what is the point?' He found himself carried away by his vehemence, but now the question loomed much larger than before.

'What is the point,' Chronos repeated.

'Now, more than ever, it seems proper for me to meet with God, not in the competitive sense, but for the sake of understanding. Perhaps we can abolish the confusion that has surrounded our endeavours. Perhaps we can hasten the process of bringing complete order to the world.'

'I favour that,' Chronos said. 'Perhaps if you talked to the other Incarnations – '

'I tried that once, in the time of one of your successors,' Parry said ruefully. 'They humiliated me. Of all the major Incarnations, only you and Nox have treated me decently, and I am afraid to approach her again.'

'Oh, I have not encountered Nox. Is she fearsome?'

'Not in the negative sense. She – but perhaps, for you, she would be all right. If you have need for a female companion who understands –'

'I do,' Chronos agreed. 'Normal women do not adapt well to my direction of living.'

'I shall send Lilah to guide you to her, if you wish. But be warned; Nox is a most seductive creature.'

'I thank you, Satan. However, do not send Lilah, for that would occur necessarily in my past. Merely allow me to borrow her without challenge in your own past.'

'Of course.' Parry, even after all this time, kept getting caught by Chronos' reversal! 'She understands, and will cooperate.' *Had cooperated*, he now realized, and had not informed him. That was best, to avoid confusion.

'But now let me see whether I can help you similarly. I do not know the route to God's domain, but I do know that the good souls find it. Perhaps if you could follow one of them –'

Parry nodded. 'I have a number that have been misallocated. I could release them, and see where they go.'

'I wish you well, friend.' But then Chronos frowned. 'However, I must warn you that in my particular time line, there is no change in the rivalry between Incarnations. This does not necessarily indicate that none will occur for you, for my past, like your future, is malleable. But it does suggest that the probability of success in your venture is suspect.'

Parry was used to his friend's circumlocutions. 'You mean I may fall on my face.'

'That is what I said,' Chronos said with a smile.

12
Heaven

Parry made sure that Hell was functioning reasonably, gave Nefertiti a holiday in mock Heaven, and collected five misallocated souls. In Hell proper they were just like living folk, but would become ethereally slight beyond. He explained the situation to them: that they were the victims of confusion, and had been held temporarily in Hell pending proper release to Heaven. Now he proposed to release them one at a time, carrying the others with him, so that he could follow them to Heaven for an interview with God.

'I am Satan, the Father of Lies,' he concluded. 'I can offer you no proof that this is the truth, and you are not required to cooperate. But it is the only way I have to find Heaven, and I hope that you will cooperate in the chance that it is true.'

They considered, and decided that if they truly were in Hell now, nothing they could do would free them from it unless they were released by the Lord of Evil. If this was to be such a release, it behooved them to cooperate; if it was merely a deception, they were lost anyway. So they agreed.

He escorted them out. As they emerged from Hell, they thinned into mere webs of themselves, patterns without substance. They had no consciousness; that was feasible only in Hell, Purgatory, Heaven, or when animated on Earth as a ghost. But when brought to an appropriate region, their souls should float. Parry wound them in like gauze and packed them into a bag he carried.

He conjured himself to Earth's surface. Then he brought out one soul and released it. Immediately it set off, attracted to Heaven by the burden of good in its makeup. He followed, using his magic to fly, keeping the pace.

The soul sailed upward, but not exactly vertically. It was not going to the sky, but to Heaven, a different matter. It wavered and swerved in the ethereal currents, its faint colour changing, and in a moment he lost it.

Undismayed, he brought out the second and released it. He had not expected to be able to follow one the whole way; if the route to Heaven were straightforward, it would not be such a mystery!

The second soul seemed to hesitate, but this was illusion; without consciousness, it was simply drifting in the pattern of good and evil, perhaps caught in an eddy. In a moment it found the way and moved out.

This one took him into Purgatory. That was perplexing; he was sure that this was a good soul, bound for Heaven. Only those in such balance that no decision was possible remained in Purgatory.

Then he realized that the way to Heaven lay *through* Purgatory. Even those souls not staying there still had to check through; there was no direct access to Heaven. It seemed obvious in retrospect.

The soul moved into a region of increasing confusion. There were trees, but they were bulbous and oddly coloured. There were paths, but they had strange convolutions. There were landscapes, unlike those of any mortal region. It was interesting; he would have to set up a region of Hell with similar configurations.

The soul moved through the middle of it – and was lost. Parry brought out the third one and let it go.

It swam through the confusion, and was similarly lost.

Parry paused. He had not been able to follow the third soul at all; it had disappeared into Limbo too quickly. He only had two remaining, having perhaps underestimated the extent of this challenge.

Limbo? He looked around more carefully. Indeed, this was like that bleak region of Hell. It was simply a field of chaotic images, with no organization.

Chaotic . . .

This was a waste, an aspect of chaos! That part of the universe with original entropy, without form and void. He had heard that Fate spun her threads of life from this substance. Now he was in it – and no wonder he was losing the souls, for there was no order here, nothing to differentiate object from background, life from nonlife. Nothing could be pursued through chaos.

He would have to get beyond it before releasing the next soul. But he paused.

Why should Fate spin her threads of life from this mélange? The good was hopelessly confused with the evil. Fate was on the side of good; she would not want this!

Yet evidently she did. And so the lives formed from her threads were almost indecipherable mélanges of good and evil, impossible to classify clearly. Thus those lives had to struggle through the horrors of mortality before finally coming to Heaven or to Hell. What a colossal waste!

But he was unsatisfied with that conclusion. Fate was a devious and unpleasant creature of many personalities, but she knew well what she was doing. She would not spin from this stuff if she had any alternative. She –

Then it came to him. Chronos had explained about entropy and chaos: that it seemed to be the duty of the Incarnations to diminish each, to bring order and comprehension to the universe. That could not be done by ignoring chaos. They were deliberately drawing from chaos, fashioning it into lives – so that these could be defined as good or evil!

All that agony of mortality – just to deal with the problem of entropy. To process the stuff of chaos through to Heaven and Hell, properly classified at last. Eventually all of it would be done, and the universe would be in order.

But at what a cost! How many thousands, how many thousands of thousands of lives like Jolie's had to be twisted and tortured and cut short, just to accomplish this goal? What a vasty cynicism!

Yet it was being done, and under God's auspices. The end justified the means! There was that treacherous doctrine that Lilah had used to corrupt him – and now it was obvious that God subscribed to it, too. The end of creating order justified the means of toil and suffering for innumerable mortal lives. He had used it to corrupt the Inquisition: the end of saving souls justified the means of torture and pillaging of the estates of those accused.

Parry sighed. He was now the Incarnation of Evil. He knew evil when he spied it, even if the other Incarnations did not. It was past time to talk to God and set Him straight on this.

Now he moved on through the confusion, closing his eyes because it would be too easy to get lost here. He knew that the extent of the void was limited; if he proceeded straight, he would in due course get out of it. A mortal might become hopelessly lost, but he was now an immortal.

He opened his eyes, and found that he was still in it. He closed them and moved on again. But when he looked, he remained in chaos.

Had he been too optimistic about his ability to escape it? Evidently it had affected his bearings, and now he was not moving the way he thought he was. What irony, if the Lord of Evil fell prey to chaos!

But there was another way. He brought out the fourth soul, and did not release it. The thing tried to move, and stretched out from his hand, but remained captive.

He moved in the direction it seemed to be trying to go. He tuned out the surrounding chaos and oriented on the soul. Wherever it wanted to go, there he would go, carrying it along.

And, without perceiving exactly when, he emerged from the void. The soul had known its destination, and brought him out.

Now he let it go. It accelerated, as if glad to be free. He followed, coursing on towards Heaven. He kept his attention fixed on it, so that he would not lose it.

Then it slowed, and he realized that they had arrived. The Circles of Heaven were forming around them.

The outermost was a blaze of light, a phenomenal brilliance, a ring of fire that resembled the outline of the sun, but became much larger, swelling to encompass the horizon. He thought there might be some challenge as he entered it, but there was not; he simply joined it and was in Heaven.

He stood on the edge of a bright cloud bank. All around stood faintly glowing folk. They did not have wings; they were souls, not angels, just as the souls in Hell lacked the tails of demons. Oddly, they did not look particularly happy; rather they seemed resigned, or even bored.

He brought out the fifth soul and let it go; he had no need for its guidance now. Instead of travelling, it unfolded into its human form: a middle-aged man, dead of the plague but no longer disfigured by it. He gazed around, perplexed. 'This is it?' he asked.

'This is it,' Parry agreed. 'Your eternal home. May you enjoy it.'

The man looked uncertain, obviously not willing to express disappointment. He drifted away.

Perhaps this was no more than the outer rim of Heaven, analogous to Limbo in Hell, where those souls drifted that were imperfect, not good enough, literally, to penetrate farther into Heaven. No wonder the soul he had released was disappointed! There really was not much difference between this aspect of Heaven and that aspect of Hell.

But he wasn't here to tour Heaven; he was here to meet God. Where would God be? Surely in the centre, the highest reach, just as the Incarnation of Evil's office was in the nethermost reach of Hell.

Parry flew up to the next level. This was not precisely physical motion, but rather a mental effort to enter a deeper circle; it was evident that the standing soul could not do it.

The Second Heaven was starkly different from the First. It was a bleak landscape, bare rock and sand, pocked by craters of every size. It was in fact the face of the Moon. Many spirits stood idle here, too, looking scarcely happier than those below.

He moved on to the Third Heaven, which was an improvement: it was the landscape of Venus, the Planet of Love.

Yet, somehow, it seemed little more illustrious than the Moon. It was supposed to be the joy of the spirits of lovers, but since carnality was forbidden in Heaven, all they could do was stand around and gaze longingly at one another. The appeal of that seemed to pall in the course of eternity.

The Fourth Heaven was the Sphere of the Sun. This was certainly brighter, and the souls were engaged in animated dialogue with each other. These were the theologians and fathers of the Church, and of course they never tired of their exercises in interpretation.

The Fifth Heaven was the Sphere of Mars, with the warrior spirits. But, of course, there was no fighting in Heaven, so they were idle.

The Sixth Heaven was the Sphere of Jupiter, with the spirits of the righteous rulers. This was sparsely settled.

He proceeded on past the Seventh Heaven of the Sphere of Saturn, with the spirits of the contemplative, and the Eighth Heaven, consisting of fixed stars. Many of the Saints were here. They lacked the passions of normal folk, so it was not surprising that they were not jubilant.

The Ninth Heaven seemed to be the retreat mostly of angels; the Tenth –

This, he realized, was where God should be. But where was He? Parry gazed about, and saw only an enormous pattern of light that could be interpreted as –

Then he realized that the light, when correctly viewed, formed the image of an infinitely monstrous human face framed within a triple halo. This, at last, was God.

Parry waved. There was no response. 'Haloo!' he called. There was no response.

God simply was not paying attention.

After some time, disgruntled, Parry gave it up. He dropped rapidly down through the layers of Heaven until he reached the outer one. He was about to depart it when there was a cry.

'My Lord Saten!'

There was a stirring among the apathetic souls of this region. From among them came the man he had last released. 'My Lord, I beg you, take me back with You!'

Surprised, Parry waited for him. 'You don't like Heaven?'

'My Lord, it is just as dull as Hell – and most of my friends are in Hell. I would rather remain there.'

'But you don't belong in Hell. The balance of your soul is positive.'

'Only marginally, my Lord. I will never get beyond this outer circle. I'd be better off in the mock Heaven annexe of Hell, if I get leave to visit there. Please, my Lord, take me back!'

Such a situation had never occurred to Parry. Yet the soul was serious. Was there a precedent for this?

There was another stirring. The other souls shrank away. 'The guardian angels!' someone murmured.

Now Parry saw them: bright winged figures in the form of big, bruising men, swiftly approaching.

'Please, my Lord!' the soul repeated.

Perhaps it was the angels that tipped his decision. Parry did not like the look of them. It seemed to him that they could readily serve similar duty in Hell. 'Very well,' he said. He extended his hand, touching the man.

Immediately the man thinned into a web, the soul discarnate. Parry wound this around his hand, compacting it so that it would fit into his pouch. Souls had no mass but did have dimensions; it would not do to have it drag out behind him.

The angels arrived. 'Let go that soul!' one ordered.

In the past century Parry had grown unaccustomed to that tone of address from either demons or damned souls. He found he liked it no better from an angel. But this was not his realm, so he let it pass. He closed the pouch, confining the soul, and turned away.

'Listen, fringe-spirit,' the angel said contemptuously. 'If you know what's good for you – '

'Hardly,' Parry said, with an ironic smile. He started to sink down through the cloud bank.

The angel reached menacingly for him. 'I warned you!' But the grasping hand passed through Parry's substance without effect. Parry dropped on down, and in a moment was out, leaving the astonished and dismayed angel behind. He was not impressed with either Heaven or its guardians. No wonder the soul wanted to leave!

He reached the vague region of chaos and plunged straight on through it. And realized too late that there was no direction in chaos. He did not emerge; he was mired in it, again.

Last time, he had used one of the souls he carried to guide him. He tried it again, appreciating the coincidence that had caused a soul to accompany him this time.

The soul oriented and stretched out. Parry followed its direction, holding on as he had before. It was working!

Soon they cleared chaos and approached – Heaven.

Now, in retrospect, he realized that this soul, being marginally good, naturally levitated towards Heaven, not Hell. The soul's private desire had nothing to do with it; it was the balance of good and evil on it. If he wanted a guide towards Hell, he would have to find a suitably damned soul.

In Heaven? Well, there could have been similar errors in classification that resulted in marginally damned souls being sent to Heaven. Perhaps he could find one of those. But would it want to go to Hell?

Parry sighed. It really would be better to find his own way. He would just have to keep trying.

He bundled up the soul again and put in the pouch. Then he closed his eyes and plunged as fast as he could.

And got lost again. Chaos took no note of direction or velocity; such concepts were valid only in a somewhat organized framework.

Maybe his own damned soul could do it! He tried to let himself go, to sink towards his natural realm as if he were a newly released soul.

After a timeless time – time was another invalid concept here – he realized that this wasn't working either. No matter what he did, or didn't do, he was stuck in the Void. Unless he gave up and used the captive soul to guide him back to Heaven. That he did not want to do!

He tried one more thing, foolish as he deemed it: he called for help. *Traveller lost*! he thought as loudly as he could, though neither loudness nor thought had validity here. Anyway, who was here to listen or respond?

Here, lost one!

Parry stopped still, though that too could not be literal. There had been an answer!

He did not, at this stage, care whom it might be. He oriented on it and went.

It turned out to be a rather old patriarchal-appearing man, white-bearded and garbed in a vaguely clerical robe. He nodded sagely as Parry approached. 'You ventured into forbidden territory, traveller.' His language was not Parry's, but here, as in Hell, all languages seemed one.

'So it turned out,' Parry agreed wryly. 'I thank you for rescuing me.'

'It is my business to rescue lost souls, when they wish it. But it has been some time since one like you appeared.' He gestured, and a room appeared around them. 'Make yourself comfortable, and perhaps we shall converse.'

'You are able to direct me from this region?' Parry asked, taking a seat in a staid but serviceable chair.

'Direct you? I am not sure. But fear not; I gladly will guide you. I use an aspect of the Llano, which is about the only force that can penetrate chaos.'

There was the Llano again! 'That I sincerely appreciate! But please, may I know your identity? I – ' Then Parry realized that the other might not be pleased to learn whom he has rescued.

'I am JHVH.' He did not actually pronounce the name; it was only a concept.

There was no help for it; Parry was not going to deceive the one who had helped him. 'I am Satan, the Incarnation of Evil.'

'Ah, the Christian variant!' JHVH said, extending his hand. 'I am glad to meet You at last.'

Parry hesitated. 'Are you sure you want to – ' Then the identity of the other finally registered. 'But you are – '

'The Hebrew Deity. Come, Satan, surely You are not shy of Me?'

Parry finally took the hand. 'I just thought – do you know, uh, do You know, I came to confront the Christian

God. I never expected – of course I should have recognized – '

'Quite all right, Satan. I do not have the following that either of You do, or, indeed, that Allah does, or any of the great Oriental Presences. I am in fact a minor Deity, and My believers suffer much from persecution.'

'But you – you are older than any of – '

'My Office is, perhaps. I myself date only from the last three thousand years or so. I was a Mountain Deity, adopted by a wandering tribe, in competition with many others. When I started, it seemed impossible to prevail against Baal, My chief rival in that region. He kept stealing My people, and – well, it is a long story, hardly of interest to You.'

'But you – You are ancient! Both Christianity and the Saracens derive from – '

JHVH waved a hand in negation. 'That is an exaggeration. The Prophet Jesus was Mine, certainly, but then his followers were diverted and a new Office was formed. I admit I did not take it seriously at first; none of us did. Splinter gods occur constantly, and few survive more than a few decades. But this faction got in with the Romans, and then it prospered, and the Office with it.'

Parry was amazed. 'You are saying that there are many Offices? That the old Gods still exist?'

JHVH smiled. 'Any Deity or Devil that any mortal believes in exists, and that entity is strengthened by the number and intensity of His believers. Thus Your Office is very strong, because great numbers of mortals believe in You, though they try to deny it.'

'I – I never realized! I thought – '

'That the Christian version of Good and Evil were all that exist?' JHVH asked with a smile.

'Something like that,' Parry admitted, somewhat sheepishly. 'Or that our mutual framework accounted for everything. You mentioned Baal; I believe he became Beelzebub, the Lord of Flies, in My Hell.'

'Yes, the Deities of one generation become the Devils of the next; the Christians adopted him for a time.'

Parry remained out of sorts. 'How is it that You, knowing this, have extended aid to one like Me? Surely you wish to abolish all that I represent!'

'We may be rivals, but We are not enemies,' JHVH said. 'We are all trying to bring order from chaos, as you know.'

Parry smiled ruefully. 'I have just had a reminder how awkward chaos can be! But You are correct; I had concluded that it was pointless to continually fight God, when actually We should be cooperating towards the common objective.'

'So You went to see Him, on that mission of amity,' JHVH said. 'And got nowhere.'

'And got nowhere,' Parry agreed. 'He is locked in a narcissistic contemplation of Himself. Apparently He is not paying any attention to the routine matter of the mortal realm, or indeed of Heaven.'

JHVH nodded. 'I fear I was no better in my heyday. I demanded above all else the adulation of Me. The first commandment of my people was "Thou shalt have no other gods before Me." When My people worshipped a golden calf, My rage was not because they were slipping back into idolatry and its uncivilized imperatives, but because it was a slight against me. I retaliated by visiting on them all manner of mischief. But I concluded after some centuries of chronic relapsing on their part that rage and punishment was not the best way to hold a clientele. It is only the most primitive of mortals who are swayed by that sort of thing. So I ameliorated My stance, and I think have been a better Deity for it, though it is true that I do not attract the same proportion of mortals that I once did. Unfortunately the young Christian Deity took Me as a role model and emulated some of the worst faults of My heyday, especially that of pride. His enormous success has given Him the freedom to indulge those propensities beyond all reason. Humiliation can indeed make better Deities of Us, because We are reminded that We do not control the universe. Pride unchecked . . .'

Parry had to smile. For the first time he saw some slight benefit in the humiliation he had suffered at the hands of the other Incarnations! His pride had never got out of bounds.

'I wonder if You, in Your contemplations, have come across the answer to the riddle I have wrestled with,' he said. 'I have been unable to decide whether, in the framework of the assignments of Good and Evil as Incarnations, it is my purpose to locate evil or to generate it. The task of sorting good from evil suggests that it is the former, but the practice seems to have been the latter. Now, in the face of God's dereliction – ' He shrugged.

'Surely it is to locate evil,' JHVH said. 'Or perhaps to evoke it. We know that evil is omnipresent; every mortal thread represents an admixture of good and evil so intricate as to be virtually inseparable. The question thus becomes not whether evil is present, as obviously it is, but to what extent it dominates the individual. You thus must do Your utmost to evoke that quality of evil that makes an individual eligible for Hell, so that no errors of classification are made.'

'To *evoke* it!' Parry repeated, wonderingly. 'Yes, of course!'

'That is what Your predecessors were doing, from the time of the fruit of the Tree of Knowledge of Good and Evil on. They were tempting mortals into sin, knowing that temptation is the surest method to evoke hidden evil. Mortals of course condemn such efforts, but consider the alternative: hidden evil would have remained in the Garden of Eden, unresolved. The Deity of that time, the ancestor to God's current office and Mine, finally recognized this, and allowed mortal man to proceed to the challenging outer world. The result has been history.'

'It has indeed!' Parry agreed warmly. 'Your perspective enlightens Me!'

'It is a pleasure to review basic principles,' JHVH said. 'So few are interested.'

'But now, with God tuned out, the separation of good from evil is becoming sloppy,' Parry said. 'Heaven hardly differs from Hell in certain respects; aimlessness seems to dominate. I have a soul here' – he patted his pouch – 'who asked to return to Hell from Heaven. Consider what that suggests for incentive! If mortals lose both their desire for Heaven and their fear of Hell, how will a proper separation of good from evil be accomplished?'

'The Buddhists seem to manage it by arranging for the extinction of all personal desires and passions, leaving the spirit perfect.'

'But it loses its identity in the whole!' Parry protested. 'Christians would never go for that! They insist on retaining their identities for eternity, good and evil and all.'

'That does seem to be their problem,' JHVH agreed.

'Which means that we can't simply extract the good and evil, we have to deal with the whole soul. That's much more difficult. That's the problem I want to address. But God –'

'Perhaps new guidance is called for. In the old days, if one Deity faltered, others were quick to take away His worshippers. The lack of such a situation may be the contemporary problem.'

Parry stared at him. 'You are not suggesting that – that I try to – to –'

'I am merely posing a notion,' JHVH said. 'Perhaps it is an unworthy one. But it may be best to consider it carefully, so as to expose its unsuitability.'

'To take over the leadership of the Christian realm

from God, so as to be able to establish an improved mechanism for processing souls,' Parry finished.

'As I understand Your framework, all that is required is the amassing of a greater number of souls than is controlled by Your opposite. God has dominated because most mortals prefer to go to Heaven when they die.'

'They wouldn't, if they knew how dull it was!'

'Then perhaps you may want to spread the word.'

Parry was uncertain. 'If my objective is to find a more efficient way to separate the threads, to evoke the evil ones instead of letting the matter drag on interminably, what would be gained by bringing an increased number of marginal souls to Hell?'

'Only power, the power brought by the number of souls in Your domain,' JHVH said. 'Would it corrupt you, also?'

'It might. I have never had complete power, and am not sure I trust myself with it.'

'A sensible caution,' JHVH agreed.

'Yet I am unwilling to let this folly continue,' Parry said. 'I wish I could simply settle it with God and be done with it.'

'In Hell, are You the sole administrator?'

'Hardly! I have a hierarchy of damned souls to handle – ' Parry broke off, catching on. 'It must be the same in Heaven! If I talked to the chief administrator – '

'That was My thought.'

'Which I think would be the Angel Gabriel. He is the one who is to blow the horn on Judgment Day.'

'Gabriel is in My service too,' JHVH remarked. 'He has been My chief messenger, and the Prince of Thunder and Fire, not to mention Death. He also revealed the sacred laws to Mohammed.'

'I am amazed at the manner he gets around!'

'Evidently God offered him a superior position, just as

Your predecessor offered one to Baal. Good administrators are hard to come by.'

'All too true,' Parry agreed. 'I thank You for Your advice. I shall go to see Gabriel.'

'Call when You wish to pass through the void again, and I will come and guide You, Satan,' JHVH said.

'I shall. But I don't know how I can repay you.'

'I have I trust passed beyond the need for repayment.'

Perhaps He had; but Parry intended to repay the debt if he ever had opportunity. He also intended to learn more of the Llano, that persuasive and powerful song, so that perhaps he could travel safely through chaos himself.

Returning to Heaven was no problem; the captive soul guided him. When they arrived, the soul reformed into the man. 'But this is Heaven!' he exclaimed. 'My Lord, I thought You were going to take me back!'

'I am,' Parry replied. 'But I am going to make another attempt to negotiate here. You may remain in My pouch if you wish, and I will release you when we return to Hell.'

'Thank you,' the soul said, and thinned to evanescence. Parry rolled it up again and returned it to his pouch.

Now he needed to locate the Angel Gabriel. From his days as a friar he remembered that there were three broad classes of angels, with Gabriel in the top rank. That was probably in the Ninth Heaven.

He was about to set off when he saw the guardian angels approaching again. They evidently recognized him, for they looked angry. Well, perhaps they could be of some use to him this time.

'Take me to your leader,' he said to the first.

'Just who do you think you are?' the angel demanded.

'The Incarnation of Evil,' Parry replied evenly.

The angel did a double take. 'You – how can you be here? This is Heaven!'

'Heaven is not as well run as it once was,' Parry replied.

'Now, are you going to guide me to the Angel Gabriel, or shall I find him myself?'

'I will have to consult with my superior,' the angel said, disgruntled.

'Do that,' Parry said. It was always better to go through channels, if that was feasible.

The angel's superior was a Dominion, a member of the intermediate class of angels. 'The Incarnation of Evil? *Here?* Impossible!'

'Then who the Hell do you suppose I am?' Parry inquired with a sardonic smile.

In a moment he was before the Dominion's superior, who was a Seraphim, an angel in the First Circle of the heavenly hierarchy. He had six wings, which were independently flexible. He also had experience and a realistic approach. 'How quickly can we cause You to depart these demesnes, Incarnation?'

'As quickly as you can get me an interview with Gabriel.'

The Angel Gabriel was there, drawing a cloak of privacy about the two of them. 'Yes?'

'I want to facilitate the processing of good and evil, so that needless suffering of souls may be abated,' Parry said. 'I attempted to talk with God directly, but he did not respond.'

'God is temporarily distracted,' Gabriel said.

'I am relatively new to My office. Only a century or so. I am not yet inured to needless suffering. I am ready to punish truly evil souls, but not to torment those whose only guilt is the coincidence of being wrought from the mixed thread of chaos. There has to be a better way.'

'That would be for God to say.'

'If,' Parry continued evenly, 'God does not say, then I shall be forced to take action on my own initiative.'

'You have the temerity to threaten God?'

'Offhand I would say that God is not doing his job, and

270

is due for replacement. I am trying to avoid taking that action myself, but will take it if you offer no alternative.'

'God does not make deals with Lucifer!'

'I am Satan.'

Gabriel was too old a hand to call a bluff he was uncertain of winning. 'God may elect to deal with this matter directly in due course. Suppose, in the interim, we arrange an alternative contest?'

This could be interesting. 'What do you have in mind?'

'We will designate a single mortal person whose influence can be critical. If You cannot corrupt that person, or that person's child or grandchild, to enable You to take power, You will forever abate Your effort.'

Parry made a soundless whistle. 'You are not an amateur at this sort of negotiation!'

Gabriel almost smiled. 'I never claimed to be. This would represent a bloodless way to settle the issue, if that is truly Your desire. Are You interested?'

Parry pondered. A single mortal person? How could such a person possibly foil the wiles of the Incarnation of Evil? It was suspiciously simple. So was Gabriel's use of the capital when addressing him. There had to be a catch. In fact, it was evident that this was no spur of the moment deal; Gabriel had come well prepared. 'Who?'

Gabriel waggled an admonishing finger. 'I did not say I would give You that information.'

Oho! 'When?'

'Nor that.'

'Where?'

'Nor that.'

The nature of the challenge was becoming clearer. How could he corrupt a mortal when he had no information about that mortal's identity? 'That is not a wager I care to risk.'

Gabriel considered. 'Perhaps if we provided one of those items of information?'

271

'Three,' Parry said firmly.

'Two.'

Parry pondered. 'I select the two.'

'You select one.'

The Angel was a hard bargainer! But the notion of this challenge had an insidious appeal. Gabriel had said that this mortal's influence would be critical, and Gabriel's word was good. That meant that Parry really could win power over God if he manipulated the situation correctly. It certainly seemed preferable to allowing the continuing and needless suffering of a host of mortals.

'Agreed,' he said. 'Tell me the name.'

'Niobe Kaftan.'

The name did not register, but of course there were too many mortal identities for him to remember. He would research it the moment he returned to Hell. 'And the information you choose to provide?'

'The time,' Gabriel said. 'That person will come into mortal existence early in the twentieth century.'

'The twentieth century!' Parry exploded. 'That's six centuries away!'

Gabriel shrugged. 'You did not bargain for a particular time.'

Parry realized that Gabriel had outsmarted him, and thereby bought six centuries of grace for his Master. He had been had – but he had to admire the finesse of it. He extended his hand. 'It is not every day that someone outwits the Master of Deception.'

Gabriel took the hand. 'I daresay such a day will not soon come again.'

'If you ever stand in need of a position – '

Gabriel smiled. 'Perhaps in six centuries.'

They had an understanding. Meanwhile, they remained opposed.

13
Niobe

Parry, having been outsmarted by the Angel Gabriel, resigned himself to several more centuries of the present order and went about his business. He did not try to take power directly, because of the covenant made, but he did do his best to find more efficient ways to evoke the evil that was in mortal folk, simplifying classification. Ozymandias reorganized Hell, dividing it into militaristic segments that were run largely by the damned souls themselves; thus those souls knew that their suffering was largely of their own making. When Ozymandias began assembling attractive concubines from among the damned souls, Lilah became restive, and finally Parry took her back, allowing Nefertiti to take an extended holiday in mock Heaven. It was nice to be back with Lilah, after this hiatus; she did know well how to please him.

The world, as it turned out, had one or two additional continents, and Parry found distraction sowing mischief in the mortal exploration and colonization of the 'New World'. Because the majority of the mortals conducting the colonization were heretical Christians, this was a singular challenge. Soon he had them acting just the way the Church had, conducting witch hunts and martyring *their* heretics. The Incarnation of Evil might not have been gaining influence in the overall scheme, but certainly he was not losing it either.

The Renaissance arrived, and now Parry saw why Chronos had asked him to spare Milan from the Black Plague. It was indeed an artistic and cultural centre, and though it spawned more good than evil, he was glad to see it.

The mortals became more clever at both magic and science, developing both to far more sophisticated applications than had occurred in the past. They would soon have seen through the devices of his mortality; now many mortals possessed similar competence.

He started an advertising campaign to make Hell seem more attractive. It remained of course a place of punishment, and everyone knew that; but it was also the place of expiation for the evil defined in the souls. It was evident that Heaven was not the place to expiate evil, so Parry simply established many levels with diminishing punishment as souls improved. Actually, after the first soul returned from Heaven with the report on its appalling dullness, few if any souls wanted to go there. The truth was that sin, particularly of carnal lust, was far more interesting than the perpetual singing of hosannas. Mock Heaven became increasingly populous, so that even those souls that qualified for release to Heaven preferred to remain. Once he got things squared away with God, he would send up a shipment; the souls would be less reluctant to go if they could go together.

He researched diligently, seeking the Llano, the ultimate song. But his success was imperfect; he was able only to acquire parts of it. The thing was somehow linked to the very foundations of the universe, not to be understood by any ordinary person.

The centuries passed. Parry went to the furnace and interviewed Lucifer, his predecessor. 'Are you ready to serve Me yet?' he inquired. 'Give up your mortal life so that it is no longer possible for you to be an Incarnation, and I will assign you to some nefarious chore that takes advantage of your propensities.'

Lucifer was proud; he declined. Parry came again, fifty years later; Lucifer declined again. But after several such visits, he finally relented, realizing that there was no hope of ousting Parry from the Office. He gave up his mortal life and became a truly damned soul.

Parry assigned him to sundry tasks, lowly at first. As time passed and Lucifer demonstrated increasing loyalty and reliability, Parry promoted him to more responsible tasks. The former Incarnation did have a talent for the business, and was excellent at evoking the hidden evil of mortals.

In this manner the twentieth century approached. 'Lucifer, watch for the appearance of one mortal named Niobe Kaftan,' he said. 'Her presence will commence the final contest between Me and God, and I want to have the advantage from the outset. You will see that it is Mine.'

'I shall see that it is Thine,' Lucifer agreed.

War had been virtually continuous in the mortal realm, but now it spread more widely, involving most of the nations of the world. Mars, the Incarnation of War, was kept quite busy, and so was Parry. But it was a seemingly minor event relating to that war that abruptly claimed his complete attention.

Lucifer had found Niobe Kaftan in Ireland. She had come into existence as that identity when she married a man some years her junior, Cedric Kaftan, and Lucifer had scrambled to set up a programme of nullification. He didn't bother Parry with the details, and Parry had been too busy with the war and the hordes of mixed souls flowing to Hell from that altercation to inquire.

'You know he botched it,' Lilah remarked one day.

'What?'

'Lucifer. He freed a demon from Hell to assassinate her, and the stupid demon got the wrong person.'

'Assassinate whom?'

'Your nemesis. That woman. Niobe.'

Now it registered. 'How could Lucifer fail? He's experienced!'

'It seems the woman's husband has a friend who's into

275

magic, and he discovered the plot, and the husband took her place. I can't think why. So he's gone, and she remains.'

Parry got busy. He fired Lucifer from the case as a matter of principle; failure in a simple mission was not to be tolerated. Then he went to spy on the young woman. He made himself invisible and entered the cabin where she dwelt with her baby.

He looked at her, and was stunned by her appearance. She was the most beautiful woman of her generation! No wonder the love-struck husband had sacrificed himself for her.

The Angel Gabriel had gained his Master over five hundred years by this deal. Now Parry understood that it was not close to ending here; Gabriel was really trying to win the contest. A woman so lovely that mortal men would gladly throw away their lives for her – and, indeed, Parry himself did not want her to die now. Not while her beauty was fresh. It would be like breaking a priceless vase.

How, then, was he to nullify her impact on the situation? For she would surely proceed to her mischief against him if he did act to prevent it.

But what form would this mischief take? If he could determine that, then he could formulate a plan to deal with it. There should be many ways to divert the thrust without actually hurting her.

He watched her for a time, but she seemed wholly innocent, merely taking care of herself, her home and her baby boy. Nothing about her, other than her amazing comeliness, indicated any potential for the defeat of the Incarnation of Evil. Her appearance would fade with the years.

Perplexed, he returned to Hell. He summoned Mephistopheles, another former Incarnation of Evil. 'You are the most sophisticated and devious of the Lords of Hell,' he said. 'Fathom the nature of this woman, the widow Niobe Kaftan, and inform Me how she can influence the tangled skein of destiny to give God the victory over Me.'

'Gladly, Lord,' Mephistopheles said, disappearing.

In due course he was back with his report. 'The woman is more than she seems,' Mephistopheles said. 'She is of only ordinary cleverness, and has no particular skill at management, but is extraordinarily attractive.'

'What else is news,' Parry said wryly. 'For days after I saw her, her face appeared in my mind every time I closed my eyes. It put Lilah in a royal snit. But beauty alone no longer launches a thousand ships.'

'I am not so sure. She finagled her way to Parnassus in the living state and interviewed several Incarnations.'

'She *what*?'

Mephistopheles smiled. 'As You said, she is beautiful. She set fire to a funeral boat she was on, bringing Thanatos, and of course he could not take her soul because she was not yet slated to die. When he saw her – he is after all a man. So he took her to his mansion and had his staff tend to her burns. Then Chronos – '

'Chronos is in on this? He's my friend!'

'She must have smiled at him,' Mephistopheles said, enjoying this. 'He took her to Fate, who was evidently quite impressed – '

'What would impress that three-headed hog?' Parry growled.

'I wouldn't know; I can't snoop directly on Incarnations. Then he took her to War, who recognized her potential. Then on to Gaea, who told her that her husband had sacrificed himself in her place because she was destined to make much trouble for Satan. That was all; they do not seem to know any more than we do in what manner she will affect You, but they assist her because of it.'

'Most of them have always conspired against Me,' Parry

277

muttered. 'But Chronos – he has always been my friend. I can't understand why he would be involved in this.'

'If he is your friend, why don't you ask him?'

'I shall.' Parry conjured himself to Purgatory and knocked on the door of the mansion of the Incarnation of Time.

Chronos had changed officeholders since the last time Parry had visited, and this new one was distinctly less friendly than the prior ones had been. What had happened?

'Your office and Mine have always got along well,' Parry said. 'Have I in some way alienated you, Chronos?'

'You gave me a real workout when I assumed the office,' Chronos said tightly. 'You posed as my friend, but you used me to achieve your own ends. I had to – but why should I tell you, and give you another chance to interfere?'

Parry sighed. 'I apologize for what I may do in your past, my future. Evidently things become very difficult then. For several centuries I have been friends with the holders of your office, and I regret learning that has changed.'

'It has changed. If that is all – '

'Please, Chronos! Certainly I will leave you alone in the interim, with regret. But I came to ask one question, and if you would be so kind as to answer that – '

'One question,' Chronos said grimly.

'Why is the mortal woman Niobe Kaftan important to you?'

'Damn you!' Chronos exclaimed. 'Are you trying to torment me worse?'

'No, no! Remember, I am from the other direction! I do not at this stage know. I had no intent to – '

Chronos straightened his expression. 'Of course that is true, though you are the realm's most consummate liar. I will answer you, though I curse myself for doing so. Niobe was my lover, and I miss her – ' He was unable to finish.

Astonished, Parry made his way out. He had never known Chronos to take a mortal lover! Evidently Niobe's widowhood had made her vulnerable, and the Incarnation had taken advantage of it despite living in the opposite direction. Now that she was, by Chronos' reckoning, about to be married, his affair with her was over, and he was hurting.

The lover of the Incarnation of Time! Now it was easier to comprehend her significance. Chronos' Hourglass was the most powerful magical instrument known, and if she were able to influence him, her mischief could be magnified in ways that Hell itself could hardly combat! No wonder the friendship between their two offices had been sundered; a woman had in her fashion come between them.

What a canny conniver the Angel Gabriel had proved to be! To select a woman so beautiful that she snared the Incarnation of Time himself! It was too bad Gabriel had not been in Hell's employ. Parry had to respect the superior nature of this ploy.

But it had not happened yet. Could he act to prevent the woman from seducing the Incarnation? This was uncertain, because of course Fate was on the other side. Parry could pluck the threads of Fate, but only when she wasn't paying attention; each Incarnation was supreme in his or her own bailiwick. Fate would be protecting Niobe, now that they had met; it would be prohibitively difficult for him to do anything directly.

He had to admire the developing prettiness of this trap. Gabriel had set him up for as nefarious a situation as any demon could have devised. Of course angels were but the positive aspect of demons, formed from ether. Evidently they were not as different from each other as he had assumed.

279

Well, there was no help for it now but to go home and wait for his opportunity. He would have a demon watch Niobe constantly, and notify him the moment she did anything significant. Meanwhile, he would proceed with his normal business.

He had to admit that despite the awkwardness of his position, he was discovering a certain infernal joy in the challenge. Niobe's beauty was not the least of it; it was much more fun to corrupt a lovely woman than a plain one.

His first alert came several months later. Niobe, after remaining quiescent, had abruptly taken a ship to America for no apparent reason. She was definitely up to something!

Parry joined her on the ship, watching her constantly. But she acted quite normally, avoiding the predatory men and remaining mostly in her cabin, reading.

Then, abruptly, Fate came to her, in the form of a spider. And, while Parry spied from cover, Fate took Niobe in as an Aspect of herself, leaving a prior Aspect of herself in Niobe's body to complete the voyage.

Niobe had become an Aspect of Fate!

Now Parry understood how she was to become Chronos' lover! The Incarnations did indulge each other in this manner on occasion, because they understood each other far better than any mortal could. Niobe was now the youngest and by far the prettiest Aspect of Fate, so this duty naturally would fall to her. He should have realized!

His problem had just been compounded. He knew from his prior observations that Niobe blamed him for the murder of her husband. Lucifer had done it, but it was indeed Parry's responsibility, for he had directed Lucifer to nullify Niobe. So Niobe was his sworn enemy, and now she had enormously increased power.

Again, he had to admire Gabriel's cunning. At every turn, this scheme became more diabolical!

How was he going to do anything about Niobe now? He had to try, lest he forfeit the contest. He could not touch her physically; even had she not become invulnerable as an Incarnation, the two wiser other Aspects of Fate that shared her body would have protected her. He needed to get her alone, and that was impossible.

Except for one occasion. Fate had to go to the Void to fetch the substance for the threads of Life. Clotho, the youngest, was the spinner of the threads; it was always her task to fetch the substance.

Parry knew what the Void was like! He knew that very few could ever face it, let alone negotiate within it. *Only* the Aspect of Clotho could do it, not the other two.

That was where he could approach her alone. That was where he could corrupt her – if he was ever to do it. Perhaps he would fail, but he had to try.

When the new Clotho made her maiden excursion to the Void, Parry followed her. He knew better than to enter that region of chaos without some kind of guide, but in this case, Niobe was his guide. He would stay with her until she emerged, perforce.

She began at the edge of Purgatory, where a road led towards the strange region beyond. Parry had not realized that chaos could be approached by a road! He followed, invisible and silent; he wanted to be sure she was alone, without her two companion Aspects, before he addressed her.

The road became a path, and the path wended through a thick forest. She spoke once, as if reflecting on something she had heard. 'The Incarnation of War, and of Nature. I wonder what business they have here?'

What business indeed! Perhaps Mars sought the raw stuff of violence here, and Gaea the stuff of nature. So they had made a path. But he was sure that they did not go all the way into chaos.

The forest became so thick and the trees so large that the path was hopelessly squeezed and the light was almost cut off. Now Parry saw that Niobe was trailing a thread. That was how she intended to find her way out – by following her thread back! It was a secure device, for no one but her fellow Aspect Atropos could cut that thread of Life. Not when Fate was paying attention. Lucifer had had to fudge the records in Purgatory to arrange for the death of Niobe – and even then, the ploy had gone wrong, taking out the wrong person and complicating Parry's challenge. It was dangerous to mess with Fate.

Niobe squeezed through the densest part of the forest, and Parry followed, having less difficulty because he was able to change his form. He became an invisible bird, flitting through crevices too narrow for his human form. Had Niobe not been an extremely slender figure overall, she would not have made it. Or was it that the path somehow accommodated her contours, which were by no means minor, so that she alone could pass?

Now the forest thinned, but the trees were misshaped and miscoloured. Chaos was drawing nigh.

He followed her on through a region of vertigo, a pin-wheel path. Then the path become a stream. Niobe hesitated, then removed her yellow cloak, laid it down, and sat on it, forming a floating craft of it. She was now in her underwear, and the contours that had been only hinted at before became fully evident. What a creature she was! He could have stared at her for a decade, while jealous fumes rose from Lilah.

That gave him a notion of how to corrupt her. He knew that she was to become Chronos' lover – lucky Chronos! – and that she was presently a widow and conservative about her relationship with any other man. If he played upon that situation, stressing the sordid interpretation, he might turn her off it before it started. She might even resign her office within the trial period. That would certainly foil much of Gabriel's plan for her.

Niobe floated out into the centre of the Void, where Parry did not dare go. He was afraid he would get lost despite being near her, and did not care to risk it. JHVH would probably rescue him again if he called, but he preferred not to impose on the Deity of the Jews again if he could avoid it.

The woman seemed to spend an eternity there, gathering the substance of chaos into her craft. She, alone of all, could spin chaos into thread. At last she emerged, hauling herself along by the thread she had played out behind.

As she came to the solid portion of the path, Parry knew it was time for him to act. He did not like what he had to do, but certainly it would be better to nullify the woman this way than Lucifer's way.

He made himself visible. 'Hi, babe.'

Niobe jumped. She caught sight of him, and stood appalled. 'I hate you!' she cried.

Parry laughed, getting into the role. 'Of course you do, you lovely creature.'

'You killed my husband!' she flared. Oh, she was as lovely in her anger as in her confusion!

He saw that he could, by the mechanism of judicious interpretation, use her very grief for her husband to turn her away from the other Incarnations.

First he explained about the nature of the substance of chaos: good and evil inextricably mixed, so that the whole of the process of mortal living was required to define and separate the two. He made sure to refer frequently to her appearance, calling her 'sweets' and 'sugar' and 'delicious' and 'luscious plum' so as to prepare her for the denouement. The irony was that it was true; she was the most delectable mortal creature he had encountered, though she was now immortal. He was using the terms for a

283

purpose, but each time he did, it reminded him of the truth of it. Niobe really was not his type, but even so, her beauty smote him with increasing force.

She was appropriately appalled. 'All life is just a laboratory to classify the substance of the Void?'

'Indeed. Beautiful, isn't it? Just like you, cutie.' If only his words were not so true! He wished he were not her antagonist, so that he could – what? Use this Aspect of Fate as Chronos would? No chance of that!

No chance? Suddenly he realized that this could be another aspect of Gabriel's ploy. To cause the Incarnation of Evil himself to be smitten by one of the Incarnations on God's side! That would surely destroy his effectiveness in opposing God! It was insidiously clever: Gabriel had made sure that Parry would take a personal interest in this woman, so as to discover how to nullify her, knowing that Parry had always had an eye for the fairest of female forms. That he had grown inevitably tired of the knowledgeability of demonesses and damned souls, and found true innocence appealing. Niobe was perfectly cast to appeal to him!

Parry steeled himself and proceeded to the necessary finale. 'The Incarnations are human, doll,' he said. 'They have human ambitions, weaknesses and lusts.'

She reacted beautifully, in the various senses of the word. 'Lusts! What are you talking about?'

'I'm so glad you asked, precious.' He went on to introduce the notion of Chronos' need for a lovely young female Incarnation. She continued to react with ideal horror. On one level he hated what he was doing, but on another he liked it, because it was all too easy to imagine himself in Chronos' position. 'You see, honeypot, we Incarnations have to get along with each other. We are not antagonists; we must cooperate. Chronos can be awkward, because he lives backward, but in this respect he is typically human.'

'I can't believe that!'

'You may verify it very simply, roundheels,' he said cruelly. 'Ask Chronos. He remembers.'

She was appalled, but beginning to believe. Now he proceeded to the lie, his specialty. He explained how the Incarnations could have cooperated to eliminate Niobe's mortal husband, so that the most beautiful of mortal women could become an Incarnation and satisfy Chronos' lust. 'I suggest you relax and enjoy it, toots,' he concluded.

'Relax, hell!' she screamed, forgetting her innocence enough to utter that foul word.

He smiled. 'Exactly.' He had really got through to her; she was now ready to kill Chronos.

He added one more detail, unable to resist. He assumed the likeness of her departed husband.

She recognized it, and screamed incoherently at him.

'Shall I kiss you, sweetlips?' he inquired. 'I, too, find you desirable, and can make you forget – '

She struck at him with her distaff. 'Get out! Get out!'

Parry resumed his normal form. 'Another time, perhaps, when you have been suitably broken in.' That was the final fillip; she would remember it the moment she saw Chronos. *First the Lord of Time, then the Lord of Evil.*

He faded out, leaving her sobbing with grief and outrage. He watched long enough to be sure she had not been feigning.

He left her, satisfied that he had done what he could. But somehow he had no joy in this operation. He hated to do this to such a lovely young woman, and he was sorry to do it to Chronos, whose other officeholders had been his only friends among the Incarnations. But mostly he was ashamed of the fact that he had been striking as much at his own sensitivities as at hers; he really did find her

285

desirable, and hated the necessity of treating such a creature with such contempt.

But the treatment was not effective, almost to his relief. The other Aspects of Fate managed to talk Niobe around, and she proceeded to have the affair with Chronos. She opposed Satan implacably, and he could hardly blame her. His effort to turn her off Chronos had been a double-or-nothing gesture; he had known that if it proved unsuccessful, all her anger would focus on him, Satan.

But her tenure as Clotho did not seem to alter that balance of good and evil in the mortal world significantly. Parry was unable to make real progress, but he did fend off the mischief of the other Incarnations. The standoff that had existed for centuries continued.

Mephistopheles continued to watch, however, for the mischief had three generations to run. Perhaps it was not Niobe but her son or his offspring that would prove to be the key.

That son grew up to be a magician of surprising potential. But he was unmarried. If he died without issue, that would end the matter, for as long as Niobe remained an Incarnation she could not have another child. Incarnations were frozen at the age they entered the office unless, as in his own case, they had the wit to choose to settle in at another age. Lilah had known, and given him the clue at the outset. But whatever the physical age, their inability to change meant sterility, for the process of gestation was an aspect of ageing.

Then the magician son decided to marry his cousin Blenda who was another mortal of Niobe's stripe: the most beautiful of *her* generation. Mephistopheles informed Parry the moment the engagement was made.

'Take him out,' Parry said curtly. He did not like such business, but he could not afford to have that third generation launched.

'I shall have to free a demon to the mortal realm, my Lord,' Mephistopheles said.

That was a complicated business; demons were hard to free for even a few hours, and the prospects were limited. But this was critical. 'Do it.'

Mephistopheles faded out with a smile; he liked dirty business.

But again destiny proved to be difficult to balk. The ploy misfired, and instead of the magician or his bride it was the bride's mother the demon killed. Gabriel's ploy continued, and Niobe was, if anything, even more implacably set against Satan.

Niobe continued to be a nuisance. She tried to save a Senator Parry had marked for extinction, and succeeded in that; Parry was, however, able to salvage the situation by destroying the Senator's reputation instead.

Then, abruptly, Niobe decided to step down from office. 'What?' Parry demanded, astonished. 'How can she interfere with Me if she steps down?'

'She can bear another child,' Lilah said darkly.

That would do it! 'Find out about this,' he snapped.

Lilah vanished. Soon enough she was back with her report. 'She plans to marry her husband's cousin Pacian, who has the magic music.'

'Music?'

'I thought that would perk Your ears, my Lord! Yes, he does not sing as well as You, but his magic enhances it so that the effect can be as great.'

There was a certain malice in her remark that annoyed him, but he kept it reined. He was getting somewhat tired of Lilah's mannerisms, though she remained his most effective sexual partner. One of these decades he would have to send her away on a long assignment so he could have a turn at some fresher female. 'Is that all?'

'Plenty more, my Lord. There is a set of prophecies in

her possession. It seems that when she was new in office, and still attached to her son, she prevailed on Atropos to pose as a grandmotherly figure and – '

'Atropos!' he interrupted. 'The senior Aspect of Fate? She cuts the threads of Life. Some grandmother!'

'Yes, my Lord. But Atropos took the little boy and his cousin Pacian to two seers who happened to be competent, and asked the same question of each: Whom were the two boys to marry, and what would become of their children?'

'That is of interest to Me,' Parry agreed. 'Why was I not advised before?'

'The demon that Mephistopheles assigned to spy on them did not realize that the prophecies were valid. Most seers are impostors, making up items to please the clients. So it was only now, when I investigated, that I recognized these prophecies for what they are: sendings from Gabriel. The Angel was giving Niobe a hint of the destiny of her line.'

'In such a way that it bypassed the demon,' Parry said with grudging admiration. 'Continue.'

'The first seer said, and I quote, "Each to possess the most beautiful woman of her generation, who will bear him the most talented daughter of her type. Both daughters to stand athwart the tangled skein, and one may marry Death and the other Evil."'

Parry's jaw dropped.

'The other seer said, and I quote again, "One to be saviour of deer, his child saviour of man; other to love an Incarnation, his child to *be* one. But the skein is tangled." More she would not say.'

Parry found his voice. 'And Niobe's son, the magician, did marry Pacian's daughter Blenda, the most beautiful woman of her generation. Now Pacian, a widower, is marrying Niobe herself, the most beautiful woman of *her* generation.'

'As I said, my Lord, they were true prophecies. So it seems there will be two daughters, highly talented, and one may marry Thanatos – '

'And the other may marry Me!' Parry finished. 'How can this be? I will never marry again!'

'Not while I'm with You,' Lilah agreed darkly. 'But there is a lot of leeway in that word *may*, my Lord.'

'Not enough leeway! This complicates the plot considerably!'

'The girls will stand athwart a tangled skein,' Lilah agreed. 'One to save man, the other to be an Incarnation.'

'The daughter of the man who loves an Incarnation,' Parry agreed. 'That would be Pacian. I must watch out for his daughter.'

'And for the other girl,' she reminded him. 'She is the one who will save man – which means You will lose.'

'I must be rid of both of them!' Parry snapped. 'One is Niobe's daughter, the other her granddaughter.'

'But each time You have tried to take out one of that line, You have failed. In fact, it was the last failure that caused Pacian to become a widower, so that now Niobe can marry him. You played into God's hands!'

Parry definitely did not like her attitude. She was enjoying this, in her covert way. 'I shall be paying closer attention henceforth,' he said darkly. 'This contest is not yet done.' Still, he heeded the warning of experience; with the amount of attention that was focusing on this matter, it would be extraordinarily difficult to eliminate those girls. He would have to try other methods first, defusing this matter in some more devious and effective manner.

His first chance was to prevent at least one of the girls from coming into existence. Therefore the next time Niobe went to gather chaos from the Void, he intercepted her. That was the one place she had to listen to him, because her other Aspects were damped out and she was alone.

'So you are quitting, cutie,' he said, as if it were of no account.

'Go to Hell,' she snapped back.

He tried to suggest to her that he was glad she was departing the office, but she was now too canny to be deceived. 'I am fated to produce a mortal child who will be a real pain in the tail for you.'

He could not fool her and, oddly, he found he did not want to. She had fought him for decades, and he had admired her for the same period. He decided to talk seriously. 'There are currents of destiny that perhaps only God comprehends. Our glimpses of the future are fleeting and imperfect, but I have taken a reading on your daughter and see only a terrible storm perhaps forty years hence. I do not know the outcome.'

'And one may marry Death, the other Evil,' she said, recalling the prophecy.

'Why should I ever bind Myself to a mortal woman?' he demanded with genuine ire. Yet he knew that had Niobe herself been interested, in her youth, he would have been sorely tempted.

But she had the answer. 'She is to be an Incarnation.'

'And what woman, whether mortal or Incarnation, would ever bind herself to Me?' There was a second level to that question, because of their past interaction. Even at this stage, if Niobe were to change her mind about him as a man . . .

'Only an evil one,' Niobe said. She looked no happier about it than he felt.

'You are indeed a good woman, as well as a lovely one,' he said with feeling. 'Yet the prophecy – '

'Satan, what are you getting at?'

Now he spoke straight from the heart. 'Niobe, there is a tangle coming in your skein that neither of us understands. Something strange is brewing. Let's avoid the whole issue, and oppose each other on conventional grounds. Keep your present office, O lovely woman! Do not generate that child.'

'You're crazy!'

'No, I am evil, not crazy. You know Me – ' he tried to stop himself, but was carried away by a surge of emotion. 'Therefore you will not do for Me what you did for Chronos.'

She stared at him. 'You – desire my favour?'

'I do desire it.' He had not realized it fully until this moment. Perhaps Lilah had, though; that would account for her creeping alienation. She tolerated his affairs with damned souls, but she realized that his love of an Incarnation, particularly this one, was mischief indeed.

'You will never have it!' Niobe said.

'That I know,' he said heavily. 'Still, I wish you would remain in office.'

She laughed in his face.

Now sudden wrath overcame him. He had spoken truth to her, and she had rejected it. That was the humiliation that stung worst! 'Then feel the brunt of My wrath!' he cried. 'And your child will suffer too. You and yours will rue this hour!' He departed.

He had made a terrific fool of himself, he knew. He had been blinded by the beauty of his opponent, and allowed his true emotion to surface. Now he was in worse trouble than ever.

More than a decade later, Parry's attention was called to Niobe again. He had not bothered with her in the interim, because her nuisance of a magician son had crafted spells to protect her and the children, and the magician knew what he was doing. But now she was taking the two girls into the Hall of the Mountain King to obtain the gifts of instruments that would greatly enhance their powers. He had to prevent that!

He sent a demon to trigger the Mountain King's defences, so that the gifts could not be removed from the premises. The demon performed, but the Mountain King himself investigated, and as Fate would have it, he recognized Niobe from her period as an Aspect and let the gifts go. It seemed impossible to impede the progress of this juggernaut!

But he continued with the routine business of his office, evoking evil wherever he could. One of the mortal organizations that interfered with his activities was the United Nations. He had succeeded in corrupting aspects of it, but the main part still stood for decency and order in the world, and so remained a problem. He worked out a plan to detonate a psychic stink bomb at its headquarters that would cause the organization to be expelled from America and moved to a hostile country. That would blunt its effectiveness.

Naturally Fate meddled in. He was ready for that. He had arranged irresistible situations that caused all three Aspects to retire at almost the same time, so that Fate was a complete novice at the moment. By the time the new office-holders became experienced and canny, he would have won a major coup. He still hoped to gain a sufficient advantage of the inattentive God before the skein Niobe had started ran its full course; then that skein would become irrelevant.

Then, at last, he would be able to take control, and commence a more efficient and gentle programme for defining the universe. The need was becoming more pressing, for in these centuries of God's dereliction mankind was getting rapidly into more trouble. Population was exploding, and the world was getting polluted, and the threat of a holocaustic war was increasing. Someone had to act to abate the situation before everything accomplished in thousands of years was destroyed.

Just to be sure that Fate did not muddle through to a victory, he arranged to have false data inserted in the Purgatory computer. The computer was a modernistic science device that now kept track of the numbers and identities of souls being processed. If the new Fate queried it, she would be sent on a spurious chase. The old Fate would never have been fooled, but the new one should be vulnerable.

All followed through as planned. He could not resist taunting Fate as the denouement of this ploy approached. She had just ventured, in the form of Lachesis, the middle-aged Aspect, into the sample Hell he had instituted on earth as part of his advertising campaign. She had with Gaea's assistance disabused one of the employees there, which annoyed him. So he broached her personally, assuming the standard Satan form, which was one of the regular alternates he used when on official business.

'So now you have nullified the last of the four threads, you meddling frump,' he said nastily. 'You think you have won.'

'Evil is never truly defeated,' Lachesis said grimly.

Not if I have My way, he thought. The irony was that though he wore the name of Evil, he was trying to do what was right; it was that God these others served who was negligent. But of course none of them would believe that. Then he told her about the manner in which he had interfered with the Purgatory computer, causing it to seem to list only selected threads.

'The penalty of being a novice,' she muttered ruefully. 'I feel very stupid.'

'Merely inexperienced,' he told her. There was an odd familiarity about her, but probably that was because he had dealt with so many mortals, and so many Incarnations too; at some time in the past six centuries he had probably encountered someone like her. Then he realized that he might be able to gain an even greater advantage from this, playing further on her inexperience. 'I can offer you a better deal.'

'You're not to be trusted!'

'Don't depend on trust; depend on common sense. Sometimes what seems good turns out evil in the long run, like the Inquisition.' Indeed, he had helped start that, working for God, and then as Satan had succeeded in perverting it to a potent instrument for evil, especially in Spain. 'Sometimes what seems evil turns out good, like the Black Plague.' That had been his pride, but he discovered too late that the decimation of the labour force which it had accomplished led to a premium on serfs and paved the way for the end of the repressive feudal system. Thus he had accomplished little if any lasting evil, in the sense that he gained no greater proportion of souls for Hell than he might have had he never made the effort. That had taught him caution. Thus he had no abiding commitment to this United Nations mischief; it was mainly a challenge, to discommode Fate.

'What's your pitch, Satan?' she asked with more alertness than he liked.

'I will cancel the psychic stink in exchange for a simple shift in employment for one person. No harm done to her, no evil on her soul, just an inconsequential change.' Would she fall for it? No reason why she shouldn't, yet his fortune in this particular matter had been so bad that he hardly trusted it now.

'Who is this person?'

She was nibbling! 'A young woman, hardly more than a girl, of no consequence, really.'

'So you say. Name the woman.'

Here was the tricky part. He knew exactly whom he meant, but could not afford to make it seem important. There were two girls who looked like twins but were actually a generation apart. One was Orb Kaftan, Niobe's daughter, with buckwheat-honey hair, who might marry Evil. Of course that qualification destroyed the validity of the prophecy; anything *might* happen! The other was

Luna Kaftan, Niobe's granddaughter, with the chestnut-brown hair. She was the dangerous one. But she was now protected by Thanatos, who was evidently smitten by her sex appeal; Parry could not touch her directly.

'Oh, she's named Moon, or some such,' he said carelessly. 'It hardly matters.' And what a lie that was! If he could nullify Luna, he could defuse the final aspect of Gabriel's ploy. 'She's actually descended from a former Incarnation. Name's – let me see – Kaftan. There are actually two girls, but I want the one with the darker hair.'

She was silent, considering this. If she caught on, the ploy was finished – but why should she? She could hardly know the daughters of a former Incarnation, so early in her own career in the office.

'You're up to something,' she said at last.

She was biting! 'My dear associate, there is no call to trust Me! You can handle it yourself! Simply give me your word that if no bomb goes off at the UN, you will modify the girl's thread to shunt her away from politics.'

'No harm will come to the girl?'

'I promise never to harm the girl whose thread you change.'

'But your promise is worthless!'

'My word is sacred when properly given.' Indeed, though he was the Father of Lies, he had never broken his given word. The same could hardly be said of the mortals who had accepted his gifts in exchange for their souls; they had used any cheap device to weasel out, after using up the gifts.

They made an oath in blood, and it was done. Victory! He had nullifed Luna, for it was in politics she had been destined to thwart his last design. He had been unable to fight the devious threads of Fate before, but this change was to be made by Fate herself; this one would be secure.

Lachesis agreed to divert the thread of the darker-haired descendent of Niobe Kaftan.

When it was done, he told her how his side of the deal was academic anyway, because Chronos had acted to notify the UN security force about the bomb.

'You know that?' she cried, outraged. 'You cheated!'

'Hardly. I agreed to spare the UN, and Niobe's non-political offspring. They will be spared.' Then he remembered something: Lachesis had been the first to name Niobe – when he had not. He had been very careful about that, referring only to 'a former Incarnation'.

Then he made the connection. That seeming familiarity – *This was Niobe!* Older, no longer as attractive physically, but definitely her. No longer Clotho, but Lachesis!

'I will see that my mortal daughter, Orb, never enters politics,' she said sweetly. 'An oath is an oath.'

'Orb? I meant Luna!'

'Luna was born with clover-honey hair, the lighter of the two. Were you not aware of that, Satan?'

He had not been. He had never examined the girls personally before Luna came to America, but had depended on reports. Luna's hair, evidently, had been dyed. He had fallen for the reversal.

'You came back – to deceive Me!' She only smiled.

He had been suckered after all! He had to admire the cleverness of the countertrap. Niobe was really paying him back for the death of her husband! All he could do now was bow out with grace. 'I congratulate you, Niobe, on an excellent counterploy.'

'That is a compliment indeed, coming from you.'

'But now I know you, and I shall not be deceived again. There are other ways.' He conjured himself away.

There were indeed other ways. He discovered Niobe's son, the magician, had managed to distort the readout on the balance of good and evil on his soul, so that he was in

Purgatory. He belonged in Hell. Parry claimed him now, quite legitimately, and put him in the fires. Then, by some intricate manoeuvring, he destroyed the message the magician had left for his daughter: how to enable Fate to prevail against Satan in future encounters. Had she learned that, Parry would have been powerless against Fate; as it was, he could continue trying to confound her, and perhaps would yet succeed in nullifying Luna.

Then Niobe came to him again, and made another deal: she put her own soul on the line in exchange for the chance to locate her son in Hell and get the information from him. This he could not decline. To have a chance to obtain Niobe's soul in Hell, subject to his will – that was the absolute stuff of dreams! He would require her to assume the form of her youth. He would not mistreat her, he would love her, and perhaps in time she would come to return the favour.

Mars supervised the encounter so that it was fair – and once again Niobe won through and got what she had come for. She had defeated him yet another time.

Yet, somehow, Parry didn't mind. He still held the image of Niobe in his mind, as she had been in her luscious youth. Had he won her soul, he could have ravished her hourly. But he knew that would have been a poor substitute for her independent love. He was satisfied to have her escape. The feeling he had for her had never really died.

14
Mars

The business with Niobe overlapped a more serious matter, which was one reason why he misplayed Fate. Perhaps that, too, had been planned by Gabriel: all the most difficult matters coming together.

This other business involved the Incarnation of War, Mars. The current officeholder had made himself expert in every form of battlecraft, and was truly competent in fomenting hostilities. He sided with God, but actually did Satan about as much good, because of the inevitable stress and suffering engendered by warfare. Refugees from a bombing, deprived of their homes, livelihoods and families, were often thrown into bare survival situations where ethics and decency were unrealistic. Evil flourished there, and souls were quickly tarnished to their maximum potential. Mars liked to believe that he was serving God by overthrowing tyrannies, but his methods fashioned gardens in which new tyrannies sprouted avidly. He, like God, had lost sight of the true nature of the doctrine of ends and means.

So it was in this particular sequence. A major war in Europe expanded to include nations in other continents, and its aftermath left such desolation that the people were ready to grasp at anything that promised improvement. There were revolutions that sprang theoretically from the roots of the common folk, but that succeeded only in installing yet more repressive regimes. One such occurred in the Russian states, and great was the carnage thereof; another occurred in the remnant of the Holy Roman Empire, now called Germany.

At first Parry encouraged the new order in Germany,

for it brought some truly ugly characters to the fore, excellent in evoking what evil lurked in the populace. But then this took a turn he should have anticipated: persecution of minorities. Parry had never had much sympathy for that, since the Albigensian crusade in France that cost him his wife. He withdrew his support.

It was too late. Mortals could be tenacious once embarked on folly. The persecution of Jews and Gypsies intensified. When the next big war erupted, these minorities were herded into camps, their properties confiscated, their bodies given over to forced labour. It was like the Inquisition, only more systematic.

Then the killing began.

JHVH appeared in Hell. Parry welcomed him in a private interview. The Deity of the Hebrews seemed emaciated; he had not been doing well. It hurt Parry to see this, for JHVH had been his closest approach to a friend, apart from Chronos in the old days.

'I simply lack the power to protect My people from Yours,' JHVH said. 'I ask whether You will consider making a change. I must confess that I went first to God, but he would not see Me.'

'He will not see anyone,' Parry said. 'He is rapt in the contemplation of His own image, while His people go wrong. Were it not for some expert management by his lieutenant, the Angel Gabriel, I would have had the advantage of him by now.'

'So I come to you, Satan, knowing that though You represent Evil, You are no supporter of pointless suffering. My people are not Yours; their corruption by circumstance does not aggrandize You, it only diminishes Me.'

'I know that,' Parry said. 'I have no onus against Your people, and I do remember Your kindness to me in the past. I have already withdrawn my support for that regime, but have been unable to turn it aside.'

'I thought perhaps You could prevail on Your associates, the other Incarnations of Your framework, one of whom is War.'

Parry sighed. 'I have never got along well with Mars. But I will try. I will do what I can to help Your people.'

'I thank you, Satan.' JHVH departed.

Parry went to the Castle of War in Purgatory. Mars was not there; he was evidently supervising combat somewhere in the mortal realm.

He went again, a few days later. And again. Mars was never there. Finally he located Mars in the field and went there.

It was not actually a battle, but a battle line. It was called the Maginot Line, constructed by France to fend off Germany. But Germany was in the process of going around it. 'Nevertheless,' Mars said with an expansive gesture, 'this line is penetrable. A fortification is only as good as the personnel who man it and the officers who direct it. The Great Wall of China never stopped a serious invasion; the steppe warriors simply bribed the gatekeepers to let them through and proceeded without hindrance. This line was built to the specifications of the last war, and is relatively ineffective against the mechanization of this one. That is the chronic folly of mortal generals.'

'I come about a different matter,' Parry said cautiously.

Mars glanced at him. 'Why should I care what you came about, Satan? I have no use for you.'

Still the same old arrogance! 'The proprietors of Germany are maltreating certain minorities. I would prefer to spare those minorities. If you would – '

Mars laughed. 'Do you think I'm fool enough to listen to you, Father of Lies? If you say you want someone spared, sure as Hell it's to corrupt three others. Get thee away from me, old Scrotch!'

Parry realized it was hopeless. Mars would not listen, and if he did, he was apt to do the opposite of what Parry

300

asked. He was arrogant in his power, and careless of the proprieties.

But if Mars would not listen to reason, perhaps he would accede to self-interest. 'Suppose I make you a deal?'

Mars suggested that he do something impolite to himself.

'Lilah,' Parry said.

Instantly the demoness was there, stunningly attired.

'This is one of My creatures,' Parry said. 'She does My bidding, always. I will assign her to you for the duration, if you will grant the favour I ask.'

Mars looked at Lilah. He was a lusty man, and she was the precise figure that evoked the maximum response in such a man. She smiled at him just as if she cared.

'I'll make no deals with you,' Mars muttered. But his gaze remained on Lilah.

'I will leave her with you for a time,' Parry said. 'When you wish, ask her the nature of the favour I want, and she will tell you.'

'A man doesn't need to talk to a creature like that,' Mars said. 'You're wasting your time, Scrotch.' Still his eyes were locked on the target.

Parry left, hoping that the man's curiosity would surface after he had sated his lusts. Lilah was very good at her business; if she could persuade him to divert the hostilities, or reshape them in such a way that the minorities would suffer less . . .

Time passed, and the carnage only got worse. Now they were burning Jews and Gypsies in great ovens, and systematically eradicating them from the continent.

Parry visited the Castle of War again. Mars was out, as usual, but Lilah was there. 'He never asked,' she said. 'How much longer must I tolerate this lout? He has appetites that would make a mortal girl nauseous.'

Never even asked? Parry realized that his ploy had

been wasted. Mars simply didn't care. He would accept the gifts of Hell, but give nothing in return. Parry had merely lost time, and done his friend JHVH no favour.

'Tell him anyway, next time,' he said.

He departed, broodingly angry. If he ever found a way to get Mars retired, he would gladly do so. But the Incarnation of War retired only when there was complete peace on Earth, and that was seldom. Certainly it was impossible at the moment.

More time passed. The war progressed, and the Axis forces were losing. But the slaughter of minorities only intensified.

Parry went again to the Castle of War. 'He wouldn't listen,' Lilah said. 'He told me I was here for only one reason, and words were no part of it.'

Parry had had enough. 'You are relieved of this duty. Return to Hell.'

She was gone so fast there was a pop in the air where she had been. Certainly she had not liked this tour!

What was he to do now? The ploy had failed, and most of the Jews and Gypsies were dead. Though the war was drawing to a close, there was no sign of abatement of the peripheral conflicts. It might be decades before this Mars was retired.

Parry realized that at this stage he had only one alternative. He would have to go to Chronos.

The officeholders of Time had changed frequently, because each was limited by the duration of his mortal life prior to his ascension to the office. But all now were hostile to him, and this one especially so. Parry could not think what had set the man off; something must have happened in the future to enrage him with the Incarnation of Evil. This made dealing difficult. But most had the same problem Mars had, only worse: no suitable women.

He couldn't assign Lilah again, for Chronos lived backward, and he would have had to assign her years ago.

The only way she could be with Chronos at this point was if she remained continuously in his mansion, living backward with him. How would that affect her stay with Mars? Parry feared that some kind of paradox would be evoked. Anyway, she deserved a rest; she had done as well as she could in a difficult situation.

What else, then?

He pondered for some time, stumped. Then at last it came to him: he would have to tell Chronos the truth – but in a way that would make the Incarnation react as Parry wanted. This would, incidentally, account for Chronos' attitude towards him.

He sent demons out to prepare his materials. Then he brought his package to Chronos.

'What brings you here, Master of Evil?' Chronos inquired coldly.

'Oh, I had some spare time, so I thought I'd gloat a bit,' Parry said airily. He was into the lie already.

'Gloat somewhere else. I am trying to be civil, even to you.'

'I want to show you the pointlessness of trying to oppose Me,' Parry said nastily. 'You control time, but you cannot eliminate the evil I have done among the mortals. Shall I present chapter and verse?'

'Merely present your backside as you depart!' Chronos snapped.

'Naturally you do not wish to know; that frees you of the onus of being unable to prevent it.'

That stung the man. 'Why should I listen to your lies?'

'Because when I gloat, I don't lie. My accomplishments are real; My lying is only a means to the end of incalculable evil. I can prove everything – if you have the stomach to admit your defeat.'

Chronos was hooked. 'What defeat?'

'Well, for example, the supposed victory of the forces of good in the recent war. You idiots with God suppose that the elimination of the Nazis makes everything perfect, but there is no way you can undo the evil they did in passing. There will soon be other calamities, as new factions are spawned and quarrel; the termination of the Nazis is only the abolition of a name, not the substance. But those who are already dead can never be revived; that evil is permanent. Thus you, with your vaunted Hourglass, are helpless against Me, and I shall inevitably prevail against your indifferent God. That is your real defeat.'

Chronos was visibly suppressing his rage. 'What dead? Soldiers in war expect to die; this is unfortunate but not necessarily evil. Many of them go to Heaven, not to Hell.'

'These dead,' Parry said. He opened his briefcase and produced pictures of piles of corpses. 'Noncombatants. Men, women, children. Civilians who did nothing to deserve this fate – but here they are, irrefutably and awfully dead. What does your kind say to that?'

Chronos stared at the pictures. They were truly horrible; Parry's minions had obtained the most effective available. They showed every stage of the holocaust against the Jews and Gypsies in hideous detail. There was no way to doubt them; they were completely real and almost tangibly evil.

'Practically every Jew in Europe,' Parry said with feigned satisfaction. 'And every Gypsy too. Do you know about the Gypsies? They are named that because they claimed to have come to the west via Egypt, but actually they came through Romania and are better called Romani. In any event, they live a simple life, always on the move, entertaining sedentary folk, blacksmithing, playing music, dancing and stealing. You might think the stealing makes them Mine, but they do it from necessity because of their poverty. The balance on their souls is positive. But now they are all dead, and there will be no more positive souls generated among them, which gives

Me the long-term advantage. It is the same story with the Jews; their extinction diminishes their God, JHVH, and so benefits Me. Meanwhile, the evil accruing to the souls of those who have destroyed these two peoples benefits Me, because – '

'Get out!' Chronos shouted, livid. He smashed his hand through the presented pictures, knocking them to the floor.

'Scream all you want,' Parry said evenly. 'You have lost, despite your powers. You cannot deny it. There is nothing you can do. Nothing!'

Chronos charged him, but Parry conjured himself away.

His stomach was knotted, but he had done what he had come to do. He had really brought the disaster home to Chronos, and repeatedly taunted him with his supposed impotence. Now he would discover whether this savage and desperate ploy had been effective. For Chronos lived backward; he would in due course be at the onset of the European disaster. If his rage at Satan carried through . . .

He returned to Hell and summoned Lilah. 'I regret the duty I assigned you with Mars,' he said. 'It was ineffective, and no pleasure for you. I am sorry that you and I have grown apart, and would make some amends if you are willing.'

'My Lord, what are You talking about?' she asked, perplexed. 'I have not been with the current Mars.'

'Demoness, don't try to lie to Me!' he snapped. 'You may be angry, but I am trying to make it right.'

'My Lord, I never lie except on direct order from You, and never to You. Are You teasing me?'

Something was wrong. 'Are you telling me you did not perform the duty with Mars I assigned you to?'

'You made no such assignment! I would have obeyed if You had, though I much prefer Your company.'

A distant thought nagged him. Was it possible?

305

'Lilah, what happened to the Jews and Gypsies in the war just past?'

Now she was really perplexed. 'Nothing happened to either group, my Lord. Do You plan some mischief for them?'

'Nothing happened? But the Nazis – '

'The what?'

'The leaders of Germany, who – '

'Do you mean the Empire? The restored Holy Roman Empire?'

So it was true! Chronos had acted to change history, eliminating the whole of the holocaust, root and all!

And of course Chronos hated Satan, suspecting what had been on that alternate time line. But the victory was, after all, Satan's. No one else might know it, for no one else could remember what had been, but Parry knew. He was the Incarnation most involved, so it could not be eradicated from his awareness. He alone would know the truth.

There was a knock at his door. Lilah went to answer it.

JHVH stood there. He was abruptly healthier. He spoke no word; he only gazed at Parry with uncanny understanding.

He, too, remembered!

Parry went to him, and the two embraced. Then JHVH departed.

'What was that about?' Lilah asked. 'Since when do You have dealings with foreign Gods?'

'Since He did Me a favour,' Parry said. 'Now I have returned it.'

'I don't understand, my Lord.'

'You don't need to.' He grabbed her, and proceeded to an act of passion so thorough that she, with her experience of millennia, was amazed.

How sweet it is! he thought, embracing a dimension more than the body of the demoness.

* * *

He had won a victory very few knew of, and changed the mortal world for the better though he would receive no credit for that. But his battle with the other Incarnations continued, as he probed constantly for his chance to win before Niobe's granddaughter ended the contest. Whenever an office changed hands, he moved in to exploit the weakness. When Thanatos changed, by assassinating the prior officeholder and taking his place, Parry succeeded in confusing the novice. But Niobe's son, the magician, managed to arrange a date between Thanatos and the magician's daughter, Luna, and thereafter Thanatos resolutely refused to let Luna die despite provocation. Mephistopheles overreached his directive and abducted Luna and tortured her, precipitating a crisis that Parry had to tackle personally. Though furious about the torture – he would never have authorized that! – Parry had to pretend it was all his own doing. Unfortunately Thanatos was so provoked that he cast off the web of delusion Parry wove and asserted himself fully as the Incarnation of Death. Parry rather admired that, but protocol required him to depart in a fury.

Then there was the business with Fate's triple changeover, foiled by Niobe herself.

Then he succeeded in retiring Mars. He picked a suitable occasion, when the mortal realm was relatively quiet, and exerted his influence to quiet it further, until for a moment the last conflict died out and the world was in complete peace. That got rid of Mars. In a moment, of course, conflict resumed, for mortals were incapable of complete peace, and a new man assumed the office. But this one was virtually handpicked. Parry had managed to manipulate some of Fate's threads to make this one the leading prospect. He was from a kingdom of India, a Prince, and he stuttered. Parry had inducements that he trusted would prove to be quite appealing to this man.

When the time came, Parry went to the Castle of War.

He set up a garden of illusion that functioned as an annexe to the Castle, and posed with Lilah as erotic statuary. 'I am assigning you to corrupt Mars,' he told her. 'For the duration you will be known as Lila or as Lilith, and you will be unable to use the terms associated with My opponent.'

'You are demoting me to ordinary demon status!' she protested.

'I am reminding you of your place. Succeed in this mission, and all favour will be restored.'

'As my Lord decrees,' she agreed, but she was not completely pleased. 'This should not be too much of a challenge.'

'It is enough of one,' he said. 'This man has a mortal concubine, a Princess, and he loves her.'

'Ah,' she said appreciatively. 'It has been a long time since I have corrupted a man with a mortal lover.'

'Seven hundred years,' he agreed reminiscently. Actually, Jolie had not really been his lover at that stage, because of her status as a ghost, but there was no point in being technical. 'I want you to corrupt him, and if you cannot, to distract him, and if you fail even at that, to tempt him into Hell. He must be taken out of circulation at the critical time. You will have several weeks, at least.'

'Plenty of time,' she said confidently. 'You forget how much experience I have had.'

'Show some of it now,' he said. 'He is coming. I want him to know you are a concubine; he can relate to that more freely than to a real woman.'

'Thank you,' she said with not altogether insincere ire.

They assumed a position of interaction and stilled into a seeming statue. The Incarnation of War walked close, and paused to inspect them with some interest. This was the type of statuary he knew from his homeland.

Parry animated, turning his head to look at the Incarnation. 'Ah, the master of the castle arrives,' he said.

Startled, the man stepped back. This was the last thing he had expected: a talking erotic statue.

Parry signalled Lilah to disengage. She sat on the pedestal, dangling her bare legs over its edge, her knees slightly spread so as to offer a suitable view for the visitor. She was in perfect form.

'Come, join me,' she invited Mars, opening her arms.

'Who are you?' Mars demanded. Then he looked surprised. Parry knew why: another of his offerings had just manifested. Here in the annexe, which was actually a part of Hell, Parry had the power to eliminate the man's normal stutter.

'I am Satan, the Incarnation of Evil,' Parry said. 'This is one of My innumerable consorts, each of whom is more luscious and tractable than the last.' Lilah was very good about the way she masked her annoyance with that description; she of course regarded herself as THE most luscious and tractable female, having no peers. She was correct, of course. But so was he; the innumerable consorts he referred to would in this case all be this one, in changing guise.

'Satan?' the man asked. 'Here in my castle?'

Parry explained about the annexe.

'Aren't you the Occidental figure of Evil? Why have you chosen to contact me?'

Parry explained that he only wished to help. Lilah bounced down from the pedestal and took Mars' arm.

'I already have a woman,' Mars protested, hardly mistaking her approach.

'But not a suitable concubine,' Parry said smoothly. 'A man of your stature needs more than one woman.'

'True. But a Prince does not take a used woman.'

'Readily fixed.' Parry snapped his fingers, and Lilah obligingly vanished. He snapped them again, and she reappeared in a new formulation. 'Lila, here, has never been touched by man.' Lilah had, of course, and Lilith, but not Lila. 'She will be available whenever you wish.' He waved her away, and she vanished again. Her duty would come during Parry's absence, now that she had been appropriately introduced.

He continued to walk and talk with Mars, quite friendly, proffering a rationale for war that the new Incarnation could accept. 'Man is not rational; he cheats and enslaves his fellow and refuses to yield to reason. In the end there is only one answer, and that is to restore fairness by force. That is war.' It was the fallacious ends and means doctrine, a marvellous workhorse for Evil.

'But war does not restore fairness!' Mars protested.

'That is why it must be supervised by the Incarnation of War.' And on; the well-rehearsed rationale flowed readily from him, finding a not entirely unwilling recipient. 'You will fashion war into a truly useful tool for the redress of inequity among mortals.'

The man was listening. Parry capped it by explaining how Mars' woman could eat the food of this region when she could not survive on that of Purgatory. This was because it was imported from the mortal realm. Mars was gratified; his woman was important to him.

It was an excellent start. Parry departed, well satisfied. He did not expect such amicable relations to last indefinitely, but there was always the chance that this Mars, like the early Chronos, could become his friend. That would be an enormous advantage.

Next day Mars brought his woman, who was named Rapture of Malachite, to the garden. Parry appeared with Lila, and explained to Rapture that Lila was available as a concubine for Mars if Rapture approved. Rapture considered, and decided to wait a few months on that. This was not spoken with irony; she was a Princess who well understood such things. The second key introduction had been performed.

In the following days Lila befriended Rapture, putting

new Occidental notions into her pretty Oriental head. This was a marvellous approach; if the woman, also, could be corrupted . . .

In due course Mars sent Rapture back to the mortal world, not fully pleased with the liberating effect Lila was having on her. It did not matter; Lila continued to work on him directly. Once she drove him to such distraction that he used his great Red Sword to cut her into segments. Even then she swayed him with her unrelenting logic, until he packed her parts into a chest and shipped it to Hell proper.

She returned, of course, on another day, intact, to tempt him some more. He resisted, but she played on him with that infinite skill she possessed. Parry knew exactly how effective that could be; that was why he had assigned her to this mission.

Yet it was not quite enough. Mars continued to perform his office, thwarting Parry's incidental mischief among the mortals. Lila had not succeeded in seducing him, despite his loss of Rapture to a mortal man, and without that, Lila's words lacked full effect.

It was time for Parry's big ploy on Earth. Mars had to be out of the way, for the ploy concerned war. Therefore Lila proceeded to the final ploy: she lured Mars to Hell proper. This was accomplished by telling him of a Princess stranded there, Ligeia by name, who was in need of rescuing. It was true; Parry had saved Ligeia for just such an occasion, and she was exactly as represented. She was indeed the perfect match for Mars. Lila had not been pleased to introduce Mars to Ligeia, knowing the likely result, but at this stage she had no choice.

Sure enough, Mars joined the Princess, came to know her in the course of his attempt to rescue her from Hell, and fell in love with her. Since she was captive in Hell, so was he, because he would not leave without her. It was one of Parry's prettiest traps.

Meanwhile, Parry got busy on Earth, freed from Mars' interference. He whipped up the forces of mortal dissention. Soon he would achieve such violence in the world that martial law would be declared in a number of governments, among them the American one in which Luna was to become critically active. That would deprive her of her political position, leaving her powerless to make the key decision that would mark his final defeat. What a phenomenal ploy this was!

But Mars, showing more mettle than Parry had expected, managed to fashion a ploy of his own. He incited the damned souls of Hell itself to rebellion. Ozymandias, long in charge of operations, was caught napping, and the situation was out of hand. Parry had to return to deal with it himself. He had to keep Mars distracted here just a little longer, until the business on Earth passed the point of no return.

He met Mars physically, when the man was deprived of his magic Red Sword. He could not of course actually hurt him; no Incarnation could injure another. But he could bluff him, and perhaps convince him that the infernal revolution was doomed.

But Mars finally caught on, and exploited the weakness of the Incarnation of Evil. 'I am going to phase in with you, Satan,' he said. That was one of the powers Mars had, to overlap mortals and read their minds. 'When I do, I will know all your secrets. All that is in your mind.'

It was no bluff. Parry had avoided direct physical contact. If Mars grappled with him, Mars would learn of his activity on Earth, and immediately act to interfere with it. Rather than allow that, Parry had to back off, though it meant the premature release of a number of souls from Hell. It was a loss he had to take, in order to preserve the situation on Earth, where the true victory was to be won. So he vacated, leaving the field to Mars. It was humiliating, but necessary.

Parry made the finishing touches on the Earthly situation, and let it be. It was now in place, and only heroic action by Mars could reverse it. Had Mars returned earlier, he could have stopped it by routine means, but it was now beyond that stage. Parry was happy to have Mars depart from Hell now, and did not attempt to delay him further.

But Mars rose to the occasion once more. He succeeded in reversing the corruption Lila was practising on him, and corrupted her instead. She deserted Parry and fell in love with Mars. She told Mars how to reverse the ploy and win the victory.

Parry was furious. He had never intended this to happen! The damage was done, but at least he could punish the demoness. She had never learned the secret of demon-banishing; like other demons, she would dissipate and be destroyed if he invoked the spell. It was psychological rather than magical; belief was what made it happen, and she believed. Every Lord of Hell had fostered that belief in all demons, her included, through the millennia. But first he had to get her away from Mars' protection.

He faced Mars again, this time by the great Doomsday Clock. He knew what Mars had not known: that Ligeia had chosen to return to mortality instead of proceeding to Heaven, so that she could be with Mars. He brought the mortal Ligeia in, offering her in exchange for Lila.

And Ligeia interceded for the demoness. That caused the wavering Mars to decide to save Lila after all. It was in his power to do so, for he threatened to drive the Doomsday Clock to the dread midnight hour and precipitate the final war that would destroy all of humanity. Parry could not tolerate that; it had never been his intent to wipe out mortal man, only to facilitate the classification of souls. He had to back off again, yielding Lila, much as it galled him to do so. Wrongheaded righteousness had won the day yet again.

How well he remembered now that when Lilah had deserted his predecessor, Lucifer, it had led to Lucifer's undoing. Now she had deserted Parry, and the time of his final reckoning with God was drawing nigh. She might already have contributed to his downfall.

Parry retreated, and Mars took over his office, defusing the situation Parry had so carefully fostered. It was yet another humiliation.

Furthermore, it left him without a woman. He did not want to call Nefertiti back from her holiday, and he had not cultivated other damned souls. The truth was that no female creature matched his memory of Jolie. How he wished he could evoke her ghost again, just to talk to!

That reminded him of Heaven, because Jolie would surely go there if she ever could get free of the drop of blood he carried. He was now releasing souls to Heaven, per the agreement with Mars; the Incarnation of War thought he was doing the souls a favour. Well, time had passed; perhaps things had improved in Heaven.

Parry decided to check. He sailed up to the Void and called for JHVH. The Deity of the Hebrews was glad to guide him through. JHVH alone knew what Parry had done for His people, and that the Incarnation of Evil was not actually doing evil.

He reached the outer circle of Heaven. Indeed, it seemed brighter than it had five centuries before. Gabriel had been doing some reorganizing, in the name of God, and now the souls were engaged in various satisfying pursuits. Some were watching the new mortal television; the shows, though edited to exclude anything inappropriate to the exalted state, seemed interesting. Others were practising various crafts, such as basket weaving with strands of ether, with evident pleasure.

All things considered, Heaven now seemed an appropriate place to be. He would make a report, and release those eligible souls who wished to go.

JHVH guided him through the Void again. Parry thanked him and descended on towards Hell. But still he was unsatisfied; he knew that he had no woman and no challenging project there, now that the business with Mars was done. The ennui of his long possession of the Office threatened to overcome him. Ozymandias was running Hell well enough, and needed no help; Parry could not blame the King for the rebellion stirred up by Mars. Only the Incarnation of War could have done it.

Was it time to retire? What was the point in continuing in an office that had become boring? He still had the challenge with Gabriel, but his successor could complete that. In any event, it seemed to be a losing cause; the massed power of the other Incarnations seemed to be too much for him.

The other Incarnations – actually they weren't all against him. There was Nox, the Incarnation of Night, with all her fascination. Lilah (now Lila) had feared that Nox would take him away from her. Well, maybe now was the time.

He oriented on Nox, and in a moment he was there in her encompassing darkness.

«What is thy business, Lord of Evil?»

Ah, that dream-memory communication! He had forgotten how evocative it was.

'Nox, I have alienated Lilah, and now have little interest in pursuing my office.'

«What would thou with me?»

'I do not know. Perhaps it is advice. Perhaps love.'

She opened her cloak and flowed about him. The intangible female nature of her encompassed him, and he felt as if he were floating. Why had he waited so many

315

centuries before coming to her? She was all he could ever desire!

Then she withdrew, as she had before. «Not yet, Lord of Evil.»

'But all I want is you!'

«Perhaps thou shallst have me, or I you. But not yet. Thou hast one more mortal woman to deal with, before me. Go first to thine Incarnation.»

The disappointment of this final rejection surged in him. 'No other Incarnation will touch me!'

«'Thou must win her, Evil.»

'Win whom?' he cried desperately as the presence withdrew. 'How? I tell you, no other Incarnation will – '

«She has been given thee, Evil, but thou must win her from the others and from herself. Win her, and all is thine.»

'Win *whom*?' he cried, but Nox was gone, leaving him with a greater emptiness than he had felt before.

He had come for relief, and had been turned away. What remained to him?

Then the significance of what Nox had sent penetrated. If he found this mysterious Incarnation and won her, all would be his. He knew from the context and significance of the thought that this meant everything. That he would at last defeat God.

Nox had directed him correctly, if deviously, before. Perhaps this new challenge would be the most significant yet.

Parry moved on towards Hell, discovering his interest in the challenge being restored. Mars might have set him back, but the larger picture had not yet clarified.

The Lord of Evil might yet have his day.

15
Gaea

First Parry spent some time thinking. He retreated to the
edge of the Void, where no one would bother him, and
reviewed what had passed. Nox had said that the woman
was mortal, and an Incarnation, and had been given to
him, but that he had to win her from the others and from
herself. There were only two major female Incarnations
currently, Fate and Gaea, and neither one of them would
touch him.

Then he remembered the prophecy he had discussed
with Lilah. The business with Mars had blotted it from his
attention. Two men, possessing the two most beautiful
women, bearing each a daughter, one of whom might
marry Death, the other Evil. One daughter to love an
Incarnation, the other to *be* one.

There was only one conclusion to be drawn from those
prophecies, assuming they were true ones. One daughter
was to associate with Thanatos, as Luna was doing; the
other was to associate with Satan, and become an Incarnation herself. What a concatenation of threads!

Which Incarnation? While it was possible for a male or
female mortal to assume any Incarnation office, the sexes
had been unchanged throughout Parry's tenure. So it
seemed likely that she would become either an Aspect of
Fate, perhaps joining her mother, Niobe, or Nature.

Nature. Gaea. The Green Mother. She had been in
office since Parry had worked her over with the plague.
She was still on the job, but might be getting tired.

If that other daughter – what was her name? Orb – if
Orb became Gaea, and associated with Parry –

It burst upon him like an explosion from the fires of

Hell. *If he won that girl, and she was Gaea, her power would be joined to his!* He could use that mergence to tip the balance against God!

No wonder Nox had elected to wait, foreseeing this! Why should she distract him from the biggest chance of his career in office! Nox preferred to see what he would do with it. If he lost, then there was time for Nox. If he won –

The prospect awed him. All he had to do was –

He quickly sobered. Orb was Niobe's daughter! She was protected by Fate. There was no way that girl would walk innocently into his embrace!

But Niobe had, in a fashion, turned Orb loose. She had agreed to divert her from politics. He had intended that to be Luna, and had been deceived. He had agreed never to harm her. But by the same token, Niobe had left her to him, because his agreement meant that she had no cause to fear what he might do to Orb. The logic was somewhat obscure, but the interpretation was viable.

But what was the girl like? He had never seen her. He knew only that in childhood she had been like a twin sister to Luna, with buckwheat-honey hair to match Luna's clover-honey hair. Luna had grown to be a beauty, talented artistically – and politically. Orb – her talent was music, for she had claimed a musical instrument from the Hall of the Mountain King. How did that qualify her to assume the office of the Incarnation of Nature?

Parry realized that it was time to take a look at Orb. He would not interfere with her in any way; he would simply observe her. After all, if she was destined to be his companion, he had a right to know!

First he had to locate her. That was simple enough; he went to Purgatory and used its computer. These new-fangled scientific devices did have their uses. He was after

318

all an Incarnation, and this was neutral territory; the computer served him as well as the others.

She was in America, on a tour with a musical group called The Livin' Sludge. That made sense, because of her music. But that group jogged a memory; perhaps he had encountered it in his quest to evoke evil among mortals.

He returned to Hell and delved into its own records. Sure enough, the members of The Livin' Sludge were considered to be prime prospects for residence in Hell after they died, because all three males were hooked on Spelled H, one of the most addictive and degenerative of modern drugs.

But what was Niobe's daughter doing with such a group? She was surely a disgustingly good girl, and would be unlikely to associate with evil in any form. This was becoming more interesting.

Then he discovered that in addition to the three male musicians, there were two young women and a succubus in the group, besides Orb herself. More interesting yet.

The succubus was of course a damned creature, a female demon who seduced men in their sleep. Her name was Jezebel, and she was not associated with Hell; she was an independent agent. The male musicians would enjoy her company, of course, but Niobe's daughter and the two other girls, who were innocent creatures, would hardly feel the same!

The group was conveyed from site to site by a huge magic fish known as Jonah. Most interesting of all!

Jonah he knew about already. He was the monstrous fish who had swallowed the Prophet Jonah some millennia back, and was being punished for it, now having assumed the name of the one he had wronged. He was forbidden to touch water; he had to swim instead through air or earth. Why would he do such a service for this motley assemblage?

Parry located the site at which they were currently performing and went there to take in a show. He assumed the form of a somewhat seedy middle-aged man, and paid for his ticket with legitimate money. This was of course an anonymous visit, just for information.

The group looked every bit as disreputable as he had expected. The boys were somewhat shaggy, and even from his distance in the rear of the audience he could sniff the aura of evil associated with their addiction to H. Ordinary H was bad, but Spelled H was truly hellish; it never let go until its victim was securely in Hell proper.

Then the girls came on. Two of them; evidently the others served other functions in the group. One of these was black and rather pretty, and she was a virgin with so little evil on her soul she seemed unreal. The other was Orb: conservatively garbed, buckwheat-honey tresses, and reminiscent of her real mother though not as beautiful. She had a little harp that seemed out of place among the more conventional instruments of the boys.

A harp? He remembered how Jolie had played a little harp. That jolted him, even after seven centuries.

They began to play, the organ, guitar and drums. There was really nothing special about it. The audience quickly became restless, and there were discontented murmurings. 'You mean this is it?' a girl near Parry whispered to her companion. 'I thought they were supposed to be hot!'

He smiled knowingly. 'They are. Just wait.'

After a moment, the black girl began to sing. Her voice was good, but not spectacular, and the fact that she sang an old folk song did not help.

'I didn't pay good money for this junk!' the girl in the audience muttered. All through the packed hall there were similar rumblings; it would not be long before balls of paper were flying.

'You'll see,' the companion said smugly.

Parry was more curious than bored. He knew that

young folk had a low tolerance for boredom, and conventional values bored them. How had The Livin' Sludge managed to develop such popularity with such ordinary stuff?

Then Orb touched her harp and joined in, adding a slight additional theme hardly audible through the existing sound.

Something happened. It was as though colour developed after an image had been established in limited black and white. The black girl's voice filled out, becoming beautiful, and the boys' instruments assumed authority they had lacked before. Suddenly the music had conviction. It spread out through the audience, an almost tangible wave, and replaced fidgeting with rapture. The mouth of the nearby complaining girl froze in mid-mutter; her eyes glazed. Her companion did not even say 'I told you so'; he, too, was rapt.

Yet the music had hardly changed. It was still the old folk song, still the motley collection of instruments.

Then it touched Parry, and he felt the magic.

Now Orb joined in singing, her voice added to that of the black girl. The magic intensified. The listeners nearest the stage seemed almost to float, and even way back here, where the effect was diminished, the sound became wondrous.

Orb had the same magic he did! But hers, enhanced by the harp from the Hall of the Mountain King, was magnified, so that its power touched thousands. It spread to the other members of the performing group, enhancing their otherwise ordinary skills. It hardly mattered what music they played; anything became marvellous.

Now Parry knew the secret of The Livin' Sludge. Magic talent enhanced by magic instrument. He understood it readily enough; after all, he himself had enraptured listeners with his voice alone on many occasions. He could depart; he hardly needed to sit through the entire performance.

But he did not move. He remained, as did all the others, silently taking it all in. At the end, he joined in the applause as ardently as the others.

As the folk departed, he remembered his mission. He wanted to know more of the situation of Orb and The Livin' Sludge. Much more!

He conjured himself to Jonah, the big fish floating invisibly in the air near the city. Jonah was aware of his coming, and shuddered, but could not protest; Parry was after all an Incarnation.

The girl Betsy was there, sitting at a desk in her office inside the fish, sorting through the voluminous correspondence the group received and dictating answers into a recorder. She was, he understood, the organist's girl. He ignored her and sought instead the succubus.

Jezebel was fixing an evening meal. Because night had fallen, she was in her exotic form, a supremely luscious young woman. But instead of seeking sleeping men to seduce, she was working patiently at this mundane chore, with seeming satisfaction.

'What are you doing here, demoness?' he inquired, materializing beside her.

She turned, annoyed – and did a humanlike double take. 'Satan! You have no call on me!'

'I have no interest in you, demoness. All I want is information: why does a creature of your kind associate in a menial capacity with a mixed bag of mortals?'

'I don't have to answer You!'

'Would you prefer that I inquire of one of the mortals? That fair girl in the other chamber, perhaps?'

'Leave her alone, Satan! She's innocent!'

'Then I think you will answer Me,' he said grimly.

It worked. The succubus knew his power, and feared for her companions. 'If I do, will You go?'

'Not only that, I will erase any signs of My visit.'

'It's the Llano,' she said.

'The Llano!' he exclaimed. 'What do you know of the Song of the Fundament?'

'Only that it will free me,' she said. 'And them. They all want it too. The boys to get off the H, and Jonah to be released from his cure, and Orb – '

He nodded. He knew of the Llano, having searched for parts of it for centuries. It was the ultimate melody of power, carrying magic that reached back into the nature of chaos itself. A minor aspect of it lent magic to his own singing.

Then he realized how this related to Orb. She too, partook of an aspect of the Llano when she sang. Naturally she wanted more of it, for a person who could tap into the Llano had the potential to do much more.

His question was answered. The quest for the Llano was indeed what unified this motley group. They were on tour not for money or fame, but to search out the Llano.

That gave him the key to his approach to Orb. He could help her to achieve a portion of the Llano.

There was a noise outside. The others were returning to the fish – or perhaps Jonah had gone to their location to take them in.

Jezebel glanced up in alarm. 'Satan, You promised – '

Parry nodded. 'You answered, demoness. Now I depart, and you will carry no memory of this interview.' He made a gesture, as of flipping something at her.

She jumped, alarmed. Then it hit her, and her expression straightened as he faded out. She had forgotten his visit.

Parry smiled. He had not been sure that a demon who was independent of Hell would react in the same way those within Hell did. Now he knew: he had the same power over outside demons as over inside demons. The power over their belief. He had not performed any magic;

323

he had simply made a gesture, and Jezebel had erased the memory herself, obeying the power she believed he had.

He remained, invisible, just to make sure she was not trying to trick him. In a moment the party boarded. One of them came straight to the kitchen chamber. It was the guitarist. He swept the demoness into his embrace and kissed her ardently, and she responded with complete abandon.

Parry was amazed. Demonesses seldom gave their love, particularly this species, but this one had. He could tell when they were deceiving and when they were true; he had had centuries of experience. Certainly Jezebel did not want Satan interfering; she just wanted to be left alone with her lover.

He would leave her alone. He remembered Lilah, who had been true to each of her lovers until they tired of her. He had lost Lilah because he had lost respect for her; he had brought it on himself.

Then Orb entered the kitchen. The two broke their kiss, remaining embraced. 'Food's ready,' Jezebel said. 'I'll get on it.'

'Finish what you're doing,' Orb said with a smile.

They returned to their kiss. Orb watched indulgently, but also with a trace of envy. She had no lover of her own.

Parry gazed at her, remaining invisible. This was the woman who might marry Evil. He had been contemptuous of that prophecy, remembering beautiful Niobe, not really able to appreciate how the baby she had after departing the office could ever interest him. But then he had heard Orb sing, in the way that he himself sang, and a dimension had been added to the prospects. Now he saw her in her natural state, and she was a beautiful woman in her own right, and a feeling one. In fact, she reminded him of her mother – and, oddly, of Jolie. Her hair was the same colour, and so were her eyes. Also, there was her little harp.

Of Jolie! He was abruptly aware of his chain of thought. A woman almost as lovely as Niobe, cast in the image of Parry's long-dead wife. Had Gabriel known it would be this way?

Parry conjured himself away from there, dismayed. Now he appreciated the potential treachery of the situation. There were two ways he could join with Orb, the potential Gaea. One was to seduce her into loving him, and adding her power to his, giving him victory over God. The other was for her to seduce him into loving her, and that would destroy all his prospects. For she was allied with God, and would not betray God unless her heart went first.

His smartest move might be to drop any consideration of any association with this young woman. To stay well away from her, and go to Nox . . .

He shook his head. He knew he could not do that. He had to settle matters with Orb, one way or the other. It was apt to be the most significant challenge of his career as an Incarnation.

Parry watched Orb for some time, attending a number of the concerts on the tour and observing her as she went out shopping or visiting. He was avoiding the issue, he knew; but he was uncertain how to approach her. Certainly he could not walk up and introduce himself as Satan; she would refuse to have anything to do with him. But if he fashioned himself into some other semblance, she would be furious when she learned the truth, and that would end the association. Either way, her mother would be trouble. Niobe knew of the prophecy, and would surely labour diligently to void it. As an Aspect of Fate, she had extraordinary power to do just that.

Yet she had, he reminded himself, in her fashion given

him leave. She knew that the issue would not be settled until the prophecy had been expended. That critical word *may* had to be settled; it had to be determined whether Orb would or would not marry Evil. Perhaps she wanted the issue settled as much as he did.

Why not start with Niobe, then? Settle with her about the manner he would settle with her daughter. Whatever she acceded to, the other Incarnations would.

He mulled it over, but found no better approach. There had to be some way to do it that would not have him at odds with the other Incarnations.

He went to the Abode of Fate. Niobe expected him, for there was a tangle in her threads at this stage. She met him in her own form; the other two Aspects were of course with her, but not evident. She was somewhat dumpy in her middle age, yet the echo of her former beauty remained. He knew that she could have changed her form to be beautiful again, but her pride prevented her. She had let her body decline, and would live with it. He respected that, though he himself had chosen to adopt a younger perpetual form when he had become an Incarnation.

'How may I approach your daughter without your malice?' he asked directly. 'To settle the prophecy.'

'Simply tell her the truth,' she said. 'That you are the Incarnation of Evil, and you have come to fulfil the prophecy. Ask her to marry you. I'm sure she will give you an answer.'

'Indubitably,' he agreed wryly. 'The same answer you gave me. I fear I would not be quite satisfied with that.'

'You must either speak the truth to her, or a lie,' she said. 'I'm sure the lie comes easier to you.'

'But the resolution of the prophecy cannot be a lie!' he reminded her.

She looked at him penetratingly. 'You're serious. You actually want to marry her!'

'Yes.'

'But not to love her, of course.'

'Of course.'

'Why, when you know she will never be corrupted to evil?'

'Because she will become the Incarnation of Nature. Her power added to Mine will give Me the balance of power in the mortal realm.'

'Satan, if you think for a moment that I will concur in that – !'

'But she must do it voluntarily. If you are certain she will not, why do you object to the trial of it?'

She considered. 'Because I do not trust you, Satan. You are devious in the extreme. You almost got my soul; I will not give my daughter's soul to you!'

'If Orb is certain of her own values, she should be able to make that decision for herself. Do you trust her or don't you?'

'I trust her if she knows the truth. But you will deceive her.'

Parry sighed. 'The truth would send her away at the outset; we both know that. I will not go into sure defeat.'

She angled her head, in a way that carried over from the days of her beauty. 'Atropos has a suggestion.'

'Put her on,' he said.

The black grandmotherly woman appeared in her place. 'Why don't you lie to her,' she said.

Parry shook his head. 'We have covered that.'

'No you haven't, old Scrotch! You just said it and never thought about it. How about this deal: you go court her – but everything you tell her must be a lie. That way you can tell her you love her. Then the moment you ask her to marry you, you must tell her nothing but the truth. Before she answers.'

'What would be the point? She would cast me off the moment – '

327

'Man, if you loved some girl, and she said she wanted to marry you but there was one thing she had to tell you, and that was that everything she'd told you before was a lie but now she would always tell you the truth what would you say?'

Parry thought about that. If Jolie had said that, would he have married her? He concluded that he would have, because he had come to know her well despite her words; he had judged her by much more than any words. He would believe that he could in time win her love, given complete honesty between them.

Would Orb judge him by other than his lying words?

He opened his mouth to ask another question, and heard himself say 'Agreed.'

Niobe reappeared. 'Now wait! *I* didn't agree!'

'I will court her,' Parry said evenly. 'Every thing I tell her will be a lie, or part of a construct of a lie. You Incarnations may watch throughout, unobserved, and verify that this is so. You will not interfere. Then, before I have her answer, I will tell her the truth. If she then decides to marry me, none of you will oppose it.'

Now it was Niobe's turn to think. Evidently an internal debate was going on between the three Aspects of Fate. 'We must ask the others,' she said at last.

'But no word to any mortals,' he cautioned. 'This must be our private deal, until I tell her the truth. Then she may consult with whom she pleases. If she decides to marry me, you accept it. If not, I accept it, and make no further suit. *She* will decide the issue.'

'We shall get back to you in a few days,' Niobe said grimly. She converted to her spider form and disappeared.

Several days later she had her answer. The Incarnations, with misgivings, had agreed. They would stand by without any kind of interference, as long as he lied to Orb.

So the challenge was on. He was the Father of Lies; if

any person could do it, he could. But *could* any person do it?

He went again to the fringe of the Void and pondered in solitude. How could he lie continually to a woman, never telling her the truth, and yet win her love – a love that would hold when she learned the truth? A stupid woman, or an ugly one, might be fooled, because she might desire to be fooled. But Orb was brighter than her mother, and almost as beautiful, and considerably more talented. That music –

And, after an instant or an eternity – there was hardly a distinction here – he saw the answer. 'The dream's the thing!' he exclaimed.

He would fashion a construct that was a lie. Within that construct everything would relate; all would be true, so as to lend verisimilitude, the semblance of accuracy. In this manner he could tell the truth to Orb, and try to win her love, without violating the agreement he had made to speak only lies to her.

First he had to learn more about his subject. He had to learn what kind of lie Orb would want to believe, so that he could fashion it for her and make her believe. He had to understand her truest motivations, so that he could play on them with his best expertise and win her love. Then he had to know how to hold that love, or at least win her acquiescence, so that she would marry him despite learning the truth.

He researched her life. Only Chronos could actually travel to past times, but there were demons in Hell who could recreate past scenes with fair accuracy by evoking them from substances that had been present when the scenes occurred. He sent his minions on a quest for such substances all along the route that Orb's physical life had travelled. He chafed at the time this took, but when the substances arrived, and he started witnessing the key evocations, he was satisfied.

Orb had led a fairly ordinary life, complicated by some extraordinary influences. She had been joined early in life by her niece Luna, who was of similar age and lineage; indeed, Orb's parents were Luna's grandparents, and the girls resembled twins. They had been raised together, and shared each others' lives. Luna had shown an early affinity for art, and Orb for music; their gifts from the Mountain King confirmed them.

Then Luna had departed with her father for America, and Orb had gone on a quest across the world for the song of songs, the Llano. That quest had taken her to the Gypsies, and she had made a close friend of a blind Gypsy girl, Tinka.

The Gypsies. There was a lever! Parry had acted to save the Gypsies from the holocaust. It was true that he had done it for another reason, to help JHVH's people; but it was also true that without his intercession, none of the Gypsies Orb had encountered, including Tinka, would have survived. If he told Orb that –

But he could not, for that was the truth. Only later, when the time for the truth came, could he tell her, and that might be too late. He had to win her love without taking credit for what he had done. What an irony!

Orb had gone on to tour India, and had made more friends there. She had come to love Mym, a fugitive Prince who stuttered, and had had a child by him.

Parry gaped, watching the animation of the sequence. *Mym was the man who had become the new Mars!* The one who had finally balked Parry by threatening to move the Doomsday Clock to midnight and bring on the final war! The one who had taken Lilah from him!

How could this have happened, and he not known of it? But he realized it was because he had not cared to know. Orb had been nothing to him then; he had been preoccupied with affairs of routine evil, and with combatting the other Incarnations as they changed office. He could not concern himself directly with every thread in the tapestry. Certainly there had been nothing at this stage of Orb's life to suggest that the prophecy of her involvement with Satan was serious.

Orb had given away the baby and travelled to America, where she joined with The Livin' Sludge, continuing her quest for the Llano. She was making progress; already she had learned to use an aspect of it to make storms. What she perhaps did not realize was that her mastery of the Llano would be far more significant than the mere satisfaction of curiosity about a song. The Llano would make her capable of assuming the office of the Incarnation of Nature. The present Gaea, it seemed, was ready to retire, and Orb was now a leading prospect to replace her.

The Llano – now there was a thing he could use! He could lie about its nature, and in the process win her gratitude by helping her to learn parts of the song she did not yet know. He could draw on his own talent for singing – a talent unrivalled until Orb herself appeared with similar magic. He could use the power of the Llano on her, even as he did her the seeming favour of teaching it to her.

But she knew about the prophecy. She could be on guard against him. How could he lay that wariness to rest?

He considered one approach, and another, and others. Finally he worked out what he felt would be most likely to persuade her. What a bold scenario it was!

She feared the prospect of marriage to Satan. Therefore he would stage that marriage – and rescue her from it. Thus the lie would preserve her from the reality, and perhaps the lie could win her love.

He scripted the illusion carefully. Everything had to be

331

just right. She had to be made to believe the lie. But whom would she believe? Not a demon from Hell, certainly! No honest person would cooperate in telling her the necessary lie. How could he develop a cast of characters that would do his bidding yet be believable to her?

By emulating the ones she trusted! The other Incarnations! With the true Incarnations bound not to interfere in any way, he could arrange to emulate them, and sugarcoat the lie. What a phenomenal total lie he was developing!

He summoned those damned souls who had talent in acting and who desired the favour of the Lord of Evil. He drilled them in the characters they were to portray, so that they could almost believe they were those folk. He rehearsed them in the script, and adjusted and refined it constantly, perfecting it. The first lie was about to be perpetrated.

When Orb returned to the Llano region of North America, Parry was ready. He watched the big fish swim low and open his mouth to let the woman out. Orb walked across the plain, seeking her song. Now was the time!

The first actor went onstage. She formed into the semblance of a spider, and the spider grew until it became the likeness of Niobe in her current form.

'Mother!' Orb cried, and hugged her. 'Luna said you had become Lachesis.'

'True. Now we must talk.' The emulation was doing very well; Orb appeared to have no suspicion.

'Did Luna tell you about my quest for the Llano? I am getting closer. I can change the weather, and I can even use it to travel across the world in an instant!'

'Yes, my dear. The Llano is the most potent theme of this realm.' That was technically true, but it was a lie because it was a false image telling it, for reason other than that presented. The best lies incorporated truth, so that they were convincing. 'But there is danger you may not have anticipated. Do you remember the prophecy?'

'That I might marry Evil! But Mother, you know I would never associate with Satan, let alone marry him!'

'But he is the master of deception.' Another truth, setting up another lie. 'Satan has set a trap for you. He means to complete the prophecy and marry you, regardless of your will.'

'But he can't – '

'He means to use the Llano against you.' Truth again – and its companion lie. 'He will stun your will and make you his love-slave. You must be on guard!'

Orb was appalled. She would not have believed this if any but her mother had said it. What an elegant lie it was! 'How can I escape?'

'I will send Gaea to you. Listen to her, Orb!' then the actor resumed spider form, and disappeared.

Beautiful! That actress deserved a commendation. Parry had found himself almost believing it was Niobe. He regretted only that no wider audience could appreciate the intricacy and craftsmanship of the pattern of lies. There was an art in lying, and not merely in that form of it termed 'fiction'.

Next he sent the emulation of the Incarnation of Nature. She formed out of mist, in the likeness of the real one. 'I am Gaea. Lachesis asked me to show you how to nullify the Llano when it is used against you. You can only do that with another aspect of itself. But there is risk. If you try the counter, and fail, you will suffer eternal madness.' There was the lie, akin to the one by which he controlled demons.

'I'll risk it!' Orb said.

The fake Gaea then explained that the countertheme was a duet that had to be sung with another person: a man named Natasha, who was the finest mortal singer apart from herself. The actress did not explain that this

333

was a monstrous half-truth, for Natasha was simply the words *Ah, Satan* merged and spelled backward; it was the immortal Incarnation Satan who was that fine singer. He had set it up this way so that he could show, when the time for truth came, that he had never completely deceived her, but had given her a potent hint as to his nature from the outset. That might make her feel at least partially at fault in her own eyes, and perhaps dispose her towards accepting him. For the lying was the easier part of this; holding her after the time of truth was the harder part.

Orb took the bait. 'This Natasha – what kind of man is he?'

'The best of men. But he may take your rendition of an aspect of the Llano as a trap of Satan's.' Nicely turning the lie on its head. Now Orb would have to try to reassure Natasha that she was not an agent of Evil!

Gaea wrote out the music and gave it to Orb. Then she departed, while Orb read the music and practised it without actually singing it, heeding the warning of its danger.

Now for the main scene. Parry crafted one of his finest illusions: a complete demonic church. In it was a damned soul mocked up to resemble the popular image of Satan: red, horned, with a tail, and clothed in flames. This scene formed around Orb, incorporating her.

'Now you will marry Me!' the fake Satan proclaimed.

'Never!' Orb cried, marvellously true to form. It was almost as though she were another actor from Hell.

The actor sang. Actually it was a recording of Parry's voice, for no other entity could perform this part of it well enough to fool a musician such as Orb.

Orb seemed stunned. Now he added the second voice, in effect singing a duet with himself. The doubled song carried phenomenal impact; it was a variant of the theme he had used to pacify demons, enhanced by the power of the Llano. The actor changed clothing magically and gestured to Orb to join him at the altar. He took her hand, leading into the ceremony.

Desperately, she sang the theme she had just learned, but it was new to her, and she was frightened, and so it lacked full effect. She tried to wrench away, but her song alone was not sufficient to free her. Gaea had carefully established that! The ceremony continued, with the demon priest readying the knife that would mingle the actor's blood with Orb's and make them one.

Orb came to the first break in her song. Now she needed the companion song, to form her own duet, or suffer madness. It seemed she had really swallowed that lie.

Now, before she could discover its falsity, Parry stepped into his own role. He conjured himself at a distance, and became Natasha: his normal human physical appearance, as it had been set from the outset of his tenure in office. Orb had never seen him; she would not recognize him. That was one of the most delicious aspects of it: any other Incarnation would have known him immediately. He sang the companion theme.

It was effective, of course; it was scripted to be. He sang; she sang. Now her voice gained strength and clarity. And what a voice it was! She was truly the finest singer of the age, a suitable match for his own ability. Slowly they came together, vanquishing the Satan figure, freeing her from the forced marriage. Her worst fear had been evoked, and blunted, thanks to Natasha. The demonic church faded out, leaving only an open field.

They stopped singing. 'You play a dangerous game,' Parry said, as if this were a minor matter. But it was all he could do to remember the script; her voice had profoundly moved him, and this was not as it should be, because it was his vision.

He saw her assessing him. Women paid less attention

to appearance than men did, but were affected by it. He knew he was a handsome man. They conversed, and he established the lie of his identity as a mortal singer. They talked about the Llano, and he taught her the ready counter to Satan's use of it. What a joy it was, to sing for an audience who could truly appreciate his skill!

Then, having suitably impressed her, he broached the subject that would be on any man's mind at this stage.

'I am unmarried,' Orb replied, flushing prettily. Oh, what a woman she was, with her delightful naïveté almost intact! Again he thought of Jolie, as she had been before death made her cynical. But in fairness he had to admit that Orb was the lovelier of the two.

'May I court you?' This was a very quick progression, but it was important to catch her in the flush of her emotion, in the hour of her gratefulness to him.

It was easy to read the play of emotions that passed through her. Then she said, breathlessly, 'You may.'

Success, for the first key stage! She was receptive.

Then he sang her the Song of Awakening, which was also known as the Song of the Morning, or the Dawning of Love. As he sang, its magic manifested, requiring no crafting of illusion on his part; this much was genuine. The scene darkened, then brightened into sunrise, bringing the sprouting of grass and the flowering of bushes. A ray of sunlight came down to illuminate Orb, making her so lovely that he hardly dared gaze at her. Her eyes seemed as great and bright as the welkin, translucently grey with a hint of greenery reflected and her bosom heaved with the excitement of her response. Niobe had been beautiful, but had left the office and aged; Orb, as Gaea, would remain forever as radiant as she was at this moment.

Then it ended, as it had to. He was surely as regretful as she. Almost, he could believe what he was telling her.

She stood. 'I will see you again,' she said.

'Certainly.' He watched her walk back towards the big fish.

The first vision had played out almost perfectly. Parry was elated. He had taken a giant step towards winning her.

He conjured himself to Hell. Soon he would organize for the second vision. But first he wanted to rest.

Nefertiti showed up. 'I fear you are lonely, now that Lilah is gone,' she said.

Parry did not have the heart to tell her that his interest in both demonesses and damned souls had diminished. 'I thank you for the thought, but you have earned your vacation and I want you to enjoy it to the full.'

'Oh. Thank you, Lord Satan,' she said, not entirely pleased at this dismissal.

When he closed his eyes, Orb was there, her honey hair flowing down about her shoulders, a half-smile on her face and that quaint small harp beside her.

He sprang the second vision on them when Jonah was swimming over the Pacific at night. The big fish could not handle water, but there was plenty of air above the ocean and the weather was clear, so it was all right. Jonah would give any bad weather a wide berth.

The vision played upon the party's awareness that a storm would be trouble for Jonah, because he could not escape it by swimming underground. Not while he was far from land. The vision included the human members of the party, but excluded the fish and the succubus, because demons were not subject to dreams and would know it for what it was. In reality, Jonah continued an uneventful swim through the air, but in the vision he encountered an expanding storm that encircled and trapped him.

The script had the fish sinking down to the surface of the sea, resting on it, unable to enter it. Jonah was helped to adapt by the singing of the group, as they essayed an imperfect rendition of the Song of Awakening.

Then the heavier element came. Skeletons danced across the surface of the water, approaching the fish. The fish, in the vision, was afraid of them, and tried to paddle away, but was surrounded. One of the dancing skeletons touched a fluke, and that part of the tail of the fish lost its flesh and became skeletal.

Horrified, perceiving the way of it, Orb did her best to halt the skeletons by singing. This was not enough.

Then Jezebel, who was not the real one but one of Hell's minions masquerading as her, introduced them to the key: the skeletons were dancing a jig called 'The Drunken Sailor's Hornpipe'. They did not seem to be distracted when Jezebel tried it, but then Orb tried a dance, the *tanana*, and danced with the nearest skeleton until it fell apart. She had found a way!

Parry, watching, was amazed. That dance was the most suggestive thing he had ever seen! How had a nice girl like her learned that? Then he remembered her association with the Gypsies. That was the sort of thing the Gypsies would have taught her. He was glad he had saved them from the holocaust.

But it was not enough. The script tightened about them. There were too many skeletons, pressing too closely. If Orb responded appropriately . . .

She did. 'Natasha!' she called in desperation.

Parry made his grand entrance, singing. The skeletons paused, hearing. He joined the party, while the skeletons hesitated, afraid of the power of his song. He was rather proud of the manner he had crafted the bones to evince living emotions.

Orb was obviously glad to see him. 'Can you stop them?'

'With the Song of Power,' he said. 'You may know it as the Song of Day.' He sang it, and it was another aspect of the Llano, whose sheer power shook the night vision. The melody banished the storm cloud and brought the light of day. The skeletons tried to flee, but the sound caught them and shattered them. The threat had been abated.

Orb flung her arms around him and kissed him. 'You rescued me again!' she cried.

'It was my pleasure.' It certainly was! But the vision was only half done.

Two figures intercepted Orb the moment she reentered the fish, alone. One was an emulation of Thanatos, and the other of Chronos. They warned her that Natasha could be a demon in disguise, and should be tested. The real Natasha, they explained, was a good man, but if a demon assumed his form . . .

Orb, concerned, took their warning at face value. She insisted on testing Natasha for demonic origin. He touched a cross and sang a hymn, proving that he was no demon. Of course the proof was a lie, because this was all a vision in which anything could happen, but Orb did not know that. She was chagrined that she had doubted him.

Natasha walked out in righteous disgust.

The script had been honoured perfectly. Now Orb was convinced of Natasha's validity, and on the defensive because of her prior doubt. She was crying when he left her.

He had made another giant step. But he hated himself, too. It had required a heroic effort not to stop, to comfort her, to tell her too much. He wished he could have told her the truth, but that would have ruined everything.

He took her on one more vision trip, an odyssey tour through the tearing pages of alternate realities that concluded at a mock-up of the Castle of War, where she encountered animations of her former lover Mym, and of his rescued Princess Ligeia, and of the demoness Lila. Naturally they endorsed Natasha but warned her to beware of Satan's tricks. Then the vision staged another crisis that Natasha came to resolve. Parry, acting firmly on the side of Right, used his song to vanquish those in the Wrong. Then he sang her the Song of Evening, the romantic theme of the Llano, and she was his. He had won her love.

But Orb had not yet assumed the office of the Incarnation of Nature. He had to wait until that was hers, because it was important that he marry not merely a mortal woman but the Incarnation. That was the liaison that would bring him the power he required to overcome God.

Then she achieved it, and he asked her to marry him. But he would not let her answer immediately. First he had to tell her the truth. This was where it could all come apart.

'I am the Incarnation of Evil,' he said.

Appalled, she stared at him.

He explained it all. Gradually she came to believe it.

'Get away from me,' she said dully.

He left her. What would she decide?

The issue was in doubt. Orb was no longer merely a woman, but was Gaea, perhaps the strongest of the Earthly Incarnations. In her rage at his deception she invoked the powers of the Llano, which she had learned with a rapidity and competence he could only envy. Her voice lent it force that he had never been able to evoke himself; that thing was dangerous! Now he truly appreciated how she had come to the office of Nature; she had enormous skill in the required music. But she was still new in office, and playing with a horrendously potent instrument. The mortal realm was rocked by savage affectations of weather – storm, flood, fire, freezing, earthquake – destroying everything. He was afraid she would finally invoke the most devastating aspect of all, and render the cosmos back into complete chaos. It was evident that the love she had developed for Natasha had been banished by her realization of his true nature. Her fury at her betrayal stemmed as much from embarrassment as from the scorning of her love – for he had not scorned it, only deceived it.

He wished he had not. What had he accomplished except the destruction of the mortal realm and the alienation of the one he least desired to? The one who had the likeness of Jolie, and the voice of rapture.

But she stopped just short of that, and repented her rage. She asked Chronos to reverse what she had done. He explained that he would have to have the agreement of all the major Incarnations before he acted so significantly.

All agreed – except Parry. He knew that his victory hinged on this: that Gaea marry him and join her power to his. It was not necessary that she love him, or he her; only that she marry him. Now he had a lever that he would never be able to use again: the fate of the mortal realm hung in the balance. Denied her love, he could still have the victory he had sought. It might be a victory that tasted of ashes, but still could be genuine.

'Will you marry Me?' he asked her again.

Desperately she looked to her mother, Niobe. 'What am I to do?'

'You now know Satan for whom and what he is,' Niobe replied grimly. 'Do you love him?'

Orb struggled with herself, but was helpless. 'God help me,' she whispered brokenly, 'for I do love Satan.'

She *what*?

Parry had a role to play, and he played it appropriately, gaining the acquiescence of all the Incarnations to the union. The victory was his!

But so was Orb's love. It had survived the revelation! That shook him profoundly.

Chronos raised his Hourglass, its sand turning blue.

Then Parry was back in Hell, alone. All was undone.

But he remembered, as he had when Chronos had changed the holocaust, because he was an Incarnation and a prime mover.

She loved him.

And he loved her. That realization smote him with peculiar force. He had never intended to; his profession of love as Natasha had been part of the construct of the lie. He had thought himself immune to true love, subject only to passing fascinations, after the loss of Jolie. He had been mistaken.

It was, he knew, her voice that had done it. He had not anticipated anything like it; it reached into the secret essence of him, moving him as his own voice had so often moved others. Had the Angel Gabriel anticipated that, too?

He realized that his careful snare for possession of Gaea's power had reversed against him. He had promised Niobe never to harm Orb; now he knew that this had assumed more than technical force. He had fallen into the trap of loving a good woman – which meant he could no longer represent Evil. For the two were incompatible on any amicable basis. He would have to try to be worthy of Orb's love, as the true Satan could never be.

There was only one way to do that.

He would have to abdicate his Office.

16
Tryst

Parry scripted the wedding ceremony as carefully as he had the three visions; it was to be a splendid occasion. He set it up in Hell's most elegant chamber, very like a cathedral. There were arches and stained glass, and seats for the major Incarnations, all of whom were invited.

Having ascertained that Heaven had improved its operations somewhat in recent centuries, he orchestrated a mass release of souls: all those who had earned their salvation but had hesitated to depart the mock-Heaven annexe. That should please Orb, and he wanted very much to please her. Those souls were organized into a massive choir; as they sang, they could come to him and be freed in glows of light.

There was to be an audience, too: all the relatives and friends of the bride, from all her walks of life. These included those who were dead; he had made arrangements with Gabriel for their temporary release from Heaven. The Angel had of course cooperated, knowing what was to occur. The same was true of the other Incarnations, who had caught on. Only Orb herself was innocent, as perhaps was fitting.

The key to the ceremony was to be two songs: Orb's and his own. The songs were to be the final keys to their love for each other. Orb did not realize how literally true that was to be.

She sang the Song of Evening, which was also the Completion of Love. It was perhaps the most evocative rendition of such a melody ever performed by a mortal, for not only was she the finest female singer, enhanced by magic; she was truly in love. The entire assembly responded to that feeling, and so did he, revelling in the delight of the free recognition of her love for him, and his love for her. All present knew that there was no way that he could match this presentation.

But he could. He was the finest male singer, and he had more than just love to express. He sang the one type of song that was forbidden to him: a hymn to God. Never mind that God was not listening, and perhaps was not worthy; the wedding party understood its significance. This was the supreme act of sacrifice: the one way Satan himself could prove himself worthy. As he sang, the choir of undamned souls joined him, and flocked to him, enhancing his music, and were released to Heaven.

Orb stared at him, gradually realizing that her belief in his falsity was in error; that he truly did love her. He sang directly to her as he concluded. Now all the souls were gone, and his own body was being destroyed by the power he had invoked. He went out, literally, in flame.

He had sung himself knowingly into his doom. He had given up his existence as an Incarnation, that she might know, at the end, that his love had been true. He would never possess her, and he had lost his challenge to God, but he had done what he had to do.

He found himself in a kind of Limbo. It was not the outer circle of Hell, but some special region evidently reserved for fallen Incarnations. There were flames, but he was hardly aware of them, for none carried the intensity of the flame of his lost love.

He was damned, of course; he would never be free of Hell. He had spent more than seven hundred years as the Incarnation of Evil. He had known at the outset that there would be no reprieve. Another person would assume the vacated Office, and perhaps in some future century would need assistance and would bring Parry out to serve. That was all he had to hope for. Yet he did not regret it.

He had loved twice: once in life, and once as an Incarnation. His demise abolished neither of these loves. His second love had not replaced his first; it had merely joined it. His feeling for Jolie now returned as strongly as it had been in life, without conflicting with his feeling for Orb. He hoped that Jolie could be at last released to Heaven, and that Orb would come to accept his necessary desertion of her at the altar. He hoped, too, that somehow the mortal suffering he had sought to abbreviate would be brought to an end despite his defection. He had been the Master of Evil, and by definition what he had done was wrong; but it had also been right, because of God's dereliction. He felt no shame in being damned for that.

He hovered indefinitely, alone. This was evidently to be the manner of his punishment: to be conscious and isolated, never to know how things progressed in the mortal and immortal realms. It was a terrible onus – but his love sustained him. No punishment could make him regret what he had done.

Then someone came. His nebulous prison assumed the form of a cell, and he became a man in chains. Some other mind was shaping his situation.

It was Orb. She came as the Incarnation of Nature, as Gaea, the Green Mother. Even Hell could not exclude her, when she chose. She was lovely in the fashion only she could be, and assured in a manner he had not observed when he courted her. Background melody surrounded her: an aspect of the Llano he had not known of before, that evidently opened the way before her wherever she chose to go. She had come into the authority of her office.

He was powerless to move or even to speak. This, too, it seemed, was part of his punishment. All he could do was gaze at her. That was enough.

She approached him and took his hand, wordlessly. Her contact was like tender fire. She lifted his hand and touched the spot of blood on his wrist.

No! he cried in sudden alarm. But he could neither voice it nor resist.

Orb took the drop of blood from him and dropped his hand. His wrist was bare.

She departed, and his cell dissolved into the formlessness of its natural state. Only one thing had changed: he no longer had Jolie.

Why had Orb done it? She could not have harboured any jealousy towards his first love; Jolie was long dead, and he, too, was dead now.

Yet perhaps this, too, was right. Jolie could not reside in Hell. Perhaps Orb had freed her for Heaven.

Abruptly he was in a loud, bright chamber. He did not know how much time had passed; part of the Hell of Limbo was its timelessness. But he recognized this place: it was the main banquet hall, where occasional entertaining was performed. Hell had very little use for such facilities other than as a mechanism to tempt potential converts: mortals with evil inclinations but as yet insufficient evil actions. A little temptation could go a long way to evoke their latent evil and cause it to manifest in ways that clarified their status promptly. Evil had to be proven in a mortal; it could not simply be assumed. Parry had developed reasonably sophisticated routines to prove it.

He stood before a fat, middle-aged slob of a man, the refuse of whose repast lay strewn all around. But a subtle kind of grandeur suffused him, too, and Parry recognized it as the stigmatum of immortality. This was the new Incarnation of Evil.

'Say, now, it worked!' the man exclaimed, wiping a

smear of gravy from his mouth. 'You're the has-been Satan!'

Parry nodded. 'I am he.'

'Listen, I need to know the spell for controlling demons,' the man said.

Parry did not answer.

'Look, schnook, I know you know it! Out with it.'

'It is a thing you must discover for yourself,' Parry said.

'You had it pretty easy these last three weeks. I can put you in some real fires, really toast your toes, know what I mean? But I'll let you off easy if you tell me that spell.'

'No.'

'Dammit, that turd Ozzy what's-his-name don't pay any attention to what I tell him. What do you want for that spell?'

'It is not for sale,' Parry said.

The man gazed appraisingly at him. 'Let me 'splain somethin', mac. When you bugged out, the office fell on the most evil mortal in the world. I got it. I was on death row for the one they caught me on – five-year-old nymphet whose head I had to bash in 'fore she'd be quiet and let me finish, and then she didn't die quite soon enough and she fingered me. My bad luck. But I'm not choosy; I can make a grown man hurt as bad as a child. It's a real thrill in the crotch, makin' some freak scream that way. I've been catching on to the ropes here, makin' the damned souls scream. They hurt as bad as live folk, would you believe, and they can scream a lot longer before poopin' out. I really like it here! But your Lucifer won't give me the time of day, and neither will Mephis-what's-his-name, and that creature Nefer-titties spat in my face. I *need* that spell! What's your price?'

Parry turned away.

'Then roast, bugbrain!' the man screamed.

Parry was abruptly in the flames. They hurt terribly, but did not actually burn him because he could not be

347

physically damaged here. No one could; pain and humiliation were all that Hell offered. He bore it; he had no alternative.

Certainly he was not going to give that child-torturing slob the secret! Such a monster might be evil, but he was no good for the running of Hell. He was evidently spending all his time gorging and torturing, not even trying to organize Hell or see to any larger purpose.

Yet despite his current agony, Parry had some satisfaction. Ozymandias and Lucifer and Mephistopheles refused to cooperate with the new Incarnation, and Nefertiti had spit in his face! Of course their attitude was routine; every new Incarnation had to earn his place. Still, it had been good to hear.

But still his major strength was in his love. He had given up his office for love of Orb, and he would do it again, though he burn in the flames forever! While his mind was on her, he did not feel the flames. He only hoped that the other Incarnations would be able to prevent his replacement from doing too much harm

Another figure came. This time the flames did not abate. Parry took this as a signal that this was not an official visit.

It turned out to be a spider, swinging on an invisible thread. The flames did not seem to affect it.

Only one spider could penetrate here: Fate. Parry tried to speak, but could not. Neither could he move. It seemed that only when he was brought out by the current Incarnation of Evil could he talk or act.

The spider formed into Niobe. 'Found you at last, son-in-law,' she whispered. 'He hid you well, but you have friends among the damned souls, and they told me.'

What was she doing here? Why should she have searched him out? He could not ask.

'As you may know, your successor is not a nice person,'

Niobe said. 'We have learned something about you. The demoness is one of ours now, and she explained some things, and JHVH volunteered some things, and our recent experience confirmed them.'

So he was to be stripped of his remaining secrets, too! Yet Niobe was not the type to gloat. This excursion had to be risky for her. What was her purpose?

'My daughter loves you, and she is your wife,' Niobe continued. 'So there does seem to be a certain familial obligation. There can never be a true union between the Incarnations of Evil and of Nature, but there may be another way. The others of us have concluded that we would prefer to deal with the old, familiar Evil, rather than the new and ugly one. Of course none of us would care to state such a thing openly.'

What was she saying? Parry hardly dared to believe!

'And I would not care to have this repeated, but there is a question in some of our minds whether the one we serve is, well, paying attention. We have operated on the assumption that He who is Good remained disengaged because He was honouring the Covenant, while He who is Evil violated the Covenant freely. Therefore we redressed that inequity by siding with the honourable one. But now we are uncertain. There is a certain interpretation that would reverse some implications.'

She shrugged. 'At any rate, the trial period for your successor is drawing to a close, and he has not found the spell he needs. He is apt to be replaced by another just as bad, unless . . .'

Unless Parry resumed the Office! He alone of the former Incarnations of Evil could do that, because he had not yet yielded his life and become a damned soul.

Niobe left her thought unfinished, knowing that he understood. But she had a qualification. 'Yet a person needs to be in an appropriate situation to assume an office. If he were, for example, lost or mute, he would be

349

unable to step in before the Office of Evil may be either grasped by the one who seeks it or will drift to the most evil. The applicant who is closest to the one who releases the Office has the first chance. Therefore it is important that an aspirant not be incapacitated at the key moment.'

She was right. The Office had to be grasped at the moment it became available, or it would be lost. He had had Lilah's guidance the first time, so had seized it without quite knowing the significance. He could not do so from the incommunicado confines of this dungeon.

'So I have brought a thread to lead you out,' Niobe said after a pause, to let him think it through. She stretched out an invisible line. 'Follow it, and – '

'Ha! Caught you, old bag!' the Incarnation cried, appearing between them. 'I may be finished, but *he'll* never profit by it!' He struck at her with a flaming pitchfork.

Niobe became the spider, and the spider vanished. She was an Incarnation, but this was Hell, and she could not oppose the Incarnation of this domain.

'And now you, pinhead!' the Incarnation cried, turning on Parry. 'You'll never get out!'

Magic flared, and Parry was carried away, helpless. The Incarnation had not learned the demon-banishing spell, but he had evidently picked up some of the lesser magic. Parry drifted through swirling smoke for what seemed like an eternity before coming to rest in a stifling environment.

He seemed to be in an aspect of chaos. Apparently the Incarnation had discovered how to incorporate a bit of the Void in Hell and buried him in it. He knew Parry could not escape it. The Incarnation was evil and ugly, but he had a certain cunning about his own survival.

The thread had been lost. The Incarnation had struck at the key moment, allowing Parry the torture of dawning hope irredeemably destroyed. He would never find his way out in time now!

Yet it was not a total loss. Though he would not resume his office, he had the comfort of the knowledge that the other Incarnations had had a change of heart about him, and that Niobe herself accepted his status as husband to Orb. It was a meaningless marriage, destined never to be consummated, yet that acceptance buoyed him immeasurably. Perhaps he had, in his downfall, accomplished part of what he sought: to gain some improvement in the processing of good and evil from souls, minimizing the suffering of the mortals involved.

It could have been a second or a century, but it seemed closer to the former. Another visitor came to him. This one was neither woman nor spider, but rather a nebulous form reminiscent of the nature of the Void. It overlapped him, and then he recognized it.

Nox! The Incarnation of Night, she who knew all secrets and preserved most of them. Parry had not known she could navigate chaos, but it made a certain sense in retrospect. She was closest of all the Incarnations to that state herself.

«Here is what you lost.»

Something touched his hand. Then the ineffable presence departed.

Parry considered what she had brought him. It was an almost invisibly thin line of a web, the kind a spider might spin. What had caused Nox to take the trouble to bring such a thing to him? What could be her purpose? She was aloof from most mortal and immortal concerns, and her business with him, by her own assessment, remained unfinished. Yet she had not chosen to complete it now.

Then he understood:

It was the thread!

* * *

351

He followed it. The thing was silken, perceptible only because he was attuned to it, hardly more than a thought. But it led through the swirling randomness, even as Fate's thread had guided Niobe through the Void. It was the single aspect of diminished entropy in his vicinity. He followed its essentially uphill guidance.

As he made progress through chaos, some anomalous formulations occurred. There were shapes of objects in no particular order of classification. The outline of a rock drawn in pastel, a squashed beer can, the curve of a naked woman's hip, the stem of a rose, a crooked ray of starlight, the left eye of a harpy, a sprouting grain of wheat, one drop of rain, a purpling bruise on the shoulder of a rabbit, a torn page of a calendar marking Friday the thirteenth. He passed it all, diverted by none of it, following the thread.

Then land appeared, a shore, and he was swimming in a disgustingly polluted stream. It was the River Acheron, the waters of woe that coursed around much of Hell proper, having no true egress. But it was familiar; now he knew approximately where he was.

He landed near the station of the three Judges, and there they were, dispensing the justice of the infernal region to arriving souls, classifying the difficult cases. Minos, formerly King of Crete, who had the Minotaur, the terrible offspring of his wife's passion for a bull. Rhadamanthus, his brother, noted for his fairness. Aeacus, formerly the King of Pythia, noted for his piety. They were good judges, and Parry had left them in place, extending their authority.

Parry could not return to Hell proper without passing by the Judges; he himself had organized Hell this way, so that no damned souls escaped proper classification. Some who came to Hell were actually destined for Heaven, and the Judges had unerringly identified these and assigned them to mock Heaven until they were willing to travel on.

Most of them had done so, at the time of Parry's wedding ceremony, but more souls arrived constantly, and the business of the Judges was never finished.

They could not fail to recognize him, no matter what form he assumed, for the Judges read not the physical appearance but the soul. If they turned him in . . .

He joined the line of souls, and followed it gradually to its head.

Minos glanced at him. His gaze paused momentarily, then moved on, as if there were nothing out of the ordinary. 'Pass to Limbo,' he said tersely.

They were not giving him away! Parry passed on, as if he were one of the regular damned souls.

He came next to Cerberus, the three-headed dog he had assigned to be the guardian of the main gate. It had been some centuries since he had had contact with the huge beast, and since the Judges passed him, he should be able to walk by without challenge, unrecognized.

'Ha!'

It was the Incarnation again. The cunning slob had been watching the main entrance, just in case.

'After him, dawg – destroy him!' the Incarnation cried.

Cerberus, not knowing any better, obeyed the voice of authority. He launched himself at Parry.

Now Parry wished the dog *had* remembered him! He had to escape – and that was no easy thing to do. Cerberus could not kill him, of course, but he could tear Parry's apparent body to bits, and it would be a day before those bits reformed. That could be too long; the Incarnation was near the end of his trial period, and could be ousted at any point. If Parry wasn't ready –

Parry dived back into the River Acheron. Cerberus followed, intent on his prey. One head watched above the surface, another looked back, and the third plunged under the surface to watch there, too. He was a good strong swimmer; in a moment he would overhaul Parry and chomp him.

Parry changed into a dirty brown fish. Now he had camouflage to match his environment, and was able to outswim the dog.

'Oh, no, you don't!' the Incarnation screamed from the bank. 'I'll take you out if it's the last thing I do, you a-hole!' He leapt into the water himself, and became a great white shark.

This was bad news! Parry had not realized that the Incarnation had learned shape-changing. It was not difficult, in Hell, for one in authority; he just had trusted that the Incarnation would have spent too much time in gorging himself and raping child souls to master it. Perhaps someone had provided the Incarnation with good advice, just as Lilah had for Parry in the early days. There were always damned souls eager to gain preferred treatment by pleasing the Master. Hell was hardly the place for honour or principle.

The shark was gaining on him, and its teeth were ready. He could not escape it by diving low, and it would be useless to remain on the surface. He would have to change form.

But there was a problem here, because it took proper concentration to change form, and his body would stop swimming for a moment while he did it. The shark was now so close that it would snap him up at the first pause. Also, he would have to change to some form that could handle the water, or else launch into the air as a bird – and the Incarnation would simply change, too, and continue the pursuit. Because Parry now had the effective status of a damned soul, he could not match the Incarnation in direct combat; his strength, agility and speed would be less even if the forms were identical.

But he could change to some similar type and size of fish with little pause, and the water was as good a way to travel through Hell as any. If he could just slip away into some bypath, so that the Incarnation would lose him . . .

No, suddenly he had a better idea! He could lead the Incarnation into a special trap, and settle the matter immediately. He surely had a better notion of the river channels than the Incarnation did, for Parry had dictated their courses. He had inherited a Hell that was archaically and inconsistently organized, and seen to its improvement; even though he had not paid much attention to such details in centuries, he knew as much as he needed to.

He shifted to a slimmer, faster form of fish, and began to gain. Here in the polluted water that was enchanted to prevent damned souls from fleeing Hell, conjuring magic did not work well; that was why Parry could not escape that way, and why the Incarnation could not banish him back to the Void. They had to settle matters right here.

The Incarnation saw this, and modified his own form. He became a slimmer, faster shark. He began to gain again. He was probably enjoying the chase, believing that the end was inevitable. After all, there was nowhere within the confines of Hell that any soul could escape the Incarnation of Evil.

But Parry knew where he was going. He dodged and turned, staying just ahead of the shark's jaws, then abruptly swerved into a tributary stream.

This was the Phlegethon, the River of Fire. Flames hovered over its surface, and its waters were boiling hot. But even as he entered, Parry modified to the form of a fire-fish, which thrived in such heat. The Incarnation, caught by surprise, paused, then did likewise, simply copying Parry's form.

That strategy would enable the Incarnation to follow him anywhere, and the Incarnation's greater strength would ensure a closing of the gap between them. But Parry had gained a critical bit of time. Perhaps more

355

important, he had established that he had to be closely followed, and by a like form, or he would escape. That would gain him a reprieve, but not victory; the Incarnation would simply reorient on his soul and chase him down again, like a cat playing with a mouse. Assuming the Incarnation had mastered the soul-tracing magic. If by chance he had not –

He looped swiftly back, swimming downstream and giving the Incarnation the temporary slip. But in a moment the other fish was back on his trail. Obviously the Incarnation had a lock on his identity, and could sniff him out anywhere. So much for that faint hope.

He reentered the Acheron, modifying his fish form again. The Incarnation followed, matching both course and detail.

Then Parry dodged into the Kokytus, the frozen river. He modified his form to handle the cold, becoming a small ice fish. The Incarnation did likewise, hardly losing time.

This time Parry did not double back. He forged upstream, under the ice, dodging boulders in the water, trying to hide in the tricky nether currents. But the Incarnation was not to be deceived. He followed every bypath, coming steadily closer. There could be no escape into the headwaters, for Parry would be slowed, or he would have to change form and leave the river, and would be caught when he tried.

As he swam, he made a spell. It was a quiet one that did not affect his form or his nature, and he hoped it went unnoticed. This was the critical stage; if the Incarnation caught on to where Parry was leading, or what the effect would be, or how to nullify it as Parry had just done, then all would be lost. But the Incarnation lacked experience in Hell; Parry was counting on that.

Abruptly he swam into a new tributary, one whose

waters were not frozen. He intensified his spell, though the effort slowed him.

The Incarnation followed, his jaws opening. Once he caught hold, Parry would not be able to escape. They both knew that. This was the finale.

Then the Incarnation slowed, seeming dazed. He began to swim aimlessly. He moved to the side to nibble at a succulent bit of vegetation.

Was it a ruse? Or was it the finish? It would soon enough be evident.

Parry reversed, and swam downriver. There was no pursuit. He came to the River Kokytus needing no further modification for the cold. He swam all the way back down to the River Acheron before venturing to the shore and changing back to his human form.

He climbed to the bank. 'I, Satan, reclaim My office,' he proclaimed. He felt the power returning to him. He had been in time. He was once more the Incarnation of Evil.

He conjured himself to the centre of Hell. Ozymandias looked up from his desk. 'My Lord, You have returned,' he said respectfully, as if it were a routine occurrence. 'But if I may inquire – ?'

'I led him into the River Lethe,' Parry explained. 'I used a spell to protect myself from its property of forget-fulness. It may be that he did not know that spell, or realize where he was.'

'That may be,' Ozymandias agreed. 'Have You new orders, Satan?'

'Revert to My standing ones,' Parry said. 'Whatever damage the usurper has done, reverse it.'

'As You wish.' Then, slowly, Ozymandias smiled. He was glad to have the old order back.

Thanks to the help of Niobe and Nox, Parry was back in office. That was a considerable gratification – yet there was emptiness, too, for he knew that his change in circumstance could not restore to him his love. He had lost both Jolie and Orb; that had been understood when the other Incarnations helped him to recover. He had a mission to accomplish, and he would try his best, knowing the others would give no further quarter and expected none. But he would have traded it all for the other. Indeed, *had* traded it all for the other, one month ago.

After a busy day of reorganizing and reestablishing, Parry retired alone. He did not need sleep, but he hoped to obtain some anyway. Perhaps it would help dull the emptiness.

Then someone came to him. He realized immediately that it was an undamned soul, for it shone in a manner no damned soul could. How had it been admitted to Hell? The guardians should not have permitted it, and Ozymandias would never have authorized it. Only another Incarnation could –

The figure came close. It was a woman of shapely proportion. 'Parry,' she said.

What? He recognized that voice! Yet it was impossible.

She drew off her hood, showing her honey hair, and then her face. Her eyes were grey-green.

Parry stared, for a moment too amazed to speak.

'Yes, it is I,' Jolie said. 'I have returned to you, my love.'

'But – I married another – I thought – '

Her expression changed. 'Parry, you know that Gaea can never have a relationship with Satan, though she be technically married to him. That marriage must remain unconsummated, so that there is no question of undue influence. But there is no need for *my* marriage to you to be so. I love you as she does. Will you accept me back?'

He got up and enfolded her. 'Oh, Jolie, yes! I thought you were forever lost. I do still love you – but I love her, too. If you can accept that – '

'I can accept that,' she said, and kissed him.

For a moment his mind wandered, piecing out what had happened. Things fell abruptly together. Orb had taken the drop of blood containing Jolie's soul. Jolie could animate a living body, if given leave by the host of the body. There was only one person who would know that, and who would give that leave. One who loved him as Jolie did, and could not come to him. One whom he could never possess, because they were forever on opposite sides.

'But I can stay only the night,' Jolie said. 'And not every night. And it must be secret. A tryst others do not know about.'

'A tryst,' he agreed. 'And – when you leave Me – if you would convey My thanks to the one whose body you borrow for what she – '

'She knows.' For that time only the voice was that of an Incarnation. But the love in it was unchanged.

He kissed her once more, knowing that he had been doubly blessed. He would never be lonely again.

Author's Note

I expect to address three types of readers in this novel. One is the person who has not read the prior five novels in this series, and perhaps has not heard of me before. For that one I need to have a story that stands pretty much by itself and is not confusing. Since this novel refers back to many episodes covered in the prior novels, shown from other viewpoints, this means I must cover those scenes adequately so that there are not gaps. I have tried to do that. Another type of reader is the one who has read some of the prior volumes but not recently; that one needs refreshment of key elements without undue repetition. I have tried to do that too. The third reader is the one who saved up all the prior volumes and has just read them rapidly in order, hitting this one fully primed with all the details fresh. For that one I should avoid repetition, because it would be wasting his time. That proved to be impossible to do. So I did what I deem to be the next best thing: I show those scenes from a fresh viewpoint, and evoke new interpretations of their significance. I realize that critics, who seem to exist on wormwood, will castigate me for supposedly running out of inspiration and copying from myself, but I hope that my real readers will bear with me on the necessary and often difficult compromises I have made. The mortal realm is rife with compromise.

This is the sixth and penultimate Incarnations of Immortality novel. The subject of the final one, *And Eternity*, may be surmised, but its approach will differ. I had originally planned on just five, but realized as I worked through them that the story was not going to be complete, so extended it. I have already been accused of doing it just for the money. Well, it is true there is money involved, and a pretty penny too; it is also true that I earn my living by my writing, and would go broke if I did not get paid for it. I am not sure why a writer should be condemned for making money when others are not. The question should be whether the money is made in a licit and socially positive manner. I remind readers of Samuel Johnson's remark on the subject: 'No man but a block-head ever wrote except for money.'

As I have mentioned in prior Notes, I have no belief in the supernatural. These novels are unabashed fantasy. Some of you have written to object to my atheism. I do not treat such letters kindly, because I am not an atheist. I am an agnostic: one who has not come to a conclusion about the validity of the existing theories of Deity and Afterlife. I regard them as unproven, and I feel free to represent them in my fiction in whatever manner is conducive to the narration of an entertaining and some-times thought-provoking story. In short, I am having fun, and I hope that my readers are too.

But as I have also mentioned, there seems to be suspicious coincidence occurring as I write these novels. No. 1 concerned Death, and death impinged on my life. No. 2 related to Time, and I had my worst time-squeeze of recent years. No. 3 was about Fate, and I described the devious route that brought me to this series. No. 4 was War, and warlike matters intruded, even threatening the publication of the novel. No. 5 was Nature, and I felt that impact too. This one is Evil, and hang on, because the curse is still viable.

You might assume that Satan would not be pleased by an exposé of his nature, since he uses deceit to forward his cause. Therefore Satan would do his best to interfere with the writing of a novel like this. This seems to have been the case, because I encountered a horrendous sequence of interferences. Some were funny; some were tragic. Let me see if I can cover this without becoming tedious.

Circumstances of a unique nature caused me to sign contracts for eight new fantasy novels at a time when I had intended to be working in science fiction, horror and a major historical project. The SF and horror had to be postponed, to my regret, but I refused to do that with the historical effort. So I undertook to catch up on the fantasy, and the historical, and certain other projects (a collaborative novel, a rework of an old unpublished novel, and some stories) in the course of three years. With the computer it is feasible, but I knew I would have to step right along.

Step along I did. This is actually the fifth novel I'm completing in this calendar year, which, along with the stories, mean about 600,000 words aggregate. That's as much as I've ever done in a single year, and more than I hope to do in any future year, because I am jammed up against the limit of what I can do without compromising the standards I maintain. There are those who assume that a prolific writer must be a hack: that is, one who churns out anything he can sell, just to keep the pot boiling. Perhaps some writers are; I am not. I care about every project I'm in, and I have changed publishers more than once when their editors interfered unduly with my text. I do not claim to be the best writer extant, merely one who is doing the best he can with his talent, situation and creative/ethical needs. I don't like to be crowded in my writing.

I allowed three months for *Evil*: OctOgre, NoRemember and DisMember, 1986. I started on schedule. But as it happened, I had got crowded in my computer, so was expanding my system's capacity. I doubled its memory to 512 K, and its storage to 20 MB. Don't worry about the figures if you are not into computers; just accept that they are solid ones in the middle range of such things. But we discovered that my operating system could not address either of these new totals. I could not use much more than I had before – unless I changed operating systems.

Back in the fourth novel of this series I discussed the two major operating systems this computer can use. One I likened to an old retired seaman, Captain Manager, known colloquially as CP/M, who maintained a sixteen-storey (as he spells it) apartment building, each floor of which could house a nice apartment complex. He called the occupants 'users' and provided well for their individual tastes, as long as they paid their rentals. The other I likened to a somewhat prim lady, Ms Dos, also called MS-DOS, who distrusted apartment buildings and preferred to maintain an intricate garden through which passed many paths. People could reside along these paths, each having his own personal access and directory of his flowers. I happened to be with the Captain, and did not try Ms Dos because she lacked a feature I liked, called MAINT, that made file housekeeping easy.

But now it was time to make the change, because while the Captain had not renovated his building in years and refused to cater to my need for greater memory and storage, Ms Dos promised to be more accommodating. So, not without trepidation, I moved out of my comfortable apartments on the lower floors and went to the Garden. My wife and daughters, satisfied with the building, remained on their upper storeys; they had no large files to process. Thus I left my family behind, though my wife did keep a certain eye on me from the window. Ms Dos, though prim by day, seems young and healthy; you never can tell.

But you don't just step from one operating system to another. Ms Dos and the Captain hardly recognized each other's programs. I had to get new software to function in the Garden. That proved to be more complicated than anticipated, and it was one of the things that slowed progress on this novel. For this is my first novel on DOS, and all the tribulations of learning occurred here.

Remember how I had to go to Finland for my keyboard, because I use a modified Dvorak that could not be generated on my American keyboard? I moved to the Finnish keyboard and reconfigured that, thanks to my wife's expertise. Well, I got Smartkey for DOS, but when I invoked the Finnish keyboard it glitched. I had to strike each key twice to make it register. My wife had no such problem. It turned out, after trial and error, that this is a phenomenon that occurs only in DOS, with the Finnish keyboard, with Smartkey. Eliminate any one of those three, and things are normal. I don't know why this effect exists, and doubt that anyone else does; I'm the only one ornery enough to go to Finland just to get my capital V's and W's. 'You know,' I told my wife, 'the Swedish keyboard is identical to the Finnish keyboard, except for some markings on the surfaces of the physical keys that would have no bearing on this. But, just in case – ' and would you believe, the interference was gone on the Swedish keyboard. Everything worked perfectly. Thus I moved from Finland to Sweden, as well as from CP/M to MS-DOS.

I still needed a word-processing program for DOS. I liked the one I had in CP/M, Edward, that enabled me to call up as many as fourteen different files at once, and allowed me to put my functions wherever I wished. I refused to give up those features. So I hired the proprietor to customize Edward for me in MS-DOS. It cost about a thousand dollars, and there were a number of glitches to debug, but I got it. I was on my way in DOS!

Now a diversion; don't worry, it does, deviously, connect.

At the end of OctOgre I attended the local science fiction convention, NECRONOMICON, as a Guest of

Honour. I had been there three years before, and this time their other GOH was Fred Pohl, a leading figure in the genre. So I arranged to interview him for an audience, and really looked forward to it, because I had some most provocative questions to which I knew he had excellent answers. But Satan struck: Fred's wife had a heart attack, and Fred had to cancel just one week before the convention. Thus the disappointed fans had to settle for just me. Oh, they were nice enough about it, but it was too bad.

At that convention my daughter Penny and I had the pleasure of taking André Norton and her associate Ingrid Zeirhut to lunch. Penny and I and Ingrid are vegetarians; André loves cats and I hate cats (but cats love me), so it was interesting, especially when we shared a panel later.

I was on several panels, and on one of them was Lois Wickstrom, co-editor of a small press magazine, *PANDORA*. I thought nothing of it until in casual conversation I learned that she was the other local writer who uses the Dvorak keyboard. Immediately we were comparing notes. I'm on the DEC rainbow computer; she is on an IBM compatible. I had a program that enabled me to call up fourteen files; hers called up twenty-four files, with windows between them. I could move my functions around; so could she, and also modify their operations. Well, now! I had just paid a thousand dollars to adapt mine to DOS, and it seemed hers was better at four hundred dollars. True, hers had a feature I didn't like, batch formatting, that requires you to plug in many codes that change the text about before printing, but it was also one of the most powerful and versatile word-processing programs extant. Satan had timed it with infernal cunning, waiting until just after I had got what I wanted before dangling a new program before me.

Her program was FinalWord II, put out by Mark of the Unicorn. In my letter ordering it, I said, 'It is the wrong reason to make a purchase, I know, but I am intrigued by the name of your company. You see, I am a fantasy novelist with whole herds of unicorns in my fiction . . .' Their response was to bounce back our cheque, because they were changing their name to eradicate the Unicorn. What a slap in the face! Satan just couldn't resist that fillip. (And here I thought that unicorns were a protected species.)

So this may be my first novel in MS-DOS and my last with Edward. But I shall remain with Ms Dos, because she has succeeded in seducing me away from the Captain. Ms Dos comes on like a cranky old bat; she even has files suffixed '.bat' to run her errands. Every time you start her up, you have to check in with the exact date and time, a nuisance the Captain did not require. You have to type in a 'Path' or she refuses to provide service to your distant sites. When you want to print something she always asks whether you mean it, the first time, and you have to agree that yes, it *is* the printer you want to use. She's like an old-fashioned school-marm: everything has to be exactly her way. But if you are willing to abide by her rules, she will do a lot for you. More than the Captain will, if you want the scandalous truth.

I see my wife is getting suspicious, so I'd better give a for-instance or two. One is that most of the software outfits have gravitated to Ms Dos. The Captain changes his clothing seldom if ever, while Ms Dos is very attentive to software. Thus the companies just naturally do more business with her. This means that if you want something like, for instance, a sophisticated interactive spelling program, you will find maybe two or three old ones mouldering on the Captain's shelf, but dozens of fancy new ones on Ms Dos's shelves. I had to go to customizing to get the kind of word-processing program I wanted in CP/M, and realized just too late that that wasn't necessary in MS-DOS. Another is those .bat files: these are little programs you type up yourself, saying do this, do that, and then do the other. Then when you summon a bat (it is actually short for 'batch'), it flies in on its leathery wings and does the job for you. There is even a vampire bat that invokes itself when you start up, and it takes care of the nuisance about the date and time and path, and anything else you want, right through setting you up with your daily program and files. In short, you can automate, and no longer be bothered with the mundane details.

But learning all the nuances, and adapting to the new ways – that does take time. My work was correspondingly slowed. It was fun learning Ms Dos's intimate little secrets, but I really would have been moving faster with the old familiar Captain. Satan knew that, and kept feeding me new distractions when I threatened to start getting ahead on the novel. For example, I obtained some freeware programs in DOS. Freeware or shareware are programs that you don't have to buy, except sometimes to pay the cost of the disc on which they come, but if you find them useful you may send money anyway; it's the decent thing to do. One was a MAINT program for DOS, so that I could handle my files as readily as I could in CP/M. Another was a Squeeze program that – no, don't get ahead of me, Ms Dos isn't *that* friendly – enables you to squish files down to about half size for more efficient storage, and to unsqueeze at need. Another was a program to translate files back and forth between MS-DOS and CP/M; that could be handy in our divided family. Nice enough stuff – but my novel was dragging.

Still, I managed to complete the first four chapters in OctOgre, which wasn't too far behind schedule. After all, I had research to do, which is always fascinating but slow. Then I hit a run of distractions, so that Chapter 5 took me three weeks, putting me a couple of weeks behind. What happened? Well, there was that convention I mentioned; I only go to one a year, and that was the one this year. Right after that I had to proofread the galleys for one of my novels, and that always takes time because I'm a slow reader and I do it carefully. We also had a morning with the state forester, because we own property we'd like to get classified as a tree farm, but first it has to be surveyed and approved for that. And a day to go to Tampa to meet my new British agent, Pamela Buckmaster. My old agent, Leslie Flood, was retiring, and she was taking over his practice, and had flown to Florida just to meet me. Virtually all of my non-American sales will be passing through her, and there was at least one six-figure deal in the offing, so this was a necessary thing. Then another slew of mail struck, taking days to answer; I answered about 385 letters while working on this novel, and though I cram most down to cards, I figure the average letter takes half an hour. There was also my big historical project, *Tatham Mound*; my sweet-sixteen daughter Cheryl was helping excavate the Mound on which the novel was to be based, and I would go out Sunday afternoons to learn new developments. It's a good and significant project, but those are afternoons that I don't make progress on this current novel. My printer glitched, printing increasingly worse, and we had to have the repairman in to fix it; yet more time expended. By the end of NoRemember I was exactly halfway through the novel, way behind schedule. Ouch; why so slow?

I made notes on a single day near the end of that three-week slowdown, just to get it straight: NoRemember 19, 1986. I was ready to start on Chapter 6, but was annoyed by a few little glitches in DOS, such as the BACKUP program that puts all your directories and files on a disc to be saved, but whose RESTORE function simply did not work. Apparently Ms Dos has a RESTORE program, but it had not been implemented on our version of DOS, unbeknownst to the writers of the instructions. That's a cute little oversight that can have decidedly uncute complications; it's like putting all your savings in the bank, then discovering that the bank will not let you take any out when you need it. My wife, after a struggle, finally figured out an alternate way to get the material back, and I wanted to make a note of the exact sequence, so that we would not have to go through this mess again. So I started my own sheet of instructions that included this and all the other deviances and omissions the engineers never bothered to fix. But this took time, because I had to test and double-check everything to be sure there was no error, because in an emergency I had to know exactly what worked. This took an hour and a half. But at least it was done, and I set up to start the chapter –

And the UPS truck chose that moment to deliver the Elite font we had ordered. There went another two and a half hours getting it ironed out. The thing worked well on letter-quality but not on draft-quality printing. Since I use both for my cards, we had to research in the manuals for a special, obscure code to fix that. Any session with a manual is time-consuming, because manuals are scripted by demons in Hell to torment mortals. Then I discovered that the font had no ¢ symbol. Now I use that on some of my cards: I have a macro that prints out a XANTH 2¢ stamp on those cards that don't require mundane postage. What was I to do with no ¢? I finally decided, with bad grace, to substitute the letter c, hoping no one would notice the difference between 2¢ and 2c. Meanwhile I did my three-mile exercise run, and then took an hour to read the mail, because another pile of letters was in; then I went ahead and used the new font to answer ten of them, washing out the rest of the day. I had never quite got down to paying work; Satan had, with magnificent timing, stepped in to introduce some new distraction every time I got close.

But my day did not end there. In the evening it rained, and when it rained it poured – and there was a leak in our roof. I remembered the day that had been made, because we had heard a thunk, and I had gone up to check where a falling branch had punctured the roofing, but we hoped it might still be watertight. It was the same day that a dead cat turned up in our yard, and I had to bury it. Our dogs don't like cats, but the neighbours' cats choose not to believe that; we heard a horrendous commotion in the night, and this was the result. So now we had the verification: the roof was no longer tight. Sigh. I went down to check our rain gauge – two inches – and on the way saw a gourd I had overlooked. You see, this year a seed sprouted from some buried garbage and it turned out to be a hypnoguard, a species seldom seen outside the Land of Xanth. Its vines grew at the rate of ten inches a day – yes, I measured – and it produced about twenty handsome gourds scattered across our yard. They look and taste rather like butternut squash. No, of course we did not look into any peepholes! But this shows how I can't even go to check rain without evoking all manner of oddities.

I turned in, reading myself to sleep on *The Blood of Ten Chiefs*, in which a story of mine appears. Then, at 1:50 A.M., the phone rang: a fan calling from Minnesota to talk with me. My wife put him off, for I was dead to the world; I keep regular hours, and am up before 6:00 A.M. regardless. Next year we plan to build on our tree farm and move there; we shall, with regret, also move to a post-office box so fans can't locate me and drop in uninvited and we shall get an unlisted phone so that we can sleep at night.

That is the story of how I failed to do any paying work that day, completing three weeks of much the same. It was obvious that Satan had no intention of allowing me to work on this novel in peace. Nevertheless, I buckled down to it, and wrapped up the novel Christmas Eve: eight more chapters in twenty-four days. Late Christmas Day I started this Author's Note.

But there were longer-range things to handle, too, all surely the mischief of Satan. One was my shoulder. During the last novel in this series I developed tenonitis (also spelled tendinitis), an inflammation of the tendon that causes pain when I move my arm beyond a certain range. I finally got a shot that reversed it, and it retreated grudgingly for about six months, then transferred from my right shoulder to my left shoulder. So now I am in the same condition, other side; the things I had to learn to do left-handed I now am relearning right-handed. After two visits to the doctor, I am now on pills that may be having some effect. Pain is a fact of my life now; I get a surge of it when I change my T-shirt or put on or off my jacket or reach for the salt. But I have discovered this about that: pain is not to be feared or loathed. I know when I will incur it, and its approximate degree, and it is under control; if it hurts too much to remove my jacket one way, I try another way, and eventually I discover a compromise that enables me to get through. When it wakes me at night, I change position until it subsides, and go back to sleep until the next time. I am used to it and can live with it. I don't like using drugs if I can avoid them, so I don't take any for this apart from the doctor's prescription. My arm exercises have been wiped out, but I discover that I feel more relaxed without those strenuous exertions; I lost my tension along with my muscle. I have always driven hard, and increasingly my body has been reacting against it; perhaps it is time to ease off somewhat. Thus the end of much of my physical programme does not after all signal the end of my health, merely the onset of a different stage of it. So there, Satan!

We still have horses, but things have been changing. Penny's horse Blue, the model for a unicorn and a night mare in my fantasies, is now coming into age twenty-nine, which is old for a horse. She's still spry, though her head is turning grey. But her companion, Misty, suffered a leg ailment, and walking or standing became hard for her. Finally I had to bring water, hay and feed to her where she lay, and for six months she survived that way. We had to fence Blue away from her, to prevent Blue from taking the food and allowing none to Misty. But horses need equine company; Blue would stand all day at the nearest part of the pasture to Misty, just watching, not grazing. This was no good for her. Misty continued to worsen, and the veterinarian said that her lung was collapsing because of her position; a horse needs to be afoot. So, with reluctance we had him give her the shot that put her away; it was our judgement that death would at this stage be a mercy for her. We buried her there in the pasture.

We needed company for Blue, and the vet had a spare horse. He brought her when he came to see Misty. This was Fantasy, a brown Arabian with a perfect white shield on her forehead two and a half inches across. She was a beautiful animal with papers who would have been an expensive show horse, but for a serious illness in her youth that caused her hind end to be somewhat deformed and perhaps had damaged her lungs. So she could not be ridden or bred, and her value was reduced to zero dollars – but she was alert and friendly and excellent company. In short, the perfect replacement companion for Blue. We liked her immediately, and after a night and day of squealing to establish just who was to be boss of the pasture, Blue did too. Now at last our farthest and greenest pastures were being grazed, and the two were always together.

Until this novel. Then trouble struck in the most painful way yet: at lovely Fantasy. She abruptly developed a heart problem. We were amazed and chagrined; if ever a horse did not deserve this, it was Fantasy. Her body was swelling as her heart was unable to clear the blood loop to her lungs, and her appetite was failing. The prognosis was doubtful; medication was not effective and it was obvious that this could not continue long. The vet came and took her away, hoping to treat her with techniques that could not be done in the field; if they were effective, she might survive. *Damn you*, Satan.

We needed company again for Blue. This time the vet brought a pony who had been left with him to be boarded for a month. Five months passed, and the owner never returned to pick her up. Her name was unknown. So we took over the boarding, knowing that at any time the owner could come to claim her. But it was a calculated risk; after all that time, the chances were diminishing. She is white (I don't care what the supposed experts say about there being no white horses) and plump, trained for children to ride, and so short that her tail drags on the ground. We named her Snowflake, after a white foal in my novel *Blue Adept*, and she fitted right in. Blue gave her the word about just who was boss of the pasture, and that was that; when frightened, Snowflake would go hide behind Blue. At this writing Snowflake has been with us a month, and this novel is just about done. The farthest pastures are being grazed again, and the two run together – Blue loves to run – and it looks as if we're all right.

There has also been human development. During this novel I received unpleasant news about Cousin Dick. Let me clarify the background. Cousin Dick is actually my fifth cousin, about fifteen years my senior; we got in touch because of a mutual interest in genealogy, researching our Jacob lineage. We had the same great-great-great-great grandfather. Cousin Dick had aspired to be a writer, and had tried a year or so doing full time writing of fiction, with the understanding that if he did not make it, he would give up that ambition and concentrate instead on making money. He did not make it, and so he went into mundane work and provided for his family quite nicely. But there was always that regret: suppose he *had* made it? How would his career as a writer have gone? There may be myriads of folk with similar ambition and similar disappointment; failed writers are a dime a dozen, and no one seems to care about their stifled dreams. But then, independently, I tried the same thing – and succeeded. Thus, in a manner, I represented the answer, for I had similar lineage and ambition, and a roughly similar personal history. We compared notes in some detail. I believe, to a degree, he regarded me as the fulfilment of his dream, while I regarded him as my alternate course, the one I did not take, about fifteen years ahead. Thus our correspondence, always amicable, had a certain extra element; we understood each other on a deeper level than is usual. He visited, and met my daughters, and of course he knew other members of my branch of the family. I believe everyone liked him. He was always alert for the appearance of my novels, and sometimes sent reviews I had missed.

But now the news was grim. Cousin Dick had lung cancer, and brain tumours, and was having seizures. 'It's a hell of a way to live,' he wrote in NoRemember, 'but after 66 years of comfortable health, it seems to be my turn.' Then, the day before Christmas, as I completed Chapter 16, I had news from his daughter: Cousin Dick was dead. One of the last conversations he had had with her was about the third volume in this series, *With a Tangled Skein*, and its Author's Note, which covered my own tangled skein of life. *Damn you, Satan!*

Let's conclude on a lighter note: the tangled skein of lesser events and impressions occurring while I worked on this novel. Satan uses honey as much as vinegar to distract me. My life is filled to the brim with minutiae. Such as requests for visits and talks. I attended a teenage girl's birthday party: she had been in an automobile crash that affected her memory, so that she could not retain new experiences. She liked my fantasy, so they hoped that if I was there, it would give her something special to remember. If she returned to the hospital, and remembered, they would know she was mending. So I went, bringing her some of my books and a Xanth Calendar, and they had video cameras of the party, so as to refresh her memory. She did improve, and I hope I helped. I also addressed a college class about story writing, reading an excerpt from my story 'Soft Like a Woman,' which is a savage antisexism commentary, because I support education and oppose sexism. Yes, I do get mail calling me sexist; some readers take my parodies for endorsements. I addressed a local Kiwanis Club meeting; the contractor we are asking to build us a nice house on our tree farm asked me, and I want him in a positive mood as he tackles that house. There's a reason for everything, but everything takes time!

Then there's the mail. Some of it affects my life and writing in devious ways. Amidst this novel, I was concerned because of the blah period in Parry's life between Jolie's death and the arrival of Lilah. I didn't want four chapters of that. Thirty-four letters arrived in one day – they come in batches – taking me three and a half hours to read and a good deal longer to answer. One was from Pat Woods with thoughtful comment about the first four novels in this series. 'You have an amazing affinity for your characters,' she wrote, and I thought darkly, *I wish that were true in* this *novel!* And then something clicked, and I realized that Jolie, who really had not been fairly treated, could in a manner be restored. Not only would this redeem her, it would enliven the dull section of the novel. Thus was introduced the Drop of Blood and all it portended. I'm really glad that happened, because I did feel guilty about Jolie. Thank you, Pat.

Two novels back I corresponded with a fourteen-year-old suicidal girl I called Ligeia, after a character in the novel, and that novel came into print in hardcover in

OctOgre. I received a number of letters expressing sympathy for Ligeia, several asking to be put in touch with her; one young man approached me directly about that at NECRONOMICON. But I could not oblige, because of the necessary anonymity and the fact that, owing to circumstances beyond my control, I lost contact with Ligeia. No, I don't think she's dead, merely incommunicado. She would be sixteen by this time. Then came one more letter: from a fourteen-year-old girl who was slashing her wrists. She had read about Ligeia . . . I do what I can, but it is quite limited, because I am no expert and even my letters are liable to be intercepted by the wrong parties in such situations. How do you answer a reader who wants advice on what her parents do not know about, when the parents read her mail? I have had this kind of letter in other connections, too.

There are also frustrations of a different nature: in this period I had about four of my cards returned 'Addressee unknown' though I had them exactly as given. If these are jokes, they are costing me valuable time; there are others who would have been glad to receive that wasted attention. I don't answer every letter I receive, but even so this year, like last year, comes to over twelve hundred I wrote. Most letters are about Xanth; next main topic is the Notes, overwhelmingly approved; it seems that the readers prefer a personal author to an impersonal one. Well, I don't claim to be a great man, but I am personal, just as my readers are. Then the ones that ask for things: contributions, mementoes for auctioning, requests for me to speak – I have to turn the great majority down. Only when the circumstances are special do I accept. For example, I have had a number of letters from prisoners. Now, I am a liberal, but I am not soft on crime; I dislike the death penalty, but I also abhor the notion of murderers going free to repeat their crimes. I suspect that there are far more guilty folk going free than there are innocent ones in prison. In addition, it is evident that prisoners have a lot more time for correspondence than I do. I can no more solve their problems than I can those of the suicides. So I tend to answer briefly and noncomittally. But one letter, in this period, made a reasonable case: the prison encourages reading as being of a rehabilitative nature, and I am a favoured writer, but their budget is limited. Prisoners cannot go out and buy their own. So – I sent a package of thirteen of my recent books, paperback and hardcover. Please, don't deluge me with requests for free books; this was a one-shot deal, about which I have mixed emotions.

As Christmas approached, I received many cards. As a rule I don't answer these, and don't send cards of my own, because if I did I would lose another critical chunk of time, but I do appreciate the sentiment. I even received a Chanuka card; I understand that occasion is becoming much like Christmas, in America. I had a letter and a painting from my youngest fan yet: six-year-old Carlitos Castillo. I did unbend enough to wish a number of correspondents 'Harpy Holiday'; I mean, what would life be without some grim humour? I received some gifts that surprised me: from a company with which I do business, and from publishers. Remember, it was only yesterday that I was beneath the notice of publishers, and I am a bit uncomfortable with first-class treatment, as any writer would be. *Do* leopards change their spots? But there is of course a price tag: now a publisher wants me to go on an Author tour to promote a novel. I hate to travel, but if it puts my novel on the hardcover best-seller lists . . . sigh.

Another problem is interviews. After four consecutive interviews from which I received no feedback – no copy, no news, except some secondhand remark that somebody had seen it somewhere – I decided that it was time to stop. If I never see a copy, I have no notion of the errors that may have been made. The main difference, as I see it, between fiction writers and journalists is that the fiction writers make sure of their facts. Then came news of a fifth: being published in a magazine with which I regard myself to be on bad terms, because of that same looseness with facts. I used to wonder why successful folk tended to isolate themselves from the public; now I am learning the answer. With interviews comes the nuisance of pictures. I had 128 little pictures of me I could send to readers who requested them; I ran out, and can't take the time to have more taken. But I have to make time to pose for photos whose rights do not belong to me, so cannot be used to replace my stock. So, after the session that occurred during this novel, I'll probably cut the line on that too. No, nothing wrong with the picture taker; it's just the time, and the fact that my dandruff reserved this occasion to come out in force. I am however conscious of the anomaly of having an attractive young woman taking pictures of a middle-aged man; sexist that I am supposed to be, I feel it should be the other way around.

While we're on the subject of evil, there is the matter of reviews. These seem to vary inversely with a writer's success, and I am getting the brunt of it now. Some of it is the arrogance of ignorance. One fan reviewer berated me for publishing a 27,000-word story as a novel. He was talking about *Steppe* on sale in paperback at this time. That novel is actually 61,000 words long. He also commented on the Incarnations series: no. 1 was wonderful, no. 2 was 'simply bad,' no. 3 was awkward because 'Anthony has always had trouble writing decent female characters.' About the Notes he said: 'Anthony's are getting longer and longer, and more and more boring and offensive.' But the pro reviewers aren't much better. *Publishers Weekly* remarked on Incarnations no. 3: '. . . The novel comes alive only at its start (set in a charming, early 20th century America, where magic has equal footing with science) and in its afterword – Anthony's cranky, contentious and revealing author's note.' The setting, of course, was Ireland; you will have to make your own judgement about the Author's Note. On no. 4 it said: '. . . In fact, most of this weak entry in the series is concerned with finding a proper mate for the hapless Mym. As before, though, the liveliest part of the book is the author's note, a 30 page open letter to his fans in which Anthony feels free to be cantankerous, boastful, whimsical and self-revealing.' Well, PW, here's another! These are actually relatively mild; reviewers get savage about my Space Tyrant series, and I believe I got my first 'killer review' on *Ghost*. At least it gives us a notion where Satan's mouthpieces are. I like Danielle Steel's comment: 'A bad review is like baking a cake with all the best ingredients, and having someone sit on it.' I have this mental picture of grouchy people walking around with squashed cake crumbling off their backsides. They might feel better if they tried appreciating the cake for what it was, rather than being asinine.

It goes on and on. We agreed to sell some small oak trees to a nursery, as those trees will have a hard time here as our pine trees crowd them out; they should be happier in individual lots. Then a second nurseryman asked. Then the first said the second was tearing up our property – and indeed, I found that he had destroyed twice as many young pines as he had taken oaks. Sigh; the simplest and most seemingly right things become complicated. I learned of the trouble a small press had with its special edition of the first novel in this series: it invested in printing and cover, then the distributor had a change in personnel and pulled the rug out. They sent me the beautiful colour-separation version of the cover; the original had somehow been destroyed. Another small press, setting up for another of my novels, got illness in the family, and an IRS audit. My American literary agent came down with strep throat and was too hoarse to speak; he does most of his business by phone. My British agent sent a large cheque, and the bank that translated it from £ to $ deleted the information about the exchange rate used; when I looked it up, I found that they had apparently shorted me by $800. I can't even update my accounts until I get that straight; just figuring it out cost me about £500 worth of my time on a £1200 entry. I heard from a beginning writer whose story was in a volume that was squelched by the prospective publisher before publication; she was warned that she would be blacklisted if she talked about the circumstances. Satan was not only working me over, he was working over anyone who associated with me! But perhaps I can do something about that last; I was blacklisted myself, in earlier days, for challenging similar dealings, and I remain militant. I mean, if the wrongdoers can win by blacklisting the innocent parties, what kind of a genre do we have? I find it hard to believe that I am the only person who objects, though that did seem to be the case before. I do sometimes get the impression that God is sleeping at the helm. Speaking of which: this was also the period in which the scandal dubbed the Reagan Watergate broke. It seems that no level is immune.

And so another novel and another year draw to a close, each with its highs and lows and ironies. Though I complain (reviewers call it bragging) about the volume of mail I receive, because it costs me the time to write approximately one more novel a year, I do appreciate the tremendous affinity and support my readers give me. Each letter is a little window into another life, and I only regret that so many of those lives are desperate ones. As the second Ligeia says: 'It's as if the whole world is moving to the key of C and I'm somewhere in B flat.' I have news for you, honey: the whole world is in B flat, but thinks that all the rest is in C. It is an illusion Satan has fostered, and we lack the wit to dispel it. But do not give up hope; things are changing all the time, and this too may pass.

One correspondent expressed dismay because he could not tell when my Notes were written and asked me to date them. Very well; this one is complete DisMember 27, 1986. I still have perhaps a week of editing and printing to go, and it may be two years before the novel sees publication, but this is now. I wish all of you a harpy new year!

Fantasy authors in paperback from Grafton Books

To order direct from the publisher just tick the titles you want and fill in the order form.

SF1482

All these books are available at your local bookshop or newsagent, or can be ordered direct from the publisher.

To order direct from the publishers just tick the titles you want and fill in the form below.

Name _____

Address _____

_____

Send to:
Grafton Cash Sales
PO Box 11, Falmouth, Cornwall TR10 9EN.

Please enclose remittance to the value of the cover price plus:

UK 60p for the first book, 25p for the second book plus 15p per copy for each additional book ordered to a maximum charge of £1.90.

BFPO 60p for the first book, 25p for the second book plus 15p per copy for the next 7 books, thereafter 9p per book.

Overseas including Eire £1.25 for the first book, 75p for second book and 28p for each additional book.

Grafton Books reserve the right to show new retail prices on covers, which may differ from those previously advertised in the text or elsewhere.